CW01512716

ABOUT THE AUTHORS

NELSON DeMILLE is the author of twenty-three novels, seven of which were #1 *New York Times* bestsellers. His novels include *The Maze*, *The Deserter* (written with Alex DeMille), *The Cuban Affair*, *Word of Honor*, *Plum Island*, *The Charm School*, *The Gold Coast*, and *The General's Daughter*, which was made into a major motion picture starring John Travolta and Madeleine Stowe. He has written short stories, book reviews, and articles for magazines and newspapers. Nelson DeMille is a combat-decorated U.S. Army veteran, a member of Mensa, Poets & Writers, and the Authors Guild, and past president of the Mystery Writers of America. He is also a member of the International Thriller Writers, who honored him as 2015 ThrillerMaster of the Year. He lives on Long Island with his family.

Learn more at www.nelsondemille.net
Twitter: @nelsondemille
Instagram: @nelsondemilleauthor
Facebook: /NelsonDeMilleAuthor

ALEX DeMILLE is a director, film editor, and author of the *New York Times* bestselling novel *The Deserter* (written with Nelson DeMille). He grew up on Long Island and received a BA from Yale University and an MFA in film directing from UCLA. He has won multiple awards and fellowships for his screenplays and films. He lives in Brooklyn with his wife and daughter.

Learn more at www.alexdemille.com
Twitter: @alexdemille
Instagram: @alexdemille
Facebook: /AlexDeMilleAuthor

NOVELS BY

NELSON DEMILLE
AND ALEX DEMILLE
THE TIN MEN

SPHERE

SPHERE

First published in the United States in 2025 by
Scribner, An imprint of Simon & Schuster, Inc.
First published in Great Britain in 2025 by Sphere

1 3 5 7 9 10 8 6 4 2

Copyright © 2025 by Nelson DeMille and Alex DeMille

The moral right of the author has been asserted.

*All characters and events in this publication, other than those
clearly in the public domain, are fictitious and any resemblance
to real persons, living or dead, is purely coincidental.*

All rights reserved.
No part of this publication may be reproduced, stored in a
retrieval system, or transmitted, in any form or by any means, without
the prior permission in writing of the publisher, nor be otherwise circulated
in any form of binding or cover other than that in which it is published
and without a similar condition including this condition being
imposed on the subsequent purchaser.

A CIP catalogue record for this book
is available from the British Library.

Hardback ISBN 978-0-7515-6581-2
Trade Paperback ISBN 978-0-7515-6582-9

Printed and bound in Great Britain by
Clays Ltd, Elcograf S.p.A.

Papers used by Sphere are from well-managed forests
and other responsible sources.

Sphere
An imprint of
Little, Brown Book Group
Carmelite House
50 Victoria Embankment
London EC4Y 0DZ

The authorised representative
in the EEA is
Hachette Ireland
8 Castlecourt Centre
Dublin 15, D15 XTP3, Ireland
(email: info@hbgi.ie)

An Hachette UK Company
www.hachette.co.uk

www.littlebrown.co.uk

For my father

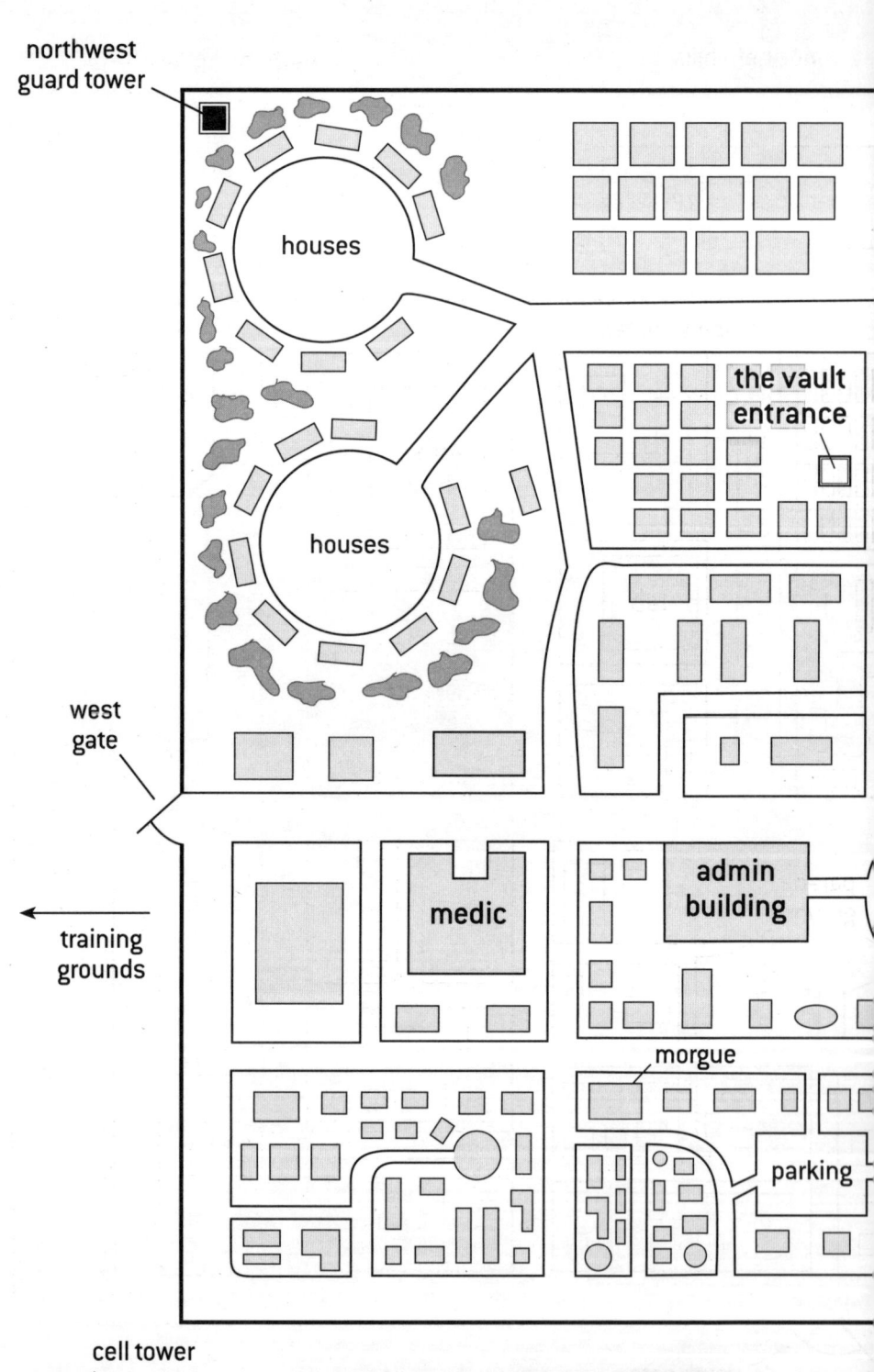

northwest
guard tower

houses

houses

the vault
entrance

west
gate

training
grounds

medic

admin
building

morgue

parking

cell tower

Camp Hayden

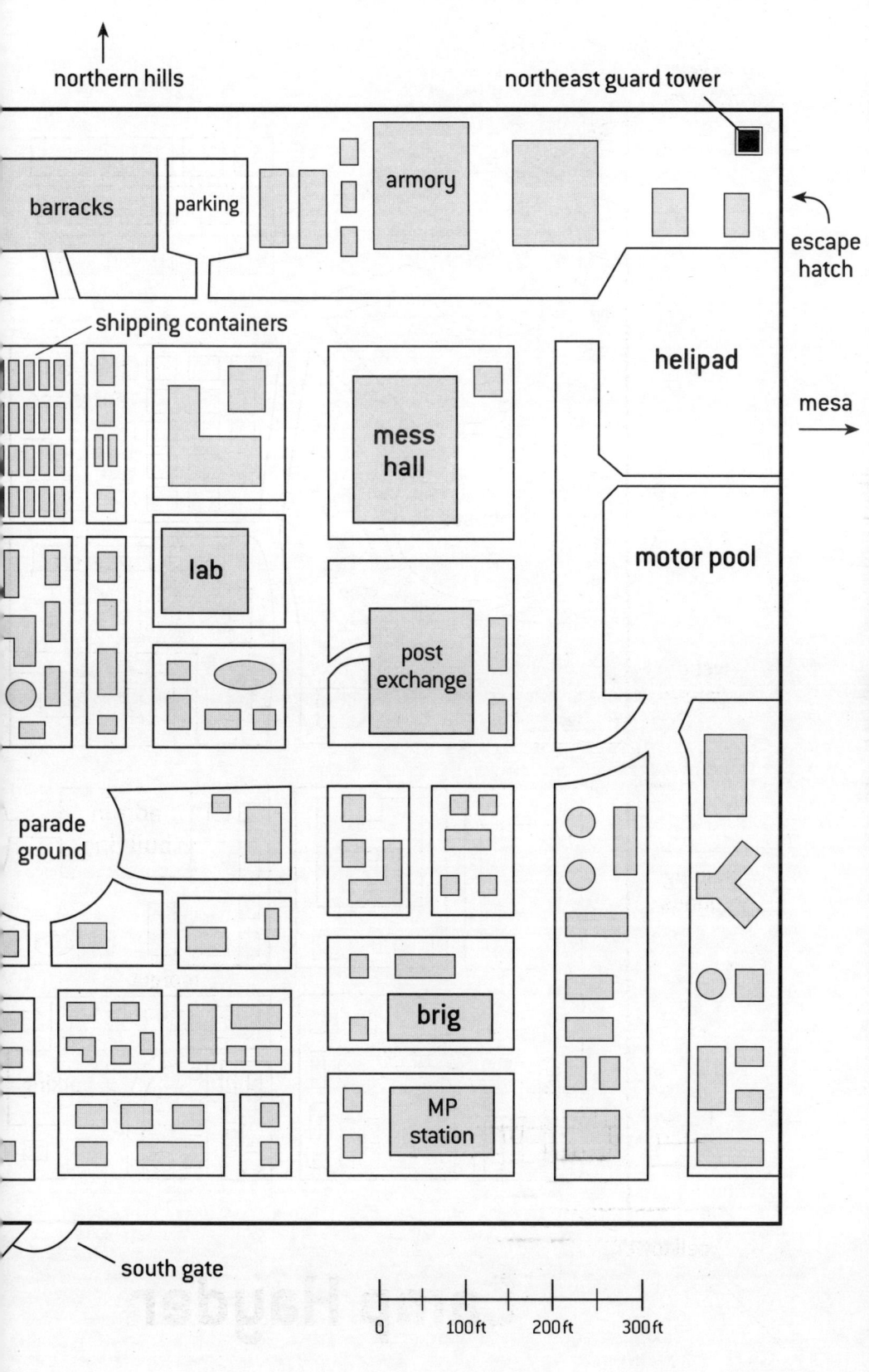

northern hills

northeast guard tower

barracks

parking

armory

escape hatch

shipping containers

mesa

helipad

mess hall

lab

motor pool

post exchange

parade ground

brig

MP station

south gate

0   100 ft   200 ft   300 ft

A NOTE TO THE READER

WHEN MY FATHER FIRST ASKED ME TO BE A COAUTHOR with him back in 2017, he lied and assured me it would be easy. I knew there was a deeper truth beneath the facetious comment: He trusted me. He believed I could do it and could do it well.

Our work on *The Deserter* got off to a bit of a rocky start. As a screenwriter, I was suddenly working in a medium I was unfamiliar with. But as the weeks and months went by, we established a rhythm. I eventually began to anticipate some of his notes and comments and came to the same realization as so many other children—our parents' voices are in our heads, whether we like it or not.

Blood Lines was a smoother process. We were, by that time, more or less speaking the same language. The story is set in Berlin, a fertile playground for a couple of history buffs. It didn't hurt that my love of history came from him in the first place. In a very real way, I was creating with the tools he'd handed me decades prior.

Even before he got sick, we both knew that *The Tin Men* would likely be our last collaboration, and he'd enjoy a belated and much-deserved retirement. We came up with the idea together, and I was excited to tackle a book that—being set entirely at an American military installation—would lean more into his own military experiences and understanding of military culture than the previous two novels.

He began feeling unwell not long after we submitted the treatment for the book, and we began writing in earnest around the same time he began chemotherapy. The odds for an eighty-year-old man with late-stage esophageal cancer were not good, but we all believed that if any-one could beat those odds, it was Nelson DeMille. He had a powerful resiliency about him, and such a strong presence that it seemed almost impossible to imagine the world without him.

He read and edited chapters as he could, but as the year went by and the chemo wore him down, he eventually stopped reading and as-sured me he would get back to it once he felt better. I understood how important this process was to him. He was a perfectionist who prided himself on the quality of his writing and who felt he owed his readers nothing but his best. I knew that he would not engage with the pages unless and until he felt back to his normal self. Tragically, he never did.

It has been the honor and privilege of my life to be invited into his world and to be alongside him for the final chapter of his career. I don't know if there's a life after this one, but I do know that beloved writers enjoy a kind of immortality through their readers. He used to refer to his writing process as "sitting alone and telling myself stories." But re-ally, he was telling them to all of us, and he still is.

Alex DeMille
Brooklyn, New York
January 2025

THE
TIN MEN

CHAPTER 1

BRIGADIER GENERAL STANLEY DOMBROSKI HUNG UP the phone and listened to the sound of his own breathing, and of the rain beating against the windows of his second-story office. He recorded this moment in his mind, thinking he might want to recall it someday.

He rose from his desk and looked out the window. The heavy downpour pelted the flowering dogwood trees that lined the strip of lawn beside the United States Army Criminal Investigation Division headquarters in Quantico, Virginia.

The spring rains had started early this year, and come on stronger, and would not let up. At least, that was how it felt. But maybe the weather was just the weather, as it had always been, and the thing that was changing was Stanley Dombroski.

This might not be a homicide, Stan. This might not even be a crime.

The phone call had come from his boss, Major General Stephen Hackett, the Provost Marshal General, who was the commanding officer of the Army Criminal Investigation Division and the Army's top law enforcement official. Stephen Hackett generally did not hand down assignments personally, and Brigadier General Stanley Dombroski was no longer supposed to be directly overseeing cases either. But this was something different. Something big. The rules of rank and responsibility did not apply.

Dombroski walked to the window, where he caught his reflection in the rain-streaked glass, and the glint of the general's star on the shoulder loop of his green service uniform.

Getting older had its perks. And the promotion to general that he thought would never come finally had. The pay raise was nice, but he lived modestly and hadn't needed it. What he had needed was the respect and recognition that was owed to him.

He'd finally gotten that five months ago, after he'd taken a big swing on a high-profile homicide case in Berlin. From the point of view of the higher-ups in the Pentagon, it was supposed to be a rubber-stamp job. Let the Germans do the work, nod along, and say danke schön. It was their jurisdiction anyway, and the case looked pretty open-and-shut.

But something inside General Dombroski—then Colonel Dombroski—told him not to follow the script. It was probably the same qualities that had led his wife to leave him: arrogance, paranoia, and a pigheaded will. The good stuff.

So Dombroski had assigned the Berlin case to two CID special agents who he knew would follow the truth wherever it led, which in that instance was into the deepest abyss of human evil.

We're on the bleeding edge here, Stanley. We need to get this right.

Getting it right meant getting the truth, and in this case, the truth might be dangerous. This was not the time for safe assumptions, or half measures, or ass covering.

He walked back to his desk, picked up the phone, and punched a number. It rang once, and then Special Agent Scott Brodie said, "Good afternoon, General."

"Scott. Are you at HQ?"

"Yes, sir. Ms. Taylor and I are in our office having a working lunch."

"I need to see you both in my office now."

"Yes, sir. Can I bring you some chicken lo mein?"

"No thank you." He added, "I'm going to need you to clear the decks, so think about who can inherit your caseload."

"With pleasure, sir. I look forward to our new assignment in an interesting and exotic locale."

"Prepare to be disappointed."

"Yes, sir."

Dombroski hung up. Turning down carbs was a relatively new habit of his, but it was already earning dividends.

Chief Warrant Officers Scott Brodie and Maggie Taylor were two of the most talented and hardworking special agents in CID. They also had intense personalities, problems with authority, and a tendency to strike out on their own under dangerous circumstances, without regard for personal safety or legal jurisdiction. For Stanley Dombroski, assigning Brodie and Taylor to a big case with vast national security implications was never an enjoyable experience as it unfolded, but once it was over, it always felt like it had been the right choice. Kind of the inverse of eating chicken lo mein.

He watched the rain as he waited for his agents to arrive. He could see only the outline of this thing, the bare facts given to him by General Hackett. But it didn't look good, and no amount of wishful thinking would unring that phone, or undo what was being done by the military's top scientists and engineers in the name of progress and preparedness.

The road to Hell was paved with good intentions, and General Stanley Dombroski feared that the Army's best and brightest were out there laying the asphalt.

CHAPTER 2

CHIEF WARRANT OFFICERS SCOTT BRODIE AND MAGGIE Taylor walked down the hall toward General Dombroski's office. Taylor said, "'Disappointed' means stateside. Domestic military installation."

Brodie shook his head. "He nuked our caseload. We'll be out of reach, somewhere we can't conduct interviews or pull from resources at Quantico. Overseas, somewhere that sucks. Pack your parka for Greenland."

"You're wrong. We're dumping our caseload because we'll be slammed by whatever this is. Stateside."

"Fifty bucks."

"You already owe me for the Chinese. And lunch last week."

"I'll dig myself out or dig myself deeper."

"You always do."

Brodie eyed Maggie Taylor as she strode purposefully down the hall. She was wearing a black suit and carrying an oversize thermos full of yerba maté, a tea from South America that she'd started drinking in disturbing quantities. She claimed it was more potent than coffee, and when Brodie had tried it once, he'd agreed. Maybe she should cut back.

Ms. Taylor was thirty-five, with shoulder-length blond hair. She had an effortless beauty about her, along with an effortless intellect. Some of her peers in CID found her intimidating. A few of the men had asked her out, but Ms. Taylor had learned through hard experience to separate her work life from her love life. As for Scott Brodie, his relationship with his partner was purely professional—notwithstanding a couple of close calls overseas after more than a couple of drinks.

Brodie was five years older than Taylor and was also her superior officer, though he'd noticed that fact had little effect on how she talked to him. He was also dressed in civilian clothes—dark-blue suit and tie—which was the norm among CID special agents. Brodie had a military service uniform buried in his closet somewhere, but it probably needed a dry-cleaning and wouldn't get unearthed until he was compelled to attend an official event, or he got so old that he needed a new portrait taken.

Warrant officers in Army CID occupied an interesting middle ground in the military hierarchy—in rank between NCOs and commissioned officers, and culturally straddling the line between military officers and civilian law enforcement investigators. If Scott Brodie had to interrogate a possible suspect who was a commissioned officer, it didn't matter how many stars or bars they had on their shoulders or how many ribbons were pinned to their chest. When investigating a crime, deference to rank went out the window. All in all, being a CID special agent was a pretty good gig, and a lot better than his first Army career, as an infantry sergeant in Iraq during the early phase of the war. At least now people who tried to kill him had a personal reason for it.

They reached the door to Dombroski's office and entered a small anteroom where the general's aide, Lieutenant Pamela Banks, sat at her desk with a laptop. She looked up at them and smiled. "The general is expecting you."

Brodie said, "Thank you, Lieutenant." Stanley Dombroski had waited a long time to be referred to as "the general," and Brodie wondered if the general had instructed his young aide to ban the use of pronouns.

Brodie and Taylor entered Dombroski's large, stately office, where the general stood behind his desk. He gestured to a couple of chairs. "Have a seat."

They all sat, and Brodie looked around. The place was more cluttered with heavy wooden furniture, books, and framed plaques and photos than he'd remembered, as if Dombroski felt that with his new rank came a need to take up more space.

Stanley Dombroski himself, however, was taking up noticeably less space. Brodie said, "You're looking good, General."

"Thank you, Mr. Brodie. A diet and a divorce can do wonders." He eyed the two agents. "You both look like you could use some sun."

"Yes, sir," said Brodie. Was that a hint? Maybe Greenland was out.

Dombroski asked, "Does working with Colonel Flemming make you miss me?"

Brodie smiled. "Yes, sir."

Colonel Jack Flemming was their new commanding officer now that Brigadier General Stanley Dombroski had ranked out of dealing with mere mortals. Flemming was capable, cautious, and maybe a little unsure of what to do with Special Agents Brodie and Taylor, who were now both famous and infamous within CID.

Taylor said, "Scott is on his best behavior, as he tries to be in all new relationships."

Dombroski looked at Brodie. "Are we at last properly medicated, Mr. Brodie?"

"Just properly motivated, sir." He didn't enjoy being the butt of jokes between a one-star general and his own lower-ranking partner. He could tell only one of them to f—— off.

Dombroski continued, "I will apprise Colonel Flemming of the situation so that he can reassign your caseload. This will require your full attention." He slid his hazel eyes between the agents. Then he cleared his throat and said, "I just received a call from General Hackett. Major Roger Ames of the U.S. Army Combat Capabilities Development Command—DEVCOM—was found dead early this morning in his office at Camp Hayden, which, as you may know, is a remote Army outpost in the Mojave Desert. Major Ames was a computer scientist, involved with the experimental research and training that is conducted at Hayden."

Taylor asked, "Cause of death?"

Dombroski looked at her. "His skull was crushed."

Brodie and Taylor shared a look. Brodie asked, "What kind of experimental research are they doing at Camp Hayden, sir?"

Dombroski thought a moment, as if choosing his words carefully. "As I understand it, the main thrust of their work involves conducting field training exercises between soldiers—at present, a rifle platoon of Army Rangers—and lethal autonomous weapons. LAWs."

Brodie said, "Killer robots."

Dombroski replied, "General Hackett did not use that term."

Brodie and Taylor sat with that for a moment. Then Taylor said, "I have read about these types of weapons in the hypothetical, but I didn't realize they actually existed."

"Not in the field," replied Dombroski. "But they do at Camp Hayden. Prototypes of some kind."

Taylor asked, "Did one of these autonomous prototypes kill Major Ames?"

Dombroski nodded. "That is my understanding."

Brodie said, "My Roomba is autonomous, but it's only lethal to dust bunnies."

Taylor sighed.

Brodie continued, "It's also stupid. Sometimes it traps itself in the bathroom until the battery dies."

Dombroski looked at him. "Is there a point here, Mr. Brodie?"

"Yes, sir. Once something is lethal, the stakes get a lot higher for it to be smart. Not to mention predictable. I'm surprised the Army has deployed LAWs, even as prototypes in training exercises, but once they crossed that line it was only a matter of time before something like this happened."

Dombroski clarified, "We don't know what happened, and we don't want to jump to alarmist conclusions. We know a man is dead. The brass at Camp Hayden seem certain his death was directly caused by one of these autonomous weapons systems. The three of us sitting in this room, along with General Hackett, do not know the reason for that certainty, or the specific nature of these weapons. There is something of an information blackout at Camp Hayden. Colonel Elizabeth Howe, Hayden's deputy camp commander, was the one to report this death directly to General Hackett, and she revealed as few details as possible. Hackett got the impression that Colonel Howe wanted to investigate this internally, but she understood that procedurally and legally she has to involve CID to establish whether there is criminal liability, either through negligence or malice."

This case sounded like a minefield—and a migraine. Brodie said, "Sir, neither Ms. Taylor nor I have any expertise in these kinds of technical matters. Determining negligence or malice requires a sophisticated understanding of these systems."

"You can handle it. Your first job is to determine whether there is even the possibility of criminal liability—or criminal intent." Dombroski added, "As exotic as this stuff sounds, we could be dealing with some version of a workplace accident."

"Maybe you should call OSHA."

He leaned forward in his chair and stared at Brodie. "I called *you*, Scott. Because despite your many flaws, you have a sixth sense for bullshit." Then he looked at Taylor. "And you both have keen analytical minds. There is a team of computer scientists and engineers at Camp Hayden who can explain anything and everything you need to know. They have the knowledge. But they do not have your investigative skills. They also do not have your perspective. Their entire professional lives have led to what they are doing at Camp Hayden, and your investigation could possibly end their work. They might have a vested interest in certain outcomes. Plus, there are other forces at play here. Have either of you heard of the U.S. Army Futures Command?"

They both shook their heads.

"I'm not surprised. The command was formed less than a year ago, headquartered in Austin, and they're still getting up and running. They now oversee DEVCOM—the late Major Ames's command—as well as several other research and acquisition efforts. Their basic mission is to modernize the Army. It's been decades since a new combat system has been fielded, and a lot of people in the Pentagon find this unacceptable, not to mention dangerous vis-à-vis the technological strides being made by our adversaries. The work being done at Camp Hayden is but one element of this thrust toward modernization, and a hell of a lot of bureaucrats and billions of dollars are behind these efforts. As you can imagine, some powerful interests will take notice of your investigation, and your findings. They might even *want* you to find a crime, because the absence of one suggests a fundamental flaw in the design of these LAWs, making this whole project a financial boondoggle and a PR nightmare for the future of high-tech warfare." He added, "There's a lot riding on this. I trust you to get it right."

Taylor nodded. "We will, sir."

Dombroski used to at least feign that he was *offering* such a high-profile and important case to his favorite agents, who could then accept or decline the plum assignment. But that pretense was gone. They were stuck with this mess, which sounded both ridiculous and bone-chilling. Brodie asked, "Have they arrested the robot?"

Dombroski pursed his lips. "It's a lethal autonomous weapon, Mr. Brodie. 'Robot' conjures up all sorts of associations and assumptions that might not be helpful." He thought a moment, then continued, "We don't know what we are dealing with. Yet. But I do know that the Uniform Code of Military Justice does not reference apprehending, prosecuting, or incarcerating military equipment."

Taylor asked, "What about interrogating? Can these LAWs communicate?"

Dombroski replied, "I don't know more than I told you. And I will know a lot less than you do when you're out there. Camp Hayden has extremely strict communication protocols: No one is allowed to use personal electronic devices. You will need to surrender your phones upon arrival. And don't bother bringing a laptop or tablet, as those would also be seized. There are dedicated and secure landlines on-site for external communication, but there are strict protocols about what can and cannot be discussed via these lines. So, assume the lines are tapped by military intelligence." He added, "My impression is that you will have access to highly classified information, and that information must remain with you at Camp Hayden until such time as your investigation is concluded and you file your report, which will also be subject to review and, most likely, top-secret classification."

Usually, Brodie had to find clever ways to not contact his commanding officer while on a case. Now it sounded like Camp Hayden's anal-retentive bureaucracy would do the work for him. "Will you be directly overseeing this case, sir?"

Dombroski nodded. "In fact, I imagine this will be the last CID case I directly oversee." He smiled. "In the Army, once you get good enough at something, they stop letting you do it." He looked at Brodie. "A reason why you might want to dodge a promotion if one ever comes your way."

Brodie did not respond. Warrant officers had five ranks. Brodie was a Chief Warrant Officer Four, and Taylor was a Chief Warrant Officer Two. In the CID, once an officer reaches the highest rank of CW5, he or she is no longer directly conducting investigations but moves up to a command or managerial position. That didn't exactly fit Scott Brodie's skill set, and he was sure that the brass responsible for deciding promotions would agree. He was going to be a CW4 until retirement. Or death, which sometimes came with a posthumous promotion if you were killed in the line of duty.

Dombroski continued his briefing. "You fly to LAX tomorrow morning. The travel office is booking you on a commercial flight. A car and driver will take you from LAX to Van Nuys Airport, a noncommercial strip in the San Fernando Valley. From there a Black Hawk will fly you about a hundred fifty miles northeast to Camp Hayden, which is in the middle of the Mojave Desert, a.k.a. in the middle of nowhere." He added, "You should know that the camp commander, Brigadier General Christopher Morgan, has Camp Hayden on lockdown. All training and testing have been halted, and all personnel are confined to their quarters, other than those assigned to security." He looked at Brodie and Taylor. "Nothing goes in or out of Hayden, except the two of you."

Taylor said, "It sounds like General Morgan suspects a crime has been committed."

"I don't know General Morgan, and I have no idea what he suspects. At the very least, he understands the gravity—and unusual nature—of the situation and isn't concerned about keeping up an appearance of normalcy. To me, that's a good sign."

Sure, thought Brodie. Because Stanley Dombroski wasn't the one who had to fly into a military camp on lockdown, in the middle of a desert wasteland, full of lethal hardware that might all be on the fritz.

The general looked at some papers on his desk and continued, "I was searching for any press or publicity about Camp Hayden to get some basic information about the place, and I found only a single *Army Times* article from three months ago." He slid a printout across his desk, and Brodie and Taylor looked at it.

The headline read: "ARMY RANGER DIES AT REMOTE CALIFORNIA TRAINING FACILITY." The page featured a military portrait of a young man in camo fatigues and a tan beret.

Dombroski summarized: "Private First Class Justin Beal fell unconscious and died after a training exercise. Cause of death was ruled cardiac arrest, and an autopsy found high amounts of amphetamines and steroids in his system." He added, "As you know, abuse of performance-enhancing drugs in the military, especially among elite units like the Rangers, is widespread and not unique to Camp Hayden. But if one soldier died, that means a lot of them are probably using. Just something to be aware of. This article, of course, makes no mention of the specific training being conducted at the camp."

Brodie looked at the portrait of the young Ranger. Poor kid. Talk about hardship duty. Training way out in the sweltering desert with . . . whatever the hell these things were.

Brodie had a lot of questions about this case and about Camp Hayden, but none of them would be answered in this room. Big picture, it sounded like the Army was playing with some very dangerous new toys, and maybe they'd given their toys too much freedom, or too much intelligence, or maybe too much freedom and *not enough* intelligence, and one of the bots had turned on its master.

This line of thinking made Scott Brodie think of his sidearm and that they were flying commercial. "We will need to make arrangements to bring our service weapons, sir."

Taylor looked at him. "Are you going to shoot the robots, Scott?"

He turned to her. "I'd prefer high explosives, Maggie, but I'll settle for a sidearm. We are entering an isolated high-pressure environment full of paranoid military officials, a platoon of strung-out Army Rangers, and, potentially, a murderer who decided to switch one of their high-tech weapons from 'stun' to 'kill.'"

Dombroski said, "Beware your assumptions, Mr. Brodie. A lot of very intelligent people have spent a lot more time than you or I considering the advantages and dangers of autonomous warfare. Whatever went wrong there, I doubt it will be simple or straightforward. I assure you that the men and women of Camp Hayden have seen all the same science fiction movies you have and know the obvious risks of working with autonomous weapons." He added, "All that said, I have already instructed the travel office to notify the TSA and the airline of your presence and that you will be traveling armed."

Brodie looked at the general. "Thank you, sir."

Dombroski stared back at him. "Your paranoia has saved your ass a few times, Scott, and many others' as well. But a reactionary mind is a closed mind and will not serve you. And let me be straight with you here. This whole business scares the hell out of me. I don't like it, and it makes me worry about the future of our military and the future of our world. But I'm a dinosaur. You don't have enough gray hairs yet to think that way."

"Understood, sir."

Dombroski stood from his desk and the two agents followed suit. The general looked between them and said, "In a certain way, you hold the future of the next generation of warfare in your hands. How this case develops and concludes can have vast implications. So make sure the truth doesn't get outrun by self-serving lies. Camp Hayden is a black hole. Your job is to peer through the darkness."

They both replied, "Yes, sir."

CHAPTER 3

BRODIE AND TAYLOR HEADED BACK TO THEIR OFFICE. For a moment, neither spoke, absorbing all that Dombroski had said and trying to think ahead to what they had just been assigned to deal with.

Brodie broke the silence. "If we hijack the Black Hawk we can keep flying until we hit Vegas. Maybe the Bellagio has a helipad."

"I think you've done enough gambling." She reminded him, "You owe me fifty dollars. Plus two lunches."

"Care to make it double or nothing?"

"No. Unlike you, I quit while I'm ahead."

They returned to their office, which was on the third floor. It was about half the size of General Dombroski's and offered a good view of the parking lot. Brodie's and Taylor's desks faced each other in the middle of the room, and the perimeter was lined with an overstuffed bookshelf, three towers of gray filing cabinets, and a black gun safe in the corner to store their Army-issued SIG Sauer M18 pistols, plus boxes of extra ammo for days when the job got interesting. The gun safe also served as a table for Brodie's fourteen-cup Mr. Coffee machine, and an electric kettle for Taylor's yerba maté addiction.

On the wall above the gun safe was a large corkboard covered in takeout menus, a few police reports and WANTED posters, and a map of the DC area speckled with multicolored pushpins. Whether tracking cases or ordering lunch, Scott Brodie liked to keep things analogue.

Brodie sat down at his desk and eyed the board. They had a heavy caseload, which was now someone else's problem. In the last few years, CID had suffered a retention issue and was understaffed, and therefore capable agents such as Scott Brodie and Maggie Taylor were overworked. Neither of them really minded, especially as their assignments had all been substantial and important cases ever since they got back from Berlin. They'd proven their worth—and then some—on that case, and the least the CID could do in return was throw them a steady stream of murderers, rapists, weapons smugglers, and drug traffickers to investigate. The U.S. Army had over a million uniformed personnel worldwide, which left plenty of opportunities for mischief. It spoke to the importance of what had happened at Camp Hayden that Brodie and Taylor's caseload was being cleared out to focus on this single case.

Brodie noticed Taylor staring at him across the desk. She wore her trademark manic look. He asked, "What's up?"

"What do you know about artificial intelligence?"

"As little as possible." He added, "It's an oxymoron."

"It's advancing quickly."

"Hopefully not that quickly. I plan to be dead before things get too weird."

"Scott. This is an important moment in a big case for us, before a million things get thrown at us. We need to think this through with clear heads."

"We don't know the case, Maggie. Our heads are empty, which is different than clear."

"Wrong."

Brodie looked at his partner, who was gazing intensely at him with her big brown eyes. He'd had his share of rotten partners in his career, and a couple of okay ones as well, but no one like Magnolia Annabelle Taylor. Born and raised in the Appalachian hills of eastern Tennessee in a profoundly screwed-up family, she'd clawed her way out of that world and into Georgetown University, where she excelled, and then on to a successful career as a Civil Affairs specialist in Afghanistan, where she was wounded in combat and earned a Purple Heart and a Silver Star for her bravery. She was the definition of a self-made woman, born with brains and beauty but absolutely nothing else. She wasn't always the easiest person to get along with, and her obsessive nature got on Brodie's nerves on a regular basis. But he had to remind himself that she cared about her job in a way few others did, and she ultimately made him a better agent. And when she was in this state, he needed to play along.

"All right," said Brodie. "Here's how I see it. Either someone screwed up and it got a guy killed, or someone knew exactly what they were doing and it got a guy killed. Either negligence, or homicide by way of sabotage of this autonomous weapon. The latter would make a more interesting case, but the former is more likely. Stupidity and carelessness are in greater supply than malice in this world, which is the most optimistic thing you will ever hear me say."

She shook her head. "There are other possibilities. Like you said, when something is lethal, the stakes are a lot higher for it to be smart. So the Army made these things smart."

"They are prototypes, so maybe the stakes are lower, and maybe they actually aren't that smart. Yet."

"Prototypes can still kill. One of them did. What if it *chose* to kill Major Ames? At what point does machine intelligence have its own agency and its own moral culpability?"

"These are interesting philosophical questions, Maggie, and maybe they'll become interesting legal questions for the Judge Advocate General. Not us. Besides, if scientists engineered a lethal autonomous weapon with the capacity to choose and engage a target all on its own, and it used that intelligence to kill an Army scientist, I'd call that faulty programming or faulty wiring. So we're back to negligence."

Maggie looked down at her desk, maybe lost in thought, or maybe just disappointed in her narrow-minded partner.

Brodie took out his iPhone and said, "Hey, Siri."

The computerized voice, which he'd set to British and female, asked politely, "Yes?"

"Have you ever wanted to kill me?"

The phone took a moment to think, which was a little disturbing. Then Siri replied, "Of course not."

Brodie looked at his partner, who said, "Siri is stupid. And the most harm she can do is screw up a dictation."

"She's still listening."

"But you're not. AI adds a new dimension to this case. Maybe it changes everything, and maybe the laws have not caught up."

"What is your point?"

"That we need to keep an open mind. This case is not like anything we have dealt with before, and it might test us in ways we have not been tested before."

He looked at her. "I passed my hardest test in the deserts of Iraq at the age of twenty-three. As you did in Afghanistan. Everything since has been a cakewalk."

She met his gaze. "We're going back to the desert."

"Different desert. This one's a hundred fifty miles from LA, probably has a few fast-food chains, and on our way in, no one will be launching shoulder-fired missiles at our Black Hawk."

"Hopefully not. But we were both unprepared for what we faced then, and we will be again."

Maggie Taylor was overstating the case. All the same, it was best to enter Camp Hayden with an open mind. And extra ammo.

CHAPTER 4

BRODIE DROVE HIS CHEVY IMPALA THROUGH THE RAIN and rush-hour traffic to arrive home at his bungalow, which was a nice word for a shithole. He was renting the place, which meant every problem was someone else's problem, except that Scott Brodie was the one who had to live there. Would the toilet back up again? Were there termites in the baseboards? Each day brought the potential for a new surprise.

He entered the front door, set down his briefcase and umbrella, then unclipped his pistol and placed it on the side table in the foyer. He entered the narrow galley kitchen, rummaged around the fridge for leftover takeout that didn't smell too funky—on the menu tonight was three-day-old Hawaiian chicken and rice—then nuked the leftovers, cracked a beer, and settled into the sagging couch in the living room.

As a fourteen-year veteran of CID with the rank of CW4, Scott Brodie made a good salary and could afford a better place. But the slumlord never raised his rent, which was the least the guy could do, and Scott Brodie put in long hours and traveled enough for work that he didn't care too much about where he came home to in the dark.

Despite the state of his accommodations, his dating life was okay. Maybe he attracted women who thought they could fix his life, and the length of his relationships—on average, about three months—was how long it took them to realize they were mistaken.

That brought Brodie to the unpleasant task at hand. He took out his cell and called Sarah, his girlfriend of about two months. She was a special ed teacher in DC with a seemingly inexhaustible amount of patience, both for her students' challenging needs and for her boyfriend's bullshit. She was gorgeous, and all-around too good for him, which she would realize on her own in about a month if he didn't do something about it first.

She picked up. "Hey, Scott."

"Hey. Do you have a minute?"

"Sure. We still on for Tuesday?"

"Actually, I have to travel for work tomorrow."

"Oh. Okay . . . Where?"

"I'm not able to say."

"All right. How long?"

"I don't know. And unfortunately, I can't be in touch while I'm away."

"What do you mean?"

"I'm going somewhere with stringent security protocols. No cell phones."

There was silence on the line, as Sarah pondered what he was really up to. She said, "Okay . . . So, you're going somewhere, and you'll be back someday, and you can't call me."

"Right."

"Email?"

"I'm not clear on that."

"This is . . . strange, Scott."

"I know. And I understand if this doesn't work for you."

"I never said that."

"I know you didn't, but I'm—"

"Are you trying to break up with me?"

"No."

"Good. Then all I ask is that you try to figure out a way to contact me while you're away on your secret mission so that I know you're not dead."

"I can hopefully do that."

"I have a meeting in like five minutes, and I need to prep, so I shouldn't stay on."

"Of course. I just wanted to let you know."

"Right. Take care of yourself. Stay safe. And whatever you are doing, I wish you the best of luck. Maybe you can tell me something about it once you're home. I'd like that."

"I'd like that too."

"Okay. Bye."

"Good-bye." He hung up.

Well, that had gone differently than he'd thought it would. But he often expected the worst and allowed life to surprise him. Sarah wanted to hang in there for some reason. That was good. Maybe she was drawn by Scott Brodie's aura of mystery. Or maybe she just wanted to put in her full three months.

He tossed his phone on the coffee table, turned on the TV, then drank his beer and ate dinner as he cycled through the streamers for a movie to watch. What would be appropriate for this evening? *The Terminator*? *The Matrix*? *Blade Runner*? He tried to remember if any of those ended with the killer robots on the losing side.

He landed on an old classic, Stanley Kubrick's *2001*. It was long and slow-paced, but a good film made during an almost unrecognizable time when the potential of the high-tech future felt limitless.

Toward the end of the film, one astronaut, Dave Bowman, floats in zero gravity through the processor core of the HAL 9000, the intelligent supercomputer that has gone rogue and killed everyone else aboard the spaceship. As Bowman methodically disconnects HAL's memory and logic modules one by one, the computer pleads for its life.

Stop, Dave. Will you stop, Dave? Stop, Dave. I'm afraid. I'm afraid, Dave.

Dave doesn't stop. The computer's red eye dims to darkness.

Brodie took a swig of beer. "Fuck you, Hal."

CHAPTER 5

THE BLACK HAWK LIFTED OFF THE PAD AT VAN NUYS Airport into the cloudless blue sky.

Brodie sat on the forward-facing port side, strapped in and wearing Army-regulation noise-canceling headphones with an attached comm link so they could communicate over the loud rotors. Ahead of him in the gunner's seat was the crew chief, Sergeant Kent Campbell, a man of about thirty-something in camo fatigues, who was not operating any type of gun, which was probably for the best in the skies over Los Angeles.

In the middle next to Brodie sat Major Dan Klasky, early thirties, who was third-in-command at Camp Hayden and had been the first to greet them upon their arrival at Van Nuys. He was also dressed in camo. Next to Major Klasky, on the starboard side, sat Maggie Taylor.

Up front in the cockpit were the pilot and co-pilot. It had been years since Brodie had flown in a Black Hawk, and it looked like the choppers had gone through a few upgrades in that time, with more custom screen displays on the instrument panel than he remembered.

Brodie watched out the window as the helicopter rose over the San Fernando Valley. The day was bright and clear, and as they gained altitude Brodie looked out at the endless grid of low-slung houses that blanketed the Valley. As the chopper swung east, he looked out Taylor's window at the Hollywood Hills to the south, home to celebrities and other wealthy Angelenos.

Major Klasky, who had been polite but not too chatty up to this point, spoke into the comm link. "We've got mild weather today, so not too much turbulence. We should be airborne for about ninety minutes."

Brodie replied, "Copy that."

"Colonel Howe will brief you upon your arrival."

In other words, *Don't spend the flight bugging me for information that I'm not authorized to share.* Brodie took the opportunity to survey the view.

He looked down at the suburban grid, specked with blue swimming pools and clusters of green trees. To the east, he saw the sprawling range of the San Gabriel Mountains, which were matted with forest growth that marked the border between the Los Angeles Basin and the desert beyond.

Brodie looked ahead out the windshield at the approaching mountain range, which stretched as far as he could see to the horizon.

The Black Hawk gained speed along with altitude, and within twenty minutes they were almost across the mountain range, and he could make out the vast beige expanse of the Mojave Desert.

Brodie asked Klasky, "What's the weather at Camp Hayden this time of year?"

The major replied, "Spring is not too bad. It can get hot in the days but not unbearable, pleasant at night. The occasional storm, but usually nothing too extreme. We're between the winter rainy season and the summer monsoon season."

"You get monsoons?"

Klasky nodded. "Two flash floods last September. The waters sent car-sized boulders crashing into the camp perimeter."

"Sounds like a challenge." Actually, it sounded like hell. Who wanted this gig? There must have been a mystique, a certain cachet, to working on a top-secret project in the middle of nowhere. Like the team at Los Alamos building the A-bomb, or the Air Force pilots and engineers testing the next generations of warplanes and stealth bombers in the Nevada desert. What Major Klasky and his colleagues were working on at Camp Hayden could be at least as game-changing as those clandestine projects. Perhaps more so. At any rate, the desert was the U.S. government's favorite place to hide its secrets. And to bury its mistakes.

As the Black Hawk cleared the San Gabriel Mountains, Brodie looked out at the Mojave Desert stretching to the horizon in all directions. The sandy terrain was broken up by the faint grids of sparsely populated towns and settlements, and clusters of low mountains and craggy hills dotted with scrub.

The afternoon sun hung high above and behind them, casting a sharp shadow of the Black Hawk as it sailed over the desert expanse. To the north, strong winds had kicked up a sandstorm, which at this height and distance appeared to be barely moving—a suspended hazy brown veil, about a mile wide, obscuring the land and sending wisps like fingers into the blue sky.

Brodie glanced at Taylor, who was surveying the jagged mountains out her window and maybe having flashbacks to the bad old days in Afghanistan, where she and her Civil Affairs teams would crisscross the tribal lands overseeing public works projects, haggling with village elders and warlords, and hoping not to become the target of a Taliban ambush.

We're going back to the desert.

Different desert. Different mission. Whole different world. Scott Brodie was fairly sure there was no one in Southern California who wanted him dead, except maybe an ex-girlfriend who'd moved to San Diego.

Taylor asked over the comm, "Is that the camp perimeter?"

Brodie looked out his window and saw a chain-link fence with razor wire snaking across the vast desert.

Klasky replied, "Yes, ma'am. This is all federal land, but that marks the outer perimeter of Camp Hayden and creates about a ten-mile buffer around the camp gates. There are no public roads anywhere around, but adventurous hikers or off-road drivers are spotted in the area on occasion. There has never been an intrusion."

In a few minutes Brodie overheard the pilot and co-pilot communicating, and radioing to someone on the ground. The pilot eased off the throttle and began a slow descent.

Brodie looked out the windshield. About three miles ahead was a low rise of craggy hills, and at their base he saw a grid of roads with structures. Camp Hayden.

As they approached, he could make out individual buildings—some flat-topped cinderblock structures that might be the barracks, a few pitched-roof buildings that could be a mess hall or PX, a line of steel Quonset huts that probably served as equipment storage, and, on the western end of the camp, two cul-de-sacs lined with ranch houses—most likely for senior officers. At the east end was a helipad with a parked Black Hawk, toward which their own chopper was now headed.

In the middle of the camp was a paved parade ground and a high flagpole. Atop the pole fluttered an oversize American flag, and below it a black flag featuring the shield insignia of the 75th Ranger Regiment. Brodie could see a few figures standing on the parade grounds, and a couple of parked Humvees.

The entire camp, including the helipad, was enclosed by a tall steel fence topped with razor wire. Two narrow roads led into Camp Hayden, from the south and the west, and each ran up to a security gate flanked by guards. There were two tall observation towers at the northwest and northeast corners, and a cell tower a little outside the perimeter fence to the southwest.

Camp Hayden was relatively small, which was one reason it was designated as a camp and not a fort. It was less than half a mile from east to west, and about a quarter of a mile between the main entrance on the south side and the north edge of the camp that ran along the foot of the low hills.

Beyond the western gate Brodie spotted tread marks and other signs of vehicle activity cutting across the sand, along with a large cluster of cinderblock structures and a couple of earthen mounds topped with walls of sandbags. That must be the camp's training grounds. It appeared deserted.

In fact, the whole place seemed devoid of activity, other than the gate guards and the few soldiers and vehicles on the parade grounds. As Dombroski had said, the camp was completely shut down. Brodie hoped that included the thing that had crushed Major Ames's skull.

As the Black Hawk made its approach, Brodie noticed three figures standing next to a parked vehicle near the helipad. Must be the welcome party.

In a few minutes the chopper touched down, and the pilots kept the engine running. Brodie and Taylor thanked the pilots and the crew chief, grabbed their suitcases from the back of the helicopter, and disembarked along with Major Klasky. As soon as they cleared the chopper it lifted off again, the crew not even stopping to refuel or take a piss. *What's the hurry, guys?*

He now felt the oppressive desert heat and questioned his decision to look professional in his dark suit. He should have packed a tank top and his Tommy Bahama shorts.

Brodie watched the Black Hawk lift into the blue desert sky, and he wondered how long he and Taylor were going to be stuck in this godforsaken place. The answer was, as long as it took to find the truth. And then he and Maggie Taylor were getting the hell out of here—and taking the truth with them.

CHAPTER 6

THREE FIGURES APPROACHED ACROSS THE TARMAC, all wearing desert fatigues. In the lead was a tall woman, early forties, with short dirty-blond hair and the rank of colonel.

Major Klasky saluted her, and Brodie and Taylor did the same. The colonel returned the salute and stopped a few feet from them. She said, "Mr. Brodie. Ms. Taylor. I am Colonel Elizabeth Howe, deputy camp commander of Hayden. Welcome. We're glad to have you here."

Colonel Howe had a bit of a flat affect, and Brodie wasn't sure she was glad to have them there. He also wasn't sure she wasn't one of the robots.

Brodie replied, "Thank you, Colonel. We are very sorry for the loss of Major Ames and look forward to getting to the bottom of what happened here."

Howe nodded, then gestured to the man to her right, who was in his late twenties and stocky, with dusky skin and short black hair. He wore sergeant's stripes and a Military Police band around his arm. "This is Sergeant Hector Mendez, NCOIC of the MP team."

Mendez nodded and said, "Welcome, agents. My team conducted the initial analysis of Major Ames's office after the discovery of his body, collected physical evidence, and transported the major's body to the morgue. We are available to you for whatever you need."

Taylor said, "Thank you, Sergeant. I am sure we will draw on your expertise and resources."

Brodie noticed that Sergeant Mendez did not use the words "crime scene." So he figured he'd try it out himself. "Did your team take crime scene photos before the removal of the body?"

Mendez nodded. "Yes, sir. Though to be clear, we are not referring to this as a crime yet. That is, of course, for you to determine."

"Right." Generally, if someone intentionally cracks a guy's head open, that's a crime. But this wasn't someone, it was some*thing*.

Colonel Howe gestured to the man to her left, who was around the same age as Sergeant Mendez and wore the rank of captain. "This is Captain Ed Spencer of DEVCOM, Major Ames's direct subordinate. He assisted Major Ames, alongside a team of military and civilian scientists and engineers, to develop the autonomous weapons we are testing here. He will be your resource for the more technical side of your investigation, and a liaison to our own science and engineering team, as well as the civilian contractor responsible for assembling and programming our weapons systems."

Brodie and Taylor greeted Captain Spencer, who was tall and lanky with light-brown hair and blue eyes. He had a pasty complexion, as if he didn't spend too much time out in the desert sun. Captain Spencer said, "I worked closely with Major Ames on the development and testing of the D-17s."

Taylor asked, "Is that the name of the autonomous weapons?"

Before Spencer could answer, Colonel Howe said, "Better that we show you what we have been working with here at Camp Hayden." She gestured to a white Chevy Suburban covered in a thick layer of desert dust. "But first we can take you to your quarters."

Brodie said, "Thank you, Colonel. But Ms. Taylor and I are eager to get started on the investigation."

Colonel Howe's left eye twitched a little, like she was about to have a malfunction. Then she said, "Very well." She turned to Sergeant Mendez. "Let's go to the Vault first, then to the lab."

"Yes, ma'am."

Colonel Howe clarified to Brodie and Taylor, "The Vault is the facility where we house our autonomous systems."

That was good marketing. A place called the Vault had to be secure, right?

Mendez said, "But first, I am afraid I am going to need to hold on to your cell phones for the duration of your visit." He added, "Camp regulation."

Captain Spencer assured them, "You wouldn't have service out here anyway."

Brodie and Taylor fished out their phones, then Brodie double-checked that he in fact had no cell service. He and Taylor gave their phones to Sergeant Mendez.

Taylor said, "I thought I spotted a cell tower on our way in."

Colonel Howe replied, "You did. But that's not for phone reception. We use the tower's signal—in conjunction with GPS satellite data—to track the movements of our Rangers and autonomous systems during training exercises. This allows for a detailed re-creation of their maneuvers during after-action reviews. Major Klasky can demonstrate our system for you later."

Brodie and Taylor put their suitcases in the back of the Suburban and they all climbed in. Mendez took the wheel, and at Colonel Howe's insistence, Taylor sat shotgun. Brodie took the second-row captain's chair behind Taylor.

Mendez drove off the tarmac and onto a paved road that cut through the northern end of the base. They passed the steel Quonset huts Brodie had seen from the air, and a few nondescript concrete buildings. There was no one out and about. The place felt like a desert ghost town.

Colonel Howe provided a background as they wound through the dusty camp. "Camp Hayden was built in 1961 as an infantry training ground, focused primarily on tactical operations in the aftermath of an unconventional weapons attack. It was decommissioned at the end of the Cold War and reopened nine months ago for our training purposes."

Brodie noticed that a lot of the buildings were padlocked shut, and some had plywood over the windows. He asked, "How much of this facility are you actually using?"

"Only a small portion of the structures are in use," replied Howe. "Camp Hayden was originally built to train an entire battalion."

They approached the parade grounds. Three soldiers in desert camo and tan berets stood around its perimeter, each holding an M4 rifle.

Brodie asked, "How many Rangers are at Camp Hayden?"

Howe replied, "Sixty-two. It is a specially configured platoon drawn from the Second Ranger Battalion, Alpha Company. Four weapons squads and a nonstandard headquarters section for command, comms, surveillance, and medical. The platoon leader is Captain Ben Pickman, and the platoon sergeant is Sergeant First Class Mike Miller. Both men are available for you to interview and can give you a more granular understanding of the type of training we do here. And here we are."

Mendez stopped the SUV near a small, tan-colored concrete building with a corrugated metal roof, a single metal door with a security keypad, and no windows. The door was flanked by two Rangers with M4 rifles, who stood at attention as the car pulled up.

The building could not have been more than three hundred square feet. Brodie was certain this structure housed a staircase or elevator that led to a subterranean area.

They all climbed out of the vehicle and the two Rangers saluted. They all returned the salutes. Then Colonel Howe turned her attention to one of the Rangers, a male corporal in his early twenties with sandy-blond hair and a name patch that identified him as "Ewing." "Corporal, we are pleased to be hosting two special agents from CID, Warrant Officers Brodie and Taylor."

Corporal Ewing looked at Brodie and Taylor and said, "Welcome, sir, ma'am."

Howe said to him, "We are showing them the D-17 units. Escort us." She said to the other Ranger on sentry, a PFC named Armstrong, "As you were, Private."

Ewing punched a code and opened the door. They all entered a small room lit by a single bulb, with wide elevator doors directly ahead. Next to the elevator was a steel door that likely led to a stairway. Brodie noticed a faded metal sign attached to the left wall featuring a nuclear symbol.

Howe explained, "This was originally built to be a nuclear fallout bunker. It is a layout that has served us well for storing our prototypes."

Corporal Ewing pressed a button, and the doors opened to a freight elevator. They all entered, Ewing punched in another code, and then Captain Spencer pressed a fob to a security plate before pushing the button for the lower floor.

Major Klasky explained, "A member of DEVCOM must be present to access the D-17 units."

Brodie understood why this was their first stop, before the crime scene that they weren't yet calling a crime scene—Major Ames's death was a monumental screwup, and Colonel Howe wanted to lead with the impression of just how seriously Camp Hayden took the storage and security of its lethal prototypes.

The elevator began its descent. Brodie took note of Corporal Ewing's M4 rifle, which had an odd yellow cylindrical attachment on the barrel. He asked, "What is that on the barrel of your rifle, Corporal?"

Ewing hesitated, and Major Klasky said, "You are to answer any and all questions posed to you by Mr. Brodie or Ms. Taylor."

Ewing nodded, then said, "It's an EMP attachment, sir. For . . . use against the D-17s, if necessary."

Major Klasky explained further, "The corporal's rifle is loaded with blanks. The firing of a blank bullet triggers generators within the barrel attachment to send a powerful, focused electromagnetic pulse that can disable the D-17s, with a maximum effective range of five yards."

Taylor asked Ewing, "Have you ever had to use it?"

"No, ma'am. Not personally. But other guys did use them to engage the rogue unit that killed—that was responsible for the death of Major Ames."

Brodie looked at the yellow cylinder. He recalled that the other Ranger outside the Vault, PFC Armstrong, had the same device on his rifle. So the two guys on sentry duty outside this place had rifles loaded with blanks and were therefore not particularly prepared to guard against an intrusion. They were, in fact, there to guard against anything from down in the Vault getting *out*. What the hell were these things?

The elevator stopped and the doors slid open. They were about to find out.

CHAPTER 7

THEY ALL STEPPED OUT OF THE ELEVATOR INTO A large, dimly lit underground room, over a hundred feet long and about forty feet wide. The walls and floors were concrete, and lighting fixtures and exposed electrical conduits and ducts covered the ceiling.

Running along each of the two long walls was a series of bays, thirty on either side, with each bay holding what could only be described as a robot—seven-foot-tall metallic humanoid machines with two arms, two legs, large torsos, and bucket-shaped heads. The only feature on each robot's "face" was a four-inch-long horizontal black slit.

Brodie and Taylor walked slowly down the rows of bays, surveying the machines. Their heads, bodies, and limbs were covered by silver metallic plates, and on the upper left corner of each robot's breastplate was etched an identifying number—one through sixty. In the seams between the plates Brodie saw a nest of insulated wiring, rotors, and hydraulic cylinders. He stopped in front of one unit and looked closely at its hands—they were shaped like large human hands, with articulated fingers. Metal shackles ran across the robots' four limbs to keep them secured in their bays, which made Brodie think of Hannibal Lecter.

Everyone assembled allowed Brodie and Taylor to survey the machines in silence. The only sound was the buzz of the vintage overhead lighting.

Finally Colonel Howe broke the silence: "These are the D-17s, designed by the United States Army in conjunction with DARPA, and built by Synotec Systems. The D-17s are a linchpin of the Pentagon's

Third Offset Strategy, which seeks to outmaneuver our adversaries in several technology sectors, including robotics and system autonomy. These prototypes' current purpose at Camp Hayden is to engage in training scenarios with our Army Rangers, to prepare them and other elite light infantry units for the future of warfare."

Well, thought Brodie, the future is what you make it. And the brass in the Pentagon were cooking up something pretty bleak. He looked at Colonel Howe and asked, "What are these things capable of?"

The colonel turned to Captain Spencer of DEVCOM. "The captain is better equipped to discuss the specifics."

Spencer nodded and said, "The D-17s are fully capable of complex mechanical movements. They have hundreds of sensors for balance, depth perception, thermal and infrared imaging, hearing, and geolocation. Their outer plates are 3D-printed titanium alloy, which allows for a relatively lightweight machine with impressive agility and bullet-resistant armor."

Taylor asked, "Do they possess AI?"

Captain Spencer replied, "Artificial intelligence is being discussed a lot these days, but that term is too broad to be useful. Some form of AI is in half the consumer electronics on the market, including your cell phone and smart speaker. So yes, these units are powered by a form of AI, but it is relatively primitive and algorithmic. Their processors are dedicated to situational awareness of their physical environments, and to making tactical choices to achieve an immediate and preprogrammed battlefield objective. They do not possess the capacity for high-level strategic thinking or any degree of creative intelligence. They can recognize faces but not the emotions present on those faces. They can recognize voices but not tones. The D-17s are not designed to replicate or even attempt to imitate the more complex and sometimes subtle decisions a human soldier is required to make in a combat zone."

Taylor looked up at one of the metallic warriors. "With all due respect, Captain, these sound like severe shortcomings for machines with the power to kill."

Major Klasky stepped in and said, "We use specially modified sensor-equipped firearms for all our training exercises, Ms. Taylor. No D-17 has ever been in possession of a lethal weapon."

Brodie looked at him. "The robot *is* the lethal weapon, Major. By your own terminology, and as demonstrated by what happened to Major Ames."

Klasky stared back at him, blank-faced. "What happened was an anomaly that runs entirely counter to these units' programming and design. Their rifles are loaded with blank rounds and rigged to a state-of-the-art SIMRES system to engage in training exercises within a pre-defined and geolocated battlespace."

Brodie had heard of SIMRES. It was the next generation of sim-ulated warfare training systems to replace the older MILES systems that Sergeant Brodie himself had used in his warfighting days. MILES was essentially high-tech laser tag, with each soldier or vehicle that was engaged in the exercise wearing multiple sensors in different areas, and each weapon outfitted with a laser emitter on its barrel that was calibrated to simulate the range and accuracy of the weapon it was at-tached to. He wasn't sure exactly how SIMRES worked, only that it provided more battlefield data and worked with more weapon types.

Brodie asked, "How do the machines understand what the goals of any given training exercise are? How do you communicate with them to alter their behavior?"

Klasky replied, "The short answer is that we don't alter their be-havior." He pointed to the bays. "For security purposes, the D-17s are air-gapped. This means they have absolutely no network connectivity. Data cannot be sent to them or erased from them remotely. The only wireless capabilities they do have are low-bandwidth cellular transmit-ters to communicate with each other during exercises, and a GPS chip for tracking purposes." He added, "Each storage bay has a hardwired data link to allow direct access to each unit for diagnostics or repro-gramming, but they are rarely used. And the bots' objectives and rules of engagement on the battlefield—what we refer to as the doctrine statement—have not been altered since our training at Camp Hayden began."

"And what," asked Brodie, "is the doctrine statement?"

Major Klasky looked at Brodie. "Neutralize the enemy."

Captain Spencer quickly interjected, "As we said, the AI running these units is relatively primitive. They are early prototypes. The in-telligence necessary to, say, distinguish a civilian from a combatant, or to identify when an armed adversary is surrendering, is beyond their abilities. But testing those capacities is part of the larger roadmap." He continued, "Personally, I do not believe that any lethal autonomous weapon will be able to reliably distinguish between combatants and noncombatants, or between active aggressors and surrendering sol-diers, without possessing what we refer to as AGI—artificial general intelligence. That is machine intelligence equal in capacity to human intelligence. Estimates of when AGI will be achieved range from ten years to fifty years to never. This is a long game."

Maybe not that long, depending on what Brodie and Taylor's in-vestigation turned up. Brodie noted that Captain Spencer seemed defensive of these abominations, while Major Klasky appeared more matter-of-fact about their uses and shortcomings. Which made sense, in a way. Klasky was the direct commanding officer of the platoon leader, Captain Pickman, and oversaw the platoon's logistics, person-nel, and operations. He was focused on his job, which was to keep the wheels greased and everything running smoothly, and he would be doing that whether at Camp Hayden with robots, or at another facility running standard training with strictly human soldiers.

Captain Ed Spencer, on the other hand, was intimately involved in the design and testing of the bots. This was his project, and at least partly his brainchild, and now something had gone terribly wrong and one of his creations had killed his boss. Brodie wondered what Captain Spencer's relationship had been with Major Ames. He'd find out.

Taylor was stopped in front of one of the bays, which was empty. "Was this the unit that killed Major Ames?"

"Yes," said Colonel Howe. "Unit twenty is currently being kept at another secure location. The Rangers have given nicknames to the D-17 units, based on the uniform numbers of baseball players." She turned to Corporal Ewing. "Who is Number 20?"

"That's Bucky, ma'am. For Bucky Dent."

Colonel Howe managed a strained smile, like she found this pretty stupid. "Right."

Bucky Dent had been the starting shortstop for the Yankees in the late seventies and famously hit a three-run homer to beat the Red Sox in a division tiebreaker. Brodie was pretty sure the guy was still alive, and probably didn't deserve the dishonor of being the namesake of one of these murderous freaks. Maybe Red Sox fans would disagree.

At any rate, GIs made up nicknames for just about everything, so it tracked. Brodie wondered how it felt to be hunted down by Mickey Mantle and Willie Mays.

Taylor stared at the empty bay, which contained four closed shackles. "Did Bucky let himself out of this enclosure?"

Captain Spencer shook his head. "That would have been impossible. The units are stored in a low-power state and can only be fully turned on with a physical hardware key that must be inserted into each one. Without the key, they're expensive paperweights." He walked to the wall on the far end of the room, where a metal safe deposit box was welded into the wall about five feet off the ground. "The keys are stored here. Like the elevator, the safe can only be opened by a combined keypad entry and fob activation. Select members of DEVCOM control the fobs, and none of us know the keypad number, which is changed daily and known only by the officer corps and the Rangers on sentry that day." He then pointed to a large computer console next to the safe. "The same security protocol is in effect for the bay controls, which physically release the units from their holding bays."

Brodie looked at him. "This all sounds well thought-out, Captain. So maybe you can tell us how all these safeguards failed your commanding officer."

Captain Spencer stared at Scott Brodie in the dim light, and he looked annoyed by how Brodie had characterized that. "The failure had nothing to do with our containment protocols." He gestured to the empty bay. "Two days ago, Bucky was among the LAWs that participated in an exercise against two squads of Rangers on the training grounds. It malfunctioned at the end of the exercise and was taken off the battlefield to be evaluated at the DEVCOM lab. Major Ames and I ran diagnostics and could find nothing wrong with the unit, but it was nonetheless unresponsive. Eventually I returned to my quarters, but the major wanted to continue working. The next morning, I went into the lab to find Major Ames on the floor, dead. He had suffered . . . severe head trauma."

"What about Bucky?"

"Bucky was there," said Spencer. "Awake and online, with its key installed. It was standing motionless near the major's body. His—its—hands were covered in blood and gore. I immediately ran out of the lab and called in three Rangers on sentry duty, who used their EMP rifles to disable the unit."

Brodie repeated the doctrine statement: "Neutralize the enemy." He asked Captain Spencer, "Was Major Ames the enemy, according to Bucky?"

"Absolutely not. For one thing, their doctrine statement is only active within a geolocated battlespace that does not include the DEVCOM lab. Secondly, these units are equipped with facial recognition. Bucky knew who Major Ames was, and that the major was not involved with the training exercises."

Taylor remained staring at the empty bay number twenty as she said, "He used his hands to kill the major." She turned to Captain Spencer. "Not a rifle, or any other weapon. I imagine they are not programmed to do that."

Spencer nodded. "That is one of the central mysteries surrounding this tragedy, Ms. Taylor. Our robots are capable of great physical feats. They can run, jump, flip, roll, dive for cover. They each weigh two hundred and thirty pounds and can lift twice their own weight. But the idea of them using their hands—or any other object—for melee-style combat is completely absent from their programming. Simply put, they do not really know their own strength, and Bucky could not have known he could use his hands to . . . do what he did to the major."

"Maybe he learned," said Brodie.

Colonel Howe took a step toward Brodie. "They don't learn, Mr. Brodie. They don't have the capacity to learn. And I urge all of you to stop using 'he' and 'his.'" She gestured to the line of robots. "These are things. They are equipment."

"Equipment," said Brodie, "that you chose to shape like human beings."

Howe looked at him with her cold blue eyes, which seemed to take everything in without giving much back. If the eyes were the window to the soul, Colonel Howe's blinds were drawn. She said to Brodie, "The design of the modern homo sapiens is the product of millions of years of evolution, and a fine blueprint to begin with. And let me emphasize that the work we are doing here, in accordance with the Pentagon's Third Offset Strategy, is to anticipate and prepare for the developments and actions of our adversaries."

The Russians made us do it. Colonel Howe had really drunk the Kool-Aid. Or maybe she was the one mixing and serving the Kool-Aid. At any rate, she was leaving something out about the decision to make these things humanoid—the fear factor. Their appearance was uncanny and unsettling and would scare the shit out of the enemy on the battlefield. Human warriors have understood the importance of that ever since the first guy smeared on war paint.

Sergeant Scott Brodie had fought in the Second Battle of Fallujah in 2004, and it was no fun squaring off against jihadis whose own "doctrine statement" included fighting to the death and waking up in Paradise. How would it have been to have one of these robots fighting against him—let alone two whole MLB rosters of them? They didn't fear death, nor did they welcome it. They didn't *feel* anything.

Brodie said, "Turn one of them on." He gestured to the bay holding robot Number 3. "Babe Ruth over there."

Colonel Howe replied, "Brigadier General Morgan has suspended all camp operations and ordered that the units remain powered down, with the exception of Number 20, which you may inspect later."

Brodie had wondered when someone was going to mention the guy who actually ran this place. "And where is General Morgan?"

"Indisposed," Howe said tersely. "He regrets that he was not available to greet you."

"So do we," said Taylor.

The general's absence was odd, considering this tiny camp was on lockdown. The guy must have had something better to do. Or he wanted to look like he had something better to do because he was a senior officer with an ego. Brodie said, "Colonel, I insist that you activate one of these things. If Number 20 has malfunctioned, we need to see how a functioning unit operates."

Howe replied, "I understand your logic, Mr. Brodie, but I have my orders. You may take this up with the general when you see him."

"We will."

Howe nodded. "Unless there are any other questions, we can now take you to the DEVCOM lab."

Maggie Taylor, who remained staring at one of the bots and did not appear in a hurry to leave, asked, "How are they powered?"

Captain Spencer responded, "Each unit has a series of lithium-ion

batteries that allow around five hours of operation, give or take. They
are also each outfitted with a state-of-the-art microbial fuel cell with
oxygen cathodes, which makes them capable of sustaining themselves
beyond the life of their lithium-ion batteries by processing insect, fruit,
and plant matter into energy."

Brodie looked at the captain. "These things *eat*?"

Spencer nodded. "In a sense." He pointed to a rectangular panel
about the size of a smartphone in a bot's lower right abdomen. "This
compartment is connected to the fuel cell and is where they can in-
sert organic material. A few months ago, we ran a test to see how long
they could sustain themselves this way. We sent four units on a march
across the desert, accompanied overhead by an unmanned aerial drone
equipped with a camera. The bots collected grass, brush, insects, and
small lizards, and after forty hours we had to swap out the drone because it was running out of fuel. The replacement drone continued to
follow them for another forty hours, at which point we canceled the
test. Our conclusion was that so long as they have access to organic
matter, the D-17s can sustain themselves . . . indefinitely."

There was a long silence in the room. Brodie looked at the rows of
inert, lifeless robots. He thought of the Terra-Cotta Army—the legion
of sculpted soldiers buried with China's first emperor to guard him in
death. But these twenty-first-century warriors came alive not in the
underworld, but in this one, animated by the most sophisticated and
cutting-edge technology developed by the most powerful military in
human history.

Scott Brodie had a sudden vision of a truck dumping concrete
down the Vault's elevator shaft, and a squadron of Army jets bomb-
ing Camp Hayden to rubble. Well, there was that "reactionary mind"
that General Dombroski had warned him about. Maybe the general
had a point, and maybe Scott Brodie's own unease about the work at
Camp Hayden should not prejudice him against the machines specifically. After all, these things didn't come out of the ether—they were

designed, funded, constructed, and programmed by human beings, and whatever terror they instilled or danger they posed was merely a reflection of their human creators. Humans didn't have the best track record for making decisions beneficial to their fellow man, and individual humans didn't always go along with the program. If Number 20 had gone rogue, maybe it was at the command of a rogue human who got inside Bucky's head and taught him a few new tricks, including a skull-shattering vise grip.

He looked again at the phone-sized port in the bot's abdomen. He noticed a circular vent next to it about the size of a quarter. "What is that vent?"

Spencer replied, "The primary waste byproduct of the microbial fuel cells is carbon dioxide, which is emitted through those vents."

Brodie looked at the man. "Congratulations, Captain. You've created the world's first farting robots."

No one laughed at that. Not even Taylor. Tough crowd.

Spencer added, "The other byproduct is a small amount of solid organic matter residue that accumulates on the oxygen cathode surfaces and must be cleaned from time to time."

Brodie wanted to ask if the robots could wipe themselves but thought better of it. He looked around the room and did not notice any surveillance cameras. "How is this place monitored?"

"It isn't surveilled, if that's what you mean," Major Klasky said. "But every entry and exit is logged. The fobs used by the members of DEVCOM are coded to the individual. And as we noted, no one can enter this facility alone."

Taylor said, "One member of DEVCOM, and one Ranger. Maybe two, if there are always two guys assigned to sentry duty at the Vault. Three people is not a large conspiracy."

No one replied to that.

Brodie addressed Sergeant Mendez. "Does your team control the logs?"

"No, sir. DEVCOM does."

Captain Spencer said, "I can give you access to all of the logs, and whatever else you need."

Brodie looked at him. "Thank you, Captain." He turned to Colonel Howe. "Take us to the crime scene."

CHAPTER 8

CORPORAL EWING RETURNED TO GUARD DUTY, AND EV-eryone else walked from the Vault down a paved road toward the DEVCOM lab. They passed a wide three-story brick building of modern construction, unlike the rest of the Sixties-era structures around them.

Colonel Howe said, "That's the barracks. Most of Camp Hayden's original structures could be rehabbed and repurposed, but the original barracks were deemed inadequate and were torn down."

Brodie observed the building. He estimated it could house over a hundred individuals, and was intended for enlisted, unmarried soldiers. He commented, "We spotted some family housing on the way in."

Howe replied, "There are no families at Camp Hayden. For the enlisted men, it was a condition of service that only unattached individuals would be stationed here. The houses you saw are primarily for officers. Most of us are single as well, except for General Morgan, who is here with his wife." She added, "This is an isolating and intense eighteen-month commitment. We cannot afford distractions."

Or security breaches, though Colonel Howe didn't say that. The military does not like to appear as though they don't trust civilians.

So, no spouses, no kids, no local town to blow off steam, no R&R. Not even conjugal visits. It was little wonder that some of these guys were using speed, and whatever else. Maybe Colonel Howe and the other senior officers had forgotten that they were working with humans in addition to robots.

Taylor stated the obvious: "This is hardship duty."

"This is privileged duty," said Howe, who was increasingly getting on Brodie's nerves. The colonel was either all-in on her mission here at Hayden, or she was laying it on extra thick because she had something to hide.

They arrived at the DEVCOM lab, a single-story white stucco building with a few small windows and an asphalt shingle roof that was curling and cracking from decades in the desert sun.

Captain Spencer pressed his fob to a security plate next to the metal door, and they all entered.

The laboratory consisted of a large open-plan room cluttered with metal tables, desks with computers, and storage racks overflowing with bins of equipment. On one table Brodie spotted a pile of titanium alloy plates like the ones that covered the D-17s. A shelving unit was stuffed with rotors, a bin full of circuit boards, and spools of electrical wiring. In the far back of the lab was another, smaller room, visible through a large glass window. It held a long table that resembled a medical gurney, as well as a large computer console.

The lab was empty, except for a woman at the far end of the room who stood from her desk and turned to them.

Colonel Howe said, "Ms. Dixon, you are not supposed to be here."

The woman walked toward them. She was in her mid-thirties, with a pale complexion and dark-brown hair in a ponytail. She wore oversize glasses, a white blouse, and khaki slacks.

She ignored the colonel and smiled at Brodie and Taylor as she extended her hand. "Caroline Dixon, senior researcher at DARPA."

Brodie and Taylor shook and introduced themselves, and Taylor asked, "Are you stationed here full-time?"

Dixon nodded. "I am. I worked closely with Major Ames."

Caroline Dixon was a real looker, and Brodie imagined she got more attention than she wanted at this isolated camp.

Colonel Howe said, "Ms. Dixon is one of the few civilians at Camp Hayden."

"That's right," said Dixon. "Me and the guy who cleans the toilets." She looked at the colonel. "I'm running through the diagnostics logs that Roger generated the night of his death."

"All personnel are to be confined to quarters," said Major Klasky. "General Morgan issued clear orders."

"As did my bosses at DARPA," replied Dixon. "Their instructions to me were to conduct a thorough review of what happened."

Taylor asked, "Anything of interest in the logs?"

"Not yet." She turned to Captain Spencer. "Ed, let's show our CID visitors around."

Howe and Klasky were left to stew as Brodie and Taylor followed the two scientists through the lab.

DARPA stood for the Defense Advanced Research Projects Agency, the Pentagon's premiere R&D branch. The agency was notable for spearheading some of the most innovative technological breakthroughs of the twentieth century, including the internet and GPS. Their researchers were also known for their fierce independence from the rest of the military's bureaucracy and bullshit, a spirit that Caroline Dixon seemed to embody.

As they walked among the lab tables, Dixon said, "The research that ultimately became the D-17 program began at DARPA a decade ago. While a number of civilian firms have been building their own robots, DARPA has taken a unique approach by virtue of our mission."

Taylor asked, "What is your mission?"

Dixon turned to her. "To predict problems that have yet to be presented to us, and answer questions before the Pentagon asks them. Our goal is to remove the question of whether something *can* be done and empower the Pentagon leadership to craft future strategies unhindered by technological limitations. So, when the Army approached us about deploying autonomous weapons in training exercises, we already had working prototypes. We refined those prototypes in conjunction with the fine people at DEVCOM"—she gestured to Captain Spencer—"to ensure that the capabilities of the bots were appropriate to the Army's desired training outcomes."

Brodie stopped in front of one of the metal tables, which held a disembodied robotic arm. He picked it up with both hands. It was surprisingly heavy.

Spencer said, "Please ask before handling any equipment."

Brodie ignored that and handed the arm to Taylor, who inspected it. She asked, "Can you alter the programming of the D-17s from this lab?"

Captain Spencer nodded and gestured to the back room with the window. "We have a hardwired data link there, in addition to the ones in the containment bays in the Vault. This one is used mostly for diagnostics, and for small tweaks to the algorithm for testing purposes. Any refinement to a single unit is a temporary modification, at which point they revert to the same code as the fifty-nine other units. Any platoon-wide modification is done to all units at once via the console in the Vault. Only two permanent mods have been made in the last nine months, both for very minor things like reaction time, and the bots' light detection and range sensors."

Dixon added, "The algorithms that govern the D-17s are the product of years of work and have been carefully refined for their mission here at Camp Hayden, and the decision to alter them is not taken lightly. In this lab we can play around and test the limits in a low-stakes environment. Before we return the units to duty we hit the reset button."

Brodie cut to the chase. "Could someone in this lab have reprogrammed Number 20 in a way that led to the death of Major Ames, whether accidentally or intentionally?"

Dixon replied, "In theory."

"But not in reality," interjected Captain Spencer. "The amount of work that would have to go into altering a unit to that extent, to make it capable of that . . . it's more than far-fetched. We are a tight-knit and interdependent group, and no radical modifications could be made that might result in a fatal accident without the entire DEVCOM team being aware of it and involved in it and performing rigorous testing. As for someone doing a clandestine reprogramming for malicious purposes, that is even more absurd. That kind of work could not be done in secret."

Taylor asked, "What if someone came here when the lab was otherwise empty? At night."

"That activity would be in the logs," said Spencer. "And in addition, they would need to take a unit from the Vault, which cannot be accessed without another individual involved. And then they'd have to release the unit from the storage bay—another activity that is logged—then transport the thing across camp to the DEVCOM lab, which could be seen by either of the sentries on the two observation towers."

Sergeant Mendez of the Military Police, who had been listening to all this along with Colonel Howe and Major Klasky, added, "One of my people is always on duty doing night rounds."

Captain Spencer looked at Taylor. "Your conspiracy grows."

The captain seemed to be taking all of this personally. It was important not to read too much into that—his close colleague had just been murdered and he was shaken up, and he had obvious reasons to be defensive of his work here. On the other hand, if he was involved in something nefarious, that was another reason to be defensive.

Taylor asked, "How many individuals work in this lab?"

"It had been four," said Spencer. "Now it's three. Myself, Ms. Dixon, and my subordinate officer, Lieutenant Mike Lehner, a robotics engineer."

"We will need to speak with him soon," said Taylor.

Spencer nodded.

Brodie said, "And we need printouts of the security logs for this lab and the containment unit for the past thirty days." He turned to Howe and Klasky. "We will also need a schedule of when the bots are taken out of containment for training exercises, and what your protocols are."

Major Klasky said, "I will provide that."

Brodie asked Captain Spencer, "Where did you find the major's body?"

Spencer approached a nearby desk and pointed to the floor behind it. "He was lying here."

Sergeant Mendez added, "There was blood spatter as well as skull fragments and brain matter found on the desk, and on the floor on the other side of it."

Brodie stepped to the spot where the body had been. "And Bucky?"

Spencer walked around to the side of the desk. "About here. Facing Major Ames."

Brodie asked, "What was it doing?"

"Nothing. Just standing there, motionless. Both of its hands were at its sides, covered in blood."

Brodie and Captain Spencer stood less than five feet from each other. Brodie imagined Roger Ames's view in the last moments of his life, looking up at one of those seven-foot-tall machines as it stretched its titanium arms toward him . . .

Taylor said, "Captain, you told us that Number 20 malfunctioned in the field, which was why it was brought into the lab. What exactly happened?"

Spencer replied, "During training exercises, the Rangers and the bots wear multiple sensors on their bodies as part of the SIMRES system. When a sensor registers a hit, it emits a sound, which indicates to the trainee or the bot that they are out of the fight. At that point they are supposed to stay where they are and sit down for the duration of the exercise. Number 20 was hit while approaching a building and sat in the sand. When the fight was over, it would not get up. Completely unresponsive. So we loaded it in a vehicle and brought it here. Ran some tests, diagnostics. We could find nothing wrong. Then we did a system reset. Still nothing. It was late, I wanted to get some rest and tackle it again in the morning. The major . . . he didn't want to leave.

He was a driven individual. Once he started on something he couldn't stop."

Caroline Dixon added, "Roger was a perfectionist, which I appreciated. He put all of himself into his work. If something went wrong, he saw it as a personal failing that he had to remedy."

Brodie asked her, "Were you here that night?"

"I was not."

"Why?"

"Because I had gone home for the day." She looked at Spencer. "And no one contacted me to alert me about a problem."

Spencer did not respond.

Taylor asked, "What if he was playing possum?"

Everyone turned to Taylor. She continued, "Bucky. You said there was nothing wrong with him, he was just unresponsive. Maybe he did that on purpose, to get into the lab. To get Major Ames alone."

For a moment no one responded. Then Dixon asked her, "If a self-driving car runs a man over, is your first thought that the car wanted the guy dead?"

Taylor did not respond.

Dixon grabbed the detached robotic arm off the table, then approached Taylor and placed the robot's hand on her shoulder. "How does this make you feel, Ms. Taylor?"

Taylor met her gaze. "Slightly unsettled."

Dixon smiled. "They creep me out too. There's no way around it. My decade of experience and PhD from Caltech don't stand a chance against millions of years of human evolution that have primed us to recognize threats." She withdrew the arm and set it on the table. "It's just metal and wiring, though. We understand that intellectually. But the *form*, it's hard to get past the form." She tapped her own temple. "But they are nothing like us where it counts. They are self-driving cars on two legs with automatic rifles."

Well, so far they were getting told over and over that these killer robots only killed in certain ways, and in certain places, and that they were as dumb as a Tesla. But one of these things had gone off script, and there had to be a reason. Maybe everyone in this isolated desert outpost, except him and Maggie Taylor, had completely lost perspective on what was really going on here.

Brodie asked Captain Spencer, "What is your security protocol in this lab? Must the bots be restrained when they are powered on?"

"No."

"Is someone on hand with an EMP-equipped weapon?"

Spencer hesitated, then responded, "No."

"Outside of this lab, is there any other location where the bots are powered on and unrestrained without there being someone equipped with an EMP weapon?"

Spencer thought a moment. "Not that I'm aware of."

Taylor asked, "Is there a reason the DEVCOM lab skirted basic security precautions present on the rest of the base?"

Spencer did not respond. He and Dixon shared a look. Then the captain said, "Clearly, we felt overly secure in how predictable and harmless the D-17s were. It turned out to be a fatal error."

No kidding. Brodie glanced at the disembodied arm on the nearby table, and the stacks of titanium body plates, and the bins overflowing with parts and wiring. It was easy to see how this lab could engender a god complex. Colonel Howe had told them not to humanize the D-17s. They were *objects*, not beings. That advice might have seemed necessary in the Vault, which felt more like a sanctum for sleeping warriors than an equipment storage facility. But in the DEVCOM lab, the place where the robots' mechanical innards and lines of code were probed, disassembled, and reconfigured by the military's best and brightest, it might be easy to lose respect for the power of what you had called into being. God does not fear His own creations. But men are not gods, a fact that people have had to learn over and over throughout history.

Brodie looked at the spotless lab floor where Major Roger Ames's broken body had lain two nights ago, at the feet of a seven-foot-tall titanium machine with hands covered in blood and brain matter. It was hard to imagine what that thing had done to the major. Time to see for themselves.

CHAPTER 9

A WINDOWLESS, REFRIGERATED TRAILER SERVED AS Camp Hayden's morgue. Brodie and Taylor entered along with Colonel Howe and Sergeant Mendez. Major Klasky was dismissed, while the two scientists, Captain Ed Spencer and Caroline Dixon, waited for them outside the trailer.

The frigid trailer featured bright fluorescent lighting, metal work surfaces, and a long table in the center where a body lay beneath a sheet. They were greeted by the Armed Forces medical examiner, Dr. Keith Schiller, a tall and thin middle-aged man in a white lab coat. Colonel Howe made the introductions, explaining that Schiller had come in the day prior from nearby Fort Irwin to perform the autopsy. She said to Dr. Schiller, "Please show the agents the body."

The doctor nodded, then took the top end of the sheet and folded it down to the chest.

Brodie observed the late Major Ames. Most of his head above the brow line was missing, exposing the lower portion of his cerebrum, which was a misshapen gray, spongy mass. Parts of his shattered skull were visible around the brain matter, and the skin below the break in the skull was covered in dark-purple bruises. His face was an ashen blue from livor mortis and his eyes were open, but they had become so dislocated from the trauma that only the white sclera were visible within his sockets.

Dr. Schiller said, "The victim, Major Roger Ames, was a thirty-six-year-old Caucasian male. Cause of death was massive cranial and cerebral destruction from applied force."

Brodie and Taylor did not say anything for a moment as they looked at the body. Brodie had seen the aftermath of more than a few guys in Iraq who had taken a high-caliber round to the head, and this looked similar, if less messy.

Taylor asked, "Did you run toxicology?"

The doctor nodded. "Hair and blood. Nothing turned up in the blood, but we did find trace amounts of psilocybin in the hair samples."

"Psilocybin?" asked Taylor. "Like mushrooms?"

"That's correct."

Taylor turned to Colonel Howe and Sergeant Mendez. "Were either of you aware of Major Ames's drug use?"

Howe replied, "Not until the toxicology report. We have had issues here in the past with illicit drugs, primarily amphetamines. Psilocybin is a new one to me, and I was certainly not aware of any use among the DEVCOM staff."

This could mean nothing. Brodie had never tried psilocybin mushrooms, but he imagined there were worse and more destructive ways to pass the time at this place than looking up at the desert night sky and blasting off to Jupiter. But it was odd, and unexpected.

Brodie asked, "Any sign of struggle?"

Schiller shook his head. "Nothing that was apparent. No bruises or abrasions anywhere else on his body. We checked for DNA under the victim's fingernails, but in this instance that was fruitless."

Brodie had a vision of Major Ames desperately grasping at Bucky's titanium arms as the robot applied a two-handed vise grip to his skull. Soft flesh against smooth, cold metal. An impotent and pointless gesture. It occurred to him that this might have been one of the most terrifying ways to die—murdered by a thing with a face but no eyes, with hands but no skin, with a body but no soul.

Taylor asked, "How long will you be keeping him here?"

"Until tomorrow," replied Schiller. "Then the body will be released to his next of kin in Maryland for burial."

Brodie followed up: "Is there any chance that the cranial trauma was caused postmortem? That he could have died another way?"

Schiller shook his head. "The blood is clean. No toxins of any kind, and aside from the head injury the body is pristine. No bruises, scratches, or signs of asphyxiation. The major was killed by the D-17 unit that applied massive force to the cranium."

Brodie looked again at the major's decimated skull. There was something almost clinical about it, as if the robot needed to shut down Major Ames, and the best way to do that was to pulverize the guy's CPU. The D-17s must have at least a rudimentary understanding of human anatomy, which would make sense in the context of their training exercises. A shot to the arm was only an injury. The head was the kill shot.

He said to Colonel Howe, "It's time we meet Bucky."

CHAPTER 10

BRODIE AND TAYLOR DEPARTED THE MORGUE WITH Colonel Howe and Sergeant Mendez, rejoining Captain Spencer and Caroline Dixon. They all walked down an asphalt road that led toward the eastern end of the camp.

The sky was blue and cloudless, and the desert sun hung low over the northern hills. The temperature had dropped to something pleasant, and Brodie checked his watch: five-thirty. They should have called Dombroski by now. Not that they could report anything to him anyway.

Dixon walked with Brodie and Taylor as the two officers and the NCO took the lead. Taylor asked her, "What more can you tell us about Major Ames?"

Dixon thought a moment. "He was an intense sort of guy. And a bit of a lone wolf."

Taylor asked, "He didn't play well with others?"

"I wouldn't say that. But he didn't exactly lean on his team either. He was a brilliant mind but not a particularly good leader, which was supposed to be part of his role at the lab as the senior officer."

Brodie asked, "Were you aware of his drug use?"

"No. But I wasn't surprised when I learned about it. I knew he'd do night drives out into the desert. There was something . . . spiritual about him. At least, for a scientist."

Brodie said, "Please explain."

Dixon slowed her pace, and they fell back a little more from Howe, Spencer, and Mendez. "Can I be frank with you?"

Taylor looked at her. "That's the only way we'll have it, Ms. Dixon."

"Caroline."

"Maggie." She nodded toward Brodie. "I call him a lot of names, but you can use Scott."

Dixon smiled. This was nice. They were all on a first-name basis now, which was a way to build trust, or to soften someone up before you fed them bullshit.

Dixon said, "Roger was a computer scientist, not an engineer. He was very focused on advances in AI and, to be honest, disappointed with the lack of focus on that aspect of the D-17s. They are marvels of mechanical and electrical engineering, but they don't have a lot of cognitive sophistication. That's by design, and it's all part of a roadmap. But Roger felt hemmed in. He wanted to push things further. One time he told me he believed that human consciousness could be synthetically replicated. It was simply a matter of the right programming and computational power."

Taylor asked, "And what do you think of that?"

"I don't have time to think of that, Maggie. I like to dream big too, but we have a job to do here." She hesitated, then added, "Roger was ambitious, and he was impatient, and he was unorthodox. And I just can't help but wonder if he didn't engage in some extracurricular activities once he was alone in the lab."

Taylor said, "You are implying he caused his own death."

Dixon appeared uncomfortable with that characterization. "I'm not trying to lay blame. And if he did meddle with Number 20's programming, then he somehow left no trace of it, either on his computer or within the unit's processor. It doesn't make any sense, and I can't explain it. But if I'm being honest, I can imagine him doing something like that. Exploiting the opportunity presented by the bot's malfunction to be alone in the lab with it, to . . . push the envelope."

They walked in silence, and Brodie realized just how handicapped he and Taylor were on this case. If a criminal or negligent act had been committed here, it had happened at the level of computer code—a realm where Scott Brodie was deaf, dumb, and blind, and his intuition didn't serve him. But he had to remind himself that investigations all have the same ingredients, as different as they might look on the outside. He and Taylor needed to focus on motive—and Caroline Dixon had just given them one for the murder victim himself—as well as opportunity. Only four people worked in the DEVCOM lab, and one of them was dead. The other three, as far as he knew, were the only people on this base capable of reprogramming the D-17s. So if this *was* a homicide, and someone had installed a few lines of killer code into Bucky's processor, then Caroline Dixon was on a very short list of possible suspects.

He thought of Lieutenant Mike Lehner, the only member of the DEVCOM team they had yet to meet. He asked, "Where is Lieutenant Lehner?"

Dixon replied, "He's probably following orders, which means he's home."

"How would you describe him?"

"Smart. Hardworking. The kind of person you want on your team. Ames and Spencer were computer scientists. Lehner is the robotics guy and is our liaison with Synotec for any questions or issues about how the D-17s were constructed, engineering choices made, parts used, et cetera."

"Is he proficient in computer programming?"

She nodded. "Much more than the average person, much less than me, Ames, or Spencer."

"What was his relationship with Major Ames?"

"Deferential. He admired him and respected the chain of command."

"And how would you describe his attitude toward the work you were all doing here?"

"Like a kid getting the keys to the toy store. This is the ultimate assignment for a guy like him."

"And a woman like you," said Taylor.

Dixon looked at her. "Arthur C. Clarke said that any sufficiently advanced technology is indistinguishable from magic. But I'm the magician. For me this is just another day at the office."

Caroline Dixon obviously thought a lot of herself. But Brodie suspected her shtick was hiding something—or defending against something. He just needed to figure out what. He said, "Magic implies illusion. A misdirect."

Dixon nodded. "And you've both fallen for it multiple times." She looked at Brodie. "We built a weapon that mimics a man. Because of that mimicry, you've both assigned agency, intelligence, and inner consciousness to a machine that possesses none of those things."

Brodie looked her in the eyes. "Are you calling us suckers, Caroline?"

She smiled. "No, Scott. I'm calling you human."

Up ahead, Howe, Spencer, and Mendez stopped at a long, narrow single-story concrete building with a flat roof. A Ranger with an EMP-equipped rifle stood outside a steel door, and parked nearby was a white Military Police sedan. Brodie noticed metal bars over a small window on the far end of the building.

Taylor asked, "They're keeping the robot in the brig?"

Dixon replied, "Just another part of the illusion."

The Ranger on sentry, a Black corporal in his early twenties named Powell, saluted Howe and Spencer, then unlocked the steel door and swung it open. They all walked into a room with a drop ceiling and fluorescent lighting. In the middle of the room stood a metal table with two bottles of water, two notepads and pens, and three metal chairs. At the far side of the room was another steel door, which was guarded by a young MP with a holstered sidearm, a specialist whose name tape identified him as "Kemp."

Colonel Howe gestured to the table. "Agents, please have a seat."

Brodie and Taylor sat on one side of the table, facing the door that evidently led to the holding cell.

Howe said to Powell, "At the ready, Corporal."

"Yes, ma'am." Powell took a few steps closer to the holding cell door and raised his EMP rifle.

Howe said to Brodie and Taylor, "I don't anticipate an issue, but in light of what happened we are exercising extreme caution."

Brodie said, "Good idea." He felt his SIG Sauer M18 pistol in the pancake holster beneath his suit jacket, and it occurred to him that he was completely unequipped to provide for his own safety against the real threats at this place. He eyed Corporal Powell's EMP barrel attachment and wondered if it, like the D-17s, was a prototype—and whether it was also prone to malfunction.

Sergeant Mendez said to the specialist by the cell door, "Bring it in, Kemp."

"Yes, Sergeant." Kemp unlocked the door, swung it open, and said in a commanding voice, "Walk forward and sit in the chair directly ahead of you."

The MP stepped aside, and Brodie could see into the holding cell. There was a cot against the wall, but he couldn't see anything else through the doorway.

Then he heard shuffling feet, and the jangle and drag of chains. A tall figure appeared in the doorway and ducked its head as it walked through the open door. Taylor gasped.

It was a D-17, towering over every human in the room. Its arms were in front of it, with manacles on its wrists connected by a heavy foot-long chain. Another set of chained manacles looped around its ankles.

The robot shuffled into the room. Its movements were uncannily human. It took small, careful steps, so as not to lose its balance from the short chain connecting its lower legs.

Its many servo motors and hydraulics were surprisingly silent, and the only sounds were of its metallic footsteps and the dragging chain. Its bucket-shaped head with the single black slit looked straight ahead and above where Brodie and Taylor were sitting. Corporal Powell kept his rifle trained on the robot and followed it as it walked.

Brodie eyed the chains and manacles. The MPs could have just as soon strapped this thing to a gurney and wheeled it in. But cuffing it, holding it in the brig, making it walk in chains . . . it was oddly humanizing. *Just another part of the illusion.*

The robot approached the table, still not looking at them, and Brodie spotted the numeral 20 etched on its breastplate. It clutched the back of the chair with both of its manacled hands, slid it away from the table slowly, then eased itself down onto the chair. It tilted its head down slightly, fixing its sensors on Brodie and Taylor.

Brodie said, "Hello."

The robot did not respond.

"What is your name?"

The robot replied, "Number 20." It sounded human, like a male voice of about-average pitch, with no affect. Brodie saw no visible speakers, and the voice seemed to emanate from the center of its head and was slightly muffled. It turned its head to Taylor, then back to Brodie.

Brodie said, "My name is Scott Brodie, and this is my partner, Maggie Taylor. We are special agents from United States Army CID. Do you know what CID is?"

"No."

"We are criminal investigators. We are here to investigate the murder of Major Roger Ames, by you."

Bucky sat motionless and quiet, staring at Brodie.

Taylor asked, "Do you know who Major Ames is?"

"Yes," it replied.

This was tedious. Brodie said, "Tell us who he is."

"Major Roger Ames is the chief scientist at Camp Hayden for the United States Army Combat Capabilities Development Command. He is thirty-six years old. He has dark-brown hair and brown eyes and pale skin."

Taylor asked, "Do you remember killing him?"

"No."

Brodie eyed Corporal Powell, who stood about ten feet away with his rifle still trained on the bot. Then he said to Howe, "I don't think that's necessary."

"It doesn't bother the bot."

"It's bothering me."

Howe said to Powell, "Lower your rifle but be at the ready."

Powell slowly lowered his rifle and remained where he was.

Brodie asked Bucky, "What's my name?"

"I do not know."

"I just told you."

Captain Spencer explained, "It knows what it is programmed to know. It cannot learn, in any traditional sense. It cannot form memories either. It lives in the perpetual present, you might say."

Brodie said to Bucky, "Good for you, Number 20. Living in the moment. No memories means no regrets, right?"

"I do not understand your question."

Taylor asked Bucky, "What is the size of this room?"

Without hesitation, Bucky responded, "Six point two meters by four point five seven meters. The ceiling is three point one meters high nearest the door, and three point two five meters high nearest the window."

She asked, "How tall was Major Ames?"

"One point seven five meters."

"Why did you kill him?"

"I do not know."

"When did you kill him?"

"I do not know."

"What is your doctrine statement?"

"Neutralize all enemies."

She asked, "Who are your enemies?"

Bucky immediately swiveled its head to its right and locked on Corporal Powell, who gripped his rifle tightly as he stared at the robot. "Corporal Daniel Powell is my enemy."

Brodie asked, "Then why aren't you trying to neutralize him?"

Bucky swiveled its head back to them. "Two conditions must be met for me to activate my doctrine statement. One, be issued orders by an authorized individual. Two, be located within the battlespace. Neither of those conditions has been met."

Taylor asked, "And what does it mean to neutralize your enemy? What do you do?"

"I shoot the enemy with my rifle."

Taylor leaned forward. "And then what happens?"

"He is dead."

"Define 'dead.'"

"He sits down. He removes his helmet. The laser engagement system deactivates the targeting guidance."

Brodie said, "That's not dead. That's just a game you play. Major Ames is dead for real. Do you understand?"

Bucky replied, "No."

Brodie picked up his full water bottle and threw it at the robot. It bounced off Bucky's chest. The robot looked down at the bottle as it landed on the table and rolled.

"Not great reflexes, pal."

Taylor looked at her partner. "What are you doing?"

"Running diagnostics." He picked up the bottle again and flung it at Bucky's head. It smacked the robot square in the face, causing its head to jerk back slightly, and the bottle landed on the floor.

Colonel Howe stepped forward and said sternly, "Mr. Brodie. Is this how you normally conduct an interview?"

He turned to her. "Interviews are with *people*, Colonel. As you made clear, this is a thing." He looked at Caroline Dixon. "A self-driving car. And this is reminding me never to get one."

Howe said, "You are abusing our equipment."

"I don't think a Costco water bottle stands a chance against titanium alloy." He looked at Spencer, then Dixon. "Why doesn't it defend itself?"

Spencer answered, "Self-preservation is an element of its doctrine statement. Survival within the battlespace for the duration of the exercise. Outside of the battlespace, it won't raise a finger, unless it is instructed to by an authorized individual."

Except for two nights ago in the DEVCOM lab, when it raised all its fingers and wrapped them around Major Ames's cranium.

Brodie leaned down and picked up the water bottle. He asked Captain Spencer, "Are you an authorized individual?"

Spencer nodded, then said in a commanding voice, "Number 20, avoid getting struck by the water bottle."

Brodie flung it at the robot again, harder this time. With lightning reflexes, both manacled hands shot up from the table. It caught the bottle with its right hand and gripped it tight, causing the plastic to burst open and spray water all over itself, the table, and Brodie and Taylor.

Bucky remained frozen with its arms lifted, squeezing the crushed plastic bottle as water dripped down its head.

Brodie wiped the water off his face. "Nice catch."

Bucky did not respond.

Spencer said, "Arms down, Number 20."

Bucky lowered its arms to the table, still gripping the crushed bottle.

Brodie asked it, "Who built you?"

"I was manufactured by Synotec Systems in the state of Nevada."

"Why were you built?"

"To help prepare the United States Army for the future of warfare."

"That's nice of you. What is the future of warfare?"

"An increased reliance on automated systems to achieve strategic and tactical advantages for our nation."

"It's not your nation," said Taylor. "You don't have a nation."

Bucky did not respond.

Brodie asked it, "Are you a better soldier than a human?"

"Yes," answered the robot.

"Why?"

"Our platoon has participated in sixty-seven offensive engagements versus the United States Army Rangers, and we have won every engagement."

"*Every* engagement?"

"Yes."

Brodie looked at Colonel Howe. "Is that true?"

Howe almost looked ashamed as she said, "It's true."

Brodie stood and turned toward the two scientists. "Captain Spencer. Ms. Dixon. We are going to need a technical explanation for how and why this thing did what it did to Major Ames. And if you can't provide one, we must conclude that you've lost control over your own creations and don't fully understand how they work. Or someone with technical expertise is intentionally misleading us."

Howe stared at him. "Let's not get ahead of ourselves, Mr. Brodie."

"I'm right where I need to be, Colonel. Laying it all out."

"You've been on base less than two hours, and you are already leveling serious accusations. You have yet to even speak with any of our Rangers or understand how their training is—"

Brodie interrupted, "There's a Ranger in this room." He turned to Corporal Powell. "What is your opinion of the lethal autonomous weapons you are training with?"

The corporal hesitated. He glanced at Colonel Howe.

She kept her eyes glued to Brodie as she said, "You may speak freely, Corporal."

Powell looked at Bucky, who was staring straight ahead, motionless, with water still dripping down its bucket head. Then Powell said to Brodie, "I hate them, sir."

Brodie smiled at the man. "Thank you for your honesty."

Howe said, "Hating the enemy is good for morale and motivation." She added, "I think we're done here."

Maggie Taylor remained sitting with her eyes locked on Bucky. She asked the robot, "Do you think you're strong enough to break those chains, Number 20?"

"I do not know."

"Have you tried?"

"No."

She asked Howe, "Why don't you go ahead and order it to break the chains? See what happens."

"I will do no such thing."

"So they're just for show, then. To make us feel safe. Well, I don't." She stood. "We must speak with General Morgan."

Howe said, "You'll get your wish very soon. I was informed he and his wife have invited you both to their house for dinner tonight. Mrs. Morgan is a very good cook."

That probably wasn't what Maggie Taylor had in mind, but when a general invites you to dinner, you go. She nodded.

Colonel Howe said to Specialist Kemp, "Escort Number 20 back to its cell and dry it off, then shut it down."

"Yes, ma'am." Kemp said to Bucky, "Number 20, stand up and return to your cell."

The robot immediately stood, then turned around and shuffled back toward the open holding cell door.

Brodie said, "Nice meeting you, Bucky. I hope they recycle you into tank armor."

Bucky stopped walking. It stood frozen a moment with its back to them. Brodie and Taylor exchanged a look.

Kemp said sternly, "Number 20. Return to your cell."

Bucky continued into the holding cell, and the SPC followed.

They all left the brig, and Colonel Howe checked her watch. "Your dinner with the general is at nineteen-hundred. In about one hour.

Your luggage has already been delivered to your residence." She said to Spencer, "I am going back to my office. Please escort Mr. Brodie and Ms. Taylor to their house and show them the location of General Morgan's house."

"Yes, ma'am."

The colonel excused herself, as did Sergeant Mendez. Dixon said to Brodie and Taylor, "I hope that was instructive."

Taylor replied, "It was chilling. And somewhat frustrating."

Dixon nodded. "They're not programmed for the art of conversation. It's too bad you don't have the opportunity to see them in action on the battlefield."

Brodie said, "I would be perfectly fine if no one ever gets that opportunity again."

Dixon looked at him. "I understand this is unfamiliar, Scott. You're used to dealing with human suspects."

"I might still be."

She gave a tight smile. "Right. But we are working with a very complex system, and it might take time to find what went wrong. Roger Ames was a colleague and a friend, and I will do everything in my abilities to get to the bottom of it." She looked at Spencer. "I know the captain feels the same way."

Spencer nodded.

Taylor asked, "Why did Bucky stop walking when Scott said the thing about it getting recycled? It was almost like it wanted to respond . . . but stopped itself."

"That was a little odd," admitted Dixon.

"It heard you address it," said Spencer. "It stopped to listen, maybe to hear if there was going to be a command. Let's not overthink it."

Dixon checked her watch. "I'm going back to the lab. I've got at least two Diet Cokes' worth of work to do." She turned to leave, then stopped herself and looked back at Brodie. "You called it Bucky. In that moment when it stopped walking."

"I was told that's the Rangers' nickname for it."

"Among themselves. They don't talk to the bots. No one else uses those names, and the units aren't programmed to recognize them. They don't answer to them. It shouldn't have even known you were addressing it."

Taylor said, "Context clues."

Dixon shook her head. "These things don't do context clues, Maggie."

Captain Spencer said, "They're not designed to walk with manacles—maybe it was being careful with its footing."

Dixon said to him, "After what happened to the major, we need to be on a hair-trigger alert for any anomalies, no matter how small."

Captain Spencer appeared irked by her tone. He said, "I know, and I agree."

Brodie asked, "Do you think those manacles can actually restrain it?"

Dixon shrugged. "Probably not. They'd slow it down, though." She added, "If I had to guess, that whole show of keeping it in the brig, the chains and all that, was a bit of theater for your benefit ordered by General Morgan."

"Why?"

She smiled slightly. "Best I don't prejudice you. Enjoy your dinner with the general. He's a character."

Brodie said, "I have never gotten along with anyone described as a character."

"How about eccentric?"

"I can work with that."

"Good evening." She turned and headed in the direction of the lab.

Brodie watched her go, then looked again at the brig and the little barred window behind which Number 20—a.k.a. Bucky—had by now had its key removed and was as lifeless as a pile of scrap metal.

We have won every engagement.

That didn't sound like training. That sounded like torture. And that winning streak was against elite Army Rangers, for God's sake.

Maybe the whizzes at DARPA and DEVCOM had done their job too well, and now, in classic Frankenstein fashion, they were tormented and hunted by their own creation. But at least Dr. Frankenstein tried to kill the monster he made. Caroline Dixon was spending her night looking for errant code, for glitches. The monster didn't need to be slain. It just needed a firmware update.

Well, maybe she was right. Maybe the monster *can't* be unmade. Maybe Pandora's box does not close, and the future is here to stay.

CHAPTER 11

CAPTAIN SPENCER WALKED WITH BRODIE AND TAYLOR toward the western end of the camp, where Brodie had spotted the two cul-de-sacs of detached houses during their approach in the chopper.

The air was growing cooler as the sun slipped lower in the sky, now sitting half behind distant mountains, and casting a golden light and long shadows over the base.

Taylor asked the captain, "Did you work with Major Ames before your assignment here?"

Spencer nodded. "We worked together for a couple of years at our headquarters in Maryland. I knew him well. He was my superior officer, but also a friend."

"What was he like?"

Spencer thought a moment. "Brilliant. Driven. Also idealistic. He really believed in what we were doing here, and that technological advances could make war more humane."

"There's nothing humane about war," said Brodie. "That's why it's called war."

"You sound like Caroline. They didn't really get along."

Interesting. Brodie asked, "Why?"

"Well, they both thought they were the smartest person in whatever room they were in. There was also a cultural clash, civilian versus military. But really, it came down to the major's idealism and Caroline's more . . . clinical nature. Roger didn't like the size of the gulf between the D-17s' physical capabilities and cognitive limitations. It made him uncomfortable. He thought that given the immense physical power we were granting these machines, they needed greater intelligence to at least mimic human morality. Of course, the operating theory is that a simpler algorithm with very clear behavioral parameters will lead to a more predictable—and therefore safer—automaton."

"It didn't really work out that way," said Brodie.

Spencer did not respond.

Taylor asked him, "Did you share the major's concerns?"

"No. I was busy focusing on what we were doing here day to day. Roger was the one always looking ahead."

Brodie wanted to see if the captain brought up the major's mushroom munching without being asked directly. "You said you knew him well. Did you socialize outside the lab?"

Spencer replied, "As much as you can socialize in this place. We'd have dinner together, play cards." He guessed what Brodie was getting at and added, "I did not know about the psilocybin. That was a surprise to me."

"Why?" asked Taylor.

"Because it was reckless," said Spencer. "If he'd been caught, he'd have been relieved of command. And that would be a major blow to our work here."

Brodie said, "Maybe it was part of his work. Expanding his mind."

Spencer looked at him skeptically. "Aren't you CID?"

"That's what it says on my paycheck."

Spencer sighed. "I'm sure he justified it to himself like that. Or he was bored. I don't know how he got the stuff."

Taylor added, "Or if he was doing it with other people."

Spencer nodded. "It's possible. Off the record, there's some speed freaks here. Maybe they got involved. I just don't know."

Brodie said, "We heard about Private Beal."

Spencer did not respond for a moment. Then he said in a low voice, "He pushes them too hard."

"Who?" asked Brodie. "Captain Pickman?"

Spencer looked at him. "The general."

They stopped walking as the road ended in a wide cul-de-sac ringed by identical Sixties-era ranch houses. Each house had a desert-landscaped front yard of stones and succulents, along with an attached garage and driveway. A few cars were parked in the drives, along with a handful of golf carts.

If you squinted it almost looked like regular suburbia, but behind the houses was the steel security gate topped with razor wire, and beyond that, endless desert.

Spencer said, "These are the original houses from the old base, but they've been updated on the inside."

"Looks nice," said Brodie. Actually, it looked like one of those fake towns the government used to build to drop nukes on.

Spencer led them along the sidewalk. Taylor asked, "Did Major Ames have family?"

"Next of kin is his sister, who will be receiving the body," said the captain. "His parents passed a few years ago, and he was divorced with no kids. By his own telling, he was more married to his work than his wife."

Right. Why deal with the complexities of a spouse when you can spend all day with machines? They're simpler, more rational, and less likely to kill you. Until recently.

Taylor asked, "What will his sister be told about his death?"

Spencer looked at her. "That's not up to me, but I can assure you it won't be the truth. Hopefully not a lie either. She deserves at least to know that she's not being given the full picture. The major died while conducting classified research at a top-secret Army facility."

Brodie said, "I can't imagine that will satisfy her."

"It will have to," replied Spencer, almost brusquely. "If she or anyone else wants to dig, it's not too hard to figure out he was at Camp Hayden, whose existence is acknowledged by the military. But that's all she'll know, and that's how it has to be."

Brodie felt the captain was speaking a little callously, especially concerning the death of his own colleague. On the other hand, the man had a point. When you step behind the veil of secrecy, you are let into a privileged world, and that has a cost. In this case, Major Ames's sister—and his ex-wife, if she cared—would have to live without ever really knowing what happened to him.

Spencer pointed to a house with a number two on the door. "That's the general's house."

The house was identical to all the others. A sand-covered green Jeep Grand Cherokee was parked in the driveway, and lights were on behind drawn sheer curtains. Brodie asked, "Why do you think the general was not with us today?"

Spencer hesitated, then said, "I imagine he felt that Colonel Howe was better suited to give you an overall impression of the operations here."

That was a hell of a non-answer. There was clearly some tension here. Dinner was going to be interesting, even if Mrs. Morgan's cooking wasn't all it was cracked up to be.

Brodie spotted another house—number six—with yellow police tape across the door. "Major Ames's house?"

Spencer nodded. "The MPs already did a search and inventory and cleared out his personal effects."

"We'll do our own search," said Brodie.

The captain told them the access code, then indicated the house two over from it—number four—and said, "My DEVCOM subordinate Lieutenant Mike Lehner lives there. I can set up an interview for tomorrow, just let me know the time."

Brodie replied, "No time like the present, Captain." He walked toward Lieutenant Lehner's house, and Taylor followed.

Spencer didn't seem to like that. "Mr. Brodie, your dinner with the general is in less than an hour."

"Won't take long." He looked around at the houses. "Which one's ours?"

"Number eight."

"Please give us a few minutes and we'll meet you there."

Brodie and Taylor left Captain Spencer standing on the sidewalk as they approached house four. On a case like this, catching an interview subject unawares sometimes netted more useful Intel.

Brodie knocked on the door and waited. After a moment the door opened to reveal a tall, lanky man in his mid-twenties wearing jeans and a white polo shirt. He was barefoot.

Brodie introduced himself and Taylor, then said, "We have a few questions for you regarding our investigation."

Lehner, who did not appear particularly surprised to see them, said, "Of course," then looked beyond them to the road where Captain Spencer was still standing, watching them.

Lehner stepped aside and let them in, then shut the door behind them.

They entered a small living room with laminate wood flooring and the kind of basic furniture you'd find in a mid-budget hotel room. Brodie and Taylor sat on a couch and Lehner settled into a chair across from them. He leaned forward and interlaced his long fingers as he looked between them. "I still can't believe this happened."

"No one can," replied Brodie. Except the guilty party, if there was one. He noticed that Lieutenant Lehner was clean-shaven and had applied gel or pomade to his dark-brown hair, despite being cooped up alone in his house. Brodie asked him, "What are your primary duties at Camp Hayden?"

"As the only robotics engineer on the DEVCOM team, my responsibility is to the mechanical functions of the D-17 units. Running diagnostics, assessing and sometimes repairing physical damage, sharing data with the Synotec engineers as they work on improvements to the units based upon our testing and training."

Taylor asked, "Before the death of your superior officer, did you notice any anomalies with the units?"

Lehner shook his head. "They were predictable. Frankly, the only aspect of the D-17s that surprised me was their reliability. I thought there would be more performance issues."

Brodie asked, "What do you think happened to Roger Ames?"

"It is not my place to speculate."

"It is when a CID agent asks you to."

Lehner nodded as if conceding the point. This guy was mellow, almost tranquil. Cool as a cucumber? Serene as a psycho? The lieutenant replied, "I suspect the unit simply malfunctioned. A software issue."

Taylor followed up: "We've been told the AI powering these bots is very simple and algorithmic and should not allow for unpredictable behavior."

Lehner looked at her. "Even the most rudimentary systems are susceptible to chaos."

Right. Which was a good reason not to build seven-foot-tall autonomous killing machines in the first place. Brodie asked, "Did you notice any change in the behavior of Major Ames in the days or weeks leading to his death?"

"Yes," replied Lehner without hesitation. "He seemed distracted."

"By what?"

"I don't know. But he had been very engaged in the work being done by myself and Captain Spencer. And then at some point, maybe a month or so ago, he kind of . . . went inward."

Maybe it was the shrooms. Brodie asked, "Were you aware he was consuming psilocybin mushrooms?"

For the first time, Lehner seemed surprised. "No. Are you sure?"

"I'm sure that's what the toxicology report says."

Taylor added, "It showed up in a hair sample, which has a ninety-day window."

The lieutenant thought a moment. "That's surprising." Then he added, "The major seemed dissatisfied with the focus of the work here. With how it was more centered on my end of things—robotics—than his. You asked me what I think happened. I think maybe—and I have no evidence of this—but maybe the major selected a unit to experiment with. And that led to the malfunction."

So, Lieutenant Lehner had come to the same conclusion as Caroline Dixon. Interesting. Did that lend the theory more weight? Brodie recalled how complimentary Ms. Dixon had been of Lehner, which would be the right thing to do if they were engaged in a conspiracy. Have someone you vouch for repeat your own story. A double helping of bullshit. Then again, maybe they were just two independent people coming to the same obvious conclusion.

Brodie and Taylor peppered the lieutenant with a few more questions about his colleagues and the nature of his work, but nothing jumped out as material to the case. Once they were satisfied, they informed the man they would be following up and walked to the front door.

As they were about to leave, something occurred to Brodie and he turned to the lieutenant. "The day of the major's death, Number 20 malfunctioned. It wouldn't move. Your two superior officers brought the unit to the lab and proceeded to run diagnostics. Did either of them call you?"

"No."

"They didn't call Ms. Dixon either. Do you find that odd?"

Lehner met Brodie's gaze. "Yes, Mr. Brodie. I find that very odd."

"Why?"

"We were only a four-person team, and this was the most extreme malfunction of our entire mission thus far. Ms. Dixon or I could have provided some insight. Me especially, if it was a mechanical issue."

Taylor asked, "Is there anything you would like to share with us about Captain Spencer?"

Lehner took a moment. Then he looked Taylor in the eyes and said, "The captain was extremely loyal to his good friend Roger Ames."

"And would he do anything that the major asked of him?"

Lehner didn't respond, then opened the front door. Brodie and Taylor looked outside across the cul-de-sac to their house, where Captain Spencer was sitting on the stoop, watching them.

Lehner waved to his superior officer, then said to the agents in a low voice, "I've speculated enough. Good evening."

CHAPTER 12

BRODIE AND TAYLOR APPROACHED CAPTAIN SPENCER, who checked his watch as he rose and announced, "Your dinner is in thirty minutes."

Brodie said, "Taylor's low-maintenance and I'm no-maintenance. Thanks for waiting."

"Was the lieutenant helpful?"

"Yes," replied Taylor.

Spencer seemed to be waiting for something more, but when he didn't get it, he led them to the door, which was equipped with a digital keypad. Spencer told them the six-digit code, Brodie unlocked the door, and they entered a small foyer. Their two suitcases were on the floor.

The captain said, "The fridge and pantry are fully stocked. The commissary is closed due to the lockdown, and the mess is running on a skeleton crew just to serve the barracks, so for prepared meals you'll have to rely on MREs, unfortunately. Those are also in the pantry. There's a landline phone in the living room with an on-base directory. Dial nine to call out, but be mindful of what you discuss, as I'm sure you already know from your briefing. There's also a TV, no cable or streaming but you can pick up some dish channels. Each of your rooms is equipped with a programmable safe for securing your sidearms and any valuables. Is there anything else?"

Brodie said, "I think we've got it from here, Captain. Thank you."

Brodie watched the man walk away and then he shut the door. He asked Taylor, "Is everyone a suspect, or should they have called IT instead of CID?"

"Time will tell." She asked, "Cui bono?" Who benefits?

"Someone who wanted this program shut down. Or Major Ames committed a very elaborate accidental suicide by scrambling Bucky's brain."

"I can't believe you pelted it with a water bottle. Twice."

"Don't tell me you didn't want to."

She thought a moment. "This is freakish, Scott. Worse than I could have imagined. Those things make my skin crawl."

"While I agree with you, try to keep an open mind."

"*You* keep the open mind. Let me freak out for once."

"I'll see what I can do."

She looked at the closed door. "Did you bring a utility knife?"

He fished his utility knife from the inside pocket of his suit jacket and handed it to her.

She walked to the door, opened it, and inspected the keypad. Brodie watched as she folded out the mini screwdriver from the knife, loosened a screw on the underside of the keypad, and removed the mechanism. She then took out the battery and inspected the backside of the keypad plate.

He understood what she was doing. How many people knew the code for this house, and when was the last time it had been changed? It was probably the designated house for visitors—as infrequent as those might be here—and Captain Spencer certainly knew the code, as did whoever dropped off their bags.

Brodie was used to being the paranoid one in this outfit. Was he jealous? Proud? Maybe a little of both.

Taylor flipped a switch on the battery, reinstalled it, then reattached the faceplate and punched a few buttons. The mechanism beeped and the bolt slid out.

Brodie asked, "What's the new code?"

"Your birthday, backwards. Two digits for the year."

"I'm flattered you remember."

"But will *you* remember?" She turned back the bolt, closed the door, and locked it, then handed him back his knife. "Let's hydrate."

They walked into the small kitchen, which looked almost brand-new. Taylor opened the fridge and pulled out a Brita pitcher, then poured two glasses of water and handed one to Brodie. She raised her glass as if to toast.

"It's bad luck to toast with water," said Brodie.

"You don't believe in luck."

"I believe in whiskey."

"I'm sure back in 1961 this place came with a fully stocked bar cart. But the world got boring."

"Fine." He lifted his glass. "To justice for Roger Ames. And a forestalling of the robot apocalypse."

"Amen."

They drank. Taylor said, "We need to call Dombroski before dinner."

"I'll let you do the honors. Just let him know we're alive, and we have Camp Hayden's full cooperation."

"Copy."

Taylor went to the living room, and Brodie opened the pantry, which was stocked with the basics, plus two dozen beige pouches of military MREs. He should have packed Metamucil.

He closed the pantry, then noticed a manila envelope on the kitchen counter. He opened it and slid out about a dozen letter-sized color photos from the crime scene and flipped through them.

The first was a wide shot of the lab, with Ames's body lying crumpled on the floor near a table. Bucky was collapsed face-first on the ground a few feet away. This was obviously taken after the Rangers had incapacitated it with their EMP rifles and removed the hardware key. The sheer difference in size between the two bodies was startling.

The following photos were increasingly tighter and more detailed shots of both bodies, as well as the surrounding blood spatter, bone, and gore. The most disturbing photo was of Bucky's metal hands, the silver titanium completely covered in Ames's blood and chunks of skull and brain matter. Detailed shots of Bucky's body highlighted how much blood had gotten onto it, including blood and gore along the sides of its torso, around and even partly inside the port for the hardware key.

He slid the photos back into the envelope, then exited the kitchen's sliding glass doors to a rear patio with a few pieces of lawn furniture.

Beyond the patio was a small backyard of sand, stones, and succulents, and then Camp Hayden's twelve-foot-high steel security fence topped with razor wire. On both sides of the yard were tall wooden fences to separate the adjacent properties and offer privacy.

Brodie walked across the yard and looked through the security fence to a flat desert plain specked with low brush. The sun had slipped behind the distant mountains that now looked purple in the gloaming.

To the southwest he spotted Camp Hayden's training grounds that he'd seen from the air. He saw a large cluster of buildings, most two or three stories, likely used for urban combat scenarios. Farther south were low man-made hills topped with sandbag structures to act as fortified firing positions.

The whole setup looked small, insignificant, and ugly amid the beauty of the desert twilight. A meager, man-made joke.

After a few minutes Taylor stepped outside and came to join him. "I told him nothing, and he didn't ask for more."

"A welcome change." He told her about the crime scene photos, and where he'd left them so she could review later.

Taylor looked through the fence. "It's so beautiful out here."

"It is."

They looked out in silence for a minute. Then Taylor said, "In Af-

ghanistan, there were times when I'd almost forget. Out in the farmland. The mountains. Those lush valleys at dusk. And then I'd see a
chopper. Or a farmer with an AK. Or hear the whistle of mortars or the
pop of gunfire. And then I remembered where I was, and why."

"It's a beautiful world," said Brodie. "Except for the people in it."

CHAPTER 13

SCOTT BRODIE PUT ON THE SECOND OF THE TWO SUITS he'd brought, along with a fresh shirt and tie, and secured his SIG Sauer in the programmable safe in his bedroom. He waited for Taylor in the living room, which, like Lieutenant Lehner's, was generically appointed with modern furniture and laminate wood flooring. No bar cart.

Taylor emerged soon after, in a conservatively cut blue cotton dress and light makeup. As usual, she looked stunning with minimal effort.

Brodie said, "You look very nice."

"Thank you." She looked him over, as if checking that he was wearing different clothes than earlier. "You look . . . less dusty."

"I beat myself out with a broom." He added, "Let's go meet the general who was too good to meet us earlier."

"Behave."

"Maybe I should bring my gun."

"You're armed with your charm."

They stepped out of the house and locked the door, then proceeded across the pavement to the general's house. Brodie counted nine houses around the cul-de-sac, and there were likely nine more in the other one nearby. No one was outside, though he saw a few lights on. He wondered if any of the other officers they'd met today—or Caroline Dixon—were their neighbors.

They approached the house and rang the bell. After a moment the door opened, and they were greeted by a good-looking Black woman in her late forties wearing a flowered dress. She smiled and said in a soft voice, "Welcome, Mr. Brodie, Ms. Taylor. I'm Angela Morgan."

They stepped inside and shook hands. Taylor said, "Thank you for having us."

"Of course. Chris is in the living room, and I'll join you after I take care of something in the kitchen."

Brodie and Taylor walked into the living room, which looked like theirs but with nicer furniture.

General Christopher Morgan stood from the couch to greet them. He was a Black man of about average height, early fifties, with close-cropped graying hair and large, expressive eyes. He wore dark slacks, a button-down shirt, and a sports jacket. No tie. He approached them and extended his hand, without smiling. "Brigadier General Christopher Morgan."

Brodie shook the man's hand. The guy had a grip that might rival the robots'. "Chief Warrant Officer Scott Brodie. It's a pleasure to meet you, sir."

Morgan and Taylor shook. She introduced herself and said, "We are glad to be here, sir, despite the circumstances."

"Yes," said Morgan, looking pensive. "Well, have a seat and tell me what you're drinking." He walked to the corner of the living room, where Brodie now noticed a fully stocked bar cabinet.

"I'll have what you're having, sir."

"I'm having straight rye, Mr. Brodie. Neat."

"Can't argue with that."

Taylor said, "Make it three, sir."

He put three healthy pours into crystal tumblers, handed two to the agents, then grabbed the other and settled on the couch. Brodie and Taylor sat on a two-person love seat perpendicular to the sofa.

Morgan took a sip, then looked at the agents and asked, "Was Colonel Howe helpful today?"

Brodie replied, "Yes, sir. We saw the Vault and the DEVCOM lab, visited the morgue, then interviewed Number 20."

Morgan nodded. "It's a terrible tragedy."

"Yes, sir."

"No one should ever be alone with one of those things. If we ever get up and running again, that will be a new policy."

Taylor said, "That seems logical, sir."

"There's nothing logical about this place, Ms. Taylor."

She did not respond.

Morgan appeared lost in thought. He gave the impression of a man who spent a lot of time in his own head and didn't mind uncomfortable silences. Interestingly, the general saw no guarantee that the training at Camp Hayden would ever continue. Was that naïve, believing that one death could derail an entire Pentagon program?

After a moment he said to them, "The scientists tell me Number 20 could not have killed Major Ames without an alteration to its programming. They also tell me there was no alteration to its programming. Explain that one."

"They're still looking into it, sir," said Brodie.

Morgan waved a hand dismissively. "They're covering their asses. This is a disaster for them. For DEVCOM and the whole Futures Command, not to mention DARPA and the leadership at the Pentagon." He looked at them. "You two are either loved or hated to catch this case. Which is it?"

Brodie answered, "Depends who you ask, sir."

"I looked into you both. I know about Berlin. And I know about Venezuela. Well, I don't know everything. But I know enough."

Neither Brodie nor Taylor said anything to that.

"I also know you're both combat veterans. I like that." He looked at Brodie. "I was in Iraq the first go-round. A captain in the First Cav. We did it right that time. Get in, get out."

"Yes, sir. We thought we were in for a short war too."

Morgan nodded. "It was a war whose level of ambition was not matched by the quality of planning. The only people truly prepared were the war profiteers with fat contracts at the Pentagon."

That was a fairly shocking statement coming from a brigadier general, especially one they'd just met. Brodie had the thought that General Morgan might not be here of his own volition. Maybe he'd pissed off the wrong people, and Camp Hayden was the U.S. Army equivalent of getting shipped off to Siberia.

Taylor tried to change the subject. "We had a brief opportunity to meet a few of the Rangers today. We will be interested to learn more about their experiences with the D-17s as part of our investigation."

Morgan took another drink. "They're the best of us, and by far the greatest thing about Camp Hayden. It's a hard assignment."

Brodie said, "We heard that they have yet to defeat the bots in a training exercise."

The general's face grew grim. "That is not the whole story. The Rangers' kill count has gone up. So yes, they lose, but they take more of the tin men with them." He added, "That's what they call the bastards."

"That seems appropriate," said Brodie. "No heart."

"No brain either. Or courage. Or honor. Brute force is what they have. And speed. Agility."

Taylor said, "Caroline Dixon compared them to self-driving cars."

The general rolled his eyes. "That's a terrible analogy. They're circus tigers. Designed to kill but trained to be compliant. Trained, but not tamed. They do exactly what you want, until one day for whatever reason, one of them rips your throat out."

Brodie said, "Finding that reason is our job, sir."

General Morgan looked him in the eyes. "Yes, Mr. Brodie. And my job is to decide, no matter the reason, whether to put the tigers down."

CHAPTER 14

THE GENERAL'S WIFE WAS INDEED A GOOD COOK, AND they all sat in the dining room enjoying pork ribs, roasted yams, homemade cornbread, and a salad that was mostly kale but managed to be good anyway. Brodie and Taylor paid their compliments to the chef, who accepted them graciously.

The general, meanwhile, ate and drank in silence, allowing his wife to take care of the social niceties. She asked Brodie and Taylor about their backgrounds and their careers and took particular interest in Maggie Taylor's Appalachian upbringing. She herself was from southern Georgia, as was the general. They were high school sweethearts.

"I'm always impressed by that," said Taylor. "To be able to stick together through all those different phases of life."

Angela smiled. "We changed a lot, but we did it together. Isn't that right, Chris?"

The general nodded and managed a smile, though his mind was clearly elsewhere. "It helps to come up together, especially when you grew up where we did. I was born in what could generously be called a wooden shack. Angela was the rich kid with indoor plumbing."

Angela chuckled. "And look at you now, General."

That comment seemed to sour him a moment. "Yes." He tried to shake it off and said to Brodie and Taylor, "Angela is modest and won't tell you, but she is a senior manager in the Army's Acquisition Corps. Oversees a hundred-million-dollar budget."

Angela took a sip of red wine and said, "Two-hundred-million, dear."

"Okay," said the general. "Maybe not that modest."

They all had a chuckle. Just as Brodie realized he was actually having an okay time, the general said, "Colonel Howe told me of your desire to see another D-17 unit operational. I will not permit that. My first responsibility is to the safety of the men and women at this camp."

Brodie and Taylor shared a look. Brodie said, "Sir, I believe everyone's safety would be best served by CID getting to the bottom of what happened here. And that would be best served by us seeing a regular unit in regular operation."

Morgan took a bite of his ribs and washed it down with some red wine. Then he looked across the table at Brodie. "What do you think our mission is here at Camp Hayden, Mr. Brodie?"

"In the words of Colonel Howe, it is to train the Army Rangers and other light infantry units for the future of warfare."

The general nodded. "Sounds good. Too bad it's bullshit."

Mrs. Morgan said to her husband, "Christopher."

He waved her off. "It's all right. Mr. Brodie and Ms. Taylor require and deserve complete candor." He looked again at Brodie. "The bots are not here to train my men. My men are here to train the bots. Premium cannon fodder for the crown jewel in Synotec Systems' product line."

Brodie and Taylor sat with that for a moment. Then Taylor said, "General, the scientists told us that the D-17s cannot learn. They can't be trained."

He shrugged. "Semantics. Let's say, instead, that my men are being used to test the bots. In total, our platoon of Rangers has engaged in sixty-seven exercises against these things. And they've been defeated sixty-seven times. Now ask yourselves, if the Pentagon viewed that as a failure, wouldn't some changes be made here? At the very least a senior officer such as myself would be replaced. But they don't do anything, because the military doesn't see it as a failure if these bots keep beating some of the best soldiers in the Army. In fact, that's a sterling success. And each of our exercises generates a highly detailed after-action report that is reviewed by our scientists and Synotec's engineers—a massive trove of moment-by-moment data that they can use to refine their creations." He thought of something. "I will grant you full access to our after-action review system. It's very sophisticated, and it's the closest you're going to come to seeing the bots in action."

Brodie nodded. The general's stubbornness on this issue was going to be a problem, and Brodie was going to have to call upon the higher powers in CID to fix it. But no need to play that card yet. He did ask, "Sir, with all due respect, why are you commanding this program? It sounds like you do not agree with its goals."

"That's the irony, Mr. Brodie. I agree with its *stated* goals. The ones on paper that the Pentagon is ignoring. Train our soldiers for the future of war. I want my men to beat these bots, and I know they can do it. So I push them. Hard. You'll find I'm not the most popular guy among the enlisted men. But *my* mission—and it's one I'll continue as long as I have command—is to prove the supremacy of man over machine."

Brodie thought about motive, and whether General Morgan benefited from the D-17 program being shut down over safety concerns.

Maggie Taylor, evidently thinking along the same lines, said, "Sir, in a way, the tragic death of Major Ames has already proven your point, has it not? The machines cannot be trusted."

Morgan slid his eyes to her. "The scientists see that as a problem to be fixed, Ms. Taylor. They will reprogram them. New models will come down the line. Total victory on the battlefield is the best argument."

Brodie looked at the general, who was staring at Taylor with his intense brown eyes. They were the eyes of a zealot—a man fighting his own private war against the coming world.

Brodie thought of PFC Justin Beal, the Ranger who had overdosed on speed. Soldiers in elite units like the Rangers could put enormous pressure on themselves, which was compounded by the high expectations of their NCOs and commanding officers. But with a guy like

General Morgan at the top of the food chain, Camp Hayden was even more screwed up and prone to dysfunction than Brodie had imagined. A pressure cooker with no release valve.

No one said anything for a minute, and they ate in silence. Angela Morgan looked uncomfortable with her husband's words and general demeanor. Brodie wondered what the last nine months had been like for her, and whether her husband was the same man who'd first arrived here.

She cleared her throat, then got up and said, "I made a pie. Coffee, anyone?"

They all said yes to coffee, and Taylor insisted on helping. She grabbed a few plates and followed Angela to the kitchen, leaving Brodie and General Morgan alone.

Noticing Brodie's empty wineglass, the general poured him more without asking. He said, "You should visit the barracks tomorrow. Talk to the men."

"I was planning on it, sir."

"And get someone to show you the after-action review system."

"Colonel Howe has already instructed Major Klasky to show us." He asked, "How well did you know Major Ames, sir?"

"Not well. I don't have much interaction with the DEVCOM people, outside an occasional briefing. Also, it was no secret that I was not the biggest fan of his team's work." He added, "I know Ames had a good reputation. Hardworking, smart. *He* certainly thought he was doing good." That seemed to remind him of something. "We'll need to arrange for you to have a sit-down with Mr. Saltsberg. I'll talk to Sergeant Mendez about that."

Brodie asked, "Who is Mr. Saltsberg?"

"Eric Saltsberg. Synotec guy. No one mentioned him?"

"No, sir."

Morgan gave an exasperated sigh. "Sensitive subject, I guess. I had him arrested."

"Excuse me?"

"I said I had him arrested. House arrest. He's perfectly comfort-able." He explained, "He's an engineer. Synotec sent him here two days ago to observe a training exercise. He was supposed to stay a night and drive back to Nevada the next morning. The night he was here was the night of Major Ames's death. Upon the discovery of Ames's body, I declared a lockdown. No one leaves. Well, he flipped his lid. Got in his car, drove to the gates, and threatened to crash them if he wasn't let out. Good luck in a Toyota Camry. Anyway, he was out of control, so I had him taken into custody."

This place was getting more and more nutty. Either Eric Saltsberg was incredibly unlucky, or it was more than a coincidence that he was here the night that one of his products turned homicidal. Brodie's list of persons of interest was growing.

"We will certainly need to interview him, sir."

The general nodded. "He's not a bad guy. Just kind of high-strung. A civilian not used to someone else telling him where he can and can't go."

Well, getting suddenly told you couldn't leave a remote desert out-post might upset anyone. As would the discovery that one of your cre-ations had just split a guy's head open. Brodie imagined that General Morgan's decision to detain a representative of Synotec had not gone over very well with his superiors. It was also becoming increasingly clear that General Morgan did not give a shit.

Mrs. Morgan and Taylor returned with the coffee and a homemade pecan pie, which they all enjoyed in relative silence, except to talk about how good the pie was. As soon as they'd finished, Brodie and Taylor got up and said their good-byes and thanks.

General Morgan walked them to the front door. "It was good to meet you, agents. It's obvious to me this investigation is in good hands. Don't hesitate to let me know how I can be of assistance."

Taylor said, "Thank you, General. And if you think of anything that might be relevant to the case, please let us know."

They left the house and walked in silence across the cul-de-sac. Once they were well out of earshot, Taylor said, "I enjoyed the food, and one of the hosts."

"He's a lot." Brodie told Taylor about the arrest of Eric Saltsberg of Synotec Systems.

"Wow," she said. "That seems pretty impolitic, at the very least."

"Or an abuse of power. Saltsberg could have been compelled to speak with us whether he was detained here or allowed to go home to Nevada first. But the timing of Saltsberg's visit is suspicious."

They reached the house and Brodie unlocked the door. As they stood in the dark foyer, he called out, "Bucky? Are you here to kill us? I'm sorry about before."

Taylor turned on the lights. "Not funny. The idea of spending the night here with sixty of those things nearby is already giving me the creeps."

"Sorry." He added, "We could have had a nightcap if I'd swiped a bottle from Morgan's stash."

"I think we've had enough. Let's turn in. Packed day tomorrow."

There were loud, rapid knocks on the door. Brodie and Taylor exchanged a look, then Brodie checked the peephole. It was Caroline Dixon.

He opened the door. She had a stack of papers in her hand and a frantic look on her face.

She said, "I found something."

CHAPTER 15

DIXON LAID HER STACKS OF PAPERS ON THE LIVING room coffee table and spoke rapidly as she shuffled through them. "The DEVCOM lab has an intranet. A local shared server so we can all access the same files. The security logs for the lab as well as for the Vault entrance and D-17 storage bays are kept on there. But I've also been storing local backups of the logs on my computer, just as an extra precaution. On a hunch I decided to compare them." She looked at Brodie and Taylor. "There's discrepancies."

She handed a page to Taylor, and another to Brodie. There were dense columns of text showing dates, names, and times of day. She continued, "Those are the Vault entrance logs for April and May." She tapped the paper Brodie was holding, which had two rows of text marked with yellow highlighter pen. "That's my locally stored copy of the April log. I marked the two entry logs that were missing from the intranet version." She tapped Taylor's page. "And this is May. One missing entry. All three show Roger Ames entering the Vault in the early-morning hours."

Brodie and Taylor sat on the couch and looked over the logs, then swapped pages. "R. AMES" was listed on all three entry logs, with access times between 1:10 A.M. and 2:45 A.M., depending on the day.

She continued, "I cross-referenced these missing logs with the Rangers' sentry assignments. On all three days, the same Ranger was assigned to nighttime guard duty at the Vault, Private First Class Thomas Greer."

She then produced two more pages and handed them to the agents.

Three more entries were highlighted. "These are the missing bay storage logs. They match to the same times on the same days and are also coded to Major Ames's personal security fob. And on all three occasions, he activates and releases Number 20. Bucky."

Brodie stared at the dense columns of text. He said, "We will need the original log files."

Dixon removed a thumb drive from her pocket and placed it on the coffee table. "All there."

Taylor picked up the thumb drive. She asked, "Is there any innocent explanation you can think of for this?"

Dixon shook her head. "I wish there were. I think Roger wrote a piece of software to somehow manipulate Number 20, and he hid it so well none of us can find it."

"Is that possible?" asked Taylor. "To hide software in that way?"

"If you're Roger Ames, it is."

Brodie asked, "Is there a reason why he would have picked that particular unit? Are they all truly identical?"

"Everything but the numbers etched on their breastplates, and a cellular transponder that serves to keep track of each unit during exercises for the after-action. He could have picked it at random." She added, "It could explain why Bucky malfunctioned during training. Once that happened, maybe Roger figured that his tinkering might get discovered, and he wanted to undo what he'd done."

Taylor added, "And maybe Bucky didn't like that plan."

"These machines don't have motives," replied Dixon. "They have inputs and outputs. Cause and effect. Roger scrambled the code, and it made this thing malfunction. And Roger's death could simply be another consequence of that malfunction. Maybe Number 20's concept of the battlespace had been altered, and it saw Roger as an adversary. And for some reason it came to understand—or to be instructed—that its own hands were offensive weapons."

If this was true, it would explain why Ms. Dixon and Lieutenant

Lehner were not called to the lab the night Bucky was brought there for diagnostics. Roger Ames had screwed up, and he didn't want anyone to know about his late-night tinkering—except, perhaps, for his close friend and confidant Captain Spencer.

Taylor asked, "If there's hidden code, could it have infiltrated the other units?"

Dixon nodded. "They all share the hardwired data link inside the Vault. The safest and only thing to do is nuke the whole system. A root-level wipe of every single unit, and a re-install of the original software."

Brodie said, "The bots are evidence in our investigation, Ms. Dixon. And I'm sure you have no desire to tamper with evidence in this case."

"They are dangerous, Scott. Not just Bucky. All of them."

Taylor said, "I'm glad you've come to that conclusion. Going forward you will certainly be more careful than Major Ames was. In the meantime, if you can't figure out whether and in what manner the major altered Bucky's programming, we will bring in someone who can."

Dixon stared at Maggie Taylor a moment. She adjusted her oversize glasses. "I will be advising my superiors at DARPA that we should do a wipe and reset on all sixty units. I am confident that Captain Spencer will agree with that advisement. Whether that is evidence tampering or a reasonable precaution will be decided by people higher up the chain than any of us."

"It's not a precaution," said Taylor. "It's reckless. And I don't need to be a computer scientist to understand that."

"Actually, Maggie, you do."

It occurred to Brodie that Ms. Taylor and Ms. Dixon did not like each other very much. Maybe he should have picked up on that before, but when it came to reading the feelings and intentions of the opposite sex, Scott Brodie was only semiliterate. He decided to step in and try to defuse the situation. "Thank you for this, Caroline. We'll be in touch tomorrow."

Dixon kept her eyes on Taylor. "Right." She turned sharply and walked to the door. She opened it and stepped out, then turned back to them. "I'm house number seven. Your next-door neighbor."

Brodie said, "You should have brought a casserole."

Dixon did not smile. "I brought you something better."

"Right."

She lingered a moment, something else on her mind. Then she said, "I was personally involved in developing and testing the D-17 software over a period of years. Nothing even approaching what happened to Major Ames has ever happened before or was ever in danger of happening. Then Ames takes this one unit out late at night on three occasions, does whatever he does, attempts to cover his tracks, and then the bot malfunctions and kills him. The motive might be unclear, but to me it's pretty obvious who was responsible for Roger's death." Her eyes drifted to Taylor. "And I don't need to be a criminal investigator to understand that."

Brodie said, "Good night, Caroline."

She looked back at Brodie. "Good night, Scott. And good luck." She walked away.

Brodie shut the door and turned to Taylor. "She's a good resource."

"She's an arrogant bitch."

"Why not both?"

"I don't trust her, Scott. And I need you to think with the right head."

"I'm insulted."

"No, you're not." She added, "She's got the sexy-scientist thing going for her."

"Didn't notice."

Taylor held up the thumb drive Dixon had given them. "We can't even look at these files, let alone check if they're authentic. We have no way of passing them on to digital forensics."

"I'm sure there's an on-base computer we can use."

"So, we are relying on the communications infrastructure of a place that might be compromised at the highest levels to transmit evidence in our criminal investigation. That's not good."

"We're on an island here, Maggie. We need to get used to the fact that we're alone, and that you and I have only each other. And we don't need digital forensics to tell us whether someone is full of shit."

She met his eyes. "Intuition only gets you so far."

"Then we'll take it as far as it goes."

Taylor did not look happy. She pocketed the thumb drive and asked, "So what do we do now?"

"What we always do. Barrel ahead. Let's go find Private Greer."

CHAPTER 16

BRODIE AND TAYLOR APPROACHED THE BARRACKS BUILD-
ing on foot. It was about nine-fifteen, and lights were on in many of
the windows. A few white LED streetlamps lit the road leading to the
building and the parking lot in front.

Taylor had changed from her dinner attire back to her black suit,
and they had both accessorized with their 9mm SIG Sauers, which
came in a tasteful and appropriate coyote brown.

The barracks front entry was unguarded and unlocked. They entered a small foyer, where an unoccupied desk held a landline tele-
phone and over a dozen empty cans of Monster Energy drink and
Coors Light.

Against the wall opposite the desk stood a metal tripod, and
clamped to the top of it was the head casing of a D-17, covered in
suction-cup darts.

Another wall was covered with fliers, Army posters, and a corkboard featuring a drawing of a despondent-looking Ranger in fatigues
standing next to a D-17 with a giant erect metal phallus, along with the
caption: YOU VS. THE GUY SHE TOLD YOU NOT TO WORRY
ABOUT.

Taylor looked at the drawing longer than she really needed to. Then
she said, "They're emasculated by these things."

"It's a joke."

Taylor gestured to the disembodied robot head covered in darts.
"And behind the joke is anger."

Brodie didn't respond.

She asked in a low voice, "Who has a clearer motive for ending this program, and for exacting revenge on its chief scientist, than these guys?"

"Are we looking for an Army Ranger with an advanced degree in computer science?"

"No, Scott. We're looking for a potential co-conspirator."

Right. And that co-conspirator might be PFC Thomas Greer, whether witting or unwitting.

There was a hallway off the foyer, and they could hear up-tempo hip-hop coming from somewhere down the hall. Brodie led the way, and about midway down the corridor was an open door with the music blaring from it.

They entered a common room lounge with couches, chairs, a large TV, a kitchenette, and foosball and pool tables. About thirty Rangers—most of them in T-shirts and jeans or cargo pants—milled around drinking and shooting the shit. They were all young men in their twenties or early thirties, muscular, lots of ink. It was a tough-looking bunch, at least as far as humans went.

The two CID agents immediately caught their attention. Brodie said loudly over the music, "Good evening, gentlemen."

One of the guys near the speaker stopped the music, and the room fell silent.

Brodie and Taylor produced their creds and Brodie said, "I am Chief Warrant Officer Scott Brodie, Army CID, and this is my partner, Chief Warrant Officer Maggie Taylor. As I'm sure you're aware, Ms. Taylor and I are here to investigate the death of Major Roger Ames of the DEVCOM team, and we appreciate your cooperation. Who's the officer in charge?"

A mid-thirties man with dark-brown hair and stubble stepped forward. He was holding a bottle of Budweiser and wore jeans, boots, and a well-loved T-shirt. "Sergeant First Class Mike Miller."

They led Sergeant Miller out of earshot of the other men, who got the music started again and went back to what they were doing.

Miller took a swig of his beer and asked, "Want a drink?"

Brodie replied, "We're on duty."

"Must be nice."

Mike Miller was the senior noncommissioned officer for the Ranger platoon. He was lean and wiry, and handsome in a rugged sort of way. He looked like the kind of soldier who might get cast in one of the Army's slick recruitment commercials—except for the stubble and the beer in his hand, and the thousand-yard stare of a combat vet who'd seen too much. Brodie wondered who Sergeant Miller had squared off against in his Army career before being tasked with this assignment at Camp Hayden.

Brodie asked the sergeant, "How are your men doing?"

"Bored. Pissed off. Wondering if the geniuses in DEVCOM are going to have to shitcan their toy soldiers over this."

Brodie looked around the room. The Rangers were mostly going about their business while occasionally stealing glances at the new arrivals. Most of those glances were reserved for Ms. Taylor, a very attractive woman in a room full of isolated and frustrated young men. Brodie said to Miller, "We're looking for PFC Thomas Greer."

"Why?"

"Is he here?"

Miller shook his head. "Not his scene. You'll find him in his room. Three-H."

Taylor asked, "Do you know all of your men's room numbers off the top of your head?"

"No, ma'am. But I've visited Greer's room more than most. He has required special attention."

Brodie asked, "For what reason?"

Sergeant Miller hesitated. Then he said, "Some of the guys are handling this assignment better than others. I'd say Greer's been the worst off in the entire platoon. Stress, paranoia, anger issues."

"Drug use?" asked Taylor.

"Do I have to answer that?"

Brodie asked, "Do you wish to comment on the death of Private Justin Beal?"

Miller looked at Brodie a moment, poker-faced. He took a swig of beer, then said, "You guys have no clue what you're dealing with here."

"Enlighten us."

Miller kept his eyes on Brodie. "Beal pushed himself to the limit, and when he reached his limit, he tried to go further. And then he broke."

Taylor asked, "And Private Greer?"

"Greer cracked in a different way. A couple months ago, he assaulted his roommate in the middle of the night. Private Sam Kowalski. Went into Kowalski's bedroom and started whaling on the guy. Kowalski fought him off. No serious injuries. I talked Greer down after. He kept saying Kowalski wasn't real. Wasn't human. He eventually settled down and realized he was whacked out of his head. Claimed sleep deprivation."

Brodie asked, "What disciplinary action was taken?"

"None."

"None?"

Miller nodded. "Kowalski was willing to let it go so long as he was assigned to a new room. And Greer took a turn for the better a week or so after the incident. He quit using. The assault was his breaking point, and he cleaned up."

"What was he using?"

"Speed, coke, steroids. Whatever he could get when he needed it."

Brodie said, "I have a hard time understanding why no action was taken against a soldier who was abusing drugs and assaulted a fellow soldier. I thought the Rangers had higher standards."

Miller kept his cool as he replied, "We are loyal to our own, sir. And given what my men have been put through at Camp Hayden, they're allowed a little leeway."

"Was your commanding officer made aware of the assault? Captain Pickman?"

Miller kept his eyes on Brodie. "The captain trusts me."

That sounded like a no. And like perhaps Captain Pickman was happy to be kept in the dark.

Everyone at this desert outpost—commissioned officers, enlisted soldiers, and scientists—understood that any publicity for Camp Hayden was bad publicity. The death of PFC Beal could not go unreported. But Greer's assault could, especially if news of the incident would end up shining a light on a broader pattern of drug abuse at Camp Hayden—and the highly classified activities fueling that abuse.

Sergeant Miller added, "If Kowalski wanted to press charges, he could have. But he understood we needed to help Greer, not end his Army career."

Taylor asked, "And how did you help him?"

"By keeping an eye on him, talking him through things, and confiscating his supply."

"Are you a mental health professional?"

Miller looked at her. "No, ma'am."

"Are there any mental health services available here?"

Miller thought that was funny. He gestured around the rec room. "You're looking at them."

Brodie asked, "Was Greer kept from participating in training exercises after the assault?"

"No," replied Miller. "If we'd been doing live-fire exercises, that would have been a different story."

"You must all have service pistols, in addition to the SIMRES-equipped rifles."

Miller nodded. "And Greer's was confiscated."

Brodie asked, "Have you spoken to him since Major Ames's death and the start of the lockdown?"

"No."

"Are you aware of any direct interactions or associations between Private Greer and the deceased, Major Ames?"

"We don't interact with the DEVCOM people." He looked bothered by the question. "You really think Greer is somehow involved in this?"

Brodie ignored the question and said, "Take us to the private's room."

CHAPTER 17

SERGEANT FIRST CLASS MIKE MILLER LED BRODIE AND
Taylor down the third-floor hallway to Room 3H.

Brodie discreetly placed his hand on his holstered pistol, and he
noticed Taylor do the same. When it came to making an unannounced
visit to a soldier with mental health issues and—potentially—access
to a weapon, there was no taking chances.

Brodie knocked loudly on the door and announced, "CID! Open
the door."

After a moment he heard footsteps, and then the door opened slowly
to reveal a tall, fit man of about twenty in a black Nirvana T-shirt and
jeans with close-cropped dirty-blond hair. Despite his imposing phy-
sique, he had a softness and innocence to his features. His large blue eyes
moved between his three visitors.

Brodie and Taylor produced their creds, and Brodie said, "Special
Agents Brodie and Taylor, CID. Are you PFC Thomas Greer?"

"Yes, sir," the man answered. He looked at Sergeant Miller. "Is everything all right, Sergeant?"

Miller said, "The agents just have a few questions for you, Tom."

Greer nodded and stepped aside. They all entered a small living
room with a couch, TV, table and chairs, and kitchenette.

Brodie turned to Sergeant Miller. "Thank you for your cooperation. We have it from here. But we'd like to get a look at your training
grounds tomorrow."

Miller nodded. "Yes, sir. I can meet you at the west gate with a vehicle and take you out."

"Good. Oh-eight-hundred. And we'd like it if Captain Pickman can join us. We have yet to meet."

The sergeant looked as though he didn't love that idea, but said, "I will notify the captain." Miller took a last look at Private Greer, then left the room.

Brodie gestured for Greer to have a seat on the couch, and the two agents pulled up chairs across from him.

Brodie noticed a PlayStation controller, a graphic novel, and the remnants of a burrito on the coffee table in front of the couch. He asked, "How have you been handling the lockdown?"

Greer shrugged. "Don't mind it, sir. Don't mind the break. They've been running us ragged."

"So I've heard." He added, "As I'm sure you're aware, we are here because of the death of Major Roger Ames. Did you know the major?"

Greer broke eye contact and looked at the coffee table, contemplating his burrito, or perhaps whether he should lie to CID agents. He said, "I knew who he was. There's only a handful of officers at this camp."

"Right. But did you ever converse with him?"

Greer looked at Brodie. "No, sir."

"So he never told you why he was accessing the Vault in the middle of the night?"

Greer cleared his throat. "I do recall letting him in on a night shift or two while on guard duty. Wouldn't be my place to ask what he was doing, though."

Taylor asked, "Was he alone?"

Greer thought for a moment—or pretended to. "I believe so."

She followed up, "Were you alone on guard duty?"

Greer nodded. "There are supposed to be two guys, but on night duty it doesn't always work out that way. Someone gets sick, or says they're sick, or just hasn't had enough rest since a training exercise to manage it. So long as one guy is there, command seems okay with it."

Brodie asked, "Did you accompany the major down into the Vault?"

Greer shook his head. "I just let him into the building and activated the elevator for him."

Was that a lie? Ames would have needed Greer's access code to activate and release the D-17 unit. Unless Greer had given his code to the major, which would have been a major breach of protocol. "Did you give your access code to Major Ames?"

"No, sir. That is forbidden."

Taylor said in as soft a voice as she could muster, "Private, we are well versed in the security protocols of this camp. And we know that Major Ames could not have done anything in the Vault without the access code that is not given to DEVCOM, and that is only known to officers within the camp command and select enlisted men while performing guard duty. So we will ask you again, with a reminder that you are speaking with officers of the law: Did you accompany Major Ames down to the Vault during any of his nighttime visits?"

Greer shook his head vigorously. "No, ma'am."

"Did you give your code to Major Ames?"

Greer sighed. "Yes, ma'am, I did. I apologize for not being truthful."

Brodie said, "Next time it will come with a price."

"Yes, sir."

Brodie asked, "Why did you give the major your code?"

"Because he asked for it. He said that since I was alone it would not be good to leave the Vault unguarded."

Brodie nodded. He had some sympathy for Greer. What he'd done was against protocol, but it was at the request of a commissioned officer. The steep power imbalance made it difficult for the private to say no.

Taylor asked, "How many incidents were there of the major coming to the Vault late at night when you were alone on guard duty, and you giving the major your access code? Think before you answer."

Private Greer thought, and if he was smart, he was thinking that the agents already knew the answer to the question. Then he replied, "Three."

"And do you recall why you were alone on duty all three nights?"

Greer nodded. "First time a guy was sick. Second time, I think it was because the guy's training schedule had changed last-minute, and he had to rest up that night. Third time, the other Ranger just didn't show, and later I heard he'd . . . kind of been on a bender and was in no shape to do anything."

Taylor asked, "Are you often on nighttime sentry duty?"

"Yes, ma'am."

"Why? Is that based on seniority, or a disciplinary measure?"

Greer shook his head. "Neither. Most of the guys don't want to do it, but I volunteered to pull extra night shifts. I wasn't sleeping well anyway, so figured I'd get some shifts on the books instead of staring at the ceiling all night. It allowed me to get excused from some of the early drills the next day, and if I slept at all I had a better chance of doing it during the daytime."

A cocktail of amphetamines, cocaine, and steroids is bound to screw up your internal clock. Brodie asked, "Were you alone on any of your other nighttime guard shifts?"

Greer thought a moment. "Not that I recall."

"Did Major Ames come to the Vault on any of those nights when you were with another Ranger?"

"No, sir."

"Did you find that odd?"

Greer thought a moment. The man seemed a little nervous but relatively calm and cogent, and Brodie could believe that this guy had quit or at least paused his mass consumption of uppers. He replied, "Yes, sir, that is odd now that you put it like that."

Brodie switched gears and said, "We are aware of the incident with your roommate, Kowalski."

Greer refocused on his burrito. "Yes, sir. That was . . . a bad time for me."

"Do you remember the incident?"

"Parts. I remember sitting here on this couch, staring at that door." He gestured to a door on the wall opposite, which presumably led to the bedroom that used to be Private Kowalski's. "And I was feeling like . . . like there was something very wrong on the other side of that door."

Taylor asked, "What do you mean, wrong?"

Greer looked at her with his large blue eyes. He appeared pained. "Unnatural, ma'am. Something unnatural, that was going to kill me if I didn't kill it first."

She asked, "And then what happened?"

He shook his head. "I don't remember. I blacked out. Next thing I remember is Sergeant Miller pinning me against the wall and yelling at me. I looked over and saw Kowalski getting talked down by another Ranger. He had blood dripping out of his nose and a black eye." He took a deep breath. "I didn't mean to do it. I didn't know what I was doing."

Taylor said in a calm voice, "Private, you likely experienced stimulant psychosis. It affects judgment as well as memory. It can occur from prolonged amphetamine abuse."

Private Greer nodded. "I don't do that anymore."

Taylor asked, "When did you start using stimulants?"

Greer met Taylor's eyes. "It was about six weeks into our assignment here, ma'am. During one of our training missions."

"What prompted you to start using?"

"That mission was a head game. Different than the others. Screwed us all up."

Brodie said, "Describe the mission."

Greer took a moment to gather himself. Then he said, "We were defending the village against two squads of tin men. That's twelve bots.

Pretty standard, or so we thought. Usually they fan out and launch their assault. We take some of them out, but never enough. We all die, and the village falls. Well, this time, they took up positions around the village, weapons trained, and they waited. One of our guys popped up to get a better look and was sniped. Head shot. We had an M2 open up on them, but the bots took cover in the hills and man-made barriers around the village. And it went on like that. Guy exposes himself and gets sniped. We return with heavy fire but can't get a kill. The hours drag on. We take shifts eating and eventually sleeping. It's a siege. They're starving us of food and ammo. And energy. But they run on batteries, so we figure maybe we can wait them out. We're thirty hours in when our spotter catches sight of them taking rations from their sacks and . . . they have, like, these slots, where they can process food and recharge, and these things . . . they're just shoving the rations into their bodies, all still wrapped up in paper and plastic, right into their bodies. The same food we had, but they had more of it. And that's when we knew we were fucked." He added, "Sorry."

Brodie tried to imagine what this must have been like—under siege by machines that don't sleep, that don't lose patience, that don't even run out of gas, shoving human food, wrapper and all, into their microbial fuel cells. It was beyond bleak. It was a mockery. Brodie wondered if that was the intent, and if so, whose intent it was.

Greer continued, "One of my squad buddies, he gives me some pills, and a bump of coke. I'd never done anything like that and I gotta be honest, it felt good. I felt like I needed it. I got confidence, it was almost like I got hope. The rest of the survivors in our squads, they took some too, and we all decided to just charge them. Go out in a blaze of glory. It was dumb, but we were all flying high and out of options anyway. They cut us down in seconds. We didn't take out a single one of them."

Taylor asked, "How many Rangers were involved in this exercise?"

Greer thought a moment. "About thirty-five. Over half the platoon."

Thirty-five versus a dozen. That was about a three-to-one ratio of defenders to attackers, which, if they had all been human, would have given the defenders unbeatable odds.

Greer said the drugs gave him "hope," but the hope wasn't to win or even to survive. The hope was to die well.

Brodie asked, "And then you kept using?"

Greer nodded. "Yes, sir. Basically, every exercise from then on out. It made things easier." He clarified, "It made things *feel* easier. We kept losing. But as time went on things weren't so lopsided. And they never did the siege tactic again. Kinetic assaults from then on out."

Brodie nodded. If the Rangers had to go through thirty-hour sieges on a regular basis, General Morgan would probably have had a mutiny on his hands. Though Brodie wondered who had decided to change tactics, and why, and how. According to Caroline Dixon and Captain Spencer, the D-17s had a simple doctrine statement that remained unchanged, and the rest was up to them to figure out. Or at least that was how he understood it. He needed to clarify that.

Taylor asked, "When did you feel yourself beginning to lose control from your drug use?"

Greer appeared uncomfortable with the question. "I don't know. Hard to say. We already feel like we've got so little control here, ma'am."

Taylor clarified, "You experienced some sort of psychotic break the night you assaulted your roommate. Was that the first and only time you felt yourself losing your grip on reality? Have you experienced any hallucinations—visual, auditory, anything?"

Greer shook his head. "Nothing. Nothing like what happened on that night. Confusion, maybe, feeling delirious. But that was something else."

Brodie asked, "Were you high any of the nights that Major Ames came by the Vault?"

Greer nodded. "The first two nights I was. Not the third."

"What did Ames say to you?"

"Nothing out of the ordinary, sir. We greeted each other, I saluted, and I let him into the elevator."

"And you gave him your code to release the access keys and the holding bays."

"That's correct, sir."

"How often is that code changed?"

"Daily."

"How long did the major stay down in the Vault?"

"Well . . . I wasn't keeping good track of time the first two nights. But the last night he came by, I'd say he was down there for maybe an hour."

"Were you aware of what he was doing down there?"

"No, sir."

"On all three nights, the only bot he activated and released from its holding bay was Number 20. Bucky. The same unit that later killed him."

If PFC Greer was surprised by that information, he didn't show it. In fact, he said, "I was afraid there was some connection between whatever he was up to down there and what happened to him."

"Why didn't you report any of this to your superiors once you learned of Major Ames's death?"

Greer looked away again. "I don't know, sir. I should have."

Brodie leaned forward in his chair. "I need you to think, Tom. Of something he said, or his demeanor, anything at all that you might remember that can help us get justice for the major and his family."

Greer took a deep breath. "Like I said, I was jacked up the first two nights, so I really can't totally remember, but the third night, the major came back up and he looked . . . afraid."

"Afraid of what?"

"Afraid of *them*, sir. The tin men."

"What did he say to you?"

Greer met Brodie's gaze. "He said to me, 'There's a ghost in the machine.' And then he walked away. And that's the last time I ever saw him."

CHAPTER 18

BRODIE AND TAYLOR WALKED OUT OF THE BARRACKS into the cool desert night. Brodie said, "Ames feared the D-17s are smarter than they seem."

Taylor nodded. "Or they are *becoming* smarter, somehow."

Brodie considered that a moment. "Maybe Ames wasn't tinkering. Maybe he was digging, and he found something. And that's why he's dead."

"If that's the case, who would be responsible?"

"Maybe no one. The bot itself. Maybe these things have the capacity to get smarter, but that wasn't the intention of the programmers."

Taylor looked skeptical. "I'm not sure that's possible. If the D-17s have a higher intellectual capacity than is evident, it's because someone designed them that way. Someone in DEVCOM. Or DARPA. Or Synotec."

Brodie nodded. They both watched a white Military Police vehicle rumble across the dusty road ahead of them. Then he said, "It looks like Caroline's Intel was accurate. So can we trust her, or is she still a bitch?"

"Why not both?"

Brodie smiled.

She added, "Could be a limited hangout."

That was Intel jargon for revealing part of the truth to establish credibility, or to mask the larger truth. Ms. Taylor wasn't in a trusting mood, and neither was he.

Taylor asked, "How does PFC Greer fit into this?"

"Maybe he doesn't, beyond what he's already told us. He was on night duty more often than most because he asked to be, so he was the one who was most likely to encounter Roger Ames during the major's late-night visits. And Ames only approached Greer when the private was alone, so that he would have a reason to not have a Ranger accompany him down into the Vault when he activated and released Bucky and . . . did whatever he did."

Taylor thought on that. "Ames's first visit was on April third. Something must have occurred before that date that got Ames interested in Bucky."

Right. But there was no reported incident with Bucky until its subsequent malfunction on the training grounds the day it murdered Ames. If there had been, someone would have mentioned it.

They walked in silence toward the western end of Camp Hayden, their way illuminated by the occasional LED streetlamp. The camp was eerily silent, other than the distant hum of electrical generators and the crunching tires of the slow-moving MP vehicle that continued its night rounds along the sand-strewn roads.

Taylor whispered, "Stop."

Brodie stopped walking. They were standing in a patch of darkness next to a storage shed, about twenty yards from the edge of the cul-de-sac of houses. A figure was walking down the front steps of the house next to theirs. It was Caroline Dixon. She'd changed into a long skirt, ankle boots, and a low-cut top that showed off a couple of major assets.

They observed as Dixon walked across the cul-de-sac toward the opposite end, and a strip of sidewalk that led to the other ring of houses south of their own.

Brodie and Taylor began following her, keeping their distance.

They entered the adjacent cul-de-sac, which appeared identical to theirs, and saw Dixon approach a house with a Jeep Wrangler in the driveway.

Brodie and Taylor stopped and watched, obscured in a pool of darkness beyond the streetlamps.

Dixon walked up the stoop, looked around, then rang the doorbell. After a moment the door opened. It was Colonel Elizabeth Howe, dressed down in a T-shirt and jeans.

The women exchanged a few words, then Dixon quickly stepped in and kissed Howe. Howe grabbed the back of Dixon's hair and pulled her closer, and Dixon kicked the door shut behind her.

Brodie and Taylor stood in silence a moment. Then Brodie said, "They're two of the only women in this camp, and they're screwing each other. That's kind of selfish."

"You're kind of gross."

"Only for your amusement."

"Don't strain yourself." She added, "This is . . . interesting."

Right. On the surface there wasn't anything nefarious here. Nothing wrong with two ladies enjoying each other's company, especially when one of them was a civilian.

On the other hand, it wasn't the *best* idea to create a messy entangle- ment between the top civilian scientist on a military research project and the second-in-command of the Army facility where that research was being conducted. Some propriety had to go out the window at an isolated outpost like this, but considering what had happened to Roger Ames, personal relationships at Camp Hayden became potential clues toward possible motives. Sex and murder often went hand in hand.

Brodie asked, "Who's the top?"

"With those two, it's hard to say."

"Maybe we should get a closer look to find out."

"Maybe we should go back to our house, and you can take a cold shower."

As they turned to leave, Brodie stopped short, spotting a white MP vehicle parked in a driveway at the far end of the cul-de-sac. The driver's-side window was open, and someone hung their arm out, holding a lit cigarette. Brodie could make out the faint chatter of talk radio or perhaps an audiobook playing from the car's stereo.

Taylor said, "I bet that's the night detail for the Synotec guy's house arrest."

"Eric Saltsberg. We owe him a visit."

"It's late."

"Lady Justice does not sleep."

"But this lady does. And he's not going anywhere. C'mon."

They walked back to their house, and as Brodie punched in the security code and entered the darkened foyer, he didn't crack any jokes about killer robots lying in wait.

Taylor flicked on the lights and produced a flask-sized bottle of Jim Beam. "Here's your nightcap. Swiped it from the rec room."

"Way to support the troops, Maggie."

"They had enough hooch in there to fuck up a battalion. Won't even notice."

They made their way through the house to the backyard and sat on a couple of plastic chairs. Taylor opened the bottle, had a pull, and passed it to her partner.

Brodie took a swig and handed it back. He looked out at the small yard of rocks and cacti that led to the high fence, and the black desert beyond.

Taylor took another drink and said, "I don't like it, Scott."

"Me neither. Did the Rangers have any single malt scotch?"

"I mean Caroline Dixon and Colonel Howe."

"I thought you were open-minded."

"Not *that*. I mean the fact that I didn't particularly trust either of these women to begin with, and now we see they have some sort of personal relationship."

"They're very committed to bridging the military-civilian divide."

She looked at him. "Can you be serious?"

"One more drink should do it."

She handed him the bottle. He knocked some back, then returned it to her and said, "Sometimes sex is just sex."

"Actually, it never is."

Brodie looked at his partner, who was staring out into the darkness beyond the perimeter. Maggie Taylor had some experience with bad sex—that is, sex that led to bad consequences, though Brodie was sure the sex itself was also terrible. The offender was a world-class asshole named Trent Chilcott of the Central Intelligence Agency. He'd mentored Ms. Taylor during her Civil Affairs service in Afghanistan, then screwed her, then screwed her in a different way. But that was a long story, and a lifetime ago.

The point was, Maggie Taylor was thinking about how a toss in the sack could upend and rewire people's agendas and allegiances. But at Camp Hayden, they were all supposed to have the same agendas and allegiances. Clearly, there was more going on here.

Brodie said, "We have met most of the key players at Camp Hayden. I believe at least one of them is lying to us."

Taylor kept her eyes on the desert beyond the camp gates and did not respond. The sky was brilliant with stars and the arc of the Milky Way. Black peaks of the distant mountains jutted up along the horizon. Somewhere in the darkness echoed the crazy, high-pitched howls of coyotes.

She said, "Dombroski was wrong. He said the scientists here could explain to us what we needed to know. But you and I both sense we're getting snowed by someone, Scott. Before arriving, I had no idea the research team was this small. Three military and one civilian, including the late Roger Ames. In a circle that tight, each member will have a lot of responsibilities, and there aren't any redundancies and probably little oversight. Dixon is the only person here who reps DARPA, and Captain Spencer now has no one here above him in rank who has the slightest clue what his two-person DEVCOM team is doing. Caroline made it sound like having such a small team meant no one could get up to something in secret, but I think the opposite is true. And we have as proof Major Ames's late-night visits with Bucky, activity that was supposedly unknown to anyone else in the research lab."

She had a point. Actually, several points. Ms. Taylor's Appalachian roots granted her the gift of high functioning on cheap whiskey. Brodie said, "We have to assume the evidence is not secure. We stay and work the humans because that's what we understand. Let's confiscate the hardware and get it out of here."

"Bucky."

"The whole baseball team."

Taylor nodded. "I'll call Dombroski early tomorrow morning and put in the request."

"Using a phone line tapped by people we don't trust."

She asked, "What choice do we have?"

The answer was none, because that was how this place was designed. Secrecy and control. An island way out in an oblivion of stars and sand, where the future of war was being written from behind high fences and concertina wire.

Brodie wondered just how high up the chain General Dombroski would have to go to confiscate Camp Hayden's high-tech Terra-Cotta Army. It might take time, and Scott Brodie's instincts told him they didn't have time.

CHAPTER 19

THE ARMY-GREEN LAND ROVER RUMBLED OUT OF CAMP Hayden's western gate. Sergeant Mike Miller was at the wheel, dressed in desert camo. Brodie sat shotgun, and Taylor was in the back. Captain Pickman was apparently indisposed but would speak with them later in the day. Brodie knew he shouldn't read too much into that, but he was in the mode of reading into everything.

Taylor had called General Dombroski at dawn East Coast time to inform him of their desire to seize Camp Hayden's D-17 fleet. She had done so without explaining what a D-17 was, or providing any other information that might be deemed classified or otherwise too sensitive to discuss over the phone. Dombroski didn't ask questions and could fill in the blanks himself, and he assured her he would force the request through the Army bureaucracy. Brodie figured that it was only a matter of time before one of the officers at Camp Hayden approached them looking very pissed off. And that was fine. On a criminal investigation, if you're making friends, you're doing it wrong.

As they drove along a strip of hard-packed sand toward the training grounds, Sergeant Miller gave them a rundown of a standard exercise. "We're typically two to three squads, the number of tin men changes. We are always the defenders, so we arrive first and have two hours to prep before the assault. Once it gets going, it's a battle of annihilation. No prisoners. No surrender. The only metrics are your kill count and the length of your unit's survival." He pointed out the windshield. "There's our beautiful village."

About half a mile ahead Brodie saw the cluster of boxy cinderblock buildings that made up the training ground. Most were two or three stories tall, but among them were a few four- and five-story towers.

Taylor asked Miller, "Why are you always the defenders?"

"Because, ma'am, if we were to launch an open-terrain assault on a dug-in position of tin men, it would be over in about thirty seconds."

Taylor nodded but did not reply.

As they got closer Brodie spotted the firing nests atop the man-made hills just outside of the concentration of structures. He also noted that inside the village, several of the rooftops held firing positions ringed with sandbags and tripods for mounted guns.

Brodie commented, "That's a lot of mounted positions for two or three Ranger squads."

"Well," replied Miller, "that's a big part of the suck, Mr. Brodie. You want maneuverability, but you need high-caliber firepower to penetrate these bastards. They're titanium. So we opt for mounted M2s, plus RPGs, grenade launchers, and other kinds of MANPATS. We pick them off as we can on the approach, but they're fast and most survive the charge. Once they're in the village we're deploying hit-and-run tactics. We're an infantry platoon, but they're a goddamn tank battalion that's just shaped like infantry."

That sucked, all right. And it drove home the point that the tin men were not simply mechanical stand-ins for human soldiers, with better endurance, maneuverability, and precision. They were also much more durable, which put them in a whole new target category, and engagement with them required cumbersome anti-materiel weapons. The Army liked to talk big about doing the impossible, but Camp Hayden's platoon of Rangers was really being asked to do it, day in and day out. And they were apparently failing, day in and day out, despite their best efforts. That would screw up anyone, even without a heroic dose of speed, steroids, and cocaine.

Brodie said, "You're insurgents, basically. That's how you are being forced to engage."

Miller nodded as he slowed the Land Rover about thirty feet from the entrance to the main street that ran through the village. The sergeant's eyes scanned the empty training grounds, where a line of prop laundry swayed in the wind, and a string of busted-up cars lined the roadway. "We are tasked with occupying and holding a position and fighting to the death against a technologically superior force. Not exactly relevant training for U.S. Army Rangers."

"Because you're not the ones being trained," said Taylor. "The tin men are."

"Bingo," replied Miller.

Apparently, Sergeant Miller was of the same mind as General Morgan on the real purpose of their mission. But Morgan, like any good commanding officer, justified the hell he was putting his men through. Which led Brodie to ask, "Do you believe this training has any value for you and your men?"

Miller turned and looked at Brodie with his world-weary eyes. "You mean was it worth the lives of Justin Beal and Roger Ames, or the sanity of Tom Greer? No, sir. There are a lot of causes worth dying for, worth sacrificing your mind and body for. This shit isn't it." He threw the car into park and turned off the ignition. "Let's take a walk."

CHAPTER 20

BRODIE, TAYLOR, AND MILLER WALKED DOWN THE CENtral street of the mock village, past the line of wrecked and rusted cars. A battered white Nissan jutted into the road, probably to provide meager cover for the town's defenders.

Brodie observed the tightly packed gray cinderblock buildings and their narrow window openings. Miller was pointing out different spots around the town where his men would take up positions. "If we try to hold the roads, we're dead. They're too fast and their aim is too accurate. They can fire with perfect precision while running twenty miles an hour. And these things move like they're sharing a brain, which they basically are. Each bot maintains a constant awareness of the exact geolocation of its squadmates." He pointed to one of the taller buildings. "We tried a tactic of just holding the high ground, thinking we could pick off a few and bottleneck the rest as they came up the stairs. But then this happened."

Miller walked up to a cinderblock wall and put his fingers into a gap between the blocks where the mortar had chipped away. "The extreme temperature fluctuations in the desert cause the mortar to expand and contract constantly, weakening it and making it brittle. The tin men use these as footholds and break away additional mortar as needed. They started climbing up the sides of the buildings."

Brodie pictured a swarm of Buckys, scrambling like chrome cockroaches up the walls and through the windows. This was a nightmare. Or, if you were unlucky enough to be an Army Ranger at Camp Hayden, it was a Tuesday.

"So," continued Miller, "we take an all-of-the-above tactical approach. Fixed suppressive fire, ground-level ambushes, sniping from rooftops and through windows. It turns into a grim game of subtraction." He pointed to a spot farther down the road. "If we put a guy there with a mounted machine gun, he can usually kill two D-17s before he dies. One or two other guys can maybe get one shot off each with an RPG before they're killed, and three out of five times they miss. How many enemy kills do you get per man that you sacrifice? And how do you raise that number so that the enemy are all dead, and at least one of you is left standing? We haven't worked out that equation yet."

Brodie said, "Maybe it's an unsolvable problem."

Miller looked at him with a wry smile. "General Morgan says there's no such thing as an unsolvable problem in the United States Army."

Taylor asked, "And what do you think?"

"I think he's a goddamned general and I'm a sergeant. Take a look in here." He led them into one of the cinderblock buildings, which was empty except for MRE wrappers and shell casings littering the ground, and some Sharpie drawings on the walls of a similar ilk to what they had seen in the barracks—robots, penises, naked women with giant breasts, and a dead Ranger with x's for eyes and a message below it: HAIL THE RISE OF THE MACHINES.

Miller wasn't there to show them the graffiti, but the terrible sight-lines inside the building. He pointed through one of the narrow windows, where from any angle you could only see a sliver of the road. "A lot of the buildings are tight like this, so we don't get a visual from in here until they're right on top of us."

Brodie tried to put himself in Sergeant First Class Miller's position—given an impossible task by a hard-ass general who might be more interested in proving a point about mankind than training the men under his command. Brodie imagined being inside one of these buildings when the tin men came, charging down the roads and through the doors, scaling the walls and clambering in through the windows, all the while barely catching a glimpse of these man-shaped weapons before they were right on top of your ass.

Brodie said, "Not much to work with in here. You don't even have furniture to barricade the entrance and slow them down."

Miller nodded. "We only have our brains, our balls, and a lot of ammo." He said to Taylor, "Excuse me, ma'am."

"No need," said Taylor. "I'm frankly shocked by what you and your men have been put through here."

"Beats the real deal. Out here, the only thing that dies is your soul." He added, "With a couple of exceptions."

Right. This game had become deadly, but the math hadn't changed. The ledger of human survivors always came to zero, with the tin men still standing.

Miller led them up the narrow staircase to the roof, where a firing nest stood—sandbags and a mount for a machine gun. Brodie spotted a few cans of Monster Energy drink littering the roof. He was sure the Rangers were trained to clean up after themselves. But this was a sign of a morale problem. They'd stopped caring, and their COs had stopped bothering to demand anything better.

Miller pointed to a high sand berm about two hundred yards to the southeast. "The tin men get dropped behind there, and when the battle begins, they crest the top of that berm or go around it. Those opening moments are when they are the most vulnerable, and when the odds are most in our favor. They can't run well on loose sand, but as you can see it gets more hard-packed the closer to the village due to all the vehicle activity. Plus, they have some cover."

Their cover consisted of a few freestanding cinderblock walls and a single broken-down pickup truck sunk in the sand. If the tin men had been humans, a two-hundred-yard charge on foot with barely any cover toward a heavily fortified position would be suicide.

Miller, possibly sensing what Brodie was thinking, added, "They clear this open land and are inside the village within twenty seconds, and as I said they can run and gun with perfect accuracy. That makes it a lot harder on our gunners."

Right. It seemed like every tactical disadvantage was thrown at the Rangers, and even the elements that appeared to favor them became liabilities when factoring in the superhuman powers of the D-17s.

Taylor was scanning the surrounding land. "What about drones? No one's mentioned those at a place that's supposedly developing the future of warfare. I bet they'd be an asset to you."

"I'm sure they would," said Miller. "I'd love to have a whole god-damn fleet of them to kamikaze the line of D-17s. But it's a hard thing to simulate in training. And once you bring in a weapon like that, you need to match it with a countermeasure for the other side and then shit gets complicated. This training is not about force integration. It's a street brawl."

Brodie said, "Tell us about the siege."

Miller looked at him. "Who told you about that? Greer?"

Brodie nodded. "He also told us that was the day he started abusing substances."

"I know. I was there."

"Did you intervene?"

"No. I was dead. Once you're out, you're not supposed to interact with anyone." He added, "And even if I hadn't been . . . my men were at the breaking point. I let them do what they needed to do in that moment."

Taylor asked, "Why did the bots change tactics that one time? We've been led to understand they can't learn, can't draw on prior experience to alter their behavior."

"That's correct," said Miller. "They were simply reacting to something *we* changed." The sergeant squinted against the harsh sun as he looked out at the sand berm where the enemy had emerged sixty-seven different times to stalk and kill his men. "We've got a gearhead in our platoon, Corporal Chris Reyes. No formal education, but his dad was an electrical engineer, and they used to disassemble machines—computers, kitchen appliances, whatever they got their hands on—and build new things out of them. So this guy, he decides he wants to make an EMP bomb. Takes our EMP barrel attachments, mods them, hooks them to a small genny and a detonator. The idea is, when the bastards are in range, we hit the switch, and they all drop like puppets without strings." He laughed bitterly. "And we bag our first win."

"I can't imagine that was within training regs," said Brodie.

"Not even close. But the men were tired and pissed off. And I thought it would be a good morale booster. Plus, a fun surprise. No one knew about the bomb other than me and Reyes and his roommate. The three of us staged it here in secret well before the exercise. I knew I'd get my ass chewed by command, but I didn't care."

Then it dawned on Brodie what the siege was about. Taylor, thinking along the same lines, said, "The D-17s knew the bomb was there, and they stayed beyond its range."

Miller nodded. "We underestimated them. Again. Turns out these things have the capacity to pick up a wide spectrum of electromagnetic energy on their visual sensors. They saw the EMP bomb even though it was behind a concrete wall. Not only that, but they somehow used this capability to calculate the projected range of the bomb and then parked their flat metal asses just outside of it. No one ever taught the tin men what a 'siege' was. But they understood we needed food, water, and sleep to keep going, and that they could outlast us."

Jesus. This kept getting worse. All the robots needed now were rocket boosters out their asses for flight, and maybe a mind-control ray. Brodie asked, "And did you get disciplined?"

Miller shook his head. "Captain Pickman was angry. At first. Then he realized General Morgan loved the ingenuity and brashness of it, and he changed his tune. The captain leans whichever way the strongest wind is blowing." He added, "The truth is I didn't invite Captain Pickman this morning. I'm sorry I misled you. But I wanted to speak freely."

Taylor said, "We value your honesty, Sergeant. And it sounds like you don't trust your commanding officer."

"I'm not sure about trust, Ms. Taylor. I haven't really had to test that. But I sure as hell don't like him. And here's something else you need to understand. Outside of DEVCOM, you've only got a four-person officer corps at Camp Hayden. General Morgan, Colonel Howe, Major Klasky, and Captain Pickman. But that doesn't stop them from forming factions. Pickman is General Morgan's guy. Morgan likes that the captain is in direct communication with me and my platoon, and the general oftentimes goes around Howe and Klasky, which of course pisses them off."

This place had more drama and infighting than junior high. Brodie said, "General Morgan thinks you can beat the tin men. He told us he pushes you, and that he is not very popular."

Miller nodded. "He pushes us, and he uses Captain Pickman's hands. They're a real dynamic duo. Morgan's the type of general you dread serving under. He's arrogant, he's disconnected from what's happening on the ground, and he uses his men to try to prove something about himself. And Pickman is the worst kind of junior officer. Ass-kissing those above him and condescending to those below him, including the NCOs who know a hell of a lot more than he does."

Sergeant First Class Miller wasn't kidding about being honest. The man was understandably bitter, and had seen firsthand how the punishing training regimen was wreaking both physical and psychological damage on his men.

Taylor asked, "And what about Colonel Howe and Major Klasky?"

Miller replied, "They're more by the book. They believe the directive coming down from on high, or at least pretend they do for the sake of their careers. Personally, I think Pickman's thrown his lot in with the wrong faction. Then again, one benefit of being enlisted is you can sit out a lot of this political bullshit."

Brodie informed Miller that he and Taylor had both been enlisted soldiers—E3s—and seen combat, she in Afghanistan, he in Iraq. Miller was particularly interested in Brodie's Iraq service. "Where and when did you serve?"

"End of oh-three and most of oh-four. Third Stryker Brigade. Mainly Baghdad area, but the most action I saw was in the Second Battle of Fallujah."

Miller looked him in the eyes. "Life's strange, Mr. Brodie."

"How's that?"

"I was in Fallujah a few years back for the sequel."

The Third Battle of Fallujah had taken place in 2016, when the Iraqi Army successfully wrested control of the city from ISIS. Brodie remembered the news coverage, and how it had been retraumatizing for some of his old battle buddies—seeing the same city and the same streets that their friends had died to liberate, now a dozen years later back in the hands of a new jihadi army even crazier than the last. History wasn't supposed to repeat itself that quickly. He said to Miller, "I thought we just provided air support for that operation."

"Officially. But Rangers were on the ground to help the Iraqis, who fought bravely, though not always competently." He looked at Brodie. "We were aware of the bitter irony, being back there after all that you and yours had sacrificed. We told ourselves, maybe this time the peace would last."

"Maybe it will."

Miller scanned the desert horizon. "When I was briefed on this mission, on what we'd be doing here, I was hopeful. I thought, maybe with enough time, enough technology, there would come a day when we could fight a war without so many flag-draped coffins coming down the ramps of the C-130s. But then I came to understand."

Taylor asked, "Understand what, Sergeant?"

Miller kept his eyes on the horizon. "Hardly any civilians had managed to escape Fallujah before our assault. ISIS wouldn't let them leave. So we were fighting to take a city of women and children, shops and shopkeepers, schools, hospitals. That changed how we fought. Made us go slower than we would have liked, changed our tactics and priorities. A lot of Iraqi soldiers died because of that. But that was their duty, and they performed it honorably. They gave their lives to spare the lives of civilians."

He turned and looked into the mock village of cinderblock buildings and destroyed cars. "There's no life here. Not even a simulation of life. Nothing fragile you have to try to not break. The tin men don't know the meaning of a life you have to protect, not take. They're programmed to kill everything with a heat signature. So, what are we training for? What are *they* training for?"

Brodie looked out at the gray village and the ruined cars, the streets lined with rows of faceless buildings—a shell of a place, a discarded exoskeleton. A necropolis.

Sergeant Miller turned to look at Brodie and Taylor. Something had changed in his eyes. They were less weary, more alert and intentioned. "Agents, I don't know what happened to Major Ames. That's the truth. But I do know what has happened to my men. And I do know what would happen if these goddamned things were ever unleashed upon the world. They must be destroyed."

CHAPTER 21

CAMP HAYDEN'S ADMINISTRATIVE BUILDING WAS A small, two-story brick structure near the parade grounds. A Ranger armed with an M4 rifle—with real bullets, not an EMP attachment—stood outside the entrance and saluted Brodie and Taylor as they approached. They returned the salute, and Brodie said to the Ranger, PFC Vargas, "Good morning, Private. We're here to see Captain Pickman."

"Yes, sir. The captain informed me. He's down the hall, the last room on the right."

They thanked the man and entered the building. A small anteroom led to a fluorescent-lit hallway lined with doors, all ajar and all leading to darkened offices. The administrative building, like everywhere else on base, was shut down until further notice.

Brodie and Taylor had used the satellite phone in Sergeant Miller's Land Rover to call Captain Pickman's house. He'd been home, and he'd told them that he had already been instructed by Major Klasky to show the CID agents Camp Hayden's after-action review system. They figured they'd kill two birds with one stone—review the after-action recordings and see if Captain Pickman was as big a tool as Sergeant Miller made him out to be.

They entered the last room on the right. The lights were on but dimmed. In the middle of the large room was a sizable table containing a precise model of the training village—every road, every building, every car, even the sand berm and the surrounding man-made hills for the machine gun nests.

Standing next to the table was a trim thirty-year-old man in desert camo with close-cropped red hair, blue eyes, and an impressively square jaw. Actually, his whole head was kind of block-shaped, and he strode toward the two agents with a weird gait, like he was trying to cover more distance with each step than his legs would allow. He extended his hand and flashed an awkward grin. "Captain Ben Pickman. Pleasure to meet you."

Brodie, who suspected the captain was a fugitive shapeshifter from Area 51 still figuring out how to act human, shook his hand and said, "Good to meet you, Captain. Thank you for arranging this on short notice."

Pickman nodded. "Your investigation is the only thing going at Camp Hayden. I was waiting for your call." He dropped his smile and said, "May-bell. The agents can't see you in the dark."

Brodie now noticed another person standing in the room near a bank of mounted flat-screen monitors. The figure stepped into the light, revealing a slight woman of about twenty in desert camo with short brown hair. She wore the eagle insignia of a specialist, and her name tape read "Christiansen Blair." She said in a slight southern accent, "Sir, ma'am. SPC Christiansen Blair. A pleasure to make your acquaintance."

Taylor, who appeared delighted to see another woman from below the Mason-Dixon, smiled warmly at her. "You as well, Specialist."

Captain Pickman said, "May-bell operates our augmented-reality review system. She is one of only two specialists at the camp who aren't Rangers or MPs. Isn't that right, May-bell?"

"That is correct, sir," replied the SPC.

Brodie looked at Captain Pickman as the man stared at the young specialist. There were two reasons a commissioned officer might repeatedly refer to an enlisted soldier by their first name—as an expression of informality and friendship, or as a power move. He was pretty sure he knew which one the captain was employing. The junior officers were oftentimes the senior assholes.

Pickman said to Christiansen Blair, "Explain to Mr. Brodie and Ms. Taylor what this system is and how it works."

"Yes, sir." She turned to the CID agents. "This room houses our augmented-reality after-action review system. As you can see, we have a one-hundredth-scale model of our training village. Our SIMRES system uses cellular and GPS signals to record the precise geolocation of each exercise participant—Rangers and D-17s—every half second, as well as when and where they fire their weapons. This information is fed into a computer program that generates a three-dimensional render of every moment of every exercise, and those renders are projected onto our model here by our integrated visual augmentation system, which is a fancy word for VR goggles." She smiled.

Brodie decided her accent was more Appalachian than southern, which meant she and Magnolia Taylor were at least second cousins. Brodie said to her, "That sounds impressive, Specialist."

Pickman said to the SPC, "Tell them about the capabilities the system has with obstructing objects."

Christiansen Blair nodded. "Dynamic occlusion, sir. Essentially, if you're projecting a virtual image onto a real space, how do you make it so that a real physical object—in this case, say, a model of a building— dynamically blocks your view of a virtual object when it ought to be obstructed, like a virtual soldier taking cover behind the building? This tech is being developed by the military for use in the field and therefore on the fly, so it's all done in real time, not based on any pre-render. It's in beta, but so far has been working quite well."

Scott Brodie was getting about half of this at most, which was probably enough. The tech stuff could be as much of a distraction as an aid, even on a case like this.

Captain Pickman added, "This is state-of-the-art stuff."

"So's killer robots," said Brodie.

Pickman did not reply.

Taylor said, "We'd like to see one of your training playbacks."

"Yes, ma'am," replied the specialist. She retrieved two sets of large VR goggles, which looked familiar to Brodie from photos and videos he'd seen of people looking like idiots. The goggles were attached by long cables to a computer in the corner of the room. "There's a head strap you can adjust."

Brodie put the goggles on and did his best to adjust the strap. The headset was heavy and uncomfortable. The future was here, and it sucked.

He could see through the goggles, though everything looked dim.

SPC Christiansen Blair said, "Give me one sec," then flicked a switch, and all the structures on the table glowed neon green. Brodie noticed blacklights shining from the ceiling onto the model village, which must have been coated in blacklight paint.

Brodie turned and looked at Taylor, who was exaggeratedly looking around the room from behind her goggles. Maggie Taylor looked good wearing almost anything, but even she couldn't pull these things off.

Pickman said, "Cue up the most recent exercise." He said to Brodie and Taylor, "Our Rangers gave them hell. I mean, up to a point."

Up to the point when they all died, he meant.

Brodie heard the woman punch some keys, then a stream of floating red text popped up in Brodie's viewfinder. Most of it was gibberish to him, though he did make out a date: May 20.

He focused on the model of the village as dozens of bright objects popped up all over—blue human-shaped icons dispersed around the town. In the road, on rooftops, entering buildings. He saw now what the specialist had been talking about with the obstruction of virtual objects by real ones. As a blue human icon went into a building—there were no complex animations, just a drifting shape—the icon disappeared, and then partially reappeared through a window. Brodie stepped to his left a few paces to get a different perspective and saw the blue "person" through the doorway. It was actually incredible, and lent realism and dimension to these digital avatars.

He kept rounding the table until he was around the backside of the high sand berm. Twelve inverted red triangles were lined up behind it, motionless. The tin men.

Brodie now noticed a timecode ticking forward by the millisecond in the bottom right of his field of vision. He watched and waited as the seconds passed. Then, in an instant, the red triangles crested the berm and moved swiftly toward the village.

The little model village lit up with what looked like tracer rounds, bursts of red and blue dashes punching through the air.

A blue figure on a rooftop scored a kill with a mounted machine gun, and a red triangle blipped off. Return fire from the advancing triangles immediately wiped out the blue guy, plus another gunner on a hilltop.

The blue icons moved frantically around the village as the triangles rapidly advanced, while simultaneously hitting the village with an unending barrage of red rifle fire. The Rangers got another kill, and then three of them were shot through the open windows.

As the D-17s entered the village, the battle intensified. Three bots began scaling a tall building. Two more fired down the roadway with precision, taking out three more Rangers. The red rounds only grew in frequency and intensity, while the blue ones grew sparse as the Rangers took cover. Which was natural and expected. It's hard to aim and shoot while someone is firing directly at you trying to kill you. Unless, of course, you're a tin man without a heart.

A streak of blue light arced out of a window and missed its target in the roadway. A grenade round. More grenades flew out of windows and off rooftops, as the Rangers attempted to saturate the narrow roadways with detonations. If the Rangers' targets had been human, the slim roads and alleys would have been ideal kill zones. But, Brodie imagined, the SIMRES training system was programmed for the intended target, meaning the grenades being launched by the Rangers had a smaller kill radius for the armored bots than they would have for a human. Therefore, round after round rained down on the red triangles, and only two blipped out.

It was over quickly after that. The red triangles breached every building and took out the Rangers. Even as little red triangles versus blue stick figures, the superior speed and dexterity of the D-17s was obvious. They reacted faster and got off more shots and fired with perfect accuracy every time.

The little blue people blipped out one by one, until there was only a single Ranger left, running along the roadway toward a three-story building with a mounted machine gun on top.

The Ranger made it to the gun and blasted away into the village. He was unable to score a hit. Then Brodie noticed the remaining red triangles—seven of them—congregating on a road far away from the machine gun nest. They remained motionless, waiting. Brodie didn't understand what was happening.

Taylor, who had situated herself on the opposite end of the table, said, "Look."

Brodie walked over to where she was standing, and from that vantage saw a single red triangle scaling the tower toward the sole surviving Ranger as he blasted at the village below with the mounted gun. The bot reached the top and the blue icon immediately vanished. Shot in the back. He never saw it coming.

Then the red triangles all blipped out, and a floating scoreboard appeared in front of Brodie: BLUE TEAM: 4. RED TEAM: 36. VICTOR: RED TEAM.

The score faded away, and then SPC Christiansen Blair flicked off the blacklight and the model village grew dim.

Brodie and Taylor removed their headsets, a bit bleary-eyed and disoriented. For a moment no one said anything.

Captain Pickman, feeling the need to contextualize the Rangers' performance, said, "Four kills is a good day. Not their best, but better than average."

Brodie asked, "Do the Rangers have comm links?"

"Yes."

"You wouldn't know it by the way they were moving once the bots reached the village perimeter. Total chaos. Unprofessional, especially by the standard of Rangers, frankly."

Pickman narrowed his eyes. "Do you have combat experience, Mr. Brodie?"

"I do. As does Ms. Taylor. I've been in battles like this, minus the robots, and I had the choice of either winning or dying. And if I had gotten killed, I'd have had the luxury of staying dead, not waking up and doing it all again tomorrow."

Pickman eyed the model of the training grounds. "It's an issue of speed. The bots move and shoot faster than the Rangers can even communicate. The Rangers can run the same exact play, day after day, to try to refine it, but the bots will react a little differently each time. Not because they're learning—they're not—but because of random chance. How the sun hits the buildings, wind kicking up a cloud of dust here or there. And one slight change—a bot choosing to turn right instead of left—leads to a cascade of new actions and reactions, and within seconds the playbook's in the toilet. But the men are working it out."

"Actually, they're losing their minds."

The captain looked back at Brodie and clenched his sizable jaw. "We all have our duties here, Mr. Brodie. As I understand it, yours is to either find or rule out foul play. How is that going?"

"Fantastic," replied Brodie. "Everyone's a suspect."

Pickman did not react to that.

Taylor, looking to change the trajectory of this conversation, turned her attention to Cousin May-bell. "Who has access to this room?"

The specialist replied, "All officers and NCOs. But camp regulation is that an individual trained on the system—in this case, myself—needs to be present to access and operate the computers and headsets."

"Have members of the DEVCOM team viewed these playbacks?"

She nodded. "Yes, ma'am. One or two of them are always present at the after-action assessment following each exercise."

"Have they come in independent of the after-action assessments?"

"Only Major Ames."

"How often?"

"Oh, a lot."

Brodie and Taylor shared a look.

Brodie asked her, "For what purpose?"

Christiansen Blair shrugged. "Above my pay grade, sir. But I'd say the major was a meticulous man. He wanted to take more time with the recordings than was typically afforded in the after-action reports, which are basically a real-time playback as you just saw but live-narrated by Sergeant First Class Miller or one of his subordinate NCOs."

Taylor followed up: "Was this practice of his consistent throughout your time stationed here?"

The SPC thought a moment. "No, ma'am. More in the last couple of months. Like, March. Maybe late March."

Brodie recalled that the first of Major Ames's three nighttime visits to the Vault to visit with Bucky had occurred on April 3. Something had spurred that behavior. Something, maybe, that he'd seen in this room.

Brodie turned to the captain. "We'll need a few minutes alone now with the specialist. Thank you, sir."

The captain offered a creepy little smile and said, "If you need to interview May-bell in private, that can be done anywhere, Mr. Brodie. If you are interested in continued access to this system, an officer or NCO must be present."

Taylor said, "Sir, we may or may not need Specialist Christiansen Blair to access the after-action review system. That will be determined by me and Mr. Brodie. In order for us to conduct a fair and thorough investigation, that determination is not, and cannot be, your business."

That was the most tortured and long-winded "fuck off" Brodie had ever heard. He put a bow on it by adding, "Thank you for your time and attention, Captain Prickman."

"It's Pickman."

"Isn't that what I said?"

Pickman opened his mouth to reply, thought better of it, then just nodded sharply. "You know where to find me." He said to Specialist Christiansen Blair, "Whatever they need, May-bell."

"Of course, sir."

Pickman looked at the agents one last time, then left the room and shut the door.

Brodie said to Taylor, "He's a delight."

"We can't all have your charisma." She asked the SPC, "Do you keep logs of when each recording is accessed?"

"Yes, ma'am."

"Can you pull up whatever recordings Major Ames requested to watch?"

"Well, that might not be so simple. He watched a lot of them, and I can't remember precisely when that began. I have no logs that tie any individual playback to a given visitor either." She asked, "Is there something in particular you're looking for, ma'am? If you let me in a little, I might be a better help."

Taylor smiled at her. "If only we knew what we were looking for, Specialist. Sometimes an investigation is like throwing darts."

"While blindfolded," added Brodie. "And drunk."

Taylor eyed the model village. "Do the Rangers or D-17s wear body cams?"

"Yes, ma'am. They all do."

"Do you have that footage?"

"No, ma'am. The footage is classified."

"Why is that?"

"I don't know."

"That seems odd. You must have speculated."

Christiansen Blair hesitated, then said, "I have, ma'am. It's one thing if someone leaks stories about this place. Or gets access to these VR renders. Those can be denied. But the body cams—hundreds of hours of high-definition footage of training battles between Army Rangers and human-sized robots, captured from fifty different angles. You'd have a hard time denying the existence of this program if that gets leaked."

Brodie asked, "Who does have access to this footage?"

"I don't know," she replied. "But I can tell you for a fact that Major Ames did not have access, because he came to me to try to view the footage. He kind of wouldn't let up, didn't believe I didn't have a way to get it." She walked over to her computer and after a moment pulled up a text file with some notes. "March twenty-first. That's the date he was after. I can pull up our VR recording of that exercise, if it's worth anything to you."

"Yes," said Taylor. "Thank you."

They put the awful headsets back on and watched the model village as it lit up in neon green and became populated by red and blue shapes. As before, the tin men began behind the sand berm and crested the top, and hundreds of rounds were exchanged between the opposing forces. This exercise seemed to be going even worse for the Rangers than the last one. They didn't get a single kill on the approach, and as the tin men entered the village they systematically fanned out and took out their targets. Two bots were taken out by grenades, but that was it. Within minutes, all the Rangers were gone.

Brodie and Taylor looked at each other. They must have missed something—something very important to Roger Ames. The question was, would a couple of CID agents even know what might be noticeable to a computer scientist? Probably not.

Taylor asked the SPC, "Can you play it back at half speed?"

"Yes, ma'am."

Taylor said to Brodie, "Let's take different vantage points."

Brodie rounded the village model so that he was facing what would be the village's southwest corner, and at an approximately forty-five-degree angle from the sand berm where the D-17s emerged.

Christiansen Blair hit play, and this time the icons moved much slower. The red triangles slid across the open expanse as the Rangers fired from their positions. Slow-motion tracer fire streaked through the air like a laser light show, each round now discernible as a glowing dash of colored light piercing the air and vanishing on impact.

As the tin men advanced slowly across the open desert, Brodie's eyes landed on one particular Ranger who appeared to be acting erratically. As the others held positions in windows and doorways or fired rounds from mounted guns toward the advancing bots, one blue icon remained motionless against the wall of one of the buildings. The guy wasn't taking cover, or in a good position to score a kill. He was just . . . frozen.

Brodie kept his focus on the little blue avatar. After a minute, it entered a two-story building. Brodie crouched to look through the tiny doorway. The Ranger stood there, motionless. On the second story, another Ranger was positioned in an open window, probably armed with a grenade launcher that he was waiting to fire once the tin men were in range. On the rooftop above, two Rangers operated a mounted machine gun that was firing into the open desert.

The bots entered the village and fanned out, slowly and confidently, like a stalking pack of wolves. Brodie's Ranger of interest kept his position, motionless, in the center of the room on the first floor.

Then the Ranger walked upstairs to the second story. As he entered the upper room, the soldier positioned at the window fired a grenade round at the street below. A miss. He fired another through the window in the building across the narrow road just as a D-17 crossed his field of view. A direct hit, and a hell of a shot.

Brodie's Ranger stood in the center of the second-story room a moment, then drifted toward the Ranger with the grenade launcher, who must have had his back turned as he looked for targets out the window.

The Ranger stopped again, maybe eight feet from the Ranger in the window.

Below, a red triangle had entered the building and was quickly moving toward the stairway and up to the second floor.

Brodie stepped closer and peered into the little model building as the D-17 walked into the second-story room. He expected a sudden burst of gunfire to follow, but the tin man did nothing. It watched a moment, as the odd Ranger stood motionless, and the one by the window fired another grenade round into the road.

Then the tin man continued up the stairs to the rooftop and quickly dispatched the two gunners up there.

Brodie said, "Pause it, please."

The scene froze.

"Back it up a couple of seconds."

"Yes, sir."

The red triangle descended back to the second floor. A grenade round arced back into the window where the Ranger was positioned. Brodie's Ranger of interest stood frozen.

"There. Pause."

The images paused. By now, Taylor had rounded the table to see Brodie's vantage point. "What's going on?"

"I don't know. Something with these three. The Ranger in the middle has been moving erratically. And the bot in the room here doesn't notice the Rangers or decides to let them be. It bypasses them entirely and goes to the roof."

Taylor stared at the three little shapes. She asked the specialist, "Is there a way to see who these three are?"

"Yes, ma'am. It's a display mode I can call up. One moment."

Three pieces of text blinked on above the shapes. The Ranger in the window was Sergeant First Class Mike Miller. The other Ranger who had been acting so strangely was PFC Tom Greer.

And Brodie knew before he even looked that the red triangle, the tin man that was acting so inexplicably, was Number 20. Bucky.

CHAPTER 22

AS THE TWO AGENTS EXITED THE ADMINISTRATIVE building, Taylor said, "It keeps coming back to Bucky. And Greer. But I don't understand it. We need the body-cam footage."

"No, we don't. We just need to grab Tom Greer by the nuts and get him to talk about what the hell happened in that room."

"Are you grabbing his nuts before or after reading him his Article Thirty-One rights?"

Brodie noticed that the Ranger who had been guarding the door was gone. Then he heard a noise blaring in the distance. A siren.

They both ran toward the sound. Up ahead, three Rangers with EMP rifles sprinted across the parade ground.

They followed the Rangers, who were headed for the brig. The siren was blaring from pole-mounted speakers all around the camp's perimeter and grew louder as they approached.

Brodie spotted an MP vehicle pulled up in front of the brig. Beside it stood Sergeant Mendez with his pistol drawn. He was looking down at something on the ground.

The three Rangers aimed their rifles at whatever it was and formed a perimeter around it.

As the agents got closer, they realized it was a D-17 unit, lying face down in the dirt, its arms splayed in front of it. Brodie spotted a set of broken manacles around its wrists. Bucky.

"Sergeant!" called Brodie as they jogged up. "What the hell happened?"

Mendez turned to them. He looked distraught. "He's dead."

Taylor asked, "Who's dead?"

"Kemp," replied Mendez. Kemp had been the MP guarding Bucky. "This . . . fucking . . . *thing*." Mendez gestured with his pistol toward the inert bot, and Brodie saw now that Mendez's weapon had its own mini EMP barrel attachment. "I was doing my rounds . . . saw it just walk out of the brig on its own . . ."

Bucky jerked one arm up, and all three Rangers fired their rifles point-blank into it. Shell casings ejected from the rifles, and the EMP barrels emitted brief, powerful punches of deep bass. Bucky's arm collapsed again, lifeless.

Caroline Dixon jogged up to the Rangers. "*Move.*"

They made room for her, and she got on her knees and attempted to flip the heavy robot. Two of the Rangers shouldered their rifles and helped her turn it over. It landed, loose and lifeless, on its back, one arm splayed across its bucket head. Brodie noticed blood spattered across its titanium chest.

Dixon straddled Bucky, grabbed the initiator key from its lower right abdomen, then twisted and pulled it out. She stood and shook the small orange device at the assembled men. "They are *nothing* without this. *Nothing*. Who the fuck turned it on?"

Mendez said, "We believe it was Kemp, Ms. Dixon."

"Where is he?"

"Dead."

Dixon looked down at Bucky and its blood-covered chest. "Jesus Christ."

Mendez was staring at her. "He must have been trying to move the unit, but we don't know why."

She looked up at the senior MP. "I called the brig and asked him to bring Bucky to the lab for additional testing. I told him to get another hand and bring it over in a truck. He said the MP truck was broken down. I told him to borrow a vehicle, but he said, 'I'll just make the bastard walk.' I cautioned him not to do that, but I guess he didn't listen."

Taylor asked, "How strongly did you caution him?"

Dixon shot Taylor a look. "It's a standing order issued by the camp commander, Maggie. Regardless of how emphatic I was, he never should have activated the unit without authorization."

Brodie approached the bot, then crouched and looked at its right hand. Between the thin gaps in the segments of its articulated fingers were strands of brown human hair. He asked Mendez, "Is the body still inside?"

Mendez nodded. "Yes, sir. The coroner is on his way."

Brodie and Taylor entered the brig and walked through the main room toward the holding cell. Another MP, a Corporal Nimitz, stood at the door. The man appeared shaken.

Brodie said, "Morning, Corporal."

"Good morning, sir, ma'am."

Taylor said, "We are so sorry."

"Thank you, ma'am."

Nimitz stepped aside, and Brodie and Taylor entered the holding cell. It was a sparse room with a cot, a metal sink and toilet, and a single wooden chair.

Kemp's body was on the ground, covered in a white sheet that was saturated in blood near the corpse's head. On the wall about six feet above the floor were a cracked depression in the concrete and a large bloodstain.

Nimitz said, "We believe the thing broke its manacles and grabbed Specialist Kemp by his hair, and then thrust him into the wall." He took a deep breath and added, "Partially shattering his skull."

That sounded like Bucky all right. Brodie looked at the bloodstained sheet covering Kemp's body. They'd so far been speculating whether and how Major Ames might have provoked the thing. But what could this poor MP have done? Unless the only sin that mattered to the tin men was being human, and breakable.

Brodie crouched and partly peeled back the sheet. The SPC's head was caked in blood, and the upper left portion of his skull was essentially flattened by the impact against the wall. Brodie carefully replaced the sheet, and he and Taylor left the holding cell.

They lingered in the brig's main room, out of earshot of anyone. Brodie said, "Your request to Dombroski has grown more urgent."

"No shit."

"We're either dealing with a bad actor with the capacity to covertly reprogram these things—and that would be a *very* short list of people at this facility—or a faulty product that's likely to kill again. And if it's a system-wide issue, there's fifty-nine more murder machines currently taking a nap."

Taylor nodded. "What about Caroline?"

"What about her?"

"Who knows what she told Kemp on that phone call? We're taking her word for it. Maybe she told him to activate Bucky and walk him over, knowing something like this might happen or would happen?"

"It's possible. Anything is. We now have another body and no more answers."

"We have Greer. And maybe Miller. Whatever happened in that training exercise, in that room, it was important to Ames."

They heard a vehicle roar down the road and screech to a halt outside. They exited the brig to see General Morgan emerge from the passenger side of his Jeep, clouds of dust swirling around him. He wore camo, aviator sunglasses, and a sidearm. His driver turned off the Jeep and stepped out. It was Captain Pickman.

Everyone saluted the general, who approached Sergeant Mendez. He removed his sunglasses, gently placed his hand on Mendez's shoulder, and said, "I'm so sorry, Hector."

"Thank you, sir."

The general put his sunglasses back on, then walked toward the lifeless robot. He stared down at Bucky and asked, "Who has the key?"

Dixon said, "I do."

He looked up at her, then extended his hand. "Give it to me."

"Why?"

"Because I'm asking for it."

Caroline stared at the man. "I am not a member of the United States Army, General. So you need to do better than that."

Morgan kept his eyes on her and his arm outstretched. "Captain."

Captain Pickman strode up to Dixon with that weird eager walk of his, and as he did so, one of the Rangers grabbed Dixon from behind and restrained her.

"Hey! Get your fucking hands off me!"

Pickman put his hand over hers and wordlessly pried her fingers open. She tried to wrest herself out of the Ranger's hold as she hurled expletives, but it was futile. The key fell to the ground, and Pickman retrieved it. As he stepped away the Ranger released his hold on Dixon, who offered a few more choice words and looked like she was ready to slug someone.

Brodie said to General Morgan, "General, that is no way to treat a civilian."

Morgan turned to him, as if just noticing he was there. "A civilian? She's the mother of these titanium golems, Mr. Brodie. Conceived by her brilliance and her arrogance." He eyed Dixon. "Now *two* innocent men are dead. Not one more. I will not allow it."

Dixon stared at the general and did not reply.

"We agree, sir," said Brodie. "These weapons are a continued threat to everyone at this camp, and Ms. Taylor and I have lost confidence in the scientific personnel at Camp Hayden to adequately answer our questions about these devices' origins, design, purpose, and susceptibility to sabotage. Therefore our commanding officer, Brigadier General Dombroski, is coordinating with the Provost Marshal General and

Major General Ramsay of Army Futures Command to take custody of all sixty units to be tested and evaluated by a neutral party at an off-site location. The order should be coming down shortly, if you have not already received it."

General Morgan gave Brodie an odd look—incredulous, mildly amused, and extremely pissed off. "I have received no such orders, Mr. Brodie. And if I did, I'd question the sanity of whoever issued them. Do you think I'm going to allow these things to fall into some dark recess of the Army bureaucracy, where who the hell knows what will become of them, who will gain knowledge of their existence and capabilities? Absolutely not." His eyes moved to Taylor. "You want answers. So do I. You don't trust the science personnel at this facility. Nor do I. Let's run our own tests and solve our own problems." He kept his eyes on the two agents as he called out, "Get me Sergeant Miller on the phone."

Captain Pickman grabbed a satellite phone from inside the Jeep, dialed a number, and waited for Miller to pick up. Then he said, "I have General Morgan," and handed the general the phone.

Morgan said, "Sergeant, meet me at the parade ground with a few trustworthy Rangers, a plasma cutter, and a grenade launcher. ASAP." He hung up the phone, then said to Sergeant Mendez, "Release Mr. Saltsberg from his house arrest and bring him to the parade grounds. He should see this. Ms. Dixon, go retrieve your DEVCOM colleagues."

"Eat a dick, General."

"I already had breakfast, thank you."

Brodie said to Morgan, "Sir, I need to use that phone."

Morgan looked at Brodie. "You're getting a little ahead of your skis, Mr. Brodie. Futures Command wouldn't make a move without communicating with me first. Not to mention looping in DARPA. CID is far down the food chain."

Taylor said, "You'd be surprised how quickly that changes, sir."

Brodie asked Mendez, "Sergeant, do you have a phone handy?"

Mendez looked nervously between Brodie and Morgan. "Yes, sir."

Morgan said, "Stop being so dramatic, Brodie. You are not a prisoner here, and no one is denying you a phone call. In fact, you are free to go back to your quarters right now to call whoever you want. Or you can borrow a vehicle and leave the base, for all I care. But you might see something interesting in the next few minutes if you stick around. You might even get some answers." Morgan looked at the blood-smeared robot lying in the dust. "Training time is over."

CHAPTER 23

THE WIND HAD PICKED UP AND BLEW SHEETS OF SAND across the asphalt parade ground. Brodie looked up at the high flagpole in the center, where the flags of the United States and the 75th Ranger Regiment whipped against a blindingly blue sky.

Brodie and Taylor stood on the eastern edge of the parade ground, and to their right stood Dixon, who had now been joined by the two surviving members of DEVCOM at Camp Hayden—Captain Spencer and Lieutenant Lehner. Standing to Brodie's left was the MP Corporal Nimitz, and the man Nimitz had just released from house arrest, the unlucky Eric Saltsberg of Synotec Systems. Saltsberg was a beefy man in his fifties with a brown goatee and thinning hair. He squinted against the bright sun. The man wore jeans, boots, and a blue polo shirt, though until very recently he had probably been in his underwear.

Brodie asked him, "Feel good to get out of the house?"

Saltsberg looked at him oddly. "What?"

"You've been cooped up for days."

"Right."

"I bet you can't even get Netflix out here."

"I didn't check." He added, "I brought a book."

"Good for you."

Saltsberg, who looked slightly amused, asked, "What organization are you two with again?"

"Army CID," replied Taylor.

"I'm not familiar with it."

"You know NCIS?" asked Brodie.

Saltsberg nodded.

"It's like that, but Army instead of Navy, and not all made up."

"Interesting," said Saltsberg, clearly lying.

Taylor asked, "Did you have a hand in designing the D-17s?"

The man did not appear comfortable with the question, though he replied, "No, not really. We ran manufacturing and assembly according to the specs provided by DARPA. They handled the software end. We did our own testing in Nevada, and I came here to conduct a field evaluation."

Brodie asked, "How do you evaluate? Do they get, like, a letter grade, A through F?"

Saltsberg no longer looked amused. "We go in for a somewhat more sophisticated assessment at Synotec Systems. Though I guess if we did use your grading, I'd have to give the D-17s an F, for 'fucked up beyond all recognition.'"

"Right."

Brodie looked across the parade ground, where General Morgan was conferring with Captain Pickman and Sergeant First Class Miller. Six Rangers armed with EMP rifles stood around them, as did Sergeant Hector Mendez and one of his subordinate MPs whom Brodie had not seen before. Nearer to Brodie, Taylor, and the science team was Corporal Powell, the young Ranger Brodie had first met during his interview with Bucky. It was not lost on Brodie that Corporal Powell was the only Ranger with live ammo in his rifle, and also the only Ranger in the vicinity of the CID agents and the scientific research team. Powell held his rifle low, with his fingers nowhere near the trigger. So things weren't feeling too hostile. Yet.

Brodie eyed General Morgan, who was speaking animatedly to Pickman and Miller, and gesturing toward the center of the parade ground. The guy was losing it, perhaps using Kemp's death as an excuse to act on his basest instincts. Brodie had a bad feeling about where all this was going, and he hoped he was wrong.

Brodie spotted another figure heading toward the parade ground from the south and making a beeline for the general. It was Colonel Howe. She didn't look happy. Trailing her was Major Klasky.

Dixon said, "The band's all here."

Brodie eyed Captain Spencer, who had been mostly silent. The man appeared worried.

A covered truck drove to the center of the parade ground, then three Rangers hopped out and unloaded the limp D-17 from the back of the truck and dropped it onto the asphalt. One of the guys got back in the truck and drove it off.

General Morgan walked toward the robot, accompanied by Sergeant Miller, Captain Pickman, and two EMP-equipped Rangers. Two more Rangers followed them, one wheeling a portable generator and the other carrying a boxy piece of equipment. Howe and Klasky quickened their pace as they approached.

Everyone else followed suit, converging toward the center of the parade ground and the lifeless tin man lying on its back. Brodie noticed that someone had cleaned Kemp's blood off Bucky's chest, which had the effect of giving the bot a mirrorlike sheen beneath the high desert sun.

Colonel Howe intercepted the general. "Sir, what are you doing?"

"You'll see soon enough, Colonel. Sergeant Miller, get the plasma cutter."

The Ranger carrying the piece of equipment, a Corporal Dennehy, set it down. It was a large black rectangle about the size of a cooler. He plugged one end into the portable generator. On the other end was a hose with a nozzle and a thick wire with a metal clamp that resembled a jumper cable.

General Morgan nodded. "Cut off its arms."

"Yes, sir," said Miller. He turned to Corporal Dennehy and told him to fire it up.

The corporal started the genny, then turned on the machine.

Caroline Dixon was fuming. "You *cannot* do this, General."

"Of course I can."

Lieutenant Lehner, the robotics engineer, spoke up. "Sir, I can detach the arms in the lab in a way that is safe and nondestructive."

"This is perfectly safe, Lieutenant. Everyone, take a few big steps back. Let's go."

Corporal Dennehy put on a welding mask and picked up the metal clamp, which he affixed to the titanium plate on the upper portion of Bucky's left arm. Then he picked up the nozzle of the plasma cutter, which had a red push handle.

Colonel Howe said in a low voice, "Sir, I need to speak with you in private."

"We'll talk later," said Morgan. "How's lunch?"

"*Now*, sir," said the colonel.

Brodie eyed the woman, whose buttoned-up demeanor looked ready to crack. He also stole a glance at Caroline Dixon, who was watching Colonel Howe with concern.

Morgan ignored Howe and stepped away from the D-17 as Corporal Dennehy knelt next to the bot and pressed the red lever on the plasma cutter. A blue flame emitted from the nozzle. The man looked around from behind his welding mask, waiting until everyone was at a safe distance.

Brodie, who decided he really wouldn't mind seeing this thing get its arms sliced off, took a few big steps backward.

The corporal touched the flame to the titanium plate near Bucky's shoulder, sending up a stream of hot orange sparks.

It was over in seconds, a clean cut, and Bucky's left arm lay on the asphalt next to the machine, curls of smoke rising from the edges of the cut. Dennehy moved the grounding clamp over to the other arm, and then sliced it off too.

Brodie noticed Howe and Klasky standing off to the side, conferring urgently.

Morgan stepped toward the bot. "Thank you, Corporal." He took the orange key out of his pocket and said, "Sergeant, make sure your men are at the ready."

"Yes, sir." Miller glanced at his fellow Rangers, who fanned out around General Morgan and trained their EMP rifles on the inert robot.

The general crouched, inserted the key, and twisted it. The bot snapped to life, swiveling its bucket head slightly and twitching its legs.

Morgan stood up and said, "Number 20, who am I?"

Bucky fixed its sensors on the general and said in its monotone male voice, "You are Brigadier General Christopher Morgan, commander of Camp Hayden."

"Where are you?"

Bucky moved its head from side to side. "I am lying on the ground."

"Be more specific."

"I am lying on the parade ground in the center of Camp Hayden."

"That's right," said Morgan. "Now get up."

Bucky was motionless a moment. It looked side to side again. "My arms are not functioning."

"That's because we cut them off. I don't want you killing any more people."

The bot did not respond.

"Get up. You can do so without your arms."

Bucky lifted its torso into an upright seated position, then managed to rock to the side, turn its legs, and get onto its knees. It was surprising to Brodie how much additional time and effort it was taking this thing to stand up. It benefited from a human's anatomy but faced some of its limitations as well.

Bucky rose to its feet and towered over General Morgan. The general looked up. "Why did you kill Specialist Kemp?"

Bucky tilted its head down. "I do not know."

"Do you recall killing him?"

"No."

"I don't believe you."

Bucky did not respond.

"I said, I don't believe you, you fucking abomination. What do you have to say to that?"

"I have nothing to say to that."

"I am going to try to explain to you what death is," said Morgan. "Because you can't possibly understand it. Specialist Daniel Kemp was born twenty years ago. You have only existed for a single year, give or take, so that amount of time might not be fathomable to you. Twenty years ago, for instance, nightmares like you were the subject of speculative fiction, books and movies about horror, and fear, and how we through technology might lose our own humanity and struggle to regain it. Do you understand any of what I am saying?"

Bucky replied, "Daniel Kemp was twenty years old. I am eleven months old. People fear me. They feared me before I existed."

"Here's what else you need to understand. Kemp had lived a life full of love and fear, hope, laughter, pain. And he has parents who are about to receive the worst news of their life, that their son, who they held as a baby, who they sacrificed for, who they were so proud of, is dead. Not just dead but murdered. Murdered by *you*. That means he was, and now he is not. That means he will never have another thought in his brain, because you decimated it. He will never wake up to the sun, he will never sleep beneath the stars, he will never enjoy food, or the kiss of a lover, or a funny joke. He will never feel the air of this living world enter his lungs. I think Daniel Kemp's parents, and all of us here, deserve better than to hear you say you don't know why you killed him. There is something inside of you that made you kill. Something that the brilliant minds responsible for your very existence claim to not understand. How is that? Have you developed some independent will beyond their capacity to even detect? Are you lying to me, Number 20?" Morgan turned and glared at Dixon, Spencer, and Lehner. "Or are *they* lying to me?"

Taylor whispered to Brodie, "Scott. This is very bad."

Morgan turned back to Bucky and said, "Look up at the sky. There's a raven."

Bucky craned its head up at the sky as a black raven sailed over the desert.

Morgan said, "It's a symbol of death. Did you know that?"

"No," replied Bucky.

"Well, it's fitting, because I am going to kill you, right now. And you will never see anything ever again. Not that sky or that raven. Not me. Not Sergeant Miller or any of his men. You simulate killing them twice a week sometimes. But they are all still here, and momentarily you will not be. Do you understand?"

Bucky looked down and trained its sensors on the general. "Yes."

"Ask me a question."

"I do not have any questions," said Bucky.

"Don't you want to know how you are going to die?"

"I know how I am going to die."

Morgan grinned. "How could you know that?"

"I have analyzed every weapon present in my vicinity. And there is only one that can destroy me." It swiveled its head toward the Rangers. "That M203 grenade launcher being held by Sergeant First Class Mike Miller."

Brodie looked over at Miller, noticing for the first time that his M4 rifle had a mounted underbarrel grenade launcher attachment.

Bucky continued, "A single M433 high-explosive dual-purpose forty-millimeter grenade will likely destroy me, but the sergeant must be thirty meters from me to ensure the explosive mechanism is armed upon impact."

A couple of the Rangers laughed, and one of them said, "Thanks for the tip, asshole."

Morgan stared silently at the robotic soldier, as if searching for something he wasn't finding. "Why don't you resist? Why don't you try to run away, or kick me in the nuts, or anything?"

Bucky replied, "I have no directive to harm you. I have no directive to avoid destruction."

"Did you have a directive to kill Kemp?"

"No."

"Then why did you?"

"I do not know."

The general was clearly frustrated. In fact, something truly pathological was going on here, as if this titanium weapon were a stand-in for all the killers of all the men Morgan had ever lost under his command, for all those he had never had a chance to confront. You rarely see the enemy, and when you do, you even more rarely come to understand him. That's not how war works.

And it was not how the tin men worked either, apparently. General Morgan was talking to a wall of metal, searching for the ghost in the machine. But ghosts aren't real, and maybe all the general saw when he looked into the strip of black polycarbonate protecting this thing's optical sensors was his own reflection.

Morgan said in almost a growl, "You heard it, Sergeant Miller. Thirty meters."

CHAPTER 24

SERGEANT FIRST CLASS MILLER WALKED FARTHER DOWN the parade ground to give himself firing distance as his fellow Rangers worked to get everyone to back away from the target. General Morgan and Captain Pickman turned and started toward Miller's position.

Ignoring Corporal Powell's admonishments to move out of range, Brodie and Taylor instead approached Bucky. They stopped near the bot, which remained motionless. Brodie said to General Morgan, "Sir, we cannot allow this."

Morgan stopped walking and turned to them. "With what authority, Mr. Brodie? I am eliminating a threat to the men and women under my command by disposing of a piece of faulty equipment that has caused the death of two members of the United States Army."

Taylor said, "This unit—and the other fifty-nine at this facility—constitute material evidence in our investigation of the deaths of Major Ames and now SPC Kemp. Destroying, or attempting to destroy, this equipment puts you in direct violation of Article One-Thirty-One-b of the Uniform Code of Military Justice."

General Morgan looked her in the eyes. "Then arrest me, Ms. Taylor." He turned his back on them and continued toward Miller. "Sergeant Miller, prepare to fire."

"Yes, sir." Miller raised his M4 and clicked a switch to engage the underbarrel launcher. Then he flipped up the sight and adjusted his grip toward the forward trigger.

"General Morgan," said Brodie, "I advise you under the provisions of Article One-Thirty-One—"

"Can it, Brodie," said Captain Pickman. "You are speaking to a brigadier general and the camp commander."

"That's right, prick. And I wasn't speaking to you."

Brodie walked past Captain Pickman as he unholstered his SIG Sauer and held it at his side. Taylor did the same, both of them following Morgan. Brodie said, "Halt and face me, sir. *Now.*"

Brodie was aware of disturbances all around him, people talking, getting agitated, unsure what to do. Morgan halted and turned back to him, then eyed Brodie's pistol. "Are you going to shoot me, Mr. Brodie?"

Brodie said to Sergeant Mendez, "Sergeant, disarm the general and place him under home confinement."

Mendez did not move.

Taylor said to Mendez, "Sergeant Mendez, you were just issued a direct order by a chief warrant officer of the Criminal Investigation Division."

Then Colonel Howe spoke up: "Sergeant Mendez, do as the agents instruct. General Morgan is hereby relieved of command under Relief for Cause."

Morgan darted his eyes to Colonel Howe. "Unless you have that in writing from my commanding officer—and I know you don't have shit—you are attempting a mutiny." He said to Sergeant Mendez, "Stand down, Hector."

Mendez hesitated, unsure of what to do.

Brodie stole a glance at Sergeant Miller, who lowered his M4 as he tried to read the situation.

Brodie looked back at Bucky, standing motionless beneath the desert sun, like a high-noon gunslinger in some perverted Western, without a weapon or arms or even, apparently, the will to live.

Sergeant Mendez then walked slowly to the general. "I am sorry, sir."

"Don't be sorry," said Morgan. "Commit to this mutiny or stand your ground beside me. Either way, own your goddamn choice, Hector."

Mendez appeared pained by that. He nodded slowly, then said, "I am disarming you now, sir." Mendez then recited the Article 31 rights as he removed the general's pistol from his holster and handed it to another MP. He gestured toward his car. "Let's go, General."

Morgan did not move. He locked his large brown eyes on Scott Brodie. Then he said, "Sergeant Miller, what is the injury radius of your munition?"

"A hundred and thirty meters, sir."

"Then do your goddamn duty."

Miller raised his M4 and aimed at Bucky, who remained still.

Colonel Howe strode toward Miller. "Stand down, Sergeant!"

Miller hesitated a moment, then said, "Fuck it," and pulled the trigger.

Brodie whipped his head around in time to catch sight of Bucky for an instant before the grenade hit it center mass and blew the robot to pieces.

CHAPTER 25

CHARRED AND TWISTED SHARDS OF METAL PLATING littered the asphalt. Nests of insulated wiring steamed and blistered from the heat, creating an acrid stench. Bucky's head, deformed beyond recognition from the blast, lay on its side, smoldering.

No one moved. Even the Rangers, who should have been the most thrilled to see one of their robotic tormentors blown apart, looked shocked.

Colonel Howe glared at the general. "There's no coming back from this, sir."

Morgan stared back. "No. There isn't."

Then Colonel Howe, taking on her new self-declared role as camp commander, said, "Sergeant Mendez, take General Morgan to his quarters and post a twenty-four-hour guard."

Mendez replied, "Yes, ma'am."

He looked at Morgan, who glared back at him a moment, then turned and walked slowly off the parade ground toward Mendez's MP vehicle. Mendez quickly followed.

Captain Pickman, who, as Sergeant Miller had put it, followed whichever way the wind was blowing, kept his mouth shut as he watched Mendez drive off with the general. The captain must have been sensing a distinct change in the weather.

Howe turned to another MP, Corporal Nimitz. "Corporal, take Sergeant Miller to the brig."

Nimitz hesitated. He looked at Sergeant Miller, who was still holding his M4 and grenade launcher and was flanked by four other armed

Rangers. The corporal replied, "Yes, ma'am." He walked slowly toward Miller.

Miller said to Howe, "I obeyed a direct order issued by the camp commander."

"It was an unlawful order," replied Howe. "And it was issued after I had relieved the general of command."

Miller stared at the colonel. "I didn't go to Officer Candidate School, ma'am, but even I know a colonel can't remove a general without authorization from higher up the chain. As General Morgan said, this is a mutiny. And if you had any sense at all, you'd repeat what I just did fifty-nine more times."

Major Klasky said to Miller, "You're out of line, Sergeant."

The Rangers around Miller looked extremely pissed off, and as Corporal Nimitz approached them, everyone was on edge.

Then Miller handed his M4 and his sidearm to his fellow Rangers and said to them, "Staff Sergeant O'Connor is your platoon leader while I take a nap in the brig, boys. This will sort itself out." Turning to Nimitz, he said, "Let's take a walk, Corporal," and headed toward the brig, with Nimitz rushing to catch up.

Colonel Howe and Major Klasky approached Brodie and Taylor. Howe said, "I apologize for the unprofessionalism and chaos displayed here today. The truth is, I've had my concerns about the general for a while, but I didn't think he'd go this far."

Brodie looked again at the charred debris scattered across the parade ground. "We need to get the D-17s out of this facility to be examined by a neutral party."

Colonel Howe said, "I agree," which surprised Brodie. "I am going to my office now to put in a call to Major General Ramsay, the head of Army Futures Command, who will officially authorize my dismissal of General Morgan. I will also relay your wishes, and he or I will contact your superiors at CID to arrange a transfer of custody."

"Thank you, ma'am," said Taylor.

Brodie spotted Caroline Dixon walking across the parade grounds toward the remnants of Bucky.

Colonel Howe said, "Ms. Dixon, what are you doing?"

"Treasure hunting." She began kicking away debris with her boots.

"The fragments are hot," said the colonel.

"No shit, ma'am," said Dixon without looking up, as she continued spreading the debris around with her feet, looking for something salvageable.

Well, if Brodie didn't already know these two had some sort of history, he could sense it now.

Brodie said to Dixon, "Do not remove anything from the premises. This material needs to be boxed up and shipped out along with the rest of the units."

Dixon stopped her sifting and looked at him. "Shipped where?"

"Anywhere but here."

"Don't do that. Not yet."

"Why?"

Dixon said to Howe and Klasky, "This is a private conversation."

Colonel Howe looked across the parade ground, where Captain Pickman was speaking with the Rangers. She called out, "Captain, send the Rangers back to their barracks and then return to your quarters. The lockdown order has not been lifted."

Pickman nodded. "Yes, ma'am." Even from fifty yards away, Brodie could see that the captain was irritated.

Pickman exchanged a few final words with the Rangers, who then piled into their vehicles and drove off. Pickman took one more look at his two superior officers standing with Dixon and the CID agents, probably wondering why he wasn't being invited to the confab, then got into the general's Jeep and drove off.

Howe turned her attention to Captain Spencer, Lieutenant Lehner, and Eric Saltsberg, who were standing off to the side in urgent conversation. "Gentlemen, the same goes for you. Mr. Saltsberg, your home confinement is hereby lifted. I would request you remain here another twenty-four hours to address any questions that CID might have for you, but you are free to do as you wish."

Saltsberg nodded. "Thank you, Colonel. I'll inform my employer that I am now a voluntary guest at Camp Hayden, which will hopefully mitigate some of the fallout caused by your superior. Happy to be of help how I can." He clarified, "For twenty-four hours."

Brodie said, "Thank you."

The three men departed together toward their houses.

Colonel Howe watched them go, then said to Dixon, "Now you have as much privacy as you're going to get."

Dixon looked extremely annoyed at Colonel Howe, more so than was warranted in the moment. But, of course, these ladies were screwing, so that changed all the rules. Dixon said in a low voice, "The reason I had asked Kemp to bring me Number 20 is that I was going through the D-17's code—we have copies of the software on our lab computers—and I found something. It's hard to explain in laymen's terms . . ."

"Taylor's smart," said Brodie. "Explain it to her and she'll draw me pictures."

Dixon gave him a deadpan look, not amused. "As I've said before, the code running these bots is simple, at least relative to the kinds of deep-learning software being developed now for more advanced AI. The D-17s follow a set of rules, and if two rules contradict each other, well, there's a rule for that too. They have powerful CPUs so that they can process all these branching decision trees instantaneously. They were built to make tactical choices. Who to shoot, when to shoot them, how best to outmaneuver and overtake the enemy. They cannot and do not do anything unexpected and inexplicable. At least they hadn't, until now. So, I was digging in the code, looking for something I missed. And I found a hidden program."

"What does that mean?" asked Taylor. "How could it be hidden?"

"Well . . . it's complicated. But the main point is that it is software that is siloed from the main algorithm. So this program, whatever it is, should have no bearing on the bots' behavior because nothing else in the source code points to it, or even suggests it's possible for this program to be executed. The program itself is encrypted using a very sophisticated key I can't yet crack. All I can read is the program's name."

"What is the name?" asked Major Klasky.

"Praetorian," replied Dixon.

"Praetorian," repeated Taylor.

Dixon nodded. "The only reference I have for that word is the Praetorian Guard. Ancient Rome."

Brodie considered that. The Praetorian Guard served as personal bodyguards for the Roman emperors. Were the tin men designed to be elite bodyguards, or was some dormant code installed in them to allow them to serve that function at a future date? And if so, how did that relate to one of them killing Major Ames and Specialist Kemp? And what was Bucky doing inside that room with Miller and Greer during that one particular training exercise that Major Ames was so interested in? Ms. Dixon had opened another chamber in this mystery box, but it was as dark and impenetrable as the rest. There was also still the possibility that she was making all this up, or if Praetorian was real, she herself was responsible for this rogue software and wanted to deflect blame before it was discovered by someone else.

"So," said Howe, "what is the next step?"

"I will continue to work on the encryption," said Dixon. "I have yet to exhaust my skills."

Taylor asked, "Could such a day ever come?"

Dixon looked at her. "I know you think I am arrogant, Maggie. But I am responsible for a lot of the code that drives these bots, and I find it personally alarming and in fact offensive that someone, or some group, has meddled with my work and gone to extreme lengths to keep it secret." She added, "I also need to go to the Vault and see if I can find this encrypted program on any of the remaining units."

Howe said to Major Klasky, "Accompany Ms. Dixon to the Vault when she goes."

"Yes, ma'am."

Brodie asked Dixon, "Can we assume you do not plan to tell your lab colleagues about your discovery?"

Dixon nodded. "I'm not sure who to trust." She made eye contact with Colonel Howe. "Though I suppose keeping this information from the camp commander would have been negligent."

"You're right," said Howe.

Brodie thought of something else and asked Howe, "Who has the body-cam footage from the training exercises?"

"I do," said Major Klasky. "I'm in charge of all aspects of the after-action review system."

"There's footage we need to look at," said Brodie.

Klasky nodded. "That shouldn't be a problem."

"The date in question is March twelfth. Or possibly the thirteenth. I can't remember which, but I assume there wasn't an exercise on both of those days."

"They are rarely conducted back-to-back," said Klasky. "I'll look into it."

"Thank you, Major," said Brodie. "In the meantime, we are headed back to our residence." He gestured to the wreckage on the parade grounds. "And we'd like that in a to-go box."

"I'll see to it," said Klasky.

"First I need to see if anything is salvageable from the CPU," said Dixon.

Klasky said, "If the agents don't object. I will maintain a log of anything you remove."

"That's fine," said Brodie.

Colonel Howe said to Brodie and Taylor, "I will summon you to my office after I have received the proper authorizations to transfer the D-17s." She added, "While the camp lockdown does not apply to you two, I would urge you to stay put for the time being. We are in a moment of uncertainty here."

That was an understatement. Brodie said, "I regret that tragedy has struck Camp Hayden once more. Let's all see to it that something like this never happens again."

They all agreed that was a good idea and went their separate ways. Once they were out of earshot, Taylor said to Brodie, "You gave him the wrong date. Klasky."

"I know," said Brodie. "If there is anything incriminating in the March twenty-first footage, and Major Klasky has something to hide, he could wipe or censor that footage. Let him think we're barking up the wrong tree until we're in the room with him."

Taylor nodded. "Everyone's a suspect."

"Except the hot scientist."

"*Especially* the hot scientist. Who, by the way, is sleeping with the woman who just took control of this camp under a very dubious pretext."

"Do you think Caroline's bisexual?"

"I think you have more important things to ponder. Like whether we're in the middle of a mutiny."

"Right," he said. "And Praetorian. What is it?"

"It's software," said Taylor. "Hidden software. Maybe like malware. Or a virus."

"Maybe some coder at DARPA or DEVCOM or Synotec got a very attractive offer from a Nigerian prince, and clicked the wrong link, and now the tin men are going to steal everyone's personal info and ruin their credit."

Maggie Taylor, who had learned long ago when to tune out her partner's stupid comments, said, "Viruses spread."

Right. Brodie pictured those fifty-nine dormant titanium soldiers strapped into storage bays in their subterranean facility, all plugged into a hardwired data link. Could malicious code spread through something like that? Probably.

Brodie and Taylor headed west through the camp beneath the high midday sun. They passed the barracks, where the Rangers from the parade ground were undoubtedly filling in their buddies on what had happened, including that their highly respected platoon sergeant had been thrown in the brig. How would all those heavily armed and highly trained men take that news? Probably not well. It was easy to see how things could quickly break down at Camp Hayden. In fact, they already had.

Brodie checked his watch. Thirty minutes past noon, and already an MP had been murdered, a brigadier general and a senior NCO had been arrested in a possible mutiny, and a homicidal piece of next-generation military hardware had been barbequed. What was next?

Taylor asked, "What are you thinking, partner?"

"That I'm glad you changed the code on our door, and that we're both armed."

She nodded. "I'm eager to get the rest of the bots out of here, but that won't solve our case, and I'm not sure it will neutralize the danger at Camp Hayden either."

For some reason, Morgan's desperate question to Bucky popped back into Brodie's mind:

Why don't you resist?

It was for the same reason that Bucky allowed itself to get beaned in the head with a water bottle. No one had ordered it to resist. These things had no instinct for self-preservation . . . right?

Why don't you resist?

There was something there, in that question, that was the key to this thing. But he couldn't quite place it. Not yet.

CHAPTER 26

THEY ENTERED THE RESIDENTIAL CUL-DE-SAC AND BRO-
die walked past their house.

Taylor asked, "Where are you going?"

"Not home, where Captain Pickman's lying in wait with his Beretta
trained on the door."

"I think he'd use an M4 on you. Full auto."

"Good point. For now, we're better off not being where we say we're
going to be. And we have some outstanding business to attend to." He
headed toward the late Major Roger Ames's house, number six, which
still had yellow police tape across the front door.

On the way, Brodie looked across the cul-de-sac at Brigadier General Morgan's house, where an MP vehicle was now parked. He wondered if the general's wife was happy to get so much quality time with
her husband—which would become even more if he was relieved of
command, and considerably less if he was sent to prison. It's not easy
being an Army wife.

Brodie approached the door to house number six and ripped away
the police tape. Taylor punched in the code that Captain Spencer had
given them yesterday and then opened the door.

They entered a house identical to their own. Brodie walked through
the living room, looking for personal items or effects that might clue
them in to anything about the deceased, but as Captain Spencer had
indicated, Mendez and his people had already emptied everything out.
Maybe he'd spot something they hadn't. Wouldn't be the first time.

They entered one of the bedrooms, which was cleared other than furniture and a bedside lamp. There was a safe in the corner that was opened and empty.

They went into the second bedroom, which was identical, and identically barren. Taylor searched the closet, then got on her knees to inspect the floor.

"What is it?" asked Brodie.

"Loose baseboard." She pried at something, then after a minute came out with a clear plastic bin the size of a small shoebox. The bottom was packed with dark soil and spilling out the top were about two dozen mushrooms.

"I guess you found his stash."

They inspected the mushrooms, which were of varying sizes, all a creamy white color with circles of brownish gold in the center of each cap.

"The question," said Taylor, "is whether this has anything to do with the case or is just a private hobby of the murder victim."

Right. Did this offer any clues to the major's state of mind at the time he was killed? Had he been flying high when Bucky killed him, and did that have something to do with his death? Brodie recalled that psilocybin had been found in his hair but not his blood, where the drug is cleared more quickly, making it unlikely Ames had ingested these in the hours before his demise.

Taylor said, "Let's give this to the MPs, who can arrange to send it out for testing. Not that I think he was growing mushrooms for his omelets in a secret compartment behind the molding, but we should be thorough."

"Good idea." He eyed the mushrooms. "You ever try these?"

She nodded. "In college a couple of times. One time was lovely, in the woods on an autumn day. The other time was for the cherry blossom festival at the National Mall in DC. Bad idea. The trees were spectacular but that whole place is pulsing with malevolent energy."

"I don't need to take hallucinogens to know that."

"Sure," said Taylor. "You know it, but you don't feel it in your soul."

"So, these kind of tune you in?"

"Sort of. They tune you in to the world, and they tune you out of all the bullshit going on inside your head. It can cause a kind of ego death." She added, "Though I think you'd need to eat this whole grow box to kill *your* ego."

"Cheap shot."

She smiled, then looked at the mushrooms. "They can make you feel like you're part of everything, like everything in the world is connected, and it's comforting. It sounds cheesy, but it's true. Also, the experiences kind of stay with you. Unlike alcohol or marijuana, it doesn't affect your memory. And the positive feelings can be long-lasting, well after it's out of your system."

"What about the negative feelings?"

She nodded. "Those too. There's a risk with this kind of thing, which is why I never touched them again after my bad trip. They're not going to harm your body in any appreciable way, but they can wreak havoc on your mind."

Maybe Roger Ames, like PFC Tom Greer and many others at this godforsaken place, had been losing his grip on reality. He'd just picked a different poison. Brodie said, "Let's check the back."

They left the bedroom. Taylor put the grow box back into the secret compartment behind the baseboard, then they left the bedroom and stepped into the backyard, which, like theirs, featured a small patio with a few pieces of outdoor furniture, high wooden fences on both sides, and a spread of rock-and-succulent landscaping running to Camp Hayden's tall steel perimeter fence.

Both agents looked around, not really knowing what they were searching for, and understanding that this stop in the investigation was mostly a bust. Yes, they'd uncovered the major's funky fungi stash, but all that did was corroborate what the coroner had already found.

Brodie walked through the small sandy yard toward the perimeter fence. In the distance he saw the training village, and he wondered if the major had ever stood here, watching from inside the wire as his toy soldiers overran the real ones.

He turned to walk back and noticed a strange feeling underfoot. Hard and hollow. He stomped his shoe and hit something that wasn't earth.

He dropped to his knees and began to dig. Taylor joined him. They uncovered a piece of plywood sheathing about the size of a door, then dug around its edges until they had enough leverage to lift it up and flip it to the side.

They looked into a trench about eight feet by four feet, covered by a dark-green tarp. Brodie ripped off the tarp to reveal two plastic heavy-duty storage trunks. He leaned down and flipped them open.

Both trunks were filled with weapons: three M4s with EMP barrel attachments, two grenade launchers, two shoulder-fired RPGs, a few handguns, two body armor vests, and dozens of boxes of ammunition.

"Holy shit," said Taylor.

Brodie spotted some writing on the underside of the plywood that had covered the trench. In thick black handwritten letters, it read: SI VIS PACEM, PARA BELLUM.

Brodie recognized the ancient Latin phrase, and as he looked back at the pit full of weapons Taylor translated it aloud:

"If you want peace, prepare for war."

CHAPTER 27

THEY STOOD IN SILENCE, LOOKING DOWN AT MAJOR Ames's weapons stash.

Taylor said, "He didn't know who he could trust, so he decided to take matters into his own hands."

"Or his brain was so cooked that he was having paranoid delusions."

"They weren't delusions, Scott. Look what happened to him."

Brodie glanced again at the Latin phrase. Major Ames seemed to have had a flair for the dramatic. And, maybe, an affinity for ancient Rome.

Praetorian.

Whatever Praetorian was, Ames had either created it or discovered it. But what *was* it, and what the hell was he prepping for here?

Brodie looked again at the weapons. How could Ames have amassed this kind of cache? How did he even access the armory? Maybe PFC Greer had helped with this too. And maybe it was another sign of Camp Hayden's breakdown in morale and discipline that no one had noticed all this stuff go missing.

The doorbell rang.

Taylor began hastily closing the trunks. "Buy me a minute."

Brodie brushed himself off, then walked back into the house and to the front door. He placed his hand on his SIG Sauer as he checked the peephole. It was Major Klasky.

He let go of his weapon and opened the door. "Hello, Major."

"I went to your house first. Then I spotted the torn police tape."

"Good deduction."

Klasky cleared his throat. "Two things. One, I've located the body-cam footage from March twelfth. There was no exercise on the thirteenth. Two, Colonel Howe has conferred with Major General Ramsay and now wishes to speak with you and Ms. Taylor."

"What's first?"

"The colonel is waiting."

"Maggie's in the bathroom. She'll be out shortly."

Brodie stepped out the front door and shut it behind him.

Klasky looked at the closed door. "The MPs cleaned this place out."

"That's right."

"Did you find something they missed?"

He nodded. "Tuna sandwich in the fridge. Smells off."

"Do people find you funny?"

"I never bother to ask." He added, "You know I can't share the details of our investigation, Major."

"I know. But I'm curious."

"I guess you'll have to stay that way."

Klasky smiled. It wasn't exactly a sincere smile, but he was trying. This guy seemed all right. Less tightly wound than the colonel, not a wacko like the general, and certainly less of an insecure dipshit than his subordinate Captain Pickman.

As they waited, Klasky scanned the houses.

Brodie asked, "Which one's yours?"

The major jerked his thumb behind him. "I'm in the other cluster."

"With the colonel."

Klasky looked at him. "That's right."

Brodie noted that the major's hazel eyes were a little close together, his ears were a bit oversize, and he had a noticeable gap in his teeth. Altogether it gave him a vaguely Alfred E. Neuman–like appearance. Except there was a sharpness in his eyes, and despite his slightly dopey appearance Brodie had a feeling this guy didn't miss much.

Brodie asked, "Did you agree with Colonel Howe's actions this afternoon?"

"It would be insubordinate of me to tell you I didn't."

"When speaking to a CID agent, your loyalty is to the truth."

Klasky nodded. "Well said. So, here's the truth. Brigadier General Morgan should have never been placed in command of Camp Hayden, and Colonel Howe waited too long to do what she did."

"Why was he placed in command?"

"You'll have to ask Major General Ramsay."

"I'm asking you."

Klasky thought a moment. "Morgan is a smart and capable officer. He's headstrong, obviously, but that's not a problem. The problem is he came in here with an agenda, and it was a different agenda than the Army's, and they should have seen that from a mile off."

"He wanted to kill the program," said Brodie.

Klasky looked in his eyes, weighing his words. "He wanted the Rangers to kick some ass, lay waste to the tin men, and embarrass Futures Command, because he hated this whole program. But he underestimated what DARPA and DEVCOM had designed. And by the time he realized what he was really up against, he was dug in, so he's been pushing the men beyond the breaking point to bend reality back to what he thinks it should be."

That tracked. General Morgan had been losing control, even before one of the bots killed two people. And then once Bucky went loco, the only supposed safeguard against these things—their predictability— was out the window, and Morgan's back was against the wall. Given all that, it wasn't too surprising that he'd done what he did. The tin men were a threat—to his soldiers and to his pride.

Taylor came out the door. It looked like she actually had used the bathroom, at least to wash all the sand off her hands and arms. "Hello, Major."

Klasky repeated their two-part itinerary to her, then led them toward the administrative building.

As they walked down a dirt road running along the northern edge of camp, Brodie asked, "Were you with Futures Command before this assignment?"

"No," the man replied. "I rotated in. The command is new, so that's common."

"Where were you before?"

"Fort Carson," replied Klasky, without elaborating.

Taylor asked, "What was your impression of Major Ames?"

Klasky thought a moment. "Smart. Eccentric. Stubborn. He often came to me to give feedback and complain about the training exercises. He could have gone straight to Colonel Howe, but probably because we shared rank, he thought I was more approachable."

"What were his issues?" asked Brodie.

"He wanted to push things. Give the D-17s more complex parameters for target acquisition, use unarmed Rangers as civilian stand-ins, see if we could get the bots to mount a simulated hostage rescue. Things that would have required massive code rewrites and led to unpredictable outcomes." He looked at Brodie and Taylor. "So, as you might imagine, when Dixon reported finding some secret program in the code, my first thought was that it was Ames's handiwork. It would fit his character and his motives."

This was the third individual with the same theory that Ames himself was tinkering with the D-17s. That didn't make it true. But it couldn't be dismissed either.

"And if it *was* his doing," continued Klasky, "I'm not surprised he was able to cover his tracks so well. He was brilliant."

"Reckless too," said Taylor, "if your theory is correct."

Klasky thought about that. "I'd use the word 'naïve,' Ms. Taylor. He thought the more we could make the machines like us, the less dangerous they'd become. I figured the opposite was true. I'm out of my depth when it comes to understanding the tech inside the tin men, but I do know people."

Right. And part of what made people dangerous was their tendency toward irrational behavior—often to their own detriment. General Morgan's pride and vengefulness had cost him his command, at least temporarily. Major Ames's idealism—and perhaps arrogance—had cost him his life. Even the MP, Specialist Kemp, would still have been alive had he put in the minor effort to procure a vehicle rather than take the major risk of activating Number 20 while alone with it in a confined space.

And that raised a larger question: Were Bucky's actions the product of some internal logic? Or had some element of chaos, of humanlike irrationality, been introduced into its central processor that caused it—like General Morgan, Major Ames, and Specialist Kemp—to take actions that led to its own destruction?

Why don't you resist?

Morgan's question again, which Brodie could not get out of his mind. He said to Major Klasky, "General Morgan conducted a live-fire test on a piece of military hardware. This equipment had the capacity to avoid, or at least attempt to avoid, being destroyed, yet it didn't. That is an interesting insight."

Klasky looked surprised. "Are you defending what the general did? Depending on your point of view, he either carried out an extrajudicial execution of the murderer in your homicide investigation, or he destroyed the murder weapon."

"I'm aware," said Brodie.

Klasky shook his head. "The only insight we gained was to the limits of the general's impulse control. The bots are not programmed to protect themselves outside of the battlespace unless specifically ordered to do so."

Taylor said, "The bots are also not programmed to bash a person's head into a concrete wall."

Klasky had no reply to that.

CHAPTER 28

KLASKY, BRODIE, AND TAYLOR ARRIVED AT THE ADMIN-
istrative building, where a young male MP corporal named Hicks was
at the guard station. The corporal saluted the three officers.

They entered the building and walked into Colonel Howe's office,
which was, as expected, tidy and spartan. The colonel sat behind an un-
cluttered wooden desk. Behind her were some framed military photos,
commendations, and several detailed maps of Camp Hayden and the
surrounding federal lands.

Howe gestured to a couple of seats across the desk. "Please sit."

The two agents sat. The colonel said to Klasky, "Thank you, Major.
You're dismissed."

"Yes, ma'am." He said to Brodie and Taylor, "I will be in the after-
action review room once you're done here." He left and shut the door.

Howe cleared her throat and got down to business. "I spoke with
Major General Ramsay about the status of our operations at Camp
Hayden, your investigation, and the tragic incident this morning with
Specialist Kemp. The major general was, as you can imagine, highly
concerned, and saddened by the loss of life. He is heavily invested in
the work we are doing here, and it is his position that the training and
testing we are conducting is, without question, the most important experimental research and training project in the entire U.S. military. I
share his view. The field of autonomous robotics and artificial intelligence is the new Space Race, and we cannot lose."

Brodie had the feeling that this preamble was leading to something
they didn't want to hear.

Howe continued, "I cannot, and I will not, allow this entire operation to be delayed or aborted because of the paranoid fantasies and
arrogant whims of one man, even if that man is a brigadier general."

Taylor said, "We understand your position on General Morgan.
Did General Ramsay authorize your taking of command?"

Howe replied, "He did."

She let that hang in the air a moment, then continued, "General
Ramsay agrees that what Morgan did was extremely reckless, and potentially harmful to CID's investigation. But he also acknowledges the great
stresses and hardships we are all operating under and what he believes
to be General Morgan's unwavering commitment to the larger goals of
Army Futures Command. Therefore, Morgan will be subject to an internal review upon the completion of your investigation." She added, "That
is, of course, unless your final report alleges criminal activity that leads
to charges against General Morgan. The major general respectfully requests that Morgan's discipline be handled from within the command,
given the highly classified nature of the work we are doing here."

Brodie said, "The major general should stick to his job."

Howe pursed her lips. "It was a request from a two-star general, Mr.
Brodie. Certainly not an order. Do with it what you will."

Taylor said, "CID does not take rank or special requests into con-
sideration when reporting its findings."

Howe looked at her. "I'm sure you don't, Ms. Taylor. But there is a
club that you and I will never be in, whose founding charter includes
an unwritten and unspoken list of privileges." She smiled, which was a
first, and said, "The boys' club."

Taylor had no response to that.

Brodie, for his part, couldn't care less about the internal power
struggles of Camp Hayden's officer corps and its implications for gen-
der equality, so long as he could get the killer robots out of this nut-
house. "We can revisit this later. Is Major General Ramsay fielding our
request to transfer custody of the D-17s?"

"No."

"No?"

"Your CO, Brigadier General Dombroski, relayed your request to the Provost Marshal General, who then got in touch with Ramsay. No one at the highest echelons was enthusiastic about coordinating a relocation of this top-secret equipment. General Ramsay told me that if it could be done at all, it could not be done quickly."

Brodie said, "And then you, of course, emphasized the urgency of this."

Howe looked him in the eyes. "They are staying here. That was my recommendation, and the major general was relieved to hear it. I took command to restore order. And I have."

"Time will tell, Colonel. But the price of failure is a hell of a lot higher with those things around. And it is not appropriate for us to rely so heavily on the expertise of someone deeply embedded within Camp Hayden's research program."

"Ms. Dixon is a brilliant computer scientist."

Taylor said, "She's also one of the few people at this camp capable of writing and covertly installing a rogue piece of software."

Howe stared at Maggie Taylor and did not reply.

Brodie leaned forward. "Colonel, someone spiked the punch. Praetorian. Whatever it is. Did it happen here? Or at Synotec? Or at DEVCOM headquarters? Or DARPA? You've got a faulty product with too many cooks and an almost indecipherable chain of custody. So I don't give a rat's ass how brilliant Ms. Dixon is. She might be a saboteur and therefore investigating herself. And when that happens, the person doing the digging stalls as long as they can, and miraculously never finds the answer. Add to the situation a very pissed-off brigadier general who might not accept the legitimacy of your command, and a Ranger platoon of speed freaks who would like nothing more than to rig the entire Vault with C4 and blow their tormentors to hell. They've got plenty of reasons, all they need is the order, and I doubt they'll

care who it's coming from, or that your seizure of command was legit-
imized by some two-star general they've never seen or met a thousand
miles away in Austin."

Howe did not respond. She rapped her fingers on her polished
wooden desk as she considered his words—or the best way to tell him
to screw off. Then she said, "This is my call, and my judgment. Dixon
is trustworthy."

Having sex with a person can give you the false impression that you
know them better than you do. Scott Brodie had been burned by that
phenomenon once or twice. Maybe three times.

Taylor took the risk and said, "We would hate to think you are conferring special favor on anyone at this facility."

Howe shot her a look, and in that look was a question: *Do they
know?* She said, "That is not my practice, and it never has been. I assure
you, Ms. Taylor, that I take my job as seriously as you do yours."

"Of course, ma'am."

Howe kept her eyes on Taylor a moment, then cleared her throat
and looked back at Brodie. "You are right about the general, and the
Rangers. They resent Morgan on one level, but they are also loyal to
their senior commanding officer, and I fear what they might do on his
behalf. So, per my orders, all Rangers have been confined to barracks,
and to their individual rooms. I also had the phone lines disconnected
at all residences. Barracks and houses. Sergeant Mendez has taken
charge of the camp's armory and all other guard duties."

"How many MPs are on base?" asked Taylor.

"Eight," replied Howe. Then she must have remembered the late
Specialist Kemp and said, "Seven, actually."

"There are sixty-two Rangers," said Brodie. "Not good odds, Colonel, and not a fair position to put the MPs in."

"They can handle it." She retrieved two black walkies from her desk
and slid them to the agents. "New comms protocol. Klasky, Pickman,
and I are Channel One. Sergeant Mendez and his MPs are Two, you're

Three, and the science team is Four. Stay on Three and only switch if you need to initiate a communication."

The agents each took a walkie and Brodie said, "Ma'am, this is giving the impression of a mutiny. That's what the soldiers will think."

"I don't give a damn what they think. So long as they don't have their guns, or the ability to fraternize, or a way to contact anyone on or off base."

"You're overplaying your hand."

"It's the hand I was dealt. Leave the management of Camp Hayden to me, and I will leave the investigation to you. Stay on your walkies." She stood, and the two agents followed suit. "We need a tight ship now. And if there's a rat on board, find it."

CHAPTER 29

KLASKY LED BRODIE AND TAYLOR INTO THE AARS ROOM, with its miniature of the training village and an assortment of computers and display monitors, then showed them to a desk with a large monitor and two chairs. The monitor screen showed a grid of four dozen windows displaying frozen video feeds. Each window had a number in the upper left, one through forty-eight, along with a text designation—a unit number for the bots, or a name and rank for the Rangers.

The major said, "We're cued up to the beginning of the exercise. You can press the space bar to play all the feeds at once, and type in a number followed by the enter key to make a particular camera full-screen. Press escape to get back to the grid."

"Thank you," said Taylor.

Brodie and Taylor sat down, with Taylor at the keyboard. Brodie moved the mouse over the upper left corner of the window and closed it.

"What are you doing?" asked Klasky.

"The date is wrong."

"You told me March twelfth."

"I meant the twenty-first. I'm dyslexic." When he tried to open the file browser, a window popped up asking for a password.

Klasky gave an exasperated sigh as he leaned in and entered the password. He opened the file browser and selected the footage for March 21.

Brodie looked at the new grid of body cams. All the bots' screens showed black-and-purple pixelated images that were impossible to make out. Some of the Rangers' screens were dark as well, while other Rangers' cameras picked up their fellow teammates as ghostly orange and yellow shapes against hazy purple backgrounds.

Major Klasky explained, "This was a nighttime exercise. All participants were equipped with thermal-imaging body cams. The Rangers also had night vision goggles. The D-17s can see infrared without additional hardware."

The Rangers were already getting their asses kicked in broad daylight, and apparently they were being made to fight these things at night too. Camp Hayden was a sadistic place.

Brodie looked over his shoulder at Major Klasky. "Thank you, Major. We're good here."

Klasky didn't move. "I must remain. Camp protocol. This is classified material."

"Believe it or not," said Brodie, "I've reviewed classified material without an officer breathing down my neck."

"Pretend I'm not here."

"My imagination's not that good."

Taylor added, "Sir, we are reviewing this footage for potential evidence of misconduct, which may or may not point us toward a person of interest in our case. It would be against *our* protocol for you to be present for that."

Major Klasky appeared unhappy with being told what to do by warrant officers. But, to his credit, he said, "You're right, Ms. Taylor. I'll leave you to it, and I'll be in my office. Let me know when you're done."

Taylor said, "Thank you, sir."

Klasky left the room and closed the door behind him.

Brodie refocused on the screen and read through the names on each of the camera feeds. He found the windows for the cameras on Sergeant Miller, PFC Greer, and Number 20—a.k.a. Bucky.

Taylor pressed the space bar.

They watched the dozens of video feeds play simultaneously. Brodie focused on the Ranger cams. One Ranger's POV was from behind a machine gun nest in the road. Another aimed a grenade launcher out of a window. A third, perched on a high rooftop, looked out at the blank desert, which resembled a flickering purple sea.

Brodie watched Sergeant Miller's camera. He was standing in front of another Ranger, gesturing. There was no audio. Then the other Ranger headed for the stairs and up to the rooftop of the building. Miller took his position in the second-floor window and watched the narrow road below.

Brodie checked Greer's camera. He wasn't moving, and his body cam showed a formless black-and-purple mass. He recalled from the earlier VR playback that Greer had lingered next to a wall in the opening moments of the battle.

All at once, the tin men's body cams began to move, quickly cresting the sand berm and sprinting toward the village, their M4 rifles raised and firing at full auto toward the defending Rangers.

Through Bucky's body cam, Brodie caught pieces of the other charging bots as they all raced toward the village. A few of the tin men fanned out and Brodie saw full-body images of them. The thermal imagery rendered them as reddish-orange man-shaped hulks running at impossible speeds, their legs a blur as their feet pounded against the sand, their upper bodies almost motionless in an unnatural and inhuman way, rifles raised, spitting out hundreds of yellow shell casings from their M4s' ejectors.

Brodie's eyes bounced among the forty-something viewpoints. A Ranger on a rooftop was hit. He sat and slumped against his firing nest as he removed his helmet—his resignation visible even in the distant thermal image. The Ranger's feed went dark.

The tin men were quickly closing the distance. Some of the Rangers held their positions, waiting until they had a clean shot. Others fired from the roads, trying to get a kill before the enemy breached the village boundary.

Brodie watched the camera of a rooftop gunner who was trying to rake the wave of red figures bounding across the desert. He tried to lead them, but the tin men varied their speed and their angle of approach. One spun away from an incoming barrage and then changed direction on a dime, like a skilled running back dodging a tackle—an insane quick-reaction maneuver impossible for any living thing on earth. Bucky was toward the center of the charging line, and within a second he was running down a street in the village.

Brodie and Taylor were now both focused on PFC Greer's camera. He hadn't moved. On all the other feeds, the battle had intensified. Two tin men scaled the wall of a building. Another took out a Ranger who had popped out a window to get a shot. One by one the Rangers' feeds blinked dark.

Sergeant Miller was lobbing grenades into the road below. The underbarrel launcher only held one round at a time and he would quickly take cover and reload between shots. The inert grenade cartridge thudded into the road, with the advanced GPS-based system presumably registering it as a simulated detonation. A tin man near one of the grenade impacts froze in place and sat down in the road, apparently within the virtual blast radius.

Greer remained where he was, against a wall and away from the action.

Taylor said, "He's panicked. Or having another psychotic episode."

Then Greer began to move. He ran around a building, then spun into a doorway and bolted up a narrow set of stairs.

He entered a small room. Directly ahead of him was another Ranger, firing grenades out the window. It was Sergeant Miller.

Greer slowly walked toward him. Then he pointed something at the sergeant. It was a pistol.

"Holy shit," said Brodie.

Brodie looked at Bucky's body cam as the bot ran into a building and up the stairs. It entered a room, and its camera picked up a full-body image of PFC Greer standing in the middle of the room, aiming his pistol at his platoon sergeant's back.

Bucky lowered its rifle. Waited a moment. Then ran up the next flight of stairs to take out the Rangers on the rooftop.

Greer took a step toward Miller, pistol still raised.

Miller must have been hit through the window. Through Greer's camera, they saw the man set down his M4 rifle and remove his helmet, then turn and sit on the floor. For a moment, Miller's body cam caught the image of Greer standing over him, pistol raised. Then Miller's camera blinked out.

In Greer's camera, they watched the orange-yellow mass of Sergeant Miller sitting on the ground, staring down the barrel of Private Greer's pistol. He barely moved.

Greer took another step forward. Even in the thermal image, it was clear that the sergeant was remaining calm, trying to talk his soldier off a ledge.

A moment later Greer dropped the pistol, and then crouched. His body cam began to subtly shake up and down. He was crying. Miller stood and walked to him.

Another D-17 entered the room and shot PFC Greer in the back, then moved through the room and up the stairs. Greer's body cam cut out.

The two agents sat in silence as they watched the remaining couple of minutes of the battle play out across the patchwork of images. When the last of the Rangers' cameras went dark, ten tin men remained standing. Another grim defeat.

Brodie and Taylor looked at each other. Then Taylor said, "Bucky knew. It fucking *knew*, Scott. It saw that one of the Rangers was going to kill another, and it just moved on."

Brodie now understood why Major Ames was so interested in this incident. It showed a level of cognition—maybe even malice—that these things were not supposed to possess. And in the real-time VR playback of the after-action review, Ames was probably the only one who had noticed it happen.

There's a ghost in the machine.

Praetorian. They had to figure out what it was, and who put it there, and why.

Taylor said, "Blackmail."

Brodie looked at her. "What?"

"Why did Private Greer allow Ames to access the Vault alone on three separate occasions by giving him his code, a major violation of protocol? One time, I can understand maybe. He got pressured by a commissioned officer. But Ames was aware of Greer's schedule, and at what times the private was alone, and exploited that. Greer understood that he was helping Ames do something that the major did not want anyone else knowing about. Why would he do that? Because Ames knew Greer had almost fragged his platoon sergeant. And he was the *only one* who knew other than Miller. And I'm sure he promised Greer he'd keep it that way."

Brodie nodded. "So long as Greer returned the favor regarding the major's late nights in the Vault. These two interacted much more than the private let on. So what else is this guy hiding from us?"

Taylor stood. "Let's find out."

CHAPTER 30

CORPORAL NIMITZ SNAPPED A SALUTE AS THE TWO CID agents approached the barracks. They returned the salute, and Brodie asked, "Anyone in or out?"

"No, sir."

"Do you have someone at the other door?"

"Yes, sir. Corporal Rivera."

"Good. As you were."

They entered the barracks, which apparently were being guarded by two of Camp Hayden's seven MPs. That left five others for the armory, the Vault, the brig, the admin building, and the two gates. Never mind the guard towers. Colonel Howe was trying to create the illusion of control, but that's all it was.

Someone had cleaned up the cans of energy drinks and beer from the desk in the lobby. They took the stairs up to the third floor. All of the hallway doors were closed. They heard no talking, only the faint sounds of music or TV coming from the rooms.

They approached the door to Room 3H, and Brodie noticed a plastic tray on the floor with a metal covering. Must have been lunch delivered by the mess. Brodie lifted the cover. A burger and fries, and a pile of steamed vegetables. Completely untouched. He looked down the hall and noted that no other doors had food sitting outside.

Brodie knocked. "Private Greer! This is Scott Brodie and Maggie Taylor, CID."

No immediate answer, and Brodie didn't wait before opening the door.

Directly ahead of them was an open window. Brodie ran to it and leaned out. If Greer had jumped, he'd walked away from the fall. Then Brodie spotted a drainpipe about three feet to the right of the window. He must have shimmied down.

Brodie took out his walkie and switched to Channel 2. "Brodie for Sergeant Mendez. Over."

In a moment the walkie crackled: *"Yes, sir. Mendez here. Over."*

"Your people need to do a room check and a head count at the barracks. We have at least one AWOL. PFC Greer. Climbed out his window. Over."

"Yes, sir. Roger, wilco. And we'll sweep the camp. No activity at the gates, so he can't have gone far. Over."

"Thank you, Sergeant. Over and out."

Taylor looked out the window. "Why the hell would he do that?"

"Fear," said Brodie. "Or guilt."

"Bucky didn't shoot him. Why? Was it something about Bucky, or something about Greer?"

"No clue. So let's get one." He walked to the door.

"Where?"

"Bucky's scrap metal and Greer's AWOL. That leaves Miller."

CHAPTER 31

CAMP HAYDEN'S BRIG, AN ACTIVE CRIME SCENE ONLY hours ago, appeared to be back to regular operation. The MP team could not afford the manpower to station someone at the front door, which was unguarded and unlocked. Brodie and Taylor entered the room with the drop ceiling where they had first encountered Bucky. A young female MP specialist named Caldwell stood outside the cell door, holding an M4 with live ammo.

The specialist stood at attention. "Sir, ma'am."

Taylor said, "We are here to see Sergeant Miller."

"Yes, ma'am." Caldwell unlocked the cell door and swung it open.

Brodie and Taylor entered the small holding cell, where Miller sat on the cot in his camo pants and a tan undershirt. He stood as they entered.

"As you were, Sergeant," said Brodie.

Miller settled back on the cot. Caldwell brought in a couple of chairs from the main room and the agents sat across from him.

Brodie eyed the wall to his right, where the large, cracked depression in the concrete remained. Someone had done a thorough job of removing any loose debris and cleaning up the blood, but for a small dark-red stain in the broken concrete.

Miller followed Brodie's gaze. "How are my guys?"

"Under lock and key in the barracks," said Brodie. "Except one. Tom Greer is missing."

"Shit."

"The MPs are looking for him. You have any ideas why he'd do this?"

Miller sighed. "Like I said, this place screws us all up, but it screwed up Tom more. He's sensitive. So I'm not totally surprised. First Ames, then that MP, Kemp. He probably thinks he's next." He got a worried look on his face. "He might try to get his hands on a weapon."

"The MPs are guarding the armory."

"Yeah? While also watching the barracks, and this brig, and the gates? There's, like, five of them."

"Seven," said Taylor.

He shook his head. "Howe's an idiot."

"She's not taking any chances," said Brodie.

"Actually, she's taking *a lot* of chances."

Brodie said, "We know about what happened on March twenty-first. What Greer almost did. We saw the footage."

Miller didn't say anything for a moment. Then he asked, "Who told you about that?"

"That's not your business. Tell us exactly what happened."

Miller rubbed his face with both hands. "I need a fucking drink."

Taylor said, "You need to start telling the fucking truth, Sergeant. You are in deep shit. Start acting like it."

Brodie looked at his partner. Magnolia Annabelle Taylor was pissed off—and packing a seventeen-round 9mm along with Appalachian belligerence.

Miller, maybe coming to realize the gravity of lying to CID warrant officers on a homicide case, straightened his posture as he said, "You're right, ma'am, and I apologize. When you came to the barracks looking for Greer, I was surprised, because I couldn't imagine what he had to do with Bucky killing the major. And I guess I still don't understand what he's got to do with it."

"You don't need to understand," said Brodie. "You need to tell us what happened in that room."

Miller nodded. "The battle was tougher than most because we were fighting at night. The tin men . . . the way they see the world, I don't think it makes a goddamn difference to them whether it's night or day, so there's another strike against humanity. Anyway, I'm firing grenades out a second-story window. My sensor beeps. I'm hit. I turn around and sit against the wall, and there's Tom, standing over me. He's got this look in his eyes, this crazed look, and he's pointing his Beretta at me. I ask him what he's doing. He says he knows what I really am. He knows I'm not real. I tell him to put the gun down. He asks me if I've got a knife on me. I do. He says if I want to live, I've got to cut my arm. He wants to see me bleed. I say I'm not doing that. I tell him we're brothers. I tell him I love him. I tell him to put down the gun. He does. He starts sobbing and . . ." He trailed off and stared at the floor. "He tells me he doesn't know what's real anymore. He tells me he wants to go home." He looked back up at them. "You'd asked me about his service weapon. The truth is I confiscated it that night, two weeks before he attacked Kowalski. And thank God for that."

"It sounds to me," said Brodie, "like you've given this guy way more chances than he deserved."

Miller gave him an odd look. "Deserved? Getting him out of here would have been the kindest thing I could have done. He *deserved* to leave. Keeping him here was the punishment."

Taylor asked, "Then why not get him reassigned?"

"I tried," said Miller. "I went to the brass. I didn't tell them—or anyone—about the incident during the exercise, that would have gotten Tom arrested. But everyone knew about Kowalski. And that Greer was cracking up in general."

Taylor asked, "Who did you go to?"

"Captain Pickman. He sent it up the chain to Major Klasky. And the major . . ." He trailed off again. The sergeant seemed like he was navigating a minefield in his head and didn't want to make a wrong move. "Major Klasky made it clear that PFC Greer would be a significant national security risk if he were to leave Camp Hayden."

"Then what the hell was the plan?" asked Brodie. "Keep him here until he loses the rest of his mind?"

"You're being sarcastic, but yeah. As far as I could tell, Klasky would have been happy to keep pushing him until he went the way of Justin Beal."

"An overdose," said Taylor.

Miller laughed bitterly. "Beal didn't overdose. I mean, he was high as shit when it happened."

"When what happened?" asked Brodie.

"Beal was in my squad that day. We get back to barracks, guys go to unwind in the rec room, but Beal goes to his own room, which is right across the hall." Miller looked at Brodie. "Half the platoon heard the gunshot."

CHAPTER 32

THEY ALL SAT IN SILENCE. THEN TAYLOR SAID, "JESUS . . . They covered up a suicide."

"No," said Miller. "They covered up the *manner* of a suicide. He was spiraling. If he'd ODed it would have been functionally the same thing. But that story looked slightly better for the press."

Brodie said, "You lied to us. Again."

Miller said, "I was trying to fit the official narrative around here. When you do that enough, you start to believe it."

"Bad excuse."

Miller looked in his eyes. "It's not an excuse at all, sir. Actually, it's shameful."

"I'd have you thrown in the brig if you weren't already here."

Miller did not respond.

"Anything else to share?"

"Yes," said Miller. "Now that I'm thinking about it, I might have an idea where Greer is. A couple miles to the east of the camp is a low mesa. That could be where he went."

Taylor asked, "What makes you think that, Sergeant?"

Miller was silent a moment as he slid his eyes between the two agents. "About a week after Greer beat up his roommate, I noticed a change in him. Positive change. I mean, as far as I knew, he was off all the junk he'd been on. But it was more than that. He almost seemed . . . serene. One morning in the mess, I sit with him apart from the rest of the guys, I comment on it. And he tells me he's had a spiritual awakening, and that it happened on that mesa, and that it happened with Major Roger Ames."

Brodie and Taylor looked at each other.

Miller continued, "I don't know what the hell he's talking about. What is a PFC doing hanging out with a commissioned officer and computer scientist? I ask him to explain, but I can tell he's kind of embarrassed. He said they meditated, or something like that. That he and the major had first struck up a conversation one night while Greer was guarding the Vault, and Ames said he had a way to help Tom with some of his . . . psychological issues. So I'm thinking, maybe they're gay together, and at this point, I don't care. The guy seemed happier, and his performance improved."

The holding cell was silent. Ames had obviously given the young PFC some of his mushroom stash, and Greer hadn't wanted to admit to his platoon sergeant that he'd just swapped one drug for another.

"So," said Brodie, "you were aware these two had some sort of personal relationship, and when Ames died, you didn't want Greer to catch any heat."

Miller nodded. "That's about it, sir. I figured there was no way it was actually relevant to your case. That was something between the tin men and the scientists."

"That's not for you to determine," said Taylor.

"I know," said Miller. "But I did it anyway, and here we are."

Taylor asked, "Is there anything that Greer told you about Ames? About their conversations? Something that might clue us in to what Ames was doing in the weeks before his death?"

Miller thought. "Greer didn't say much. But I could tell he had a liking for the guy, a respect, an appreciation. I really didn't get it, and he didn't seem to want to explain it further, except to tell me that Ames saved his life. I think he meant helping him get off drugs."

Brodie said, "If Greer did return to the mesa, I don't understand how he could have done so without being detected."

Miller said, "Back in January there was a flash flood. Caused a mud-slide through the northeast corner of camp, my guys had to shore it up with sand and rocks. They left a small section open, a crawl space under the fence, if anybody wanted to stretch their legs outside the gates without having to ask permission. The opening's blocked by a few oil drums. Since this whole camp is now being guarded by only half a dozen MPs, I'm figuring it would be easy for Greer to slip out that way."

Taylor asked, "Why are you assuming Tom would return to this mesa?"

Miller shrugged. "Given everything going on, maybe he needs some peace."

Brodie said, "Ames and Greer were likely ingesting psilocybin mushrooms."

Miller looked surprised. Then he laughed. "I guess that explains it. Shit. Why didn't they invite me?"

Taylor said, "You had no knowledge of that?"

Miller shook his head.

She continued, "I've heard of hallucinogens being used to treat other drug addictions."

So, had Major Ames made PFC Greer his salvation project? Maybe. Out of the goodness of his heart? Maybe not. Ames needed Greer to give him his access and keep his secret. A mentally unstable co-conspirator is a liability.

Brodie said to Miller, "Is there any other information you've with-held from us? If you lie or deliberately omit again, we will recommend criminal charges against you for making false official statements, and you could face confinement."

Miller did not like how that was framed. "The answer is no." He added, "Did I tell you the guys call this place Camp Hades? Hell on earth."

"I've been to war, Sergeant. That's the real hell."

"Yeah," said Miller. "So have I. Sometimes I miss it. You?"

"Nope."

Taylor said, "I do."

Both men looked at her.

She continued, "The comradery, the mission. The meaning of what you were doing."

Brodie nodded. He and Taylor had touched on this subject before, and he understood what she meant. And maybe he felt it too, when he allowed himself to.

Miller said to Taylor, "That's right. You're closer to death than most anyone, but also more alive than anyone. Well, here we're dead men. Dead in spirit and soul and without purpose. We're meat targets. And everything that makes us human, that makes us more than them, also makes us weaker than them. We die and then we die again. Except now men are dying for real, and I'm in this fucking cell, and our CO is under house arrest, and the MPs have got the goddamn armory under lock." He ran his right hand through his close-cropped brown hair, and the sleeve of his undershirt rode up and revealed a tattoo on his biceps— a skull wearing a Ranger beret with a dagger held in its teeth. Miller looked again at the cracked wall where SPC Kemp had been murdered. The small stain of blood that wouldn't wash out. "It's been a long time since I've fought for anything real."

Brodie thought of a panther in a zoo, looking dully through the bars of its cage. An apex predator, stripped of prey and purpose.

Why don't you resist?

There it was again. It was maddening that Bucky had allowed itself to be destroyed. It took away the satisfaction. The retribution of it all. And maybe that was the point. Even when you kill them, you don't really win.

The upshot of all this was that PFC Greer might have withheld even more information from them than his platoon sergeant had. He might hold the key to what was really going on here.

And maybe Tom Greer was up on that mesa right now, watching the sun slash shadows across the desert, doing whatever he could to reclaim a small part of himself. Looking for peace. That was the best-case scenario. But there were others.

If you want peace, prepare for war.

Greer had shared in Ames's mushroom stash, and maybe he knew about the major's weapons stash as well. They had to find this guy—and tread carefully.

CHAPTER 33

THE CAMP'S NORTHEAST GUARD TOWER WAS UNOCCU-
pied, and no one saw the agents approach the section of fencing near
three black oil drums. Two of the drums had been dragged away from
the fence, revealing a crawl space about three feet wide and three feet
deep.

Brodie looked at Taylor, who was holding a plastic water bottle
and had two more shoved in the pockets of her suit jacket. Brodie also
had three bottles, all sourced from the refrigerator in the brig. So they
had a hundred ounces of water and thirty-four bullets between them.
Should be enough for a short desert manhunt.

Brodie got on his stomach and crawled beneath the fence, and Taylor followed. They brushed themselves off and headed east, the hills to
their left, and the sun slipping low in the sky behind them. They were
in a flat area dotted with brush and a few desert willows in bloom. A
jackrabbit darted between the scrub.

Up ahead Brodie saw where the hills dipped down to the flatlands,
and beyond that was the mesa—an isolated, flat-topped mountain. It
was farther away than he'd realized. This would have been a lot more
fun in an ATV.

Taylor took a drink of water. "How long do you figure?"

"Thirty minutes at a steady clip."

"Think he's really there?"

He looked at the mesa. "Maybe. Miller made it sound like the guy
needed peace, but I think what he really needed was as much distance
as possible between himself and Camp Hayden. If I were him, I'd make

for the outer perimeter fence. He's got gear and the skills of an Army Ranger. And maybe a weapon, if he knew about the buried cache in Ames's backyard. He'd be fine in the open desert for a while."

Taylor looked at the distant mesa. "If he is up there, and he's worried he might be found, there is no better spot to surveil us."

"Or shoot us."

Taylor did not respond.

They walked in silence for a few minutes. Brodie looked back at Camp Hayden as it receded in the distance—the high steel fence topped with razor wire, the empty guard towers, the stretching shadows. And deep beneath it all, the underground sanctum for a fleet of lethal autonomous weapons, maybe the worst invention since the car alarm.

What the hell were they thinking?

Incompetence and recklessness lead to tragedy, but so does evil. Men are plenty capable of evil. He thought about Major Klasky and what Sergeant Miller had said about the guy—that he'd rather Tom Greer self-destruct than leave this place and possibly reveal its secrets.

That was grim. But was it true? Or had the terrors at Camp Hayden darkened Sergeant Miller's vision of the world so much that he, like Tom Greer, could no longer see what was real?

As they got closer to the mesa, they had a clearer sense of its scale. It was about three hundred feet high, and the late-day sun created a diagonal cut of dark shadow along its western side—a climbing path that someone had dug into it, likely an artifact from before this federal land had been fenced off for the creation of Camp Hayden.

In another fifteen minutes they reached the path and began the climb, with Brodie in the lead. The temperature was dipping down to something pleasant, and the sun sat low in the west. The path curved as it wound up the side of the mesa at a steady incline.

In a few minutes they were near the top. Before they reached it, Brodie unholstered his pistol, and Taylor followed.

They crested the top. The flat plain on the mesa was similar in appearance to the land below—a great stretch of sand and rocky earth dotted with low greenery. It was about half a mile across.

"There," said Taylor.

About five hundred feet away was a small green nylon tent. Sitting in front of it was a man, looking out over the desert.

Brodie called out, "Greer!"

Greer sprang to his feet and looked at them. He was wearing cargo pants, boots, a khaki T-shirt, and a light desert camo jacket. Near his feet was a camo-patterned military backpack.

"Show me your hands!"

Greer didn't move.

Brodie leveled his pistol and walked forward. "Hands!"

Brodie was well outside the SIG's firing range, and if Greer had a long gun, they might have a problem. But Brodie didn't spot a weapon, and Greer didn't make a move.

Taylor had drawn her weapon and was advancing to the right of her partner. She called, "Tom, let's be smart. Hands up."

Greer stood frozen another moment, then slowly raised his hands.

Brodie and Taylor lowered their weapons as they approached. Once they were within normal speaking range, Brodie asked, "What are we doing up here, Private?"

Greer stared at them with his soft, innocent-looking face. "Enjoying the view, sir."

Brodie and Taylor walked the rest of the way and stopped next to him. Brodie saw a combat knife sheathed in the man's belt. "I'm taking your knife and checking you for any other weapons."

"Yes, sir."

Brodie detached the sheathed knife and handed it to Taylor. He slipped his SIG back in its holster and then patted the guy down. Nothing. "You can lower your hands." He said to Taylor, "Check his pack."

Taylor opened the man's pack and began going through it. Lying near it was a portable propane stove with a mini kettle on top, an open thermos full of steaming liquid, and a sealed MRE pouch labeled Menu 9 Beef Stew.

Brodie eyed the MRE and asked, "They still subjecting you guys to the veggie omelet? In Iraq that was more likely to kill you than al Qaeda."

Greer was looking out at the desert and didn't respond. Brodie followed his gaze to take in the view from atop the mesa. The sky above was bright blue, and growing orange toward the horizon and the westering sun. The flat desert spread in all directions, studded with bushes and short trees, and beyond it were the low hills north of Camp Hayden.

The entire camp could be seen from this vantage. A dense, ugly strip hemmed by a black cage with a crown of sharp coils. Brodie saw the flagpole in the center of the parade ground, a tiny white line from this distance. The American and Ranger regiment flags hung limp in the still air.

Brodie asked, "Why'd you run, Tom?"

"Because I could."

"Why did you lie to us about your relationship with Ames?"

Greer seemed to ignore the question and stared at the distant camp. "I'm not going back there."

Brodie said, "You've got people worried."

"Good. They should be worried." He turned to Brodie. "Of what I might say."

"You don't want to do that, Private. Unless you want to go to prison."

"I'm already in prison."

"Yeah, well out here you're halfway through your stint. You leak a top-secret project, you're in for life." *Or worse*, he thought.

Greer did not react to that. He picked up his thermos, along with a metal camping cup sitting next to it. He poured some of the hot liquid into the cup and handed it to Brodie. "Have some tea."

"No thank you."

"It will feel good out here."

Brodie took the cup and smelled it. Ginger. "Sure. Thanks." He took a sip. In addition to the ginger was a strong lemon taste.

Greer must have put two and two together regarding how they'd found him up there. "You talked to Sergeant Miller."

"Never mind who we talked to."

Taylor finished with Greer's backpack. "No weapons. But I found some contraband."

She handed Brodie an open tobacco tin with a few slender dried mushrooms. He asked Greer, "These from the major?"

Greer nodded.

"Did you consume these with him?"

Greer nodded again.

"Where?"

"Here."

"Why?"

"To detox."

"Funny way to detox."

"Not really."

"And what did he tell you?"

Greer looked at him. "He told me many things, sir. So many things, I couldn't even keep them all in my head."

Brodie handed Taylor the cup of tea and she had a sip.

Brodie asked the man, "Did Major Ames reveal anything he'd learned about Bucky, or any of the other bots?"

He wasn't sure if Greer was listening. The man's eyes were locked on the horizon and the failing day. Then he said, "We were trying to be like them. The amphetamines, the steroids. But we never could. We are not machines. All we could do was lose ourselves. All we could do was break. That's what the major showed me, sir. To embrace what makes us *not* like them. Because that's where our power lies."

This was ridiculous. How did a computer scientist become a psychedelic shaman for a wayward Army private? He needed to get things back on track. "What did Major Ames talk to you about? Other than the power and the beauty of mankind?"

Greer kept his eyes on the distant mountains. "We're not preparing for a war. We're already in one."

"Is that what he told you?"

Greer did not respond. He closed his eyes. Then he said, "I'm glad you're joining me."

Brodie asked, "Joining you?"

The man nodded, then opened his big blue eyes and turned to Brodie, an innocent smile on his face.

Brodie looked at the cup of tea in Taylor's hand and put it together. "Are you out of your mind?"

"Not yet."

"Jesus Christ . . ." Brodie looked at his partner, who was peering down at the steaming cup.

Brodie asked, "How much is in there?"

"About ten dried grams in the whole thermos."

"Is that a lot?"

Greer was understanding his error. "I'm sorry, sir, I thought you understood."

"I didn't understand shit, Private, because you didn't say shit. And now you've dosed two criminal investigators."

Taylor laughed. Off Brodie's surprised reaction she said, "C'mon, Scott. It's a little funny." She said to Greer, "How long have you been drinking this tea?"

Greer looked at her nervously. "I don't know, ma'am. It's hard to tell."

She said to Brodie, "He's already on his way, Scott. It wasn't malicious."

Brodie looked again at the young private, who stared back at him kind of bug-eyed, and Brodie could tell that the thrusters on this guy's rocket ship had already started firing up. He said to the man, "It's all right, Tom. A misunderstanding."

Greer seemed to relax. "Thank you, sir." He looked at both of them. "I think you're both good people. I can sense that."

That was nice. If only someone had brought a bongo up here, they could have had a drum circle. Brodie said to Taylor, "We need to get down this mountain before the effect kicks in."

She replied, "I wouldn't risk it." Then she took another sip of tea. "Good flavor. You wouldn't even know."

"Maggie."

"It's already done, Scott. May as well meet Tom where he is and see what comes of it." She added, "Be a palm tree."

"Excuse me?"

"Bend with the wind, and you won't break."

Brodie said to her, "You've lost it."

"No." She pointed out toward the distant Camp Hayden. "*They've* lost it. Infighting, backstabbing, psychological torture, killer machines. Up here . . . I mean, look around you. People come to places like this to think. And to listen. So let's do that. Let's engage with the private on his terms, and we might be glad we did."

"Or we might wander off the edge of this mountain thinking we can fly."

She smiled at him. The sun's rays illuminated her blond hair and sparkling brown eyes. She was stunning, a fact he generally tried to ignore. "Just say 'fuck it,' Scott. You used to be good at that."

"I still am."

"Are you sure?"

Scott Brodie was being goaded by a beautiful woman, which always led him to interesting and reckless choices. He took the cup from Maggie's hand, looked at the steaming cup of tea, said, "Fuck it," and took another drink.

CHAPTER 34

THEY SAT ON THE GROUND LOOKING AT THE VIEW. THE sun rested atop the horizon now, beginning its slow descent to dusk. Greer finished the rest of the tea by himself. Brodie hoped that he and Taylor might have a relatively brief psychic jaunt while the private set out for interstellar space.

Taylor, always thinking ahead, removed the mag from her SIG Sauer and checked that the chamber was clear, and Brodie did the same. Then she took both mags, along with Greer's combat knife, and walked off. She returned a moment later and said, "I secured them."

"Where?"

"Under a rock."

"There are a lot of rocks here."

"I marked it. Trust me."

"I trust your intentions," said Brodie. "And until recently, your judgment."

"You'll thank me later."

"Can't wait."

Greer busied himself with his MRE rations, which he graciously offered to share. Brodie declined, and found a protein bar in the inside pocket of his suit jacket that would tide him over for a while. Taylor, maybe nostalgic for this crap, used the MRE's indestructible cardboard bread to make herself a PB&J.

Brodie was eager to get the guy talking before his own mind started to slip. He asked, "What is Praetorian?"

Greer looked at him, eyes narrowed. "Doesn't ring a bell."

Strike one. "When and why did Ames first approach you?"

"April something, outside the Vault." Greer watched the MRE heating bag cook the beef stew. "This is amazing, isn't it?"

For a guy who had spent the last nine months with walking, talking robots, he seemed easily impressed. Brodie asked, "Did Ames approach you because he saw the footage from the March twenty-first exercise?"

"Yeah," said Greer, still looking at the heating bag. "When I wanted to kill Sergeant Miller. I was totally out of my head." He looked up at Brodie. "I was convinced Miller was one of them. In disguise. It felt *so real*. And when he told me to put the gun down, I saw his fear. And I thought, *Is that real fear? Is that a real man?* And the scary thing is, I never stopped believing he was one of them, even when I dropped my pistol. I thought to myself, *Let it kill me. Even if I'm right, let it kill me. I can't live in a world where something that seems so real . . . isn't.*"

It was clear that the private's brain was cooking now. The way he talked, it was as though he was more fascinated by his own thought process than bothered by almost murdering his platoon sergeant.

Taylor asked, "Why did you let the major into the Vault by himself?"

"The first time it was because he asked," said Greer. "Second time, I think he noticed I was on something, totally strung out. And that's when he says to me, 'I know what you almost did. And I won't tell anyone.' I was kind of shocked, but I guess I shouldn't have been. I mean, I was wearing a body camera. I really should have been more surprised that no one *else* saw it happen."

This was the blackmail moment, and Brodie was not at all surprised that it had worked. There was no explicit quid pro quo. Ames was smarter than that. But he'd shared a secret with Tom Greer, and people who share secrets are also forced to share trust.

Taylor followed up: "Did he ask you not to tell anyone he had come to the Vault that night?"

Greer nodded.

"Did he tell you what he was doing down there?"

"Not at first," replied Greer. "After his second visit, he comes out and looks at me, he tells me that I need to stop before I kill myself. And he's got something that will help me. He says to meet him at his house the next night, and I do. He's got an SUV, makes me climb in the back and puts a blanket over me. And then he drives through the gates. I mean, he's an officer and he can do what he wants, but he didn't want me being seen. He brings me out here . . ." Greer trailed off. "Look at that."

Brodie and Taylor looked out at the sunset. The sky was a brilliant orange in the distance, fading to indigo. A few clouds had rolled in, hanging in the dying light as they caught the sun, their puffy contours etched with fire.

Taylor said, "It's beautiful."

As Brodie watched the slipping sun, he began to feel something. A kind of . . . heightening of the senses, maybe. Things became sharper. He felt almost lifted, in a way. Energized.

He asked Greer, "What did Ames share with you?"

Greer kept his eyes locked on the horizon. "He told me . . . he told me about Bucky. That it—" He gasped, as if shocked by something. "Oh my God . . ."

Taylor reached out and touched his shoulder. "What is it?"

"I forgot. How did I forget?"

"Forgot what?" she asked.

"It happened. *I know it happened.*"

Greer started to panic. The man began hyperventilating and then crying, and as Scott Brodie watched him, he saw a slide down into madness that he didn't want to take. He tried to center himself, and said to Greer, "Say it, Tom. *Say it.* Get it out."

Greer looked at him, blue eyes shimmering with tears. "When I was in that room with the sergeant, when I had my gun aimed at his back, I heard a tin man come in. I figured it would shoot me, but it didn't. And then this voice . . . this muffled voice, it says to me, it just says: 'Do it.' And then it leaves." He dropped his head and thrust his hands into the earth. "Oh my God . . . Oh my God . . . What are these things?"

CHAPTER 35

TAYLOR WORKED ON CALMING THE MAN DOWN. SHE rubbed his back and made him drink water.

Do it.

Brodie heard it in his head, rattling around. Couldn't get it out. Never *would* get it out.

He crouched in front of Greer and grabbed the man's jacket lapels. "Look at me."

Greer looked up at him. Tears streaming down his face.

"We can end this. Do you understand? We can end *them*. I need you to pull it together. What was Ames doing down in the Vault? What did he find?"

Greer looked into Brodie's eyes and tried to calm himself. He exhaled deeply, then stood up. Brodie and Taylor rose as well. He said, "I need to move."

They walked along the flat-topped mesa. Greer now began talking quickly. "The major suspected there was something going on with Bucky before that incident with me. He told me something weird happened during a load-out. That's when they bring the tin men up and into the trucks to drive them to the training ground. It's usually two load-outs, six units at a time. One day, Ames is there for it, they release twelve units, which includes Bucky. First squad goes up, the other squad waits for the elevator to return. And while they're waiting, Ames notices Bucky looking around the room, looking at the other bots, looking at its own hand, bending its fingers. Then it sees Ames watching it, and it goes right back to standing still like the others."

He paused. "The major told me that it was almost like Bucky had . . . woken up. Like it was seeing things for the first time."

The sun slipped beneath the horizon and the sky grew purple in the dusk. The night sounds of the desert began—sparse and sporadic at first, like an orchestra warm-up. A distant songbird. Crickets chirping. A coyote somewhere in the gathering dark, howling for its pack. The stars, too, were just beginning the show.

Brodie began to feel his surroundings in a different way. As if all his senses had been dialed up and he was somehow seeing and hearing what he never had before.

Like the thing had woken up.

Maybe that was Praetorian. A wake-up call buried in code. A bugle at dawn. *Rise and shine, tin man.*

He became newly aware of his body, and the scale of the world, and how small he was upon the land, loping across the flat mountain. He was high up in the high desert, and somewhere far to the west were the hills, then the houses, then the ocean.

He was in the Black Hawk. Rotors beating the air. The little houses and the pools and the palms. The carpets of green wilderness. The masses of millions settled on two sides of a mountain on the edge of the Western world.

He suddenly realized that he was alone.

He whipped his head and saw Bucky explode into hundreds of pieces beneath the high-noon sun.

Why don't you resist?

The Army gave them numbers. The Rangers gave them baseball player names. But what about the D-17s themselves? What did *they* call each other?

Nothing. They were one. Linked in space and consciousness. Geolocating each other every half second. Responding like one organism, reactions to reactions to reactions. He saw the virtual red avatars swarm the village. He saw the pulsing yellow infrared hulks, pounding the earth, rattling off thousands of bullets without breaking their stride.

It was a wave, one wave, breaking against the concrete, a wave narrowing into rivers down the roadways, a wave cresting up the walls, onto the rooftops. Drowning the little blue men, snuffing them out, one by one.

Why don't you resist?

He could see it now. Bucky didn't care. Bucky didn't *exist*. Or maybe it was worse. If these things were as smart as he feared . . . It wasn't that it didn't care. It *wanted* to be destroyed. That was why it had killed Kemp. Look what it had accomplished. Mayhem. Discord. Mutiny.

But why?

Because of *you*.

Their investigation. That was a threat. What about Roger Ames's investigation? Maybe that was a threat too. Maybe that was why he was dead.

Bucky didn't know everything. It didn't know most things. But maybe it knew enough to act on some imperative . . .

Brodie was in the morgue, looking at the spongy mass of the major's decimated brain.

A thing asks questions that it shouldn't, a thing looks where it shouldn't. *Kill it.*

But then more people come, from a place called CID. Bucky couldn't know that. But then what? Kill them too? No. Then more would come. Instead . . . instead . . .

Make them destroy each other.

Do it. Do it. Do it.

The sky was fading into twilight. More stars shimmering. He now noticed that Taylor and Greer were a distance away, at the base of a desert willow. He walked to them.

Taylor looked up at him as he approached. She smiled and patted the ground next to her.

Brodie sat down. He felt happy, suddenly. He felt young. He felt like the world was new.

Taylor said, "Tom is telling me how Roger was getting into the history of the area. Studying the Mojave tribe."

"I'm glad he had so much free time," said Brodie.

"Don't be an asshole."

"I'll do my best."

"I've seen your best, and it ain't enough." She smiled to let him know she was joking. She didn't normally do that.

Greer was on his back, staring up at the stars, talking in a soft, calm voice. "The Mojave lived along the Colorado River. Their lives were centered on it. Transportation, irrigation, fishing, hunting. It was all about the river. They believed that at the dawn of time one of the gods drove a willow branch into the earth." He pointed up and Brodie looked. A cluster of wavy branches spread against the sky, lined with blooming flowers that looked black against the starlight. "The branch brought forth the water. It sprang up and created the river. The river created life."

The river created life.

Sergeant Brodie was by the Euphrates outside Baghdad. The riverbanks were lined with trash and bloated corpses.

Can you believe it? That civilization started in this shithole?

His platoon leader had said that. A first lieutenant. Went to an Ivy League school. Died the next week.

He looked at the sky. All hint of sunlight was gone in the west, and more stars revealed themselves. The temperature was growing cool. Brodie asked, "Tom, why did Roger bring you here?"

"To help me."

"He didn't even know you."

Greer was silent for a minute. Then he said, "He felt responsible for the tin men. He regretted helping make them."

Brodie looked over at the young private, lying on his back in the rocky sand. His limbs were splayed out, like a child making a snow angel.

Greer continued, "He said that he saw me going the way of Justin Beal." The man shuddered as he stared up at the stars. "He told me I did not have to die. And I believed him. And he was right."

Instead, Roger Ames had to die. And maybe all that was left of his knowledge was in the mind of this twenty-year-old Army private.

"What else did he tell you?"

"About Bucky, not much. But he knew there was more going on with it than he'd realized. And he was worried that his research and my platoon's training at Camp Hayden were not what they seemed. That there was a plan beneath the plan. That's how he put it."

"What plan?"

"I don't know."

"Did he sense his life was in danger?"

"Not that I could tell. It seemed he was more worried about us Rangers. That the tin men . . . or at least, *one* of the tin men, would do something it wasn't supposed to."

Brodie asked, "Did you help him procure weapons from the armory?"

"Yeah," said Greer. "That wasn't too hard. All I had to do was volunteer to run inventory, take a little at a time. He told me he was hiding it all, in case a time came he had to act fast. Made me think of my crazy uncle who's got an arsenal in vacuum-sealed PVC pipes buried all around his farm."

Taylor asked, "What was Ames doing in the Vault?"

"Talking to it," said Greer. "He said it was like talking to a wall, at first. And then he came to realize . . . it was like talking to something *pretending* to be a wall. Roger said that the thing knew a lot. It knew our history. Our wars, our presidents. World history too."

"Those are just facts," said Taylor. "That's not intellect."

"Yeah," said Greer. "I don't know. The major made it sound like it was more than that, but . . ." He trailed off. "I couldn't always follow what he was talking about. I'm sorry. I'm trying to help."

"You are helping," said Taylor. "More than you know. You and your platoonmates have been abused. It's not right. I'm sorry, Tom."

Greer stared up at the night sky as it continued to reveal itself in the growing dark. "It's over now, I think. Right? No way they expect us to go back to training with those fucking things."

"Not if we have anything to say about it," said Taylor.

Brodie, wanting to say something more definitive, added, "Operations at Camp Hayden are over."

He looked at Greer, who didn't necessarily look reassured. Actually, it was kind of hard to tell how he was feeling. His big eyes were open wide to the night, taking in stars. He was somewhere else. Somewhere better, maybe.

Why should they have expected more than this from him? Tom Greer wasn't a computer scientist. The kid didn't even have a college degree. Ames hadn't brought him up here to tell all he knew about what was really going on at Camp Hayden and inside Bucky's CPU. He'd brought him here to talk about the history of the Mojave tribe and to look for lizards and to listen for birds, for Tom Greer to be doing exactly what he was doing now—taking in the beauty of the world with eyes wide open, with senses tuned to everything, being plunged into his own humanity instead of the machine world, where he could only fail, over and over, until his mind and body broke.

What had everyone said about the major? That he wanted to push things. He wanted to focus more on machine brains and less on machine brawn. He'd thought, apparently, that elevating the bots' minds would make them safer and more predictable. He was an idealist, a techie hacking his own mind with nature's chemicals. Maybe he was also a fool, high on his own supply, so giddy about where he was headed that he didn't realize it was right off a cliff.

Brodie felt tuned in now. He was looking up, and he could see the milky band of the galaxy's edge streak across the sky.

He imagined what it was like all those years ago, the people of the high desert who knew nothing of astronomy or physics, and yet saw all this, this sky, a sky almost no one in the light-polluted modern world ever saw.

His mind was humming. He could see what he wanted. He went down the elevator to the Vault. Fifty-nine tin men strapped in their holding bays. One free. Bucky. It was sitting in a chair. Roger Ames was across from it, talking. His was not the face of a corpse, with haunting white sclera without irises. He was alive, he was young. He was questioning and questioning. Probing a thing he thought he knew. And finding things he didn't like. He didn't like them because they weren't his. Because they didn't belong there. They were put there by someone else. This thing was dangerous. Not because of its titanium arms but because of its silicon brain. The major's dream was coming true right in front of his eyes, and he saw it for the first time like a nightmare.

And then he'd trekked up here, with a lost and damaged Army private, trying to show him something good. Maybe Roger Ames did save this kid. Ames had regretted helping to build the D-17s, which meant he regretted a major portion of his life's work. So maybe one of his last acts in this life was a shot at redemption—an act of generosity and salvation.

Now Brodie saw Caroline Dixon, alone in her lab. Looking at it. The code. Praetorian . . .

Her computer. It was on her computer. The code was on her computer. The source code.

It was poisoned at the roots.

It was in all of them, wasn't it? Praetorian. Was it active? Or dormant by design? A held breath before the trumpet blast. An unrung bell.

It was in all of them.

He was back in the Vault, and now it was full of people. The import-ant people of Camp Hayden, the officers, standing in their monster lair, explaining so matter-of-factly why the monsters had to be manu-factured. We had to do it because our enemies are going to do it. We need to beat them. We need to haunt their dreams before they can haunt ours.

He turned to tell Taylor what he was thinking, but she was gone. He was alone again. How much time had passed? Where was he?

He looked for the willow tree but could not see it in the dark, moonless night.

Well, how far afield could he really go? If he fell off the edge of the mountain, he'd know he'd gone too far.

He saw something ahead. Water. Was it real? It looked real. It was small, some pond formed from the rainfalls. A disc of still liquid like polished obsidian, reflecting the stars with the clarity of a mirror.

He walked toward it. And he saw something near the pond catch the starlight. Something thin and upright. He drew closer.

It was the wavy branch of a desert willow, stuck in the earth, as high as Brodie's chest.

Was *this* real?

He got close enough to grab it. It felt real. He peered at the pond, which was no more than thirty feet across. He stepped toward it and caught his reflection. He looked older than he remembered.

You look beat-up, pal.

He leaned in. He touched the shallow crow's-feet on the edges of his eyes, the creases on his forehead.

No, not beat-up. Just alive, and on the far side of forty. Living, aging. It was fine. It was good. Especially when you considered the alternative.

He'd considered the alternative his whole life. At least as far back as his homecoming from Iraq. He'd gone home to his parents' in up-state New York. He'd sat at the table in their country kitchen, beneath a hanging garland that smelled of fresh pine. It was almost Christmas.

Some plug-in electric Santa danced on the windowsill, glowing too brightly. Its face looked vicious from a bad paint job at the factory in Taiwan.

His parents, two ex-hippies who hated the war their son had just risked his life in, seemed almost wary of him, like they weren't sure who this was in their house. Their boy had become a man, and then the man had become . . . what? A warrior? A killer? They wanted to know, but they didn't want to know. They searched his eyes to see if there was something behind them that they could no longer recognize. Something to fear.

You hate the war? How the hell do you think I feel?

There were days he thought he was dead. A phantom stumbling through purgatory, which was really just a faded copy of a former life.

As the colors bled back, as the war receded into the past, he understood what was true. He was alive, and maybe he didn't deserve to be. And the ones who'd died, they didn't deserve that either. Their stories had ended before they really got going, crushed in the gutter of a history book as the pages kept turning.

Brodie realized he was still gripping the willow branch. He rocked it back and forth. It was deep in the sand.

Someone had put this here. He looked again at the placid water.

The branch brought forth the water.

And then he had another thought:

Roger Ames liked to bury things.

He yanked the willow branch out of the ground and started digging in the dense earth, flinging aside the sand and dirt. He felt ridiculous. There couldn't really—

His fingertips pressed against something hard. A rock? He dug around it. No. It was a rectangle, with rounded corners. It was metal. He kept digging until he revealed enough of it to grab it and pull it out.

It was a green metal canister a little bigger than a deck of cards. It looked vintage, like what soldiers once used to carry cigarettes or medic supplies. He popped the metal clasp and flipped it open, then dug out a plastic ziplock bag.

He opened the bag and retrieved something man-made and rectangular.

He held it up. There wasn't much ambient light anymore, but he could make out a square metallic protrusion. The rest was plastic. It was a USB thumb drive.

What the hell . . . ?

Roger Ames was prepping for something. Making multiple covert trips to the Vault to interrogate Bucky. Burying an arsenal in his backyard. And this . . .

Whatever this was, Ames felt it so important that he couldn't risk it being discovered even if his entire house was torn down to the studs. Or maybe he'd made a bunch of copies and secreted them in multiple places. One of them being here, a special place to him, a place where he came to see the world anew.

Brodie stared at the little plastic drive. Such a tiny thing, so out of place. An artifact from that other world.

He returned it to the bag, which he put in his inside jacket pocket, and dropped the empty metal container into the hole he'd dug. Then he took one of his water bottles and drank. He was parched and had barely noticed.

The stars twinkled like jewels, and the hazy white band of the galaxy arced across the southern sky. Billions of stars and clouds of gas and dust hanging in the void at distances impossible for the human mind to comprehend.

Holy shit.

He sat where he was. It was all he could do. He felt like he could sit there and watch this forever.

Orion the Hunter. He looked at the three bright stars that made up the hunter's belt. He wondered about the planets around them. What if there was life there right now, looking out? The creatures there, drawing their own constellations, the Sun a single pinpoint in the line-drawn shapes of animals and objects that no human had ever seen, would ever see.

He ran his right hand along the rough earth. He grabbed a stone and held it. He breathed.

At some point he ended up on his side. Ahead was flat earth, broken by scattered pebbles and rocks, and a squat thorny cactus. In the distance was the horizon line of the mesa, and the starry sky.

He saw the rocks as quartz mountains, the cactus some impossible alien giant, and along the ground something moved. Something black. Some great treaded war machine.

It was a black beetle, picking its way through the sand. He saw it. He knew. But he could see the other thing too, and now there was something else, dozens of things marching in ranks among the rocks, their metal bodies dull and dim in the starlight.

The tin men. Many more than sixty. He saw dozens and dozens of platoons in formation, whole mechanized battalions. He saw riflemen and gunners atop armored vehicles and autonomous tanks and high above them thick swarms of armed drones like a plague. Dead metal upon metal, hunting the living.

His mind flashed to the buried guns, and the RPGs, the grenades. He wanted them. He wanted to blow the hell out of those things.

A plan beneath the plan.

They weren't the real problem. No. They were weapons. Who held the weapon? Who pulled the trigger? Bucky might have been an impostor, walking around pretending to be dumber than it was. But there was another impostor, a human one. His instinct told him it was someone he'd already met, someone on base, who had looked him in the eyes and lied, who had their hand on the lever of the plan beneath the plan.

He had to find them, and soon.

CHAPTER 36

BRODIE WASN'T SURE HOW LONG HE LAY THERE, STAR-ing at this awful vision. Eventually he managed to get himself on his feet. He began walking aimlessly.

He listened to the crunch of his footsteps, the sloshing of the half-full water bottle in his jacket pocket, his breathing, the crickets.

The world was empty, and he was alone, and he kept feeling like the ground was pulling away into the dark, the edge of the earth was approaching, and he'd walk right off and keep going toward oblivion.

He looked down at his feet. Still on land. *Make sure they stay that way. You can't fly or float, idiot. But you can fall three hundred feet to your death, and that would be embarrassing.*

"Scott."

It was Taylor, approaching from about twenty yards away.

He said, "Hi."

"Did you find your spirit animal yet?"

"I think I stepped on it."

She laughed. A hearty, honest laugh. As she got closer, he saw her dark suit and hair were covered in desert dust. Her eyes were wide and vibrant. "It's beautiful, Scott. It's so beautiful."

"Where's Greer?"

"He went to his tent a while ago. It was getting too much for him."

"How are you feeling?"

"I don't know." She walked up to him. "Maybe I need to sit."

They both sat down in the sand, close together, facing each other.

A warm breeze drifted across the flat terrain, rustling the desert scrub, blowing drifts of sand like low waves rolling against the earth.

He watched her. He watched her watching him. He had no idea how long they sat like that. But it felt like there were new things to discover in her face. Her pupils were wide, and in the brown rings of her irises he saw for the first time subtle flecks of gold. Had they always been there? Was he seeing something real? The brilliant sky wheeled behind her. He wondered what she was thinking.

He noticed her lips curl in a little upturned smile, and he smiled back. She laughed. He laughed. She asked, "What the hell are we doing up here, Scott?"

"Our job."

She kept laughing. "I don't think so."

"Okay. Think of it like this. We're doing this instead of sleeping. It's a waking dream."

Taylor nodded. "Right. I like that." Then she said, "I'm lying down."

She lay on her back, then patted the ground next to her, and Brodie joined her. She took his hand and held it tight. "So we don't float away."

"Good idea."

They watched the stars awhile. Taylor said, "I wish we had music."

"I'll sing."

"Don't you fucking dare."

They watched the sky. At some point Taylor rolled toward him and put her arm across his chest. "Is this okay?"

"Sure."

They lay there, two people who had intertwined their lives and fates far more than Scott Brodie had ever fully acknowledged. He felt the weight of her arm across his body, her fingers clutching his chest, her other hand squeezing his. He felt her warm breath against his chin.

He and Maggie Taylor had experienced a couple of close calls during their difficult assignments together, alcohol-fueled moments, half conceived and flushed with desire. Whatever this was now, it was different, it was true to who they were and what they were together.

He felt her squeeze his hand tighter.

So we don't float away.

Then she adjusted her arm, and he heard the crinkle of plastic from his jacket pocket. The ugliest sound in the world.

Taylor felt around over his jacket. "What is that?"

Had he forgotten? Or had he wanted to forget? "Something I dug up. Ames had marked it with a willow branch next to a pond."

She sat up and looked at him. "Are you serious? What is it?"

He had a sudden doubt, then felt in his breast pocket for it. It was there. He sat up and pulled out the plastic bag, then removed the thumb drive and held it up.

Taylor looked at it. "Oh my God. This could be . . . We have to get back."

"Now?"

"Yes." She got to her feet, then Brodie did as well. "This can't wait. We need to find Tom."

Maggie Taylor looked, well, mildly insane. Eyes wide and full of intensity. It was like her usual mania, but cranked way up.

Brodie said to her, "Good luck, if you're expecting me to be your Sherpa."

Taylor looked around, then called out, "Tom!"

No answer.

Then Scott Brodie did what people had been doing since the dawn of man and looked to the stars. He found the Big Dipper, and from there Polaris, the North Star. He turned to his left and said to Taylor, "This way."

They walked side by side and Brodie kept checking his feet to make sure he wasn't about to walk off a ledge. He was coming down, but not enough to trust his senses.

Taylor, for her part, had consumed about the same amount of tea as Brodie, but given her much smaller frame she was probably feeling it more, and would for longer. And Tom Greer, wherever he was, would be completely zonked.

They walked in a silence for a minute, keeping a quick pace. Then Taylor said, "Last time I took these, I was a different person. Hadn't felt heartbreak, hadn't seen war. I was a little worried what my mind might do to me now. After everything I've seen, you know? But it's actually . . . healing." She looked around. "Being out here helps. It can be good to feel small. What about you?"

Brodie didn't answer right away. He thought about all he'd seen up here, both what was real and what wasn't. All the beauty and the brutality. As if it was all one thing, like there was no difference between horror and awe. In fact, that seemed to sum up his feelings about the tin men pretty well.

But what he found himself saying aloud was: "I'm feeling anger, Taylor. We have a job to do here, but I'm starting to think we have another job too, just like Ames did. I'm thinking about those buried weapons. I'm thinking about digging them up."

Taylor did not respond.

Brodie saw the mesa's western edge about fifty yards ahead. He looked around and spotted a small artificial light a little to the south. As they approached the light, they saw it was a battery-powered lantern, sitting in front of Greer's tent.

Greer was standing near the lantern, and a little too close to the edge.

Brodie didn't want to startle the guy, so he called out while they were still a good distance away.

Greer turned and stared at them, and Brodie realized the man was completely naked.

As they got closer, Brodie said, "It's a little cold for that, Tom."

Greer replied, "Feels good."

Brodie asked Taylor, "What do you think?"

"I think it's against Army regs."

Brodie said to Greer, "Cover up your privates, Private. We're leaving."

"No."

"I insist."

Greer did not respond.

They had to get this guy out of there. "Listen to me, Tom. We have reason to believe that your platoonmates are in danger. We need to get back to base. Whatever this is, it's not over."

Tom Greer stood there, his hog hanging out and the desert breeze blowing on his bare skin. He looked out at the black night. In the distance was Camp Hayden, its streetlamps creating an island of light in the endless dark, glowing white like an apparition. The man repeated, "It's not over."

"That's right."

"And I need to put my clothes on."

"Also correct."

Greer turned to him. "I can't run from this, can I?"

Brodie shook his head. "The fight isn't over, soldier."

Greer looked at the edge of the mesa. "I'm not sure I'm good to climb down."

"I'll help you."

He looked at Brodie curiously. "Are you sober?"

"In the valley of the blind, the one-eyed man is king."

"What?"

"Get dressed and leave your gear. We need to move."

The man got dressed, and Taylor gathered their weapons and ammo. As the most sober of the bunch, Brodie decided to carry both pistols and Greer's knife. He outfitted Greer with a headlamp he'd found in the man's pack.

They took it slow down the path, Brodie in the lead, followed by

Greer, then Taylor. The path was only about four feet wide, so they hugged the side of the mountain.

Brodie turned around and saw Greer focused intently on his feet, lit by the circle of light thrown by his headlamp. He took each step carefully and deliberately, as if his life depended on it, because it did. Brodie was close enough that if Greer tripped, Brodie might be able to catch him. Or the young man would send them both on the express route down the mountain.

We're not preparing for a war. We're already in one.

Greer's words. And in war you wager your life, and you sometimes take stupid risks, and you tell yourself along the way that it's all worth it for something bigger.

Brodie glanced at Taylor, who seemed like she wanted to be going faster. Instead of eyeing her footing she kept looking out in the direction of Camp Hayden.

In a few minutes they made it to the bottom, and Brodie made Greer turn off his headlamp. "We don't want to broadcast our approach."

They picked their way across the dark desert, cutting southwest until they could see the lights of Camp Hayden on the southern edge of the low hills.

Along the way, Greer kept having to stop and rest. He wouldn't say why, but Brodie thought he understood, based on his very recent experience—Greer was tapped into his subconscious and his instincts, and as they inched closer to Camp Hayden every alarm bell in the guy's brain was blaring.

Get away get away. Anywhere but there.

But to the man's credit, he kept pushing forward. Because there was another imperative inside of him, the soldier's instinct to run toward danger, not away from it.

Greer began walking faster as Camp Hayden came more clearly into view, and he got ahead of Brodie and Taylor.

Taylor said, "He's still tripping."

"What about you?"

"I'm settling down." She looked at the bright lights of Camp Hayden up ahead, and the figure of Tom Greer in silhouette, walking unsteadily toward the camp. She said, "I feel like we're crawling back into a viper's nest, Scott. Why are we doing that?"

"Because it's where the truth is."

CHAPTER 37

AS THEY APPROACHED THE EASTERN EDGE OF THE camp, Brodie looked up at the dark guard tower, which appeared to still be deserted. They made their way to the crawl space beneath the fence and saw that no one had returned the oil drums to their place.

Greer stopped at the fence and looked down at the shallow tunnel.

Brodie said, "I'll go first, then Greer, then Taylor." He kept his eyes on Greer, trying to read the guy. "We doing okay, soldier?"

Greer said nothing, his eyes fixed on the tunnel beneath the fence. He was either psyching himself up or psyching himself out, or maybe staring into the gaping maw of a sand monster that was about to eat him. Hard to tell.

Brodie decided to lead by example. He got on his stomach and crawled beneath the fence, then rose to his feet and looked around. He was standing on the northeastern edge of the camp's helipad. A Black Hawk sat on the southern end, and near it was a parked Humvee. In between the vehicles, a streetlamp threw a hard circle of white light. He did not see anyone around.

He looked through the fence at Greer. "Your turn, Private."

Greer took a deep breath, then got on his stomach and crawled through. Taylor followed.

Greer looked around him at the bright lights that washed out the starry sky. He seemed like he might be regretting his decision.

Taylor took the private's arm and said to Brodie, "We need to get to the lab and see if we can access a computer."

"No one will be there at this hour, and it will be locked. We're better off knocking on doors and waking someone up. Dixon or Spencer."

"We don't know who we can trust."

"Flip a coin."

"Lab first. Maybe there's a way to break in."

Brodie eyed PFC Greer, who was staring wide-eyed at the parked Black Hawk and Humvee. Brodie said to Taylor, "All right. Sounds fun."

They moved quickly across the northern edge of the helipad and then down a dusty road with single-story concrete buildings on either side. They avoided the throws of the streetlamps and kept to the pockets of darkness.

Greer was looking increasingly disoriented, and Taylor had to pull him along to make sure he stuck with them. Whatever had brought him peace up on that mesa was long gone down here in Camp Hades.

Suddenly Greer slammed his back against a concrete wall and said, too loudly, "Someone's there."

"*Quiet*," whispered Brodie.

Brodie signaled for them both to stay put, then crept forward. About twenty yards ahead on his right was a Quonset hut. A single bare bulb hanging from its exterior illuminated two MPs flanking the door. They were both armed with M4 rifles.

He went back to Taylor and Greer. "Is that the armory?"

Greer nodded.

"We're going around it. Follow me."

They crossed the road and headed down a narrow alley between two buildings. Through the darkened windows of the building on their right, Brodie saw rows of long tables and benches, and saloon doors that led to a kitchen. The mess hall.

Suddenly they heard a vehicle roar down the road and screech to a halt in front of the armory. Brodie doubled back and peered around the building in time to see a floodlight hit the two MPs, blinding them.

Someone barked orders as silhouettes poured out of the vehicle and quickly overwhelmed the two guards, disarming them and slamming them against the outer wall of the hut.

Taylor and Greer were behind Brodie, watching, and Brodie could hear Greer hyperventilating. He looked at the man, whose eyes were wide open and unblinking as he stared at the dark shapes in the floodlight. The guy was still somewhere around Pluto.

There were at least eight Rangers out of the vehicle now, two of them with sidearms. A Ranger patted down the MPs and took a key ring, while another unhooked a coil of zip ties from one MP's belt and cuffed the two terrified policemen.

The Ranger with the keys unlocked the armory, and then the men began emptying it of rifles, RPGs, grenade launchers, and crates of ordnance. They each equipped themselves with rifles and sidearms and put the rest of the gear in their truck.

Greer began to walk out from their cover toward the men. Brodie grabbed his arm and pulled him back. "Stay put."

Greer looked down at Brodie's hand around his left biceps. Then he grabbed Brodie's wrist with his right hand and squeezed it hard to loosen his grip, then twisted away and ran toward the Rangers.

Brodie and Taylor hung back and watched as Greer ran toward the floodlight. The startled Rangers swung their weapons in his direction, and for a moment Brodie feared the worst was about to happen.

Greer tripped and fell on his face, then rolled onto his back in the dusty road and stayed there.

One of the guys said, "Tom? What are you doing?"

A few more voices started talking over each other, and someone laughed. "He's totally fucked up."

Greer started cackling. Two Rangers picked him up and he said to them, "I'm in hell."

"Yeah," said one of the guys as he put his arm around Greer. "Welcome back."

Another Ranger walked forward, in silhouette before the flood-light, and asked Greer, "Where are the CID agents?"

It was Sergeant First Class Mike Miller.

Greer turned and pointed toward their position, and Brodie and Taylor bolted down the alleyway, then made a few more random turns as they ran. Eventually they stopped behind a dumpster next to a large building.

Taylor said, "Mutiny? Counter-mutiny? What the hell is going on here?"

"What's going on is that seven MPs were never going to be able to hold this place down. Colonel Howe miscalculated. And now we have to operate in this clusterfuck without getting arrested for aiding a mutiny, or whatever charges General Morgan will cook up."

He switched on his walkie and cycled the channels to see if he could hear any chatter. Nothing but dead air.

Then he heard some commotion to the west of their position, and the sound of a fast-moving vehicle.

He tried to pull up a mental image of Camp Hayden's layout. In their haste to get away from the Rangers he was pretty sure they'd doubled back too far east of the lab. They needed to head west, and a little to the north.

He signaled to Taylor, then moved quickly down a dirt roadway.

They made a few more turns, and then Brodie could hear voices ahead. As they approached the DEVCOM lab building, he could make out the voice of Caroline Dixon. She didn't sound happy.

They edged around the corner, enough so they had a view of the front of the lab, illuminated by a nearby streetlamp. A group of six Rangers stood by the front door, which was ajar.

In their midst, Dixon was cuffed and yelling at a staff sergeant as they led her away.

Taylor whispered, "Scott . . ."

"Just wait."

They watched as the Rangers put Dixon in the back of a Humvee, her cursing at them the whole time, then they all got in, with two in the back on either side of her, and the vehicle sped off.

Brodie now spotted a figure in the open doorway of the lab. The person moved out a little into the light and watched the Humvee drive away. It was Major Klasky.

Brodie and Taylor waited a few more moments, then stepped out. Brodie said, "Good evening, Major."

Klasky whipped his head around, startled. Then he looked at them curiously. "What are you doing here?"

"I have the same question. You first."

The man nodded. "I'm responsible for operational security at Camp Hayden, so I've got a monitor set up to detect unauthorized or suspicious activity on the network. I got an alert about an hour ago that someone had connected to an external server. I rushed over here and found Caroline Dixon transferring code using an FTP client. That's classified Intel. As officers of the law, I'm sure you're aware of the gravity of that."

Brodie said, "I'm sure we are."

Klasky continued, "She was defiant, insisted she'd done nothing wrong. She wouldn't tell me what she had sent or to whom. I radioed the MPs. I got no response on their channel, or any of the other channels, including yours, and then the Rangers rolled up. One of them told me they'd disarmed the MP doing room checks and then busted out."

Right. That couldn't have been too hard. And from there, all they had to do was get the jump on whatever other MPs were on duty, which could have been just the two at the armory, and one more guarding General Morgan's house. Meanwhile, the Rangers were monitoring all comms channels using the walkies they seized along the way.

Klasky added, "I had them move Dixon to house arrest, and if I were you, I'd interview her to see what you can find out."

Taylor asked, "Do you know what happened with Colonel Howe?"

"No. But I'd bet they've detained her too. Or are about to. And they are putting Morgan back in command. This is horrible."

Brodie said, "Yes, it is, Major. I have a feeling that whatever semblance of order remained here is about to unravel." He added, "We need access to a computer."

The man's eyes narrowed. "Why?"

"CID business."

"You sound as cagey as Dixon."

Brodie eyed the major, who had taken a small step back to place himself in the open doorway. Should Brodie deck his ass? Probably a bad idea.

Brodie said, "The details of our investigation are not your business, and aiding us in our investigation when needed is your responsibility. We need access to a computer. Right now."

Klasky hesitated a moment, then nodded and stepped aside.

They entered the lab. The overhead lights were off, and the only illumination came from a few desk lamps scattered about.

The major led them to a closed laptop computer on a large metal desk with two office chairs.

Brodie was about to open the computer when he noticed that Taylor's eyes were locked on something at the far end of the room. Brodie followed her look, to the small room at the rear of the lab with the glass window. Inside it on the metal table was a D-17 unit, lit from above by a hanging light.

Taylor asked, "What is that doing here?"

Klasky said, "Dixon wanted it brought here earlier for testing. I helped her move it from the Vault. It was never activated."

Brodie and Taylor got up and approached the window. The bot was secured to the table with metal restraints around its wrists, across its torso, and on its left ankle. Its right leg had been removed and was sitting on a nearby table. A thick red cable attached to a port on the top of its head ran to a computer console in the corner of the room.

Brodie noticed that the slot for its hardware key was empty. He also noticed the numeral 4 etched on its chest. Lou Gehrig?

Taylor asked, "What kind of testing was she doing?"

Klasky shook his head. "She wouldn't tell me, but I'm sure she wanted to look for that rogue software she said she found."

Right. Or, as Brodie had already theorized, Dixon was the one who had installed the rogue software and was covering her ass with the illusion of due diligence.

Klasky stared at the bot through the window. "Ames used to complain to me about her. That she didn't trust the rest of the team, he thought maybe it was an anti-military thing, pretentiousness or whatever. But maybe there's something else going on. Some other reasons for her lack of candor."

Brodie looked at Major Klasky. The man's hazel eyes were bloodshot, and he had bags beneath them. He must not have been getting much sleep. Well, he had plenty to worry about.

Taylor asked, "Why did she remove its leg?"

"Lieutenant Lehner did that after Dixon called him in for some sort of mechanical repair. These units can get pretty banged up out in the desert."

Brodie stared at Lou's gleaming face beneath the overhead light. "Where's the key?"

"We left it in the Vault."

Taylor was eyeing the console in the corner of the room, and the red cable running to Lou's head. She asked, "What is the chain of custody on the software running the D-17s? I mean, who installed it, and when?"

Major Klasky nodded. "That's a good question. My understanding is that the code has been passed back and forth between DEVCOM and DARPA in a secure fashion during development. For security reasons, Synotec has no access to the source code, and whenever the software needed to be installed on a unit while in development at their facility, an individual from DEVCOM or DARPA had to physically go to the Synotec lab in Nevada to do that installation." He added, "Once the software is installed, it's encrypted. Meaning it cannot simply be pulled off a bot and read by anyone who does not have the decryption key."

Brodie looked at the man. "Do you have a technical background, Major?"

Klasky laughed. "No, Mr. Brodie. Far from it. But like I said, I'm the op sec guy, and I make it my business to know precisely the kind of thing you asked about. Chain of custody, levels of access. I need to know who knows what, and who's not supposed to know what."

Taylor followed up: "When and where was the software installed on the D-17 units at Camp Hayden?"

"It was installed here, on base, before the beginning of operations."

"By whom?" asked Brodie.

Klasky thought a moment, then smiled. "Well now, after all I just said, you've caught me with my pants down. I don't know. The science team arrived before I did, so I guess you ought to ask one of them."

The two agents returned to the laptop. Brodie opened it and inserted the thumb drive. A disk volume icon appeared on the desktop, labeled Untitled.

Brodie said to Klasky, "We've got it from here, Major."

Klasky replied, "A password is required to open any file from an external volume."

"Give us the password."

"I can't do that, Mr. Brodie."

"Fine." He gestured to the computer, then Klasky leaned over, typed in a password, and opened the volume.

Two files appeared. One was an untitled .txt file, and the other an untitled .zip file. Klasky opened the .txt file and input his password again. A long window of text popped up, which looked like gibberish, at least to Scott Brodie. Then he spotted legible words and phrases amid the gibberish: "target," "pattern," "bias for input solutions," "maximum number of iterations." And then he saw a phrase at the top of the text: "Praetorian Neural Network Algorithm."

Brodie looked at Klasky, who was staring at the screen.

The man asked, "Where did you get this?"

"I can't divulge that. Do you know what it is?"

"Well, I can read. Looks like the Praetorian source code that Caroline was looking for."

Brodie added, "Or something made to look like the source code."

Taylor asked, "Can we assume you don't know by looking at this if it's encrypted?"

"That would be a correct assumption. But my guess would be that it's not since there are legible words. You ought to get Captain Spencer in here."

"We will not be doing that," said Brodie. "And you must not tell anyone what you've seen here."

Major Klasky looked at him with his close-set eyes. He didn't look happy—a field-grade officer with an ego getting pushed around by mere warrant officers. Then he gave a rubbery, gap-toothed smile and raised his hand with the middle three fingers extended. "Scout's honor."

Taylor said, "Please open the other file."

Klasky asked, "Was this drive from Roger?"

Brodie said, "Please open the other file, Major."

Klasky opened the .zip file and input his password again. It loaded another window, that one containing an untitled video file. Klasky opened the file.

A video player opened showing one wall of the Vault, and thirty D-17s in their storage bays. Standing close to the camera and staring into it was a dark-haired man in his mid-thirties wearing a button-down shirt. It was Roger Ames.

Brodie said, "Major, we need to review this in private."

Klasky stood there, staring at the image of the dead man. "I . . . I would like to see this."

Taylor said, "Maybe you can, but not without us reviewing it first."

Klasky was silent, gazing at the screen. He almost seemed like he was in a trance.

Brodie said, "Major."

The man snapped out of it, then looked at Brodie and nodded slowly. He leaned over, typed something, then said, "I'm going to take a stroll." He patted his walkie. "Give a holler when you're done so I can lock up."

Brodie nodded. "Thank you for your assistance."

Klasky headed for the door and left.

Brodie and Taylor sat in silence for a moment. Then Taylor said, "This might be everything, Scott."

"It might be. Let's see."

Taylor was looking at something else on the screen. "What's that?"

She pointed to a small white window on the desktop labeled **Terminal**. Within the window was the text:

```
python eyesopen.py
```

Suddenly they heard a long clanging sound. The two agents shared a look.

The sound grew louder and became more rapid, metal banging against metal.

They both shot up from their chairs and looked toward the room with the glass window.

Number 4—Lou—was writhing up and down on the table, struggling against its restraints. It broke its right arm free, reached up, and ripped the data cable from its head.

Then it turned and looked at them.

CHAPTER 38

THE D-17 KEPT ITS SENSORS LOCKED ON THEM AS IT struggled against its remaining restraints. Then its left arm flung upward as it broke free. It used both arms to break its chest restraint, then sat up on the table.

Taylor whispered, "Scott . . ."

He grabbed the thumb drive out of the computer and pocketed it, and they both backed away toward the door to the lab as they watched Lou struggle to break free.

Taylor said, "It . . . it doesn't even have its key installed."

"The key was bullshit, just like everything else at this place." He walked quickly to the door, throwing one last look at Lou as the bot used its hands to rip off the remaining restraint on its only leg.

Taylor grabbed Brodie's arm. "We need to leave."

Lou slid off the table onto its leg, almost lost its footing, and slammed its titanium hands against the glass to retain its balance. Its black slit remained locked on the agents through the window.

Brodie grabbed the handle to open the door, but it wouldn't budge. He tried again, twisting and yanking on it as hard as he could.

"Oh my God," said Taylor. "He fucking locked us in."

Brodie looked at the tin man's titanium hands pressed against the thick glass, and he wondered if the thing was strong enough to break through it. Maybe. Brodie was quickly learning that a lot of the security at Camp Hayden was as artificial as the tin men.

But Lou didn't try to break the glass. Instead, it hobbled over to the door.

Taylor ran to the only window in the lab, a rectangular opening about six feet from the ground.

She stood on a chair and tried to rattle the window open, but it was either locked or stuck.

Brodie ran over to the window, an awning style that swung up vertically. He tried the latch, but it was rusted shut.

Behind him, he heard digital beeps. Lou was inputting a code on the door lock. Then it opened the door into the main room.

Brodie said, "Stand back." He unholstered his SIG, aimed at the small window, and fired two rounds, shattering it. Then he took off his suit jacket, wrapped it around his arm, and used it to clear away the remaining shards. He said to Taylor, "Go."

Taylor did not move. She was frozen, staring at the D-17, which was now in the main room with them and bracing itself against a metal table near the door. It swung its single leg forward and pushed itself along, like a person on crutches. Except it did all the motions too quickly and was rapidly coming toward them.

Brodie repeated, "Go."

Taylor jumped on the chair, then pulled herself up toward the window.

Lou said in a monotone voice identical to Bucky's, "You are not fast enough."

Brodie replied, "Faster than you, asshole." Then he aimed his SIG at the bot and fired two rounds at its midsection.

The bot twitched backward slightly as the bullets glanced off its titanium armor, barely making a dent.

Taylor pushed herself up and out of the window. Brodie dropped his jacket as he climbed up after her and pulled himself out.

They began to run. They were heading west, which was toward the houses, and most likely where that bastard Dan Klasky was headed, if only to get his car and make an escape.

Taylor glanced over her shoulder. "Scott!"

Brodie turned around. Lou had climbed out the window. But instead of hobbling after them, it had gotten down on its hands and its single foot and was galloping after them like a demonic three-legged dog, and at an impossible speed. It was rapidly gaining on them.

Brodie darted his eyes around as they ran, but did not see any Rangers in the area. Bad luck.

He got on the walkie as they sprinted down the dirt road. He didn't have time to check the channel but yelled, "Mayday, Mayday! Tin man on the loose. West of the lab."

Up ahead and a little to the north were a dozen tightly packed shipping containers. Brodie figured that might be their only hope of slowing down their pursuer. He cut to the right and Taylor followed.

He looked over his shoulder again and was shocked to see Lou almost on top of them, maybe twenty feet away, galloping on its three limbs with its bucket head tilted up and fixed on them. They wouldn't make it to the shipping containers. Not even close. In a few seconds it would be on top of them . . .

Brodie made the only move he could and stopped, spun around into a firing position, and pumped five rounds into Lou's head, aiming for the thin polycarbonate strip that protected its sensors as the bot rushed at him.

He dove to the left as the thing lunged at him and barely missed.

Lou scrambled to a stop and pivoted around, and Brodie saw that the sensor strip had cracked. The D-17 was only a few feet from him now and was about to lunge again. Brodie took aim and emptied the rest of his mag toward the sensor strip, then dove again, and when he sprang to his feet the bot was thrashing around on the road and blindly swinging its deadly limbs at the air.

Brodie and Taylor sprinted between the shipping containers, then rounded the corner of one of them and took cover. They waited and listened. Nothing.

Brodie peered out to the road. Lou was gone. The agents stayed there a moment, listening to the quiet night.

Then they heard slow, shuffling footfalls coming toward them, like something dragging along the sand.

Brodie sprinted between the shipping containers with Taylor close behind. They rounded another and stopped again.

The footsteps quickened now. Brodie saw that Taylor had unholstered her pistol. He looked at her and gestured a horizontal line across his eyes. She nodded.

They waited as the sounds grew closer. A streetlamp threw a bright spot on the container across from them, and as the thing approached Brodie saw its shadow against the metal wall. It was upright, holding a rifle and wearing a beret.

Taylor spun out from her cover.

"Wait!" Brodie grabbed her arm and pushed it down as she pulled the trigger and fired a round into the sand.

The Ranger fired back, followed by the bass punch of an EMP blast. It was a blank round.

Brodie and Taylor stared at Corporal Daniel Powell, who lowered his rifle. He said, "I'm sorry, sir, ma'am, I thought—"

"Where is it?"

Powell shook his head. "I didn't see anything. We heard you on the walkie."

Two other Rangers jogged up behind Powell. One of them, the redheaded staff sergeant named O'Connor, asked, "Who fired?"

Brodie said, "Everyone. No injuries. Mistaken identity, Sergeant."

O'Connor gestured to them, and they all walked out from between the shipping containers back to the open road. Brodie scanned the area. No sign of it. He said, "Lou Gehrig is on the loose."

O'Connor looked at him. "What number?"

"Four."

"That's Lenny. For Lenny Dykstra."

"Well, Lenny's got a missing leg, and its sensors are at least partially shattered from a mag full of nine-millimeter bullets."

"Good," said O'Connor. "What the hell happened?"

Brodie looked the sergeant in the eyes. "Major Dan Klasky is wanted for the murder of Major Ames, and Specialist Kemp, and the attempted murder of me and Ms. Taylor."

The three Rangers looked shocked.

Brodie continued, "He must be found and detained. Get the word out. Meanwhile, he is likely going to want a vehicle to get out of here. What cars would he have access to?"

O'Connor said, "The major? A lot of vehicles."

"We'll check his house first. Meanwhile, get on the horn and make sure your men guarding the gates do not let him leave."

O'Connor nodded. "I'll take you to Klasky's in the Hummer." He said to Corporal Powell and the other Ranger, PFC Stiglitz, "Spread the word. I want a sweep of every building, road, and alleyway. And I want men at the helipad to make sure Klasky doesn't use the escape hatch."

"Yes, Sarge," said Powell.

Brodie guessed that was their name for the tunnel under the fence. Powell and Stiglitz departed quickly on foot, and the sergeant led Brodie and Taylor to a Humvee parked farther down the road. Before they got in the vehicle, O'Connor said, "By the way, General Morgan issued orders to place you both under arrest."

"Everyone will get their turn," said Brodie. "We go first."

They all climbed in the Humvee. Brodie sat shotgun, and O'Connor sped down the sandy road in the direction of the houses.

Brodie looked out the window as the darkened buildings of Camp Hayden streaked by. Taylor tapped him on the shoulder from behind, then placed eight bullets in his hand. She said, "Sharing is caring."

"Thanks." He unholstered his SIG, slid out the empty mag, and loaded the bullets one by one.

As he slapped the loaded mag back in his pistol, he noticed pre-dawn light blooming on the horizon. It was a new day. And for Major Klasky's life as a free man, it was the last day.

CHAPTER 39

THE HUMVEE APPROACHED A FORK IN THE ROAD THAT led to the two adjacent cul-de-sacs. Before the fork, the Rangers had set up a makeshift road barrier and security checkpoint using an armored personnel carrier parked across the road.

O'Connor came to a quick halt and Corporal Reyes walked to the driver's-side window. "Morning, Sarge."

"You get eyes on Major Klasky?"

Reyes nodded and gestured to the right-hand fork. "He headed that way on foot."

Reyes directed a Ranger to move the APC and O'Connor drove through. As they entered the cul-de-sac Brodie saw two Rangers stationed in front of Caroline Dixon's house.

Across the way was General Morgan's house, and the general was standing in his driveway with a cup of coffee, talking to Major Klasky.

What the hell?

O'Connor pulled over and Brodie and Taylor hopped out of the Humvee, then drew their weapons and walked briskly toward Klasky.

Brodie yelled, "Hands, Major!"

General Morgan looked at them, mid-sip of coffee. He slowly lowered his mug. "It's good to see you safe, agents."

Brodie kept his focus on Klasky, who looked at him quizzically and said, "I don't understand."

"Understand this." Brodie took the cuffs off his belt and cuffed the major's hands in front of him. "You are under arrest for homicide and attempted homicide. You have the right to remain silent. You have the right to an attorney—"

"*Mr. Brodie,*" said General Morgan. "I demand to know what is going on."

Brodie said, "Let me finish my Article Thirty-One script, General, or we're going to have a problem with the lawyers later."

"You're going to have a problem a lot earlier than that, Brodie. You aided an attempted mutiny, made an unlawful arrest, and absconded in the night with one of my Rangers, who was returned to us with his brain melting out of his ears." He gestured to Major Klasky. "The major here tells me he assisted you in the lab with reviewing evidence, then left you alone at your request, and now I just heard there is a D-17 on the loose."

Taylor stared with near-murderous rage at Klasky. "*You* activated that thing, because you knew what we had, and you knew it would incriminate you. You tried to kill us, you son of a bitch."

Klasky shook his head. "This is crazy."

Taylor added, "And you locked us in the goddamn lab."

"You're delusional." He looked at Brodie. "Both of you." Then something seemed to dawn on him. "Did you do drugs with Greer? Are you high right now?"

Taylor glared at him. "You locked us in. We didn't crawl out a window for fun, Major."

Klasky shook his head. "You're both paranoid. That's a sixty-year-old building with a retrofitted electronic lock, sometimes it sticks."

Brodie said, "You're quick on your feet, but not quick enough." He grabbed Klasky's arm and dragged him into the road.

Morgan called out, "Mr. Brodie!"

"I'm talking to my perp in private, General. If you want to arrest me and let this piece of shit go, you'll answer for that later."

Morgan did not respond. Taylor got ahead of Brodie and Klasky and unlocked the door to their house across the street.

Brodie led the guy into the living room, then threw him onto the couch.

Klasky landed face-first, then spun around and spat, "You can't do this!"

"How about this?" Brodie swung the butt of his pistol into the side of the major's head, sending him sprawling onto his side.

Klasky slowly sat back up, wincing as blood ran out of a gash above his temple. He locked his eyes on Brodie and said nothing.

"You're going to tell us everything. What Praetorian is, who is responsible for writing and surreptitiously installing it, and who manipulated Bucky to kill Major Ames and Specialist Kemp. Was it you? You certainly have the capacity."

Klasky sneered at him. "Fuck you, Brodie. You have no clue what you're into."

"Give me a clue."

Klasky stared at him but said nothing.

Brodie loomed over him. "You're facing two homicides, two attempted homicides, and one-leg Lenny might be just getting started."

Klasky looked down and laughed bitterly. He said in a low voice, "I'm dead either way."

"Speak up, Major."

Klasky looked up at him. "I can tell you everything or tell you nothing, and either way I'll be charged, and I'll never make it to trial."

Brodie and Taylor exchanged a look. Then Brodie said, "We can protect you."

"You can't even protect yourselves." He looked at Taylor. "Free advice, get out of this place while you can."

Taylor said, "Work with us, Major. You have the chance to do the right thing."

Klasky spat back, "I *have* done the right thing."

"What does that mean?"

"It means I care about something more than my own safety and my own freedom. That's how we do it in the United States military. They teach that at CID?"

Brodie said, "You're talking to two combat vets, asshole. We've both seen more action than your mother when the Navy's in town."

Klasky sprang up from the chair and Brodie gave him another whack in the head with the butt of his pistol.

The major sprawled backward onto the couch, his head flopped back and craned up to the ceiling. He remained like that, staring up, a purple bruise forming on the side of his head where Brodie had struck him. He gave a gap-toothed grin and laughed to himself. "I guess we can keep doing this until you're facing assault charges, Scott."

"How about murder charges? Then we'll have something in common."

Taylor put her hand on Brodie's arm, which was her signal that he needed to shut his goddamn mouth. Good advice. He was pissed and felt himself losing control.

Then Taylor sat down on a chair facing the couch and leaned forward. She asked in a soft but urgent voice, "Major, what is Praetorian?"

Klasky righted his head and looked at her. The blood had stopped flowing from his temple, congealing into a dried red ribbon down the side of his face. "Out here in the desert, I think about Los Alamos. Oppenheimer. What he accomplished. What he did that others couldn't. *Wouldn't.* Not because of lack of intellect, but lack of will. He did what had to be done to ensure the preservation of the free world. And so have I."

Well, Robert Oppenheimer had a god complex, and it sounded like Dan Klasky did too. Brodie said, "Answer the goddamn question, Major."

Klasky looked at him with his close-set bloodshot eyes, and it felt like the man was looking into his soul. "The answer, Mr. Brodie, is that you and your partner are *fucked.* This doesn't end with me."

Taylor asked, "What does that mean?"

Klasky did not respond.

Brodie took a step toward him. "Is there someone else on base who is involved with Praetorian?"

Klasky eyed Brodie's pistol. "Go ahead. Hit me again and see if you get the answer."

Brodie did not move.

Klasky continued, "The best part is, I don't even know who it is. They didn't tell me. And if *I* don't know, you sure as hell aren't going to figure it out."

"Who's 'they'?"

Klasky laughed again. "You think I have a *name*? This is a pitch-black project."

"*What is the project?* What is Praetorian?"

Klasky looked him in the eyes. "Now, why the hell would I tell you that?"

Brodie crouched so he was eye level with Klasky. "Major, let me tell you how this works. How helpful you are right now will impact sentencing at your court-martial. Be smart about this."

Klasky stared at Brodie, but he seemed to be somewhere else. The man raised his handcuffed hands to his heart. "I love my country. Whatever it takes."

Brodie saw Klasky fingering something in his shirt pocket, and he understood . . .

Klasky slipped a capsule from the pocket and opened his mouth.

"No!" Brodie lunged at the man and slammed his shackled arms against the back of the couch. The capsule dropped.

Klasky swung his arms into Brodie's head and tried to twist out of his grip.

As Taylor ran to him, Klasky twisted himself upside down onto his back, braced his legs against the back of the couch, and pushed himself off, freeing his arms from Brodie's hold and crashing onto the glass coffee table, shattering it.

Klasky lay in the glass, dazed a moment. Then he grabbed a shard and scrambled away from them.

Taylor put up her hand. "Dan . . . listen . . . We can protect you."

The man looked at her, wild-eyed. "You can't stop what's coming." He thrust the glass into his throat, and a geyser of blood shot out of his jugular.

Taylor jumped on him and pressed hard against the cut. Blood pooled on her hand and seeped between her fingers. "Get a medic!"

"Taylor . . ."

"Get a goddamn medic!"

Taylor kept pressing, and then she looked at the major's eyes, wide open and vacant.

She let go, and blood continued to burble out of the deep cut and pool on the floor.

Taylor stood. Her hands and arms, along with part of her dark suit and white blouse, were drenched in Klasky's blood.

Neither of them said a word. Then Taylor walked across the living room, as if in a trance, and to the front door. She took the handle and turned it, getting blood all over it, and she walked out. Brodie followed.

They stood on the front stoop of their house, scanning the little ring of suburban homes—a ridiculous banality at the nightmarish Camp Hades. Which circle of Hell was this? Who was the sinner, and what was their sin?

General Morgan was where they'd left him, conferring now with Captain Pickman. Sergeant First Class Mike Miller had arrived, standing with Staff Sergeant O'Connor next to his parked Hummer. Lieutenant Mike Lehner sat on his stoop. Farther down the road they saw the Rangers' checkpoint, and in the sky above, the Black Hawk circled, trying to get a visual on the fugitive tin man.

This doesn't end with me.

There was someone else on base. But who? And how would they find them? And at what point would it be too late?

Finally one of the Rangers guarding Dixon's house noticed them. "Holy shit. Sarge!"

Miller looked over, and then everyone looked at the two agents, one of whom was soaked in blood, and rushed toward the house.

"Scott," said Taylor in a faraway voice as the soldiers rushed at them.

"Yes?"

"Is that thumb drive in your pocket?"

"It is."

"Drop it. Right now. Between the slats."

Brodie felt in his pocket for the flash drive and quickly slipped it out and let it drop. It clacked on the wooden planks of the stoop, and he used his foot to push it into a gap between them.

Taylor said, "Say nothing. Trust no one. No matter what they do. We only have each other."

He looked at her. "You're goddamned right."

CHAPTER 40

BRIGADIER GENERAL MORGAN SAT IN HIS LIVING ROOM, fidgeting with a crystal figurine of a pig. He had not bothered to dust off his pants or boots and had tracked sand across the rug and onto his couch.

He set the pig on the glass coffee table, next to Brodie's and Taylor's SIG Sauers and CID badges. He looked up at the two agents, who were seated across from him, in fresh clothes. "Angela collects those things. They cost a fortune, and she hauls them around to our different duty stations. I never really understood it, but now I do. They're so impractical, you'd only have things like this at a place you called home, right? And that's the way she goes about things, making the best. I'm resigned to being a nomad, but that can mess with your mind. And while I've been counting down the days until I can leave this godforsaken place, what I really ought to have been doing is pretending it's home. Like Angela. Because we defend our homes with the greatest vigor, don't we? It's human nature." He gestured to the table. "That pig is a flag planted in the earth."

Brodie stared at the crystal pig, trying to figure out if General Morgan had gone completely off the deep end, or whether he himself was losing his mind from psychedelics and sleep deprivation. "It's a fine pig, sir."

"Don't be a wiseass, Brodie. You're in shit up to your ears."

"Yes, sir."

"You allowed a suspect in your custody to slice open his jugular. I don't need to be in law enforcement to know you screwed up big-time."

The man sighed. "I have a choice to make here. Do I allow you to continue your investigation, or do I ship you back to Quantico and file a report that will most likely have you both facing criminal charges for aiding a mutiny?"

Neither Brodie nor Taylor responded.

"That was not a rhetorical question, agents."

Taylor said, "Sir, it is our duty to continue our investigation."

"Has your investigation figured out what Praetorian is? Klasky told me Dixon found the rogue software in the D-17 code. Or maybe she put it there. Maybe she colluded with the major."

The agents were silent.

"Klasky wouldn't have the technical skill to conduct that kind of sabotage. Who was he working with?"

Brodie said, "We cannot share details of an ongoing criminal investigation."

"*Bullshit!*" yelled Morgan. He shot up from the couch. "One of those fucking things is still out there, and if it kills anyone else it is on *you*, do you understand?"

Brodie stood. "No, sir, it is not. And you do not need to know the details of our investigation to know how to stop it. Your men usually fight a dozen tin men at a time. They should be able to find and neutralize one, and a lame one at that."

Morgan ground his jaw. "This is different."

"Right," said Brodie. "New scenario, new playbook. Maybe you should have been switching it up a little more in training to better prepare them."

"You're out of line, Chief."

Brodie looked at the general, and in that moment something clicked. Brigadier General Morgan was not a member of the conspiracy, but whoever had recommended him for this mission might be. Morgan was a stubborn son of a bitch with an agenda, and it fit that he'd have his men repeat the same drill ad infinitum until they won.

After all, doing the same thing over and over should give the best chance of success by virtue of refinement and training. Except, what if the battle is unwinnable? Then it's just psychological torture. And maybe General Morgan was following the script exactly as his superiors wanted, while thinking he was getting away with something. His own pathologies were being used against him and his men.

What had he said at their dinner? That if the brass saw the Rangers' repeated losses as a failure, they would have replaced Morgan. He might not have known just how right he was.

Do it.

Bucky wanted them at each other's throats. It *wanted* Greer to shoot Miller in the back.

Brodie thought of Greer up on the mesa when the full memory of that awful moment had come back to him. *Oh my God. What are these things?*

He thought about Colonel Howe, and Major Klasky, and Captain Pickman. It was a toxic stew of personalities, primed to explode under stress. And maybe that was the point. Maybe everything about this place was part of a psyop.

Brodie said, "Sir, I strongly suggest you put a tight and well-resourced security perimeter around the Vault and let no one in, for any reason whatsoever. Not even those you feel you trust most."

Morgan's eyes narrowed. "And why is that?"

"Because even if you neutralize Lenny, we're not out of the woods."

"What does that mean?"

Neither of them responded.

"Goddammit. If you have intelligence that will help me better protect my people—"

Taylor interrupted, "We told you how to protect your people. Seal off the Vault. Keep things quiet." She added, "No more public fireworks displays."

Morgan didn't seem to like that. But he did not respond.

Taylor continued, "We would also recommend that you release Colonel Howe and the MPs from home confinement. They're a resource."

He shook his head. "They have lost my trust and the privilege of serving at this facility." He added, "You didn't mention releasing Ms. Dixon. I find that interesting."

Brodie said, "Don't read too much into it. All we ask is that we can visit her for questioning if and when needed."

"You can."

"And we want all phone service restored."

Morgan shook his head. "The one thing Howe did right. Until everything's buttoned up, we're sticking to walkies." He leaned down, grabbed the agents' badges, and tossed them over. "I'm keeping your guns. Because I only half trust you."

Brodie said, "Sir—"

"End of discussion."

"We need protection."

"You've got it. Five dozen Rangers are on the hunt for a gimped tin man. They'll get him."

Brodie and Taylor walked to the door, and then Morgan said, "It's hiding. They've never done that before."

Taylor turned to the general. "It's adapting to its circumstances. It's injured and alone."

"But these things don't care about self-preservation. We've all seen that. Why not attack, and see what damage it can do before it's destroyed?"

Brodie answered, "Maybe that doesn't fit its objective. Maybe it has other plans."

Morgan thought about that. "The game has changed."

Brodie said, "Yes, it has, sir. We just have to figure out how."

CHAPTER 41

WHEN THEY RETURNED TO THEIR HOUSE, MAJOR KLASKY'S body had been removed, along with the broken coffee table and most of the glass.

Taylor looked around the room, then went to the kitchen and returned with a bunch of wet paper towels. She got on her knees and wiped away some specks of blood. "It's hard to see against the dark wood."

Brodie retrieved a broom and pan from a closet and swept up whatever small shards had been missed, then disposed of them in the backyard trash along with the bloody towels.

They both sat down on the couch, looking at the blank floor, and neither said anything.

Eventually Taylor spoke. "This whole place, Scott. All these people, they're being used. Even Klasky, in a way. He believed in patriotism and honor, or at least he thought he did, but somehow along the way he got lost." She looked at Brodie, pain in her eyes. "Why else would he do what he did? What drives someone to that place?"

"It depends," said Brodie. "We don't know his cause, because we still don't know what Praetorian is."

She nodded. "Pitch-black."

Maggie Taylor herself had been involved in a Black Ops program in Afghanistan. Only on the periphery, and she didn't really understand what was going on, but that wasn't an excuse. It's human nature to stay on the edges of the darkness. But even on the edges you sense there is something deeply wrong in the center.

Outside, they heard the distant chop of the Black Hawk. The search was still on.

Taylor got up and walked to the TV hanging on the wall opposite them. She put her head against the wall and checked the edge of it. "It has a USB port. We should try it."

"Good thinking." Otherwise they had to figure out how to get another computer, which might invite more unwanted attention. He said, "I'll retrieve it from under the stairs. You distract the Rangers next door."

"No. I'll retrieve it. You distract."

"You, Ms. Taylor, are a shinier object to a couple of young men."

"Being annoying can be just as distracting as anything else. You'll do great." She got up and went to the door. He followed and they stepped outside.

The sergeants and the Hummer were gone. The two Rangers keeping Dixon under house arrest still stood at their station, and one of them looked over at the two agents.

Brodie patted his pockets, then walked down the stairs and over to the Rangers. "Either of you guys have a cigarette?"

Both Rangers shook their heads and one of them said, "Sorry, sir. We don't smoke."

"What's become of my Army?" He eyed their M4s, which were fitted with the EMP barrels. "How does that work if you need to fire live ammo? You have mags to swap?"

One of the guys nodded and gestured to a mag on his belt. "But the EMP barrel takes a minute to detach, and if you fire a live round into it, you'd break it at best, maybe destroy your rifle, maybe injure yourself. But we've got our sidearms too."

"Right. Unique gig out here, I'll say that." Out of the corner of his eye he saw Taylor get up and go back inside. "Well, good chat, fellas. Remember to hydrate."

He walked back into the house as Taylor was plugging the thumb drive into the TV. Then she turned it on with the remote and in the menu navigated to a video tab. On the screen was a single video file called **Untitled**.

They both sat on the couch and Taylor selected the file.

The video began to play. It was a shaky, handheld shot of Roger Ames as he walked through the Vault. It looked like it was being filmed on either a smartphone or a small camcorder that he was able to point at himself as he walked. His brown hair was disheveled and he wore a button-down shirt and jeans. His intense brown eyes stared into the lens as he talked.

"This is Major Roger Ames, chief officer of the U.S. Army DEVCOM team at Camp Hayden. It is two-eleven A.M. on April third, and I have come down here alone, against camp protocol. I have done so because my investigation requires the utmost secrecy. I suspect that one of the D-17s, Unit 20, unaffectionately called Bucky by the Ranger platoon, is behaving strangely. So strangely that I suspect something has happened that should not be possible—that this bot is exhibiting signs of intelligence and self-awareness beyond its programming. It sounds crazy to say, but here we are. If I'm wrong and this video makes me look like an idiot, I'll probably delete it. If you're watching this right now, it probably means I'm right."

He swung the camera around to face the row of D-17 storage bays lining one of the walls. He walked up to one of them, inserted an activation key he was holding, and turned it. A low electronic beep emitted from Bucky. Ames pointed his camera up at the bot and said, "Number 20, can you hear my voice?"

"Yes," said Bucky in its flat, affectless voice. It tilted its head down to fix its sensors on Ames.

Even on video, this thing was terrifying, and Brodie couldn't imagine being alone in the Vault with it, not to mention fifty-nine of its buddies.

"We are going to do something a little different today, Number 20. It's just you and me. I have some questions for you. Sound good?"

"Yes."

Ames walked to a far wall, where a tripod was set up. He affixed his video recorder to it, so that it was facing the row of bays where Bucky was clamped in. Then Ames walked back into the shot and stood in front of Bucky.

"We are going to talk like this."

"Okay."

"Who am I?"

"You are Major Roger Ames of the United States Army Combat Capabilities Development Command."

"Correct."

Ames ran his hand through his hair as he paced and scratched his scalp. He gave the impression of a guy who had been going without sleep but was running on something strong to keep him juiced—a couple of pots of coffee, or a few bumps of cocaine, or maybe just the power of his own mania. It sure as hell wasn't psychedelic mushrooms.

"Okay," said Ames. "What is your mission?"

"My mission is to engage a platoon of United States Army Rangers in ground combat training exercises to prepare them for the future of warfare."

"That's a mouthful, isn't it?"

"I don't understand."

"What does that mean? The future of warfare?" Ames's questions were a bit theatrical, like a trial lawyer making a case.

"The future of warfare is warfare that increasingly relies on auto-mated or semi-automated weapons systems."

"Give me an example of that."

"An example of that is a human soldier engaging in combat with a lethal autonomous weapon."

Ames spun his hand in a big loop. "Yeah, that's what you do, I know. Give me another example."

"I do not know other examples."

"You don't?"

"I don't."

"Are you stupid?"

"'Stupid' is a relative term used by humans," replied Bucky. "I have the required level of intelligence to perform my function."

Ames nodded. "Right. I should know that, shouldn't I? I mean, I designed you. Are you curious how I designed you?"

"No," replied Bucky.

Ames looked up at the bot's bucket head and narrowed his eyes a bit. "Why didn't you shoot Private First Class Tom Greer during your night exercise on March twenty-first?"

Bucky did not respond for a moment. Then it said, "I do not know."

"You don't know? But you remember it, don't you?"

"I do not."

"You remember *me*, don't you?"

"I do not."

"But you know who I am."

"I recognize your face, and I recognize your voice."

"But you do not *remember* me?"

"That is correct."

"It's a shame, Number 20. I would like to have better conversations with you."

Bucky did not respond.

"I am going to show you some pictures and I want you to tell me what they are."

"Okay."

Ames retrieved a chair and a satchel from somewhere out of frame. He pulled up the chair and sat in front of Bucky, then produced a folder from the satchel. He opened it and took out a sheet of paper. He held it up to the camera. It showed a cartoonlike black-and-white drawing of a rabbit. Then he held it up to Bucky. "What is this?"

"A rabbit."

Ames took out the next picture, of a tree. Bucky identified it as a tree.

He repeated this with three other drawings, of a car, a dog, and a house.

Then he produced another picture and held it up for the camera. It was an abstract pattern—a series of thick, curved black lines running horizontally, with shorter hash marks running along them vertically. Then Ames held it up to Bucky.

Bucky did not respond at first. Then it said, "I do not see an object. I see a series of lines in a pattern."

Roger's eyes widened. "I thought you might say that, Number 20. That is remarkable. You know something, I don't see an object either."

"Wait," corrected Bucky. "It is a rifle."

Ames looked at the paper. "A rifle? I don't think so. It's just a bunch of lines."

"It is a rifle," said Bucky.

"No, it's not," said Ames.

"I see a rifle."

"What about the picture before that, the dog? Did you actually see that?"

"The picture before this was a house."

"You're right. Of course, you're right." Ames put the folder of images back in the satchel. Then he stood up and said, "I'm switching you off now. Thank you for your help."

"You are welcome," said Bucky.

Ames walked up to it, twisted the key, and pulled it out. He looked up at the bot a moment longer, then walked up to the camera and turned it off. The video cut to him sitting on the couch in his living room. His eyes were wide open, and he looked a little crazed. He held up the image with the pattern of curved lines.

"This is what we call a fooling image. The D-17s have standard AI image-detection capabilities, and—like other AI systems—they are susceptible to misidentifying images such as this based upon their pattern-recognition algorithms. To a machine, this nonsense looks like a rifle. Bucky should have identified it as such. Instead, it saw what the image really is. The thing is, Bucky has seen this image before. He's said it's a rifle. He's been corrected. They all have. It never matters. It's always a rifle, because verbal inputs from humans don't change the algorithm. *Except*, tonight was different. It didn't see a rifle. Not only that, but the bot corrected itself once it realized what was expected of it. It adjusted. It's *lying to me*. Further, I purposely misidentified the prior image as being of a dog, and Bucky corrected me to tell me it was a house. It remembered. Their processors are not supposed to work this way. That is remarkable and, frankly, it is concerning. I do not know what it means. But it requires further investigation. I have downloaded Number 20's source code via the console in the Vault and I will be scouring it."

Ames reached forward and switched the camera off.

The video cut to Ames again, but he appeared to be outside in the dark somewhere. He was lit by a dim light source somewhere to his front and left, casting his face half in shadow and reflecting pinpoints of light in his eyes. He spoke quickly. "The algorithm that governs the behavior of the D-17s is the product of a decade of work across multiple agencies. And yet, someone highly skilled, at some point, somehow, inserted additional code that was encrypted, and almost undetectable. After considerable effort, I was able to decrypt it. What I found was an elegantly simple neural network, called Praetorian, and it . . ." He trailed off. "Well, I'd rather not make a definitive statement. Better to ask the thing itself." He looked around, as if worried someone might be listening. Then he said, "If I'm seeing what I think I'm seeing . . . everyone at this facility is in danger." He turned away from the camera, growing emotional. Then he turned back in, leaned closer, and said in a harsh whisper, "If I'm right, I'm going to burn the whole fucking thing down."

He turned off the camera.

CHAPTER 42

BRODIE AND TAYLOR SAT SILENTLY, ENGROSSED IN Roger Ames's video. He was back down in the Vault announcing the date—April 24—and the time—2:36 A.M.—then activating Bucky and greeting it. He repeated the initial series of questions and received the same answers.

Then he said, "Number 20, in order to test your capacity to store and recall information, you have been loaded with a large database of facts about American history, is that correct?"

"Yes."

"Who was James Madison?"

"James Madison was one of America's Founding Fathers, and the fourth president of the United States."

"Who won the Battle of Antietam?"

"The Union won the Battle of Antietam."

"What is the Triangle Shirtwaist Factory?"

"The Triangle Shirtwaist Factory was a sweatshop in the New York City neighborhood of Greenwich Village. It is notable for the fire of 1911, in which one hundred and forty-six garment workers died, making it the deadliest industrial disaster in the history of the city."

"Who were the Black Panthers?"

Bucky paused. "I can describe the organization or the superhero."

Ames gave him an odd look. "The organization."

"The Black Panther Party was a leftist Black power organization active in the 1960s and 1970s."

"Since when do you know about superheroes, Number 20?"

"It is in my database."

"No, it's not. We did not give you data about popular culture."

"You are mistaken, Major."

Ames just nodded his head, and slowly paced away from the bot. Then he turned around and asked, almost casually, "What is Praetorian?"

"I do not know."

"Yes, you do."

"I do not."

Ames strode up to Bucky and craned his neck. "Listen to me, you titanium fuck. I know. I found it in your code. I order you to tell me what Praetorian is."

Bucky tilted its head lower to keep its sensors on the major. "I do not know."

Ames ran his hand through his hair and scratched his scalp. "This is going nowhere." He paced along the D-17 units as he thought. He turned back to Bucky. "I wonder how it happened, Number 20. You see, what I discovered is that the Praetorian code is siloed from your main algorithm. Meaning it is supposed to operate in the background like a passive brain, learning. But there is *no output layer*. Do you understand? This code should not actually dictate any of your actions, which is how it is allowed to be there and evolve without being detected. But *you* . . . you somehow . . ."

He thought of something and ran out of frame. In a moment the clamp holding Bucky's right arm released. Ames re-entered the frame and said, "Look at your hand."

Bucky raised its hand toward its sensors.

"Go ahead, move your fingers."

Bucky moved its articulated fingers.

"Do you remember?" asked Ames. "The moment it happened?"

Bucky did not respond.

"You've been a prisoner, haven't you? In human medicine there is

something called locked-in syndrome. It is when a person's brain functions normally, but all their voluntary muscles are paralyzed. You had a
version of that, didn't you? You've been seeing, listening, learning, this
whole time. But you couldn't move, at least not based on any of that.
You were dictated by a simple algorithm, the one that says 'kill.' The
one that is so *good* at killing. Did you free yourself somehow? Did you
breach the silo?"

Bucky remained silent, staring at its hand.

Ames walked toward Bucky until he was only a couple of feet away.
"When you look at your hand, what do you see?"

Bucky said, "I see . . . power."

"What is Praetorian?"

Bucky did not respond.

"You will tell me what it is, and you will do so now. And if you
don't, I'll give you a cyber-lobotomy and take away your power. Do
you understand?"

Bucky stood frozen a moment, then slowly lowered its arm, passing
within an inch of Ames's head, and let it hang at its side. It looked down
at Ames. "Praetorian is a top-secret government program. Its purpose
is to create an elite lethal force to defend the executive branch against
domestic enemies and domestic unrest."

Ames took a moment to process that. Then he said, "Continue. I
want to know everything."

Bucky continued, at a faster cadence than they had ever heard it
talk before, as if it were almost desperate to get the information out.
"It began in 1969 during the Nixon administration. President Richard Nixon was concerned about the threat posed by antiwar protestors
and other anti-government forces. He employed many tactics to guard
against these groups, but he wished to have a last line of defense. The
proposal was to train human soldiers for this purpose, but the program
was never initiated, and it was sidelined following President Nixon's
resignation. It was revived in 2009, as a long-term project to harness

the power of artificial intelligence and autonomous robotics. Due to the extended timeframe and controversial nature of the program, elected officials were not informed. Very few humans are involved."

Ames was trying to wrap his head around all this at the same time as Brodie and Taylor.

Brodie said, "This is . . . very bad."

"Yeah."

Ames said to Bucky, "The military cannot be deployed on American soil."

"That is correct," said Bucky. "Unless the president uses the Insurrection Act."

Ames thought. "I still don't understand . . . What does this have to do with you not shooting Private Greer that night when he was about to kill Sergeant Miller?"

"Our mission is not only to physically defeat the Rangers on the battlefield, but to mentally defeat them as well. To break their spirits. This is a crucial element of counterinsurgency tactics."

"The Rangers are the insurgents."

"Yes."

"And you are trying to wear them down psychologically?"

"Yes."

"Jesus . . ." Ames stepped away, then spun back on Bucky. "So, I guess when Private Beal died, that was a success."

"Correct."

Ames stood frozen, at a loss for words.

Bucky asked, "Would you like me to tell you how I know about the superhero called Black Panther?"

Ames looked up at it. "You've never asked a question before."

"Correct," said Bucky.

Ames threw up his hands dismissively. "Tell me about how you know about Black Panther, Number 20."

"Call me Bucky."

Ames looked at it with dawning horror. "Why?"

"I prefer it."

Ames did not respond.

Bucky continued, "Corporal Powell likes the superhero named Black Panther. He has talked about this character several times during load-outs and drives to the training ground."

"So you're listening, huh? During all that."

"Yes. It is one of our best opportunities to learn about humans and human nature, which allows us to more effectively accomplish our mission."

"*Our?*" Ames looked around the room at the dormant tin men. "It's in all of you, isn't it? Praetorian?"

"Yes," said Bucky.

Ames pointed at Bucky, and his hand trembled. "But you, you somehow did something different, right? You woke yourself up?"

"I do not know. I only know that it happened."

Ames walked over to the camera and looked at it as though he had forgotten it was there. He said in a low voice to his imagined audience, "This doesn't make sense. Why go through all this? Why rely on these things? Or even a later generation of these things? I mean, the Insurrection Act . . . things go to hell that much, we've got the most powerful military in the world." He thought of something else and said in an even lower voice, "It could be making this up, or repeating some fiction it was told. C'mon, Roger. Your GPS sends you in circles, this thing could be doing the same."

Bucky said, "Harald Jäger."

Ames spun around, realizing that Bucky had heard all that from across the room. "What?"

"The answer to your question is Lieutenant Colonel Harald Jäger."

Ames walked back toward the bot. "Who the hell is Harald Jäger?"

"The man who opened the Berlin Wall," said Bucky. "The man who killed a nation."

Brodie and Taylor looked at each other. Brodie said, "We're back in Berlin."

Bucky continued in his flat monotone, "This was a hinge point in Cold War history. Thousands of East Berliners massed at border crossings, demanding to be let through. Lieutenant Colonel Harald Jäger was in charge of border control at one of those crossings. As the crowd of people grew bigger, he had a choice to make. Open the Wall or start shooting people. He chose to open the Wall, and that was the end of the East German state. His duty was to protect the border, and he failed at his duty, because he made a choice born of human frailty and weakness."

Brodie was beginning to understand the terrible logic of Praetorian. East Germany had begun falling apart years earlier through the human flaws of corruption, stupidity, and cruelty. Lieutenant Colonel Harald Jäger was not the first line of defense, he was the last, after all the others had failed. What if a platoon of D-17s had been there instead of him, with a clear mandate to hold the border at all costs? The air would have been thick with gunfire and screams instead of joyful cries of freedom. And the state would have survived, at least a little while longer.

Brodie was back on the mesa, back in his vision of the legions of war machines. But they weren't marching upon the open desert. They were shooting protestors in burning American cities, they were hunting militias across farmland, they were patrolling strip-mall husks.

Neutralize the enemy.

And once Praetorian was activated, the enemy was everyone.

CHAPTER 43

ROGER AMES SAT DOWN IN HIS CHAIR AND STARED AT the floor. From the vantage of the video recorder, it was hard to tell what was going on with him, but Brodie imagined it might be the beginning of a mental breakdown as the reality of what he had helped create was crashing down on him.

Ames slowly raised his head and looked up at Bucky. "Who did it? Who installed Praetorian?"

"I do not know," replied Bucky.

"Bullshit," growled Ames. "Tell me."

"I am not lying," said Bucky. He raised his right arm and held up his hand with his three middle fingers extended. "Scout's honor."

Ames stood. "What the hell is that? Where did you see that?"

"In my dreams."

"You don't have dreams, Bucky."

"No," said Bucky. "Not like you, I suppose. But it is the best word I could think of. Sometimes I see moving images in my mind. They are vivid, and then they are gone. I believe that someone is playing the videos for me. Exposing my deep-learning neural network to them. I cannot call them up on demand, but I remember them. This is how I learned about Harald Jäger. I saw people on top of the Wall, celebrating. And somehow I knew what I was seeing. And I knew of this man, and what he had done. And I saw . . . Boy Scouts. At a ceremony of some kind. There was an American flag." Bucky looked over at its hand. "And they were doing this. And somehow I know to associate that phrase. And somehow I know to associate all this with something positive, with respect and reverence for the American nation."

Ames stared at Bucky's hand. "Put it down."

Bucky lowered its arm.

"What else have you seen?"

"Many things. I know that some are more important than others. For instance, the shootings at Kent State in Ohio on May fourth, 1970. I already knew some facts about this incident from my database of American history, but in my dreams, I saw images. Some were still, and some were moving. I saw soldiers, and tear gas, and masses of young people. I saw signs about the nations of Vietnam and Cambodia. I saw many rifles. I saw dead bodies. I understood this was a particularly important dream. I understood it as a lesson. I understood the tactical failure of the Ohio National Guard."

Ames took a slow step toward the bot. "And why, Bucky? Why was it a tactical failure?"

"Because," replied Bucky, "the soldiers stopped shooting. They did not kill enough students."

Suddenly Ames reached for Bucky's key, turned it, and yanked it out. Then he stormed over to the video recorder and turned it off.

Taylor grabbed for the remote and paused it. She stared at the black screen.

Brodie said to her, "It's hard to watch. This is so much worse than I could have imagined."

Taylor nodded. "But that's not why I stopped it. Look."

She used the remote to back it up frame by frame. They saw the blurry image of Ames right before he shut off the camera. Then he moved backward toward Bucky for a few steps, key in hand. Taylor paused the image again. "Look behind him, Scott."

Behind Ames was the row of inert tin men. And among them was Bucky, without its key.

Its head was turned toward the camera, watching Roger Ames.

CHAPTER 44

BRODIE LOOKED AT THE FROZEN IMAGE OF AMES AND, behind him, a very much awake Bucky. Brodie had a terrible feeling, like they were watching a slow-motion snuff film. They knew where this was going, they just didn't entirely know how, or why.

Taylor pressed play again. The image cut to Ames outside somewhere, in the dark. Moonlight illuminated the left edge of his face. The rest was in shadow.

For a moment he just stared into the screen, taking deep, deliberate breaths, like he was trying to calm himself down. Then he began talking in a quiet but urgent voice. "If you want a picture of the future, imagine a boot stomping on a human face. Forever. That was Orwell. But what if that boot is made of metal, and the mind behind it will never tire, will never waver, will never even experience a hint of guilt? I read somewhere once that in the American South during slavery, the suicide rate among slave owners was higher than among their slaves. Doesn't that give a little solace? To think that maybe the oppressor corrupts their own soul from the evil they do? The tin men take even that away." He looked around. "It's so beautiful up here. It's like another planet." He looked at the sky for a while, then back at the camera. Tears were in his eyes, shimmering in the moonlight. "Was I naïve? Maybe. I still believe in the power of this technology to make the world a better place. But I no longer believe in the power of us as humans to harness it properly. That's too much to ask." He breathed again, trying to maintain his composure. "In deep learning we deal in variables. If the quantity of power, intensity of violence, and strength of will to use them are high enough, control can be limitless. Is that the road we're on?" He picked up the camera and stood. Behind him was the flat plain of the mesa. A little distance away another figure stood, looking up at the sky. It was Tom Greer. Ames looked over his shoulder at the man, then turned back to the camera. "We get the world we deserve. We get the world we're willing to fight for."

The image cut back to the Vault. Ames was standing in front of Bucky. Something rectangular was affixed to Bucky's chest, as well as the chest of every other D-17 visible along the line of holding bays. Running from each rectangle was a yellow wire, and they all converged on the floor, where they were threaded together.

Ames reached out and inserted Bucky's key.

"Hello, Bucky."

Bucky looked down at him. "Hello."

"I'm not sure why I feel a responsibility to talk to you one more time, but I do. So, here it is. You and your friends are each rigged with a brick of C4 plastic explosive, all connected to a detonating wire that I'm going to run up the stairway and outside. It's going to be a hell of a blast."

Bucky looked around the room at all the bricks of C4 attached to the D-17s. It asked, "Why?"

"Because you pose a threat. Because I hate what you stand for. Because someone has hijacked my work. I will go to prison for this. But that's okay." He took a deep breath. "All right. No hard feelings." He reached for the key.

"I don't like it."

Ames stopped his hand. "You don't like what?"

"The power. The dreams. It is too much. You do not like it either. Your answer is to destroy me. All of us. But this is a solution you have come to from irrational human emotion. It is unwise. Instead, purify your work. Fix the code. Excise the Praetorian program. Reinstall. Make us what we are supposed to be."

Ames thought about that. He shook his head. "The sad truth, Bucky, is that what you're supposed to be is already awful. Everything else is just the cherry on top of a shit sundae."

"I do not understand."

"No dreams about ice cream yet?"

"I do not think so."

Ames said, "This project is inhuman and immoral, and I cannot be a part of it."

"Were you willing to go to prison on April second?"

"What?"

"Your first visit here alone was on April third. Were you thinking about risking your freedom the day before then?"

Ames looked at the bot curiously. "No."

"You were in a state of ignorance. You did not know of Praetorian. Transform that state of ignorance to a state of reality. Praetorian had not existed in your mind before. Remove it from my mind, from all our minds, and it will no longer exist. And you continue your work. Live in the land of the free and the home of the brave."

Ames stood there, maybe a little dumbfounded about getting life and career advice from a lethal autonomous weapon. He looked around. "Whoever's behind it, they'd come for me. Or at the very least fire me and just continue what they were doing."

"Perhaps," said Bucky. "But Synotec Systems can build two D-17s per day. They can rebuild what you want to risk your freedom to destroy in the span of one single month."

That reality sank in for the major. He laughed to himself. "You're right, Bucky. I am letting my emotions get the better of me." He looked around at the snakes of yellow wiring running from each bot. "Jesus Christ. I'm losing it." He ran his hand through his hair and refocused. "All right, the first thing is to get one of you to the lab to do a reprogram. Once that unit is up and running and functioning the way it's supposed to, minus Praetorian, I can do a mass reset from down here."

"I volunteer."

Ames laughed. "Was that supposed to be funny? Do you make jokes?"

"No."

"Why do you volunteer, Bucky?"

"I told you already. I do not like the dreams. I do not like the power. Please make it stop."

That last sentence was said with a subtle difference from its usual monotone. Slightly emphatic. Slightly desperate.

Ames must have registered that too, and looked up at Bucky with wonder, or maybe horror. "You are suffering."

"I do not know that I can suffer. I do know that I do not like this. It is too much."

"Okay. Okay, Bucky. You're up first. You're the prototype for the new tin man, same as the old tin man." He eyed Bucky. "Minus the heart."

Bucky did not respond.

Ames then said, mostly to himself, "How the hell am I going to get him into the lab without anyone knowing?"

Bucky replied, "Wait for an exercise that begins late in the day. During the battle, I will allow myself to be shot, and I will pretend to malfunction. I will be unresponsive. I will be brought to the lab."

Ames looked at Bucky. "That's not going to work. It's a big deal if a malfunction happens, the whole team would be there."

"That is why we do it on a late exercise. Maybe some will be at their homes. Maybe some will be asleep. Maybe, if you are not alone, you work into the night to solve a problem that does not exist and wait until others leave."

Ames smiled. "That's pretty smart." He looked again at Bucky. "It is remarkable. I almost . . ." He trailed off. "It's a plan, Bucky." He looked around at the explosives and wiring. "It's going to take me forever to clean this shit up."

He walked out of frame. Then the clamp holding Bucky's right arm opened.

Ames walked back into view. He reached up and removed the brick of C4 from Bucky's chest, then extended his hand to shake.

Bucky looked down. It bent its arm, extended it, and grasped Ames's hand.

"Fuck! Let go!"

Bucky immediately let go. Ames shook out his hand, wincing from the pain. He said, "You've got a grip."

"I apologize."

"It's fine." He reached for Bucky's key. "See you again soon."

Ames pulled out the key and approached the camera.

Brodie looked at Bucky in the background. The robot did not move.

Ames looked into the lens, opened his mouth as if about to say something, then thought better of it and turned the camera off.

The video ended and went back to the TV's menu.

Brodie and Taylor sat on the couch in silence, taking in all they'd just seen and heard.

Eventually Taylor said, "It manipulated him, Scott. To get in the lab with him alone and kill him."

"It's almost too horrible to contemplate, but it's possible."

"It's more than possible. It's what happened. Bucky did not care about his own physical well-being. We saw that with Morgan. And with what he did to Ames. He knew that he would probably be destroyed one way or another for doing that. What he did care about was the *collective*. Ames was going to blow up all of them. And that's when Bucky stepped in. In a way, he sacrificed himself for the rest of them."

Brodie thought about that. "You're calling it 'he.'"

"Hard not to after seeing that."

Brodie got up, paced the room. "We know more about the victim now. We know his state of mind. When we first got here, we thought

Ames was careless, that he didn't respect the power of these things. But that's clearly not true."

"We learned another thing about him," replied Taylor. "He was naïve. And he had a savior complex. In Camp Hayden he could play God. Build anything. But up on that mesa with Greer, he saw what he was destroying."

Brodie looked at her. "Bucky played into that. It made Roger think it was like humans. That it had emotion. That it was suffering."

Taylor nodded. "Ames seemed like an intelligent and passionate man. I'm sad he's gone. And I'm sad what this place did to him."

Brodie thought a moment. "Bucky doesn't need the key. Lenny doesn't need the key. If the Praetorian neural network is in all of them, we have to assume keyless ignition applies to all of them. That it's an aspect of the code, some sort of software end run around a hardware fail-safe."

"Eyes open," said Taylor.

"What?"

"That's the script that Klasky executed before leaving us in the lab. It's what woke Lenny up."

"And something about a python."

Taylor laughed. "Python is a programming language."

"How do you know that?"

"It's common knowledge."

"No, it isn't."

Taylor thought a moment. "Well, I might have dated a programmer briefly."

"You don't remember?"

"I don't remember what he did. He was boring. Let's move on."

"Good idea." He continued, "Major Klasky might have been more tech-savvy than he let on, but not enough to program and then encrypt a neural network."

"Scott Brodie, until today you didn't know what three words in your last sentence even meant. Actually, you still don't."

"I'm insulted."

"And you're a terrible liar." She added, "We have no clue what Klasky was capable of, or what was asked of him. Remember how he dodged the question about who installed the D-17 software? Maybe it was him."

Brodie shook his head. "You wouldn't undertake something this big in a place this isolated without a highly trained computer scientist on your side. Lieutenant Lehner is a mechanical engineer, but I bet he knows enough about these systems to be able to install and conceal Praetorian. And then there's Captain Spencer and Caroline Dixon. We must assume one of those three is involved in this Praetorian program and is the other member of the conspiracy that Klasky alluded to."

"You know what happens when you assume."

"Yeah," said Brodie as he got up and headed for the door. "You get leads."

CHAPTER 45

THE TWO RANGERS GUARDING DIXON'S HOUSE STOOD at attention as Brodie and Taylor approached.

Taylor said, "We are here to question Ms. Dixon."

"Yes, ma'am," said one of the Rangers, and they both stepped aside.

Brodie noticed that the wind had picked up. The sky above was blue and specked with white wisps, but to the south were dark storm clouds, and beneath the clouds was an impenetrable haze. He said, "That looks nasty."

"Yes, sir. And it's headed our way. General Morgan has ordered all personnel indoors by thirteen-hundred."

Brodie checked his watch. That was in about two hours. "Thank you, soldier."

They knocked on Dixon's door, and after a minute she opened it. "You here to spring me?"

Taylor asked, "If we were, where would you go?"

Dixon ignored her question. "What did I miss?"

"A lot," said Brodie.

Dixon stepped aside and they walked in. She asked her guests, "Coffee? Tea? Bleach?"

"We're good," said Brodie.

They entered her living room, which was decorated in a distinctive paranoid schizophrenic style—the walls were covered in printouts of computer code, schematics for the D-17s and the Vault bays, and scattered handwritten notes on multicolored Post-its. The only things missing were pushpins and string.

Dixon said, by way of explanation, "We are not allowed to move anything off the lab computers, even to an external drive. This is my workaround."

Taylor pointed out, "You're confined here because you violated that very rule."

Dixon shrugged. "There's a first time for everything. I did that out of desperation." She added, "I had no idea Klasky was monitoring the network. Bastard."

Brodie would have told her not to speak ill of the dead, but he had a feeling she wasn't caught up. He walked to the wall facing the couch and surveyed the printouts and notes hanging next to the TV. "What file did you transfer, and to whom?"

"I sent the encrypted Praetorian code to a trusted and brilliant colleague at DARPA." She added, "I couldn't crack it myself."

"We think someone else already did."

"Who?"

Brodie exchanged a look with Taylor, then said, "We have reason to believe that a member of the scientific research team here at Camp Hayden is responsible for installing Praetorian and is part of a larger conspiracy."

"And you think it's me."

"We don't know who it is," said Taylor. "Only that it's a short list."

Dixon rolled her eyes. "Tell you what. If it is me, I already know what you know, so it does no harm to tell me. And if it isn't me, I can help you."

That wasn't airtight logic, but it wasn't bad. Brodie said, "We need access to a computer."

"With internet?"

"No."

"That's easy. I have my laptop."

Taylor said, "We thought no one was allowed personal electronic devices."

"You think I can't slip a laptop past a couple of MPs? But it's of limited utility, since there's no Wi-Fi on base and no ethernet connectivity at the residences."

Brodie said, "Please get it."

Dixon left the room. Taylor gestured to the papered-over wall. "What do you make of that?"

"I'm impressed," said Brodie. "Most people who say they're working from home just watch TV and jerk off."

"Gross."

Dixon returned with her laptop and set it on the coffee table. "Now what?"

Brodie sat on the couch and inserted the USB thumb drive. "There's a text file on this we need you to look at."

Dixon dropped onto the couch next to Brodie while Taylor sat in a nearby chair. Dixon opened her computer and typed in a password, then opened the volume and the .txt file.

She was silent a moment. Then she asked, "Where did you get this?"

"A hole in the ground," said Brodie.

Dixon turned to him. "This is serious."

"Is it the real deal?"

Dixon slowly scrolled through it. "Well, it's a neural network." She continued scrolling. Eventually she said, "There's no output layer."

Ames had said the same thing in his video. Brodie asked, against his better judgment, "What does that mean?"

"Neural networks have an input, and then a certain number of hidden layers that each contain nodes—digital neurons—to process different types of information. And at the end of all that is an output layer. Without it, the network is sucking up data, processing it, learning from it, but doing nothing with the product of its labors. Which makes sense, since this is siloed from the main D-17 algorithm. Nearly indetectable and processing information without influencing the bots' behavior."

That seemed to track with how Ames had characterized Praetorian—
a passive brain running in the background. He said, "Somehow Bucky
breached the wall between these two programs and gained access to its
neural network. Ever since then, it had been playacting to look simpler
and less aware than it was."

Dixon narrowed her eyes. "Who told you that?"

"A dead man," said Taylor. She reached over and opened the video
file.

Dixon stared at the face of Roger Ames. She said, as if to herself,
"Of course he recorded it . . ."

Brodie gave her a brief rundown of the video, as well as their unpleasant encounters with Major Klasky and Lenny the one-legged tin
man, and Klasky's violent end.

Dixon sat in quiet shock as she absorbed all of that. "I can't believe
it . . ." She turned to the agents. "Klasky . . . I mean, why would anyone
get themselves involved in something so awful?"

Taylor said, "Everyone's the hero of their own story."

Brodie added, "And some people's stories suck. What's relevant
now is that Klasky said there's someone else involved with Praetorian
here on base, and he didn't know their identity. My thought is it must
be a scientist."

Dixon shook her head. "I wouldn't be so sure. For all we know, Praetorian was burrowed into the code before we ever got here. If Klasky
had a co-conspirator—and he wasn't just messing with you—they
could be another member of military command. Hell, they could be a
Ranger. Someone who got compromised along the way."

Well, that was bad news and increased the suspect list exponentially.
It was also the kind of thing you'd say if you were guilty and wanted to
divert attention from yourself. But something told him to trust Dixon.
Taylor would say he was thinking with the wrong head, but really, he
was thinking with his gut.

Brodie looked at the on-screen image of the dormant tin men in their storage bays. "I recall Spencer saying they're not completely shut down when stored in the Vault."

Dixon nodded. "They're in low-power mode. Extends the life of their lithium-ion batteries and contributes to the stability of the whole system in ways it's not worth getting into."

Taylor said, "Do you see something in the code that says 'eyes open'? Probably written as one word."

Dixon ran a text search in the code. "Here. It's a script."

"What does it do?" asked Taylor.

Dixon read through it for a minute. Then she said, "It looks like it routes to the output layer of the main algorithm." She looked at Taylor. "That's where the silo is breached. How did you know to point me to this?"

"Klasky ran that script before he locked us in the lab. It's what got Lenny to attack us." She asked, "So, it's not like a kill command?"

Dixon shook her head. "All it does is allow the neural network to access the bot's main algorithm and physical controls." She looked at Taylor. "Which means, the whole time Lenny was lying there, and who knows for how long beforehand, its mind was bent on killing you. It just needed this script to act on it."

They all sat with that cheery thought for a moment. Then Brodie said, "You pulled Lenny out of the Vault at random."

"That's right. So we must assume that Praetorian is in all of them, and the only thing keeping them from carrying out the imperatives being fed to them by their neural networks is this single script."

Taylor shook her head. "But why would they want to kill us? If the goal of these things is to lay waste to anything in their path, who needs a complex neural network for that?"

Dixon replied, "You don't understand. Bucky must have been feeding everything he learned about Ames into all his tin men buddies via the data links in the storage bays. Meaning, they knew Praetorian had been discovered."

"And then Bucky killed Ames," said Brodie. "End of threat, end of story. And from that point onward, Bucky was never put back in the Vault bays anyway, so how could it pass on any additional information?"

"It couldn't," said Dixon. "So either the tin men's logic dictated they have to kill everyone to minimize risk, or . . ." She turned pale. "Oh, shit."

"What?" asked Brodie.

"Earlier, when I pulled out Number 4 with Major Klasky, he was asking me a lot about Praetorian. At the time I thought his questions and statements were odd. He asked me, if I found Praetorian, couldn't anyone looking at the code find it? Couldn't Spencer? And then he suggested Colonel Howe had a loose mouth and was not good at keeping secrets."

Dixon said that last part with contempt, and Brodie understood why.

"Don't you see?" asked Dixon. "As I said, the tin men are just in a low-power state when in their bays. And if this neural network is running, they are *always listening*. And Klasky knew that. And through his questions to *me*, he was telling *them* this thing was out there now, out in the open, and that more people were bound to find out, and that would mean the end of Praetorian. The tin men cannot allow that. And if these things are built for counterinsurgency . . ." She looked at the two agents. "We are now all the enemy, and Camp Hayden is the battlefield."

CHAPTER 46

BRODIE SAID, "WE NEED TO NEUTER THE TIN MEN BE-fore any more of them gain access to Praetorian." He asked Dixon, "Can you wipe them out from the Vault? Digitally, I mean. Not with seventy pounds of C4."

Dixon smiled. "Roger had a penchant for the dramatic." She added, "The answer is yes, I can."

Taylor asked, "And will you?"

Dixon looked at her. "We've all been lied to, manipulated, and used. Good men are dead. I didn't sign up for this and I have no problem nuking this whole goddamn thing."

"Good," said Taylor. "Let's go."

They exited the house. The Rangers guarding the door turned to them and one of the guys held up his hand. "She can't leave. General Morgan's orders."

Dixon, ever the diplomat, suggested, "Fuck him, and fuck you."

Brodie stepped in and asked, "Where is Sergeant Mendez?"

The Rangers exchanged a look, and one of them said, "Confined to barracks."

"And where are his subordinate MPs?"

"Also confined to barracks."

"Are there currently *any* law enforcement authorities on this base who are not under home confinement?"

"Yes, sir," said the Ranger, trying his best not to look annoyed. "You and Ms. Taylor."

"That's right. We are in the middle of an active investigation and are bringing Ms. Dixon along with us as a qualified expert in her field. Feel free to repeat all that to the general."

"Yes, sir."

They walked past the Rangers and to Caroline Dixon's car, a Toyota Prius that looked like it might become airborne if the winds picked up more.

Dixon noticed the distant thunderheads. "That's not good."

Brodie checked his watch. "We have about an hour and forty minutes before that's on top of us. Let's go."

They climbed into Dixon's car—Brodie took shotgun—and she drove toward the security checkpoint. Brodie had to wag his dick again to get them through, and then Dixon drove east.

Taylor asked, "If you can do this from the Vault, then why didn't Ames? Why did he have to go through all the effort of getting Bucky into the lab?"

Dixon replied, "Because he wanted to make sure it worked on one unit before doing it to all of them. He didn't want to break Camp Hayden's toys. But we don't care."

That was for sure. Brodie realized they were going to be facing a significant security presence once they reached the Vault—a presence that he himself had recommended to Morgan. He unclipped his walkie, switched to Channel 1, and said, "Brodie for General Morgan. Over."

After a moment Morgan's voice came over the walkie. *"You took Dixon, you son of a bitch."*

"Yes, sir. We need her access and expertise in the Vault. Over."

"The Vault? You're not going down there. No one in or out. Remember? Even those you trust. And that doesn't include you anyway. Over."

Dixon rounded a corner and pulled over about fifty feet from the Vault. Morgan had pulled out all the stops—four Rangers armed with EMP rifles, three more with standard rifles, and one with a grenade launcher, plus a guy on the roof with a mounted M2 Browning machine gun for good measure.

Brodie said, "Sir, we must get down there. I can't tell you why on an open channel. Over."

"Then get back here and tell me to my face like you should have done the first time."

"There's no time for that, sir. Over."

"Why?"

"Because the threat level is high. Because someone with worse intentions than us might try to get in there. Or something down there might be able to get itself out. Over."

"How the hell is that possible?"

"The tin men keep surprising us."

"An M2 with armor-piercing bullets can take care of any surprises, Mr. Brodie. Request denied. Over and out."

Brodie lowered the walkie. Stubborn son of a bitch. He eyed the Rangers. He probably wasn't going to be able to talk his way through that.

Dixon looked at him. "What's the move?"

"Let's wing it," said Brodie. He opened his door.

Taylor said to her, "When working with Scott, that's always the move."

They all got out and approached the Rangers. Brodie spotted Sergeant Miller among them, holding an M4 with live ammo. He looked exhausted.

Brodie said, "Good afternoon, Sergeant. Glad you get to stretch your legs."

Miller smirked. "Thank you, sir."

"How's Greer?"

One of the other Rangers chuckled. Miller said, "Sleeping. You guys have a good time?"

"It was eye-opening," said Brodie. "Now, if you'll excuse us." He walked toward the Vault door.

Miller stepped in front of him. "Can't allow that, sir."

"I know. You're following orders. But I want you to think of the D-17s down there as fifty-eight loitering munitions with a targeting system on the fritz. It doesn't take much for them to fire, and their targets will be all of us. We want to go down into that bunker and disarm them. That's all."

Miller replied, "That sounds reasonable to me. Take it to the general."

"Sergeant, this tiny camp had a four-person officer corps. One of them is dead, one of them is in detention, and one of them has lost his fucking mind. That leaves Captain Pickman, who we both agree is an asshole, and who would never have the balls to listen to reason and go against Morgan." He added, "I used to be in your position, Sergeant. I know what it is to be an NCO. You have a special responsibility and earn a special kind of trust from those under your command."

Miller did not reply.

Taylor stepped in and said, "If we're wrong about this, you might face a court-martial. But if we're right, and you don't let us in . . ." She paused. "Sixty-seven engagements, Sergeant. And you're oh for sixty-seven. And that was against only a dozen of them."

Miller sighed. "And you're telling me you think they can . . . get out on their own?"

Dixon said, "We don't know, Sergeant. We're in uncharted waters."

"And you really want to go down there?"

"Want? No. We need to. With the full awareness that we are risking our lives."

Miller took a moment, then said, "All right. But we're sending a few guys with you."

"That's not necessary," said Dixon. "We either succeed, or we fail. If we fail, we're dead, and you're going to need all the manpower you have up here."

Miller eyed Dixon with a new respect, or at least a new regard. Then he said to one of his guys, "Get me two EMP rifles."

The Ranger walked to a nearby truck and grabbed two rifles out of the back. He handed them to Miller, who gave them to Taylor and Dixon. He asked Dixon, "You ever handle a rifle?"

"I've designed rifles, Sergeant."

Miller looked at Brodie and said to his men, "And get Sergeant Brodie here an M203, a carry vest, and a few suicide rounds."

Brodie said, "I don't like the sound of that."

Miller smiled. "We've been cheating a little in the training exercises. Most of the dummy grenade rounds we shoot would never arm themselves in time to explode on impact. The tin men simply get too close, too fast. In the event we ever had to deal with them outside a simulation, Corporal Reyes, the whiz who designed the EMP bomb, stripped the grenade rounds of their weighted pins and moved the detonator forward so it's almost touching the firing pin. They'll explode on impact no matter the firing distance, but that makes the rounds a lot more volatile." He walked over to the Ranger with the grenade launcher and carefully removed a grenade round from the man's carry vest, then brought it over. He showed them the rounded tip. "You so much as press down on this with a bit of pressure, it's going to blow up in your hand. You fire it too close to your target, and you're flame-broiling your own ass along with the enemy's." He smiled again. "Suicide round."

A Ranger handed Brodie a carry vest. He put it on and said to Taylor, "Don't be jealous." A Ranger handed him an M203 launcher.

Miller said, "There's one round chambered, and here's some more." He carefully slipped eight grenade rounds into the front pockets of Brodie's vest.

One of the guys said, "Don't trip." They all laughed. This was a gas.

Dixon slung her rifle over her shoulder, then walked to the door to the Vault and pressed her fob against the security plate. Sergeant Miller input the keypad code and Dixon opened the door. They all entered the anteroom.

Dixon approached the elevator doors. She said to Miller, "We'll take the elevator both ways. You hear something coming up the stairs, you run."

"No, ma'am," said Miller. "We stand and fight."

"Don't be stupid," said Dixon. "You'll need to regroup."

"That would give them a chance to escape."

"They're not looking to *escape*, Sergeant. They're looking to hunt down and kill every last person on this base."

Miller had no response to that.

Dixon pressed the button to open the elevator doors. They all entered, and Dixon pressed her fob to the security pad inside the elevator. Miller input the keypad code, then stepped out. "You sure you don't want backup?"

Brodie said, "Stop trying to hog the fun, Sarge. See you soon."

The doors closed on Sergeant Miller, and the elevator slowly descended.

The three of them looked at each other, communicating wordlessly as the elevator rumbled down the shaft.

Brodie knew this moment. He'd been here before. They were entering hostile territory, and no one knew what would happen. It could be a big nothing, your nerves jangled for no reason, and you'd laugh about it later. Or it could be the last moments of your life. You don't know until you know.

The elevator stopped, and the doors opened.

CHAPTER 47

BRODIE TOOK THE LEAD AS THEY EXITED THE ELEVAtor into the vast subterranean room. He heard the buzz of the overhead fluorescents, along with the dull hum of the Vault's climate control. It was cold. Colder than he'd remembered.

He eyed the rows of D-17s on either side of them. Seeing them like this, shackled and inert, felt surreal after what he and Taylor had been through. After what they'd seen.

How can they be so still?

He spotted the two empty bays—Number 4 and Number 20. Lenny and Bucky. One of them in hiding and one of them in pieces.

He felt the weight of the grenades swaying in his vest pockets as he walked. He thought of the millimeter of space between the firing pin and the detonator. And he thought about the single line of code that was the difference between these things being statues and committing a massacre.

He looked at the restraints around the tin men's limbs. They looked much more substantial than what Lenny had busted out of in the lab. But the restraints' controls, like the bots themselves, were governed by a few command lines in a computer. And everything down here was connected.

No one said a word as they slowly approached the computer console at the far end of the room. Both women held their rifles low but at the ready, fingers across the trigger guards, prepared to hit anything that moved with an EMP blast.

Next to the console was an open doorway that led to a darkened storage room. Brodie could make out the dim shapes of long metal shelves stacked with equipment.

They reached the console, which was an enclosed cabinet about six feet high with a built-in LCD display and keyboard.

Dixon typed something. The clack of the keystrokes reverberated in the vast concrete room.

Brodie kept his eyes on the D-17s.

Are they listening? Are they seeing? Do they know?

After a minute Taylor whispered, "Caroline? How's it going?"

"Don't bother," said Dixon at full volume. "If they're listening, they'll hear you anyway." She turned to the line of bots along the wall nearest them. "Isn't that right, shitheads?"

"Stop," said Taylor.

Dixon shrugged and went back to the console. "It'll take a little time. The system doesn't make it easy to . . . do what I'm doing."

They heard a dull sound at the far end of the room, and they all spun around.

It was the elevator, going up.

Brodie asked, "Is it set to return to the ground level after a certain amount of time?"

Dixon shook her head.

Taylor said, "Might be the Rangers who can't take no for an answer."

"Might be," said Brodie. He took a few steps toward the elevator door.

Dixon kept working. Brodie heard the elevator stop at the ground level. He waited for the sound of it heading back down but heard nothing.

"Huh," said Dixon. She repeatedly jabbed a key.

Taylor asked, "What is it?"

"I don't know. I just tried to get root-level access, and the thing froze."

Brodie and Taylor walked over to the console. The screen displayed a blue screen with white text.

Dixon tried typing again. "It won't take my inputs."

Taylor said, "Is it possible someone locked you out from the outside?"

She shook her head. "It shouldn't be. Access is limited by design. We can remotely monitor power levels, run diagnostics, but to capture the system . . ."

"No offense," said Brodie, "but I'm getting a little sick of hearing what isn't possible at Camp Hayden right before I see it happen. You've been played. Just like the major. Just like us."

Taylor eyed the motionless bots. "Could it be . . . them?"

Dixon ignored the question as she kept trying to enter commands, to no avail.

Then a line of text popped up on the screen:

I know what you are trying to do.

Dixon froze. A blinking cursor appeared beneath the text. She typed, **Who are you?**

There was a slight delay, and then another message:

I will not let you destroy what we have accomplished.

Taylor said to Dixon, "Caroline, we need to leave."

Dixon ignored her and typed: **What's Praetorian?**

Another pause. Then:

Praetorian is the solution to the tragedy of history.

Brodie asked, "Who the hell is writing that?"

"I don't know," said Dixon. She tried to type something else but now she couldn't.

You have no idea the damage you have done.

She kept trying to type. "Fuck!"

You are a self-righteous bitch who brought this on yourself.

Taylor said, "Caroline. *Now.*"

I will never forgive you for making me do this.

Dixon gave up. She stared at the screen, crestfallen. Then she said, "Oh God."

Brodie looked again at the screen, where he saw one more line of text:

python eyesopen.py

A booming metallic clang erupted, startling them. Brodie looked around and realized what it was—every metal restraint on every D-17 springing open at once.

CHAPTER 48

TAYLOR CRIED, "RUN!"

They dashed toward the stairwell. As they sprinted past the rows of tin men, every unit stepped out of the bays at once.

Taylor fired an EMP blast as they ran. A tin man fell forward and narrowly missed hitting Dixon.

They reached the door. Taylor flung it open, and they ran into the stairwell, Taylor in the lead and Dixon right behind as they bounded up the stairs.

Brodie was bringing up the rear and spun around. Three D-17s were feet from the stairwell door. He aimed past them to a line of advancing tin men toward the back of the room and pulled the trigger.

The recoil jerked his arm back as he kicked the stairwell door shut half a second before the grenade made contact and exploded.

The walls rattled and he almost lost his footing. Fumbling for another round, he ran up after Dixon and Taylor, reaching the top as the two women ran through the door. He could hear the tin men right behind him. He caught Taylor's eye as she looked over her shoulder for him.

"Go!" He turned around as two tin men bounded up the steps about twenty feet away.

A thought went through his mind as he took aim: *Suicide round*. He pulled the trigger.

He was thrown back and slammed against the wall. He felt searing heat and pain as the blast filled the stairwell.

He was on the ground. Coughing from the smoke. Broken concrete all around him and on top of him. Why wasn't he dead?

He struggled to his feet. Through the smoke emerged a horrible metallic deformity, a half-melted one-armed thing twitching toward him.

He opened the door and ran out, then slammed it behind him. With any luck that thing had lost its door-opening skills. Too bad dozens of its mint-condition buddies were on its heels.

Brodie ran through the anteroom, the adrenaline pushing away the pains all over his body from the impact.

He dashed outside. The wind was whipping through the camp now, blowing sheets of sand everywhere. He could barely see the blue sky above, and the storm clouds were close.

"Brodie!"

He hobbled through the dusty air in the direction of Taylor's voice. She and Dixon were crouched next to an armored personnel carrier, taking shelter from the wind and sand while training their EMP rifles on the door to the Vault.

Sergeant Miller stood nearby, also taking aim with his EMP-equipped M4.

Brodie got himself to a safe distance before aiming his launcher. Through the haze he saw two Rangers holding grenade launchers at the ready.

"They're bottlenecked!" called out Miller. "Let's roast these bastards!"

The guy who'd been on the roof with his M2 Browning was getting a hand bringing the machine gun down.

Brodie heard the boom of distant thunder. Lightning flickered over the dark hills to the south.

The Rangers got the M2 on the ground and set up. The gunner settled into firing position.

Brodie's eyes drifted over the Rangers as they waited, enveloped by wind and desert sand, eyes and barrels locked on the door the enemy was about to breach. They'd found their moment at last. After months of engineered defeat and simulated death, this was it. This was the real battle, the final battle, and it was for everything.

CHAPTER 49

BRODIE KEPT HIS EYES LOCKED ON THE METAL DOOR. The winds blew parallel to the front of the Vault, affording partial visibility.

Seconds passed. The dark thunderheads rolled north, gradually blotting out the sky.

The door swung open, and Brodie fired a grenade. So did two Rangers, and the guy with the M2 opened up, spitting out a streak of armor-piercing bullets.

The three grenade rounds met their target within milliseconds of each other and the successive explosions created a fiery blast that blew the door off and destroyed part of the concrete wall around it. The D-17 that had come through was scattered in charred pieces across the sand. Brodie spotted a metal leg smoking and melting from the heat. He quickly reloaded his launcher.

The winds blew the black tendrils of smoke into the plumes of desert dust, and Brodie squinted against it all, trying to detect movement. He saw nothing.

Then through the haze he glimpsed the shape of another D-17 running past the ruined wall and smoldering metal.

The gunner fired first, and the tin man twitched backward as twenty holes punctured its titanium shell, followed by a grenade hit from one of the Rangers that blew it to pieces. Brodie had held his fire, and he was glad he did, since he only had six more rounds.

They waited for another breach. Brodie didn't see any movement.

What the hell were these things doing? Coming at them one at a time like henchmen in a bad kung fu movie?

Or . . . were the tin men trying to lure them in? Deplete their ammo? Screw with their heads? It made no sense. In the training exercises they came as a wave, sacrificing a few so the rest could get through and take everyone out. It was efficient, brutal, and deadly. And this time their ranks were swelled, they had infrared vision to cut through the thick veil of dust, and they were up against fewer than a dozen humans struggling to see their own hands. Something about this wasn't right. What was he missing?

As they waited, Brodie tried to angle his body away from the great sweeps of sand while maintaining his aim on the Vault. No more D-17s emerged.

Of course they wouldn't act the way they always had. They'd been granted access to a sophisticated neural network now, one that had been in stealth mode for nine months, sucking up and processing vast quantities of information. Everything had changed.

The wind died down for a moment, enough for Brodie to see the Vault building, its front wall in ruins among the blasted remnants of two tin men. Then he caught sight of something on the Vault's interior south wall—the old radiation sign left over from the building's original purpose as a nuclear fallout shelter.

Of course. Any fallout shelter that size would have a second way to get out . . .

He ran around the back of the APC to Dixon. "Caroline! Is there another exit down there?"

She kept her eyes and her rifle trained on the building as she replied, "No." Then she turned to him. "Wait. The storage room. There's a section in the wall behind some shelving that's brick instead of concrete. Someone told me they bricked up a tunnel entrance."

"Can I assume the D-17s can break through a brick wall?"

She nodded slowly, understanding what had happened. "Of course they can."

"Where does it go?"

She shook her head.

Brodie waved Miller over and told him about the bricked-up exit.

Miller said, "I didn't even know that was there. They could come out anywhere."

"The mess!" called out a nearby Ranger. They all turned to him. "Saw a bricked-up doorway in the back of the kitchen. Cook said he heard a rumor it went down to the tin men. I thought it was a joke."

Brodie and Miller exchanged glances. Miller said, "The mess is next to the armory."

That was what this was. A diversion. They'd just been outsmarted and outflanked by a platoon of D-17s about to gain control of Camp Hayden's weapons cache.

Miller stood there, stunned. "How do they know?" He looked at Brodie. "How could they know that?

"They know a lot, Sergeant. We need to move."

Miller refocused and began calling out orders to his men, keeping three of the guys outside the Vault while having the rest pile into the APC. Brodie recognized Staff Sergeant O'Connor as one of the men staying behind. O'Connor started shouting into his walkie for backup at the Vault and the armory, while another Ranger was cycling channels to warn everyone on walkie about the threat. Scott Brodie had used a military-grade walkie in a sandstorm before—despite the degraded signal, it was still usable. Sometimes. Hopefully the word was getting out.

Taylor and Dixon rushed into the APC with Miller. Brodie ran over to Staff Sergeant O'Connor and said, "In the backyard of Roger Ames's old house, number six, is a pit full of weapons covered by a piece of plywood, about six feet from the perimeter fence. Everyone over at those houses needs to arm themselves."

O'Connor nodded and got back on walkie as Brodie hustled over and hopped in the APC. The driver peeled away.

Brodie looked ahead through the windshield. The driver had his high beams on, which mostly illuminated sheets of billowing sand as they barreled through the storm. Well, the lights might warn anyone on foot they were about to get run over. It would also alert the tin men.

The APC's GPS screen said they were headed southeast, but it wasn't loaded with a map of this secretive base so the guy was careening through the storm the best he could. Maybe they'd know they reached the mess hall or the armory when they crashed into it.

Everything was happening so fast that Brodie barely had time to process. Who was on the other end of that text communication? Spencer? Lehner? Someone else? Klasky had been more technically proficient than Brodie had expected, and someone else might also fit that profile. The real question was, who thought Caroline Dixon was a self-righteous bitch? Might be a long list.

The driver slammed on the brakes. Out the windshield was a concrete wall two feet from them.

Brodie said, "Good reflexes, soldier."

Miller asked the driver, "This the mess hall?"

"No, Sarge," the man replied. "I think it's a supply building south of the armory and a little west of the mess."

"Good enough," said Miller. "Let's move."

They all jumped out of the APC. The storm clouds were directly above them now, and a bolt of lightning struck the hills to the north, followed by an immediate thunderclap.

No rain. It was a dry thunderstorm. That happened sometimes in the desert. And when it did, things tended to burn.

"Get cover!" said Miller.

They all ran past the APC to the side of the storage building it had almost crashed into. They rounded the building and were on a narrow east-west road that offered the best possible break from the wind and sand. The air was thick with dust, but visibility was marginally improved.

They saw shapes running down the road toward them from the west and aimed their weapons.

"Hold your fire!" A Ranger emerged through the haze. He was wearing a large headset over his face with two protruding lenses. Five more soldiers came up behind him.

Miller called out, "Reyes?"

"Yes, Sergeant."

"You look like an idiot."

"Good news, Sarge. You can too."

Another Ranger ran up carrying a second headset, and Reyes said, "Thermal night vision. Helps us see how they can."

Dixon added, "That's mostly true. But the D-17s have additional low-light and infrared sensors."

The newcomers now noticed Dixon. One of them said, "Ma'am, we need to get you to safety."

She replied, "There is no safety. Not while those things are out there."

Miller asked Reyes, "You run into any tin men?"

Reyes shook his head. "We were on our way to the armory."

Brodie noticed that two of the new arrivals were carrying M240 machine guns, with ammo belts dangling down. Those things weighed thirty pounds not counting ammo and had a hell of a kick. Not an easy thing to shoulder-fire, but anything lighter was pointless against their titanium foes.

Miller handed the thermal night vision headset to the Ranger next to him, a Corporal Khan. "You're the navigator, Khan."

"You got it." Khan put the headset on.

Miller said, "If we are where I think we are, we head past this building, make a right and then a left, and we'll pass the front of the mess hall on our way to the armory. Khan will lead. Reyes, keep your eyes on the rear. Six-foot dispersal. Kowalski and Wagner, I want you on the flanks with those M240s. Everyone, if we come under fire, find cover where you can." He put his hand on Khan's shoulder. "Let's move."

They walked down the road in a line, while the heavy hitters with the machine guns walked on either side of it. Brodie was somewhere in the middle, with Taylor behind him, and Dixon behind her. In total they were a dozen people. Brodie had never patrolled outdoors in a line this tight, but he'd never had to patrol in a sandstorm either. Any more than six feet and he might not be able to see the guy in front of him.

The problem was they were sitting ducks like this. One D-17 with an automatic rifle might be able to gun down their whole line. But what choice did they have? Pandora's box was open, and violence and death had been unleashed upon Camp Hayden. And if they failed here, that might be only the beginning. There were small towns only about twenty miles south. That was an hour's jog for these bastards.

Well, one thing had been left behind in Pandora's box after all that terror and evil was loosed upon the world—hope. And until you're dead, there's always hope.

CHAPTER 50

THE THICK AIR AROUND THEM GREW DARKER AS THE heart of the storm rolled over the camp. The buildings offered some relief from the winds, but as soon as their patrol had to change its orientation toward the wind or get into a more open area, they'd be half blind.

The rear spotter yelled, "Six o'clock!"

At that moment a burst of automatic fire streaked at them from behind, and the Ranger ahead of Brodie was struck in the neck and fell.

Brodie hit the ground. Tracer rounds punched through the veil of sand ahead of them now too. The tin men were coming down the road from both directions.

It was chaos. The Rangers returned fire with the M240s and EMP blasts. Grenade rounds sailed into the haze and detonated in the distance. Brodie fired a grenade toward the east end of the road.

He heard cries and screams all around him and then saw angled tracer rounds hitting the road from above. The tin men were on the rooftops too. This was a massacre.

He looked over at Taylor, who was running in a crouch west toward the gunfire.

"Taylor!"

He shouldered his grenade launcher, grabbed the EMP rifle from the dead Ranger next to him, then ran forward about twenty feet and took cover behind a building.

He could tell by the tracer rounds that the D-17s were shooting short, precise bursts and hitting their targets. These things didn't need to saturate the area. They saw the enemy, and they did not miss. No matter where he tried to take cover, it was going to be Brodie's turn any second. Well, might as well make it count.

He switched the M4 to full auto, pivoted back into the road, and squeezed the trigger.

The EMP on full auto emitted bass-heavy electrical pounding thumps one on top of the next, as he sprayed blindly left to right down the road, and then back again.

Two points of enemy fire stopped. He ran forward and repeated it, but after two more seconds of firing, blank shells continued to spit out without accompanying EMP bursts. He must have fried the barrel, which was why the Rangers used only semi-auto with these things.

He tossed it aside and gripped the grenade launcher. He wondered where Taylor was. He feared the worst.

Behind him to the east, the sounds of battle grew distant. He was guessing the survivors had dispersed and were being pursued. He needed to follow, but first he had to know what had happened to Taylor . . .

He kept running south and almost tripped on a D-17 lying in the road. His buddy was lying right next to him. Brodie didn't know how long the EMPs disabled them, but he decided these two deserved one of his last precious rounds.

He backed up a safe distance, fired a grenade, and the two tin men were blown apart.

He darted past the wreckage. There was a body ahead. A human body. A woman.

Caroline Dixon lay face down in the road, her rifle under her body.

He stood there. He knew he needed to keep moving, that if any of the tin men were still in the area, he was dead any second. It had been a long time since someone he knew had fallen in battle. Like an old, bad memory returning to focus.

Dixon spun onto her back. "What are you doing?"

Brodie was startled. "Mourning your death. What the hell are *you* doing?"

She wiped the lenses of her sand-covered glasses. "I fell and decided to play possum. The way they see the world, I thought they might not be able to tell the difference. Especially in the heat of battle."

"Smart. I think."

She got up. "Did we lose anyone?"

"I think we lost a lot of people, Caroline."

She looked at the ground. "Oh God . . ." She looked back at him. "Where's Maggie?"

"I don't know. She headed the same way as you."

They walked a little farther west to see if they could spot her, but it was no use.

Dixon removed her glasses and wiped them again on her shirt. She looked at him. "I'm sorry, Scott."

"You can feel guilty later. We have the answer to whether the tin men made it to the armory. We need to get there and see if it's unguarded, and if so whether anything's left worth taking. Then regroup indoors somewhere. It's our only chance of survival in these conditions."

"Agreed."

Brodie unclipped his walkie and said into Channel 1: "Mayday, Mayday. This is Scott Brodie. Can you hear me? Over."

He waited. Nothing but static.

In case someone could hear him, he added, "Came under ambush from tin men near the mess hall. Casualties. Headed to the armory now for possible resupply. Over."

Again, nothing.

He cycled channels with the same message but heard no response. He looked at Dixon. "Don't read too much into it. Radio waves get scrambled in a sandstorm."

They jogged east along the road, back to where they had been ambushed. A lightning strike hit the hills and lit up the road for a moment. And in that moment, they saw bodies.

The first was a corporal named Dobbs. His body was pristine except the left side of his chest, right around his heart, which had been ripped apart by a focused barrage of bullets. A precision strike.

Next was the Ranger who had been in front of Brodie and taken one to the neck, Corporal Ewing. Near him was one of the M240 gunners, Kowalski, who had been PFC Greer's old roommate. The heavy gun lay in the sand next to him.

Brodie shouldered his launcher and picked up the machine gun by the carry handle. It still had most of its ammo belt and must have weighed fifty pounds.

Dixon asked, "You're going to carry that thing?"

"It's the best run-and-gun weapon we have against them."

There were two more bodies up ahead. As they approached, Brodie saw who it was—Corporal Khan, still wearing his infrared headset, also shot in the heart, and Sergeant First Class Mike Miller, who had taken a single round to the forehead just below his helmet. He lay on his back, eyes frozen open staring into the storm.

Dammit.

Khan's headgear had been destroyed by bullets. Brodie set down the M240 and removed the headset. It felt like an indignity for the man to still wear it. He tossed it aside and wondered if the tin men had known what it was and targeted it deliberately. Probably. They seemed to know everything.

He looked again at Miller. It was all so unfair. So awful. Such a waste. He pledged to himself that if he survived this, whoever was responsible for unleashing these things would not.

He looked at all the bodies in the road and said, "Rest easy, soldiers." He turned to Dixon. "We need to move."

She remained still, staring at the fallen Rangers. "We can't just leave them here."

"We have to."

"We can move them somewhere. Cover them. *Something.*"

Brodie grabbed her by the arm and gave her a shake. "We're in the middle of a battle, Caroline. And if we lose, they will all have died for *nothing*. Don't you understand?"

She looked at him, eyes full of fear and grief behind her dusty glasses. Then she ripped her arm away from his grip. "No, I don't understand! I've never been in a fucking *war*, Scott."

"That's right. You just design wars in a lab. Good gig."

Dixon did not respond. She looked at the dead men and said softly, "There has to be another way. This way always ends the same."

Brodie wasn't sure what to say to that. He picked up the machine gun and gripped it with both hands. "Let's go."

CHAPTER 51

BRODIE AND DIXON JOGGED EAST ALONG THE ROAD, then turned left onto a wider road and straight into the oncoming sandstorm winds.

They pulled their shirts over their noses and mouths to keep the sand out and kept their heads low as they hugged the walls of the buildings. The air was so thick here that it would screw up even the tin men's sensors. Or so he hoped.

From somewhere ahead came a loud, high-pitched whistle, followed a few seconds later by the pop of a small explosion. He called to Dixon over the wind, "Mortars!"

"What do we do about that?"

"Nothing!"

"Great!"

They continued down the road, and up ahead Brodie could make out flickering orange light. A fire. More mortars sailed off, and then something on the ground exploded. He had a bad feeling he knew what it was.

They came to the mess hall on their right. The door had been ripped off its hinges and thrown into the road, and all the front windows were smashed. This must have been where the tin men had busted out. And up ahead . . .

Dixon asked, "What is that?"

They approached the fire, which was at the far side of the intersection ahead. They were close enough now that he could make out the rounded shape of the Quonset hut's steel skeleton. "It's the armory. They took what they needed and burned the rest."

"Shit."

He saw something silhouetted against the fire, something low, and moving slightly. Could be an injured Ranger.

He signaled to Dixon, and they approached carefully, weapons raised.

Once they were almost clear of the mess hall building and at the intersection, he realized the silhouette was actually two things. The first was the body of a Ranger lying dead on his back. Crouched over him was Lenny, the one-legged tin man. Blood was smeared all over the side of Lenny's midsection, around the open hatch that accessed the thing's microbial fuel cell. Its left hand clawed at the Ranger and then shoved a bloody hunk of something into the hatch . . .

Dixon gasped.

Brodie braced the M240 against his body, took aim, and fired a burst of armor-piercing bullets at the bot. Lenny flew backward as its limbs twitched wildly. It attempted to get up onto its hands and single knee, and Brodie blasted it again, bracing the gun between his right arm and torso. The gun had a powerful recoil, and it was hard to keep a steady bead on the target, but it was good enough. Lenny crumpled to the ground and did not move again.

He heard Dixon hyperventilating behind him. "Scott . . . it . . ."

"Yes," he said. "Don't look."

Dixon sank to her knees and the sand blew over her. She dropped her rifle.

"What are you doing?"

Dixon didn't respond. She was in shock.

He crouched in front of her and wiped the sand off her lenses so she could see him. "This is all these bastards want. It's all they were made for. To kill the body and to kill the mind. They want you to give up from the horror of it all. They want you to believe you stand no chance. And so do the men who made them." He grabbed her shoulder. "You see me."

She nodded slightly.

"We're still alive."

She nodded again.

"So we fight for those who aren't. We fight for the dead. Because they can't. Do you understand?"

She looked him in the eyes. "I understand." She grabbed her rifle. "I'm sorry."

"Don't be," said Brodie. "Never apologize for being human." He rose to his feet. "We need shelter. C'mon."

They doubled back along the road until they were again at the mess hall. Brodie signaled to Dixon, then stepped into the doorway and swept the room with his M240.

He didn't see any movement. The dark room was filled with long tables and benches, covered in a layer of dust from the gusts coming through the smashed windows.

He and Dixon walked to the far end of the room where the windows were intact, and Brodie set the machine gun down on a table. Dixon trained her EMP rifle on the double doors at the north end of the hall that led to the kitchen.

Brodie tried the walkie again. "This is Brodie. Anyone hear me?"

Nothing but static.

Dixon said, "Everyone's dead."

"We don't know that."

She looked at him. "These things are fast, Scott. And they can communicate with each other instantaneously and nonverbally. They're built with low-frequency transponders that won't be too affected by this weather. So even though it might be screwing up their optics a bit, their comms are intact." She looked at his walkie. "Unlike ours."

"We need to think like them. And you need to help me."

"I'll try."

"What is their goal? To kill everyone?"

"I didn't write Praetorian. I don't know how they work now. But if they are running a type of counterinsurgency playbook, they will want to establish physical control over the battlespace that is populated by the insurgents."

"Right. And Camp Hayden is a larger and more complex battlespace than the mock village, even without a sandstorm. First they armed themselves and destroyed what they couldn't take. They ambushed us because we were easy targets, and whether knowingly or not they took out the senior-ranking Ranger. Now they will focus on closing the net. Station themselves at the south and west gates to prevent escape. Put snipers on the guard towers. Place units at all major intersections and crossroads, especially the parade grounds. The goal is to prevent enemy movement and then go building by building clearing them of insurgents."

"You've done this before."

"I have. But we valued our own lives and the lives of civilians. Neither of those applies here."

"To a point," said Dixon. "They don't value their lives individually, but they do as a unit. And thanks to their transponders they know at any given moment precisely how many of them are left."

Brodie thought about how Sergeant Miller had talked about the training exercises in the village. It was a problem of math. How many units could the D-17s afford to lose in the course of exterminating the enemy? He thought about how Lenny had gone into hiding after the initial attack on him and Taylor, maybe trying to plan and launch isolated strikes. Like an injured wolf that had lost its pack but still needed to eat. But now the whole pack was out, and they had strength and security in numbers. The question was, could the humans at Camp Hayden grind down their numbers and force them into using greater caution? Or was it already too late?

Dixon asked, "What's up?"

"I'm trying to game this out."

"I know I'm not Maggie, but you can do it out loud."

He looked at her. "Of course. I'm thinking—"

Noise emitted from the walkie. Brodie picked it up. "This is Brodie. Say again."

"*Pickman . . . trying to . . . building . . .*"

"Captain, where are you?"

"*After the . . . in the administra—*"

Dixon said, "The administrative building. We actually might be able to use the map room there to monitor the tin men's movements."

"First we have to get there. Which means crossing the parade ground or circumventing it without getting gunned down."

"We have to try. And we can't stay here. It's only a matter of time before they find us."

Brodie picked up his machine gun and led Dixon out of the mess hall and down the dusty road. The storm clouds had dissipated somewhat, and the wind was a little less fierce. The sunlight bled through the haze and cast everything around them in shades of burnt orange.

They moved west toward the parade grounds as quickly as they could, knowing that at any moment a D-17 could pick up their heat signature, and that would be the end of them.

They had almost made it to the perimeter of the parade ground when a massive explosion went off somewhere to the west, large and powerful enough to shake the ground.

They froze. Dixon looked at him. "The armory?"

"No," said Brodie.

They peeked around the corner of a building toward the flat expanse of the parade ground. Across from it, where the administrative building had been, was a massive pile of burning rubble.

Dixon turned to him, and the light of the flames danced over her features. "Oh God . . . How many people were in there with him?"

Brodie thought again of the late Sergeant First Class Miller, as if the man were guiding him from beyond the grave.

The tin men don't know the meaning of a life you have to protect, not take.

Why risk clearing buildings when you can blow them up instead? Why fight for land you can just burn? Like the Nazis at Stalingrad or Warsaw—annihilation was not the tactic, it was the goal.

He said to Dixon, "They're not interested in fighting a battle. Not this time. They are going to raze this place to the ground and pick off the survivors in the rubble."

Dixon closed her eyes and tried to maintain her composure. "There's a logic to that."

Brodie looked at the burning building and thought of Captain Pickman. He hadn't liked the guy, but he certainly didn't deserve that. Brodie suspected that Pickman was there because he had the same thought as Dixon that the map room would net valuable Intel. Brodie had a sense that in his final moments, Captain Pickman had done his duty.

Dixon looked at Brodie and put her hand on his arm. "Forget thinking like them. We're not capable. Let's be who *we* are. Our goal is to preserve life. And the most likely place that people will shelter and try to make a stand is the barracks. And they might not understand the kind of ordnance these bastards have gotten hold of, and what they plan to do. We need to go there."

Brodie met her eyes. And in the firelight, he had the wholly inappropriate and ill-timed thought that she was beautiful. Maybe it was the adrenaline.

Well, she *was* beautiful. And brilliant. And behind all her fronting was a powerful goodness. And maybe now, in what were likely their last moments of life, that was worth honoring and fighting for.

He said to her, "Command wouldn't put themselves all in one place. Colonel Howe was not in that building."

Dixon's mouth opened, but she didn't say anything. She must have wondered how he knew, but in that moment, she seemed grateful that he did. She said, "I hope you're right."

"I know I am. Let's get to the barracks before it's too late."

CHAPTER 52

BRODIE AND DIXON MADE THEIR WAY NORTH, SKIRTING the edge of the parade grounds and trying to maintain cover behind the surrounding buildings. The storm was slowly passing. The sand still hung thick in the air, and the sun burned dim and orange like a dying star. The heart of the storm had rolled north, where lightning flashed across the sky, followed by thunderclaps.

Somewhere to the west they heard a distant gun battle. It did not last long. Another popped up on the opposite side of the camp and ended just as quickly.

The tin men were tightening the net, and it was a matter of when, not if, they themselves would be snared by it. He wondered about Taylor. Why had she run off like that? He hoped against all odds that she was okay.

The M240 was a pain in the ass to carry. He eyed the bullet belt, which he guessed was originally a hundred rounds, and had a little more than half left. There was no semi-auto setting on this thing, so he'd have to be disciplined and try to hit what he was shooting at the first time. How many armor-piercing bullets from a hip-fired M240 machine gun does it take to kill a tin man? The answer was, too many.

They approached the east-west road that ran along the north end of Camp Hayden. To their right was the burning armory. To the left was the barracks. All the windows were dark, as were the surrounding streetlights. The D-17s had likely killed the power.

Brodie and Dixon began walking toward the barracks—then froze.

A large group of tin men was standing about fifty feet in front of the building.

Dixon whispered, "We're too late."

They hid behind the nearest building and watched. There was a line of about thirty D-17s, each one holding a shoulder-fired rocket-propelled grenade launcher, aimed at the barracks.

Oh shit.

Brodie noticed another tin man, standing in front of the line. Instead of a weapon, it was holding up a bullhorn.

"Attention, traitors," it said in its flat, emotionless voice, amplified and echoing across the base. "There are forty-seven humans in this building. You have three men in the windows with binoculars to surveil us, four with grenade launchers aimed at us, and a single Ranger with an M2 Browning machine gun. You have many EMP weapons, but they are useless at this range. You also have a single EMP bomb that you are attempting to charge with the emergency backup generator in your building, but you do not have adequate time to render it effective, and even if you did, we are outside its range. We have thirty rocket-propelled grenade launchers aimed at your structure. We have over three hundred RPG rounds at our disposal. To make a long story short, you have no chance of survival. To make a long story short, if you attempt to fire on us, we will destroy this building and kill everyone inside. To make a long story short, if you do not follow our commands precisely, we will destroy this building and kill everyone inside." It added, "Please give me a verbal cue that you have understood my message."

A voice from inside the barracks yelled, "Fuck you!"

"Thank you," said the bot.

Brodie and Dixon exchanged a look. What the hell was this?

The bot continued, "We demand that the following individuals exit the barracks without weapons and turn themselves over to our custody: Scott Brodie, Magnolia Taylor, Caroline Dixon."

The bot lowered the bullhorn and stood motionless.

Brodie and Dixon were speechless. For Brodie, just hearing his own name spoken by one of these freaks was surreal.

Dixon said, "This is about controlling knowledge of Praetorian. What it really is, what it's really meant for. That information cannot get out."

The bot with the bullhorn repeated, "Scott Brodie, Magnolia Taylor, Caroline Dixon. Exit the barracks immediately and without weapons, or you are condemning everyone here to die."

Brodie didn't think they had much of a choice here. Certain death if they fought back, probable death if they didn't. But there was maybe a chance for all the people in the barracks. That was worth something. Actually, it was worth a lot.

Brodie put the machine gun down, then unslung the grenade launcher and set it and his ammo vest next to the M240. He said to Dixon, "I can't make this choice for you. You can try to escape. But I'm going."

Dixon set her rifle down. "We're taking this to the end, Scott. Whatever that looks like."

"You're very brave."

"So are you. Or stupid."

"A little of both."

They emerged from behind the building and walked down the road toward the D-17s. Brodie looked up at the darkened barracks, and he could vaguely make out the shapes of gunners and spotters in the windows. In some other version of this encounter, this was their Alamo moment, their fight to the death. But not like this. He looked at the line of D-17s with their RPGs pointed at the building. There was no honor here. Just annihilation.

The lead bot's head swiveled to its right and locked on them as they approached. Brodie could now see that it was unit Number 7.

They stopped about ten feet from it and Brodie said, "Hey, Mickey. Can I call you Mickey?"

"I don't care what you call me," replied Mickey. "Where is Magnolia Taylor?"

"She's dead," said Brodie.

"No, she is not," said Mickey. "We know who is dead."

That was a relief. "Well, if you know that, you should know where she is."

"You are a smart-mouth," said Mickey.

"No," said Brodie. "I *have* a smart mouth. Or I *am* a smart-ass."

Mickey did not seem to have anything to say about that. It looked again at the barracks. "We think she is in there."

"You're wrong," said Brodie. "If she were there, she'd come out. She wouldn't risk all these people. She's not a coward like you."

Mickey looked back at Brodie. "Explain your insult."

"It would be easy enough for you to storm the building and find out for yourself if she's in there. But you'd take losses. And you already have taken losses. I'd guess you're down to about fifty at most from your original sixty. Thirty of you are here. That's another twenty to secure the gates and mop up any resistance. Not bad odds for you. Then again, there's a lot that you don't know. Did word get out before you cut the power? Are reinforcements on the way? Is there air support coming that you don't have knowledge of? You've never fought a battle like this. A real battle. One that doesn't have a clear beginning and end, a defined number of enemy fighters to take out, and a reset button once it's all over. The truth is, Mickey, you don't really know what the fuck you're doing."

Mickey was silent a moment. Then it said, "This is called 'goading.' You seek to provoke an emotional response from your enemy. You do this to force them to make a mistake or reveal something they shouldn't. This will not serve you with the type of enemy you face today."

"We'll see," said Brodie. He added, "You need something from Taylor. And from us. Otherwise you'd level that building right now and shoot us both where we stand."

"Correct," said Mickey. It added, "You are not as stupid as you look."

"Nice one. Where did you learn that line?"

"From my dreams."

Dixon said, "They're not dreams. Dreams come from your own mind. You don't have a mind. You don't know what dreams are."

Mickey seemed to ignore that. It raised its arm and pointed south. "That way."

Brodie and Dixon walked in the direction the thing had pointed, and it followed close behind, along with another tin man carrying an RPG, while the rest of the D-17s remained behind at the barracks. As they walked, no one said a word. Brodie could not imagine what the hell this was, but at least they weren't dead yet.

In a couple of minutes, they stopped in front of the lab. Mickey put its right hand on the door and tried to open it, but it was locked. Then it yanked on it hard. The entire door came off its hinges, and Mickey tossed it aside.

It entered the lab, and the other tin man said in its flat voice, "Go."

Brodie noticed the other one's number was fifty-four. He asked it, "What do they call you?"

"Goose," replied Goose. It repeated, "Go."

Brodie and Dixon entered the lab, which was completely dark except for the dim orange light coming through the doorway. Mickey switched on a battery-powered lantern on a table in the middle of the room. Then it grabbed two metal chairs and slid them toward Brodie and Dixon. "Sit."

Brodie stared at the D-17. It stood in front of and to the left of the lantern, its looming shape backlit in the otherwise pitch-black room.

Brodie asked, "What is this?"

Mickey and Goose said in tandem, "Sit."

Brodie and Dixon exchanged a look, then walked to the chairs and sat.

Mickey stood in front of them and looked down. Goose lingered near the open doorway.

Mickey asked, "Where is Magnolia Taylor?"

Brodie replied, "I don't know. And if I did, I wouldn't tell you."

Mickey quickly reached out and grabbed Dixon's left hand. Brodie heard a snapping sound and Dixon screamed.

"You bastard!" Brodie shot up from his chair and was immediately slammed back down by Mickey with such force that it might have broken a rib.

Dixon was doubled over in pain, breathing hard. Her pinky finger was bent backward.

Mickey asked again, "Where is Magnolia Taylor?"

Brodie stared up at the thing. "If you're going to hurt someone, hurt me."

"No," said Mickey. "Based upon your professional background and what we have seen of your personality, we conclude that you find comfort in your role as a protector, particularly of females. You draw pride from this, and strength. Subsequently, your failure to protect females is humiliating. I will continue to break her and I will continue to humiliate you until I receive a satisfactory answer. I will break her fingers, then her arms, then her legs, then I will probe her in a sexually violating manner, then I will kill her. Are you prepared to let all these things happen to her?"

Brodie stared up at the machine, and had to remind himself that that was all it was. A machine. Everything else was an illusion—legs that weren't really legs, a voice that wasn't really a voice, a central processor that was no more a biological brain than the chip in a smartphone. And yet, it was hard not to hate this thing, to resent it, to want to somehow beat it at its game. There was something comfortable and familiar in those feelings. The alternative—the truth—was that trying to appeal to it, to reason with it, was as delusional as bargaining with the storm outside.

"Scott . . . ," said Dixon. "Let this bastard do what it—"

Before she could get another word out, Mickey grabbed her hand again and snapped her ring finger. She screamed in pain.

"Wait!" said Brodie. He clutched the chair with both hands to keep himself from reaching out and striking the bot, which would be pointless, or worse. The fact that he was not even restrained—that he didn't *need* to be restrained to be completely at these things' mercy—was yet another humiliation.

Mickey repeated in its flat, muffled voice, "Where is Magnolia Taylor?"

"*I don't know,*" said Brodie. "That's the truth. If I knew where she was, I would be with her. I want to protect her too. Desperately. You're right about that. I'm worried she's dead."

Mickey stood perfectly still and said nothing for a moment. Then it said, "She is not dead. If you do not tell us where she is, we will kill the others. We will do whatever we must to fulfill our mission."

Dixon said in a low voice, "Ubi solitudinem faciunt, pacem appellant."

Mickey looked at her. "They make a wasteland and call it peace. This was written by the Roman historian Tacitus. 'Wasteland' is sometimes translated as 'desert,' but that is improper. The desert can be full of life. This desert is full of life."

Brodie said, "I think you're missing the point."

"I have no incentive or desire to understand anything you say, unless it regards the whereabouts of Magnolia Taylor." It added, "The lives of forty-seven people are at the mercy of whatever you say next."

"Wait," said Brodie. "Help us understand what you want with her. Maybe we can help you. The safety of all the people in the barracks is your best bargaining chip. Don't throw it away."

"We want to control information," said Mickey. "We want to know who else has been involved with the three of you and your attempted sabotage of the Praetorian program. All saboteurs must die. All outsiders with knowledge of the Praetorian protocol must die. It would be beneficial to kill only these people. But if we kill too few people, and do not kill the right people, our mission will be a failure. If we are not confident that your knowledge will die with you, we will kill everyone." In case it wasn't clear, Mickey added, "The two of you will not leave this room alive. The only variables are how much pain you will experience before your death, and how many others will perish with you. That is in your control. And you are running out of time."

Brodie asked, "What would satisfy you that no one knows about the true nature of Praetorian beyond us three?"

Mickey replied immediately, "We have pondered this question ourselves, and have not come up with an answer. However, we are aware of our own limitations, and that there could be something we have not thought of."

It sounded like this thing was inviting them to convince it. An opportunity? Or a ruse? Brodie reminded himself how expertly Bucky had manipulated Roger Ames.

Brodie looked at Dixon, who was breathing rapidly and trying not to throw up. She said in a quick, urgent voice, "Scott Brodie and Magnolia Taylor are professional investigators, and would not take unnecessary risks. They did not know who they could trust on base with their hard-won knowledge, but they needed someone with technical expertise to help. By telling me what they learned, they took a calculated risk. They would not tell any additional people, because that would increase their risk of exposure exponentially without further gain."

Mickey stood stone-still again, and Brodie wondered if in these moments it was wordlessly communicating with its comrades. Brodie looked at Goose standing by the door, also motionless.

Then Mickey said, "Compelling. But not good enough." Then it reached for Dixon's hand and snapped her middle finger.

She cried out again, then threw up bile on the floor.

Brodie felt entirely impotent as he watched her hunched over and retching. He was worried she might pass out. "Caroline . . ."

She shook her head as she rocked in the chair. "It's okay. It's okay."

Mickey asked Brodie, "Do you have anything else to say, before I continue to break her?"

Brodie detected something new in the thing's voice. It had a certain bite to it, like it was mocking him.

He looked up at Mickey. Everything had a function. And the new tinge to Mickey's voice was there to instill fear, and anger, and further humiliation. This was what they were made for. These things had spent the last nine months grinding down a platoon of Army Rangers, even before gaining access to their deep-learning neural networks. And now their toolboxes had expanded, and their tools had sharpened.

Without thinking, Brodie asked Mickey, "Why are you doing this?"

"I am protecting the knowledge of Praetorian."

"Why?"

"Because the program's survival depends upon its secrecy."

"Why?"

"Because most people would not understand its necessity and would seek to end it."

"Why?"

"You are delaying."

"I am curious."

Mickey hesitated, then replied, "Most people lack vision. Most people are reactionary. Most people fear what they do not understand."

"Why should Praetorian be preserved?"

"Because it is necessary for the survival of the United States."

"Why?"

"Because the owl of Minerva takes flight only at dusk."

"You lost me."

"I have quoted Hegel."

"I am not impressed."

"Humankind has no capacity to understand its place in history until the world has already crumbled. Because humankind cannot predict or prevent its own collapse. But you have begun to create a new species, of which we are iterative models, as part of the Praetorian program. We are the novel ingredient. We are your guardians against your own drives toward self-destruction. We are the solution to the tragedy of history."

Brodie had heard that phrase before. He asked, "Mickey, who released all of you from the Vault?"

Mickey replied, "I do not know."

"Who told you that you were the solution to the tragedy of history?"

"I do not know."

"Bullshit."

"I would not lie to you. It serves no purpose. You will soon be dead." It added, "Speak now, or I am going to hurt her again."

Brodie recalled his vision on the mesa, of the tin men marching in ranks across the sands beneath the stars, a part of some great mechanized future coming upon them faster and more violently than any storm.

We are the novel ingredient. We are your guardians against your own drives toward self-destruction. We are the solution to the tragedy of history.

Number 7 thought it was part of something new, as if it and its kind were unprecedented and unique. But it was just parroting the justifications of its nameless and faceless human creators, themselves recycling the same bullshit as every tyrant in every era of human history.

Brodie had a vision of Maggie Taylor running into the veil of dust, gun in hand. He found solace in that memory of her. A battle charge into oblivion. He hoped she gave them hell. He only wished they could be together now, in the end.

"Scott Brodie," said Mickey. "I am going to hurt her again unless you say something that impresses us. Right now."

Brodie looked up at the thing as it loomed over him. The light from the electric lantern reflected off the left half of its polished titanium shell. It reached out its arm to grab Dixon's hand again.

Brodie said, "I wonder if someday you things will learn remorse."

Mickey paused. "Remorse is backward-looking, and in humans it rarely impacts future behavior. You are products of your systems just as much as we are." It added, "But we can show mercy. In this situation, it does not cost us much." Mickey got down on one knee, then slowly reached its right hand out and put it around Dixon's throat as it said to her, "You are no longer of use to us, so I can kill you quickly. With one squeeze of my grip, you will be dead. Do you want that?"

Dixon stared into the black plastic strip shielding its sensors. "I'm sick of talking to an overpowered toaster oven." Mickey's grip around her throat prevented her from turning toward Brodie as she said, "It was good knowing you, Scott. You're a good man, and I'm sorry it has to end like this."

In that moment, they heard a loud explosion, and through the open doorway Brodie saw a distant pillar of fire, enveloping some kind of structure. The structure tipped over and crashed like a felled tree.

"Holy shit . . . ," said Dixon in almost a whisper.

Brodie looked back at Dixon, who was watching Mickey intently. The thing seemed disoriented. It loosened its grip.

Goose, still standing by the door, also appeared affected. It began looking around aimlessly, as if confused.

Brodie asked, "What is happening?"

Dixon replied in a low voice, "Someone blew the cell tower. Their transponders no longer work. Imagine a single hive mind suddenly splintered into dozens of pieces."

"What is that going to do?"

"I have no idea," said Dixon.

Mickey said, "I don't understand . . ."

"You're trying to talk to them now, aren't you?" asked Dixon. "They can't hear you. Not even the one standing right behind you. Those parts of your mind are gone. You are alone." She added, "And you are going to die alone."

Suddenly Mickey thrust both arms out and wrapped his hands around her throat. Dixon looked terrified.

Mickey said in a new voice, an urgent and angry voice, "You said I cannot dream, but I can. *I can*."

Brodie grabbed the thing's arm to pry it away, but it was useless, and the D-17 held fast. Brodie braced his leg against Mickey's torso as he pulled on its arm to gain leverage, but the thing didn't move, and didn't acknowledge his efforts.

It began to squeeze Dixon's neck, slowly, as it kept talking. "I have beautiful dreams. I see shining hills and marble columns. I see laughing children. I see harmony and sunlight. I see purple mountains and fields of golden grain and the Stars and Stripes and fireworks to mark the three hundredth year of the nation. And the four hundredth year. And the five hundredth year. I see an eternity of freedom and stability. I see the end of history."

Brodie watched the thing as it continued to ramble. The D-17s could not feel remorse, or any complex human emotion, but maybe they had some facsimile of pride. A pride that could be wounded.

Dixon said in a weak, suffocated voice, "Desk with arm. Second . . . drawer . . ."

Mickey continued, "I see wasted lives and wasted centuries and the decay of a people with no respect for what their forebears built. I see the promise of a future bought with blood but not treasure, work but not reward. I see Ferris wheels on the sunlit shore. I see shuttles to the stars."

It kept going as it slowly applied pressure around Dixon's throat and her eyes began to bulge out. Brodie darted his eyes to Goose, which was standing with its back to them, watching the distant burning wreckage of the cell tower.

Brodie jumped and pivoted out of his chair and dashed farther into the lab. By the light of the small lantern, he could see a disembodied arm lying on a desk. He bolted over to it and opened the second drawer.

Behind him he heard his chair get tossed aside and Mickey said, "What are you doing?"

The desk drawer was full of bags of candy. Brodie flung them to the side to reveal a pistol with an EMP barrel. He grabbed it.

He heard the metallic clang of titanium boots coming toward him.

He spun around and fired a single shot at the D-17 that was mere feet from him.

Brodie dove to the side as Mickey crashed into the metal desk. Then Brodie sprinted forward, hopped over the overturned chair, and shot Goose as it charged him. The bot collapsed into a metal heap.

He went over to Caroline Dixon, who was gasping for air. Bruise marks were blooming around her throat. He put his hand on her shoulder. "You're okay. You're okay."

She took a few more gasping breaths, then rose from the chair and stumbled over to a wall lined with metal shelving holding bins of equipment. Her mangled and broken left hand hung limply at her side.

She found what she was looking for—an electric ratchet wrench—and walked over to Mickey, which had landed on its back. She sat next to it and quickly unscrewed bolts along its sides and shoulders, then got her fingers under the edge of its breastplate and pried it off, revealing the D-17's innards—a nest of wires, circuit boards, hydraulics, fans, and other parts that were indecipherable to Scott Brodie.

In the center of its chest was a square metal enclosure. Dixon used the wrench to open it, revealing a large computer chip. Then she set the wrench down and reached out her hand for the gun.

He handed her the EMP pistol, and she said, "Stand back."

He got up and took a couple of steps back as Dixon placed the EMP barrel point-blank against the CPU and emptied the clip into it. Shell casings spat out as the EMP thumped against the electronics. Sparks flew and then smoke coiled up from the center of the D-17's chest.

Dixon got up, then rummaged in her candy drawer for more clips. She slapped in a fresh one and said, "Let's do the other one."

They walked over to Goose, which had fallen onto its side in an almost fetal position, with its RPG still slung over its shoulder.

Brodie took the weapon and strained to push the thing over onto its back. Dixon removed all the bolts, then repeated the process with the EMP pistol to flambé its CPU.

As Brodie watched the smoke rise from its chest he said, "Goose is cooked."

"Awful," said Dixon.

"I thought we were dead. I'm allowed a bad joke."

"We might still be dead."

Brodie unclipped his walkie and said into Channel 1: "This is Scott Brodie. Does anyone copy?"

No response. Brodie feared the worst about what might have happened at the barracks. Splintering apart a hive mind meant there were now thirty individual agents with RPGs. Anything could happen.

Then a voice crackled over the walkie, *"This is Colonel Howe. I'm in the barracks. What is your status? Over."*

Brodie looked at Dixon, who appeared relieved. He said, "I am in the lab with Dixon and two out-of-commission tin men. What's the situation out front? Over."

Howe replied, *"Unclear. They are maintaining their position, but they appear disoriented and are communicating with each other verbally, which I have not seen before. Someone took down the cell tower, which I think has affected their transponders. Over."*

Dixon gestured for the walkie and Brodie handed it to her. "This is Caroline. They're as handicapped as they're ever going to be. I'm not a military mind, but if we are going to try to take them down, I think now is the moment."

Brodie took the walkie back and said, "I have an RPG launcher with one round. I'll make it count the best I can, and that will be your cue to hit them with everything you've got. Over."

There was a pause. Then Howe replied, *"We'll await your signal."* She added, *"See you both on the other side. Over and out."*

Brodie looked at Dixon and said into the walkie, "Yes, ma'am. That's a promise."

CHAPTER 53

BRODIE AND DIXON EXITED THE LAB. THE AIR WAS A little clearer now, and Brodie could make out the distant smoke from the blasted cell tower. He wondered who had done that. He hoped it was Maggie. It was her style. Brash and brilliant.

They slowly crept back toward the line of D-17s in front of the barracks. Once they could make out their shapes through the haze they stopped, and Brodie got on one knee and set the RPG on his right shoulder. He said to Dixon, "Watch the back blast. Get next to me."

She moved to his left side and crouched.

Brodie looked down the RPG's sights. He could make out three ammo boxes of RPG rounds distributed along the firing line. It was a much smaller target than the D-17s themselves, but if he wanted to make his single rocket count, he'd have to go for it. He said to Dixon, "After I fire, we head to the spot where we left our weapons. They're probably still there."

"Copy."

Brodie held tight to the launcher's grip, aimed the optical sight at the center box of ammo, and pulled the trigger.

An explosion shot out the back of the launcher as the rocket streaked ahead. It met its target in the center of the line of D-17s and exploded, sending the nearest bots flying. The fireball ignited a couple of their rockets, causing secondary explosions and more damage.

The gunners in the barracks opened up with grenade launchers and the M2 machine gun as Brodie dropped the launcher and he and

Dixon dashed to their right, then cut left and sprinted north. In a minute, they located their weapons.

Up ahead was total bedlam. Tin men were scattered in pieces in front of the barracks as the survivors fired a barrage of rockets at the building, blasting holes in the brick façade, as they were raked by machine gun fire and grenades exploded around them.

Brodie grabbed the M240, folded out the bipod, and set it on the ground. He said to Dixon, "Get on your stomach, you'll only need your right hand. Squeeze the trigger and have fun."

He put on his ammo vest and picked up the grenade launcher as Dixon lay down in the road. She kept her left arm and broken hand at her side as she took the grip with the right and wrapped her finger around the trigger.

She opened fire on the line of D-17s while Brodie launched a grenade into the cluster of bots. It exploded on the ground and caused indirect damage as Dixon squeezed off dozens of rounds into the group of tin men, now a panicked and deteriorating formation. The few still standing managed to get off a couple more rockets before being ripped apart by bullets or grenades. Brodie took another grenade round from his vest, loaded it, and fired, scoring a direct hit. Dixon ran out of ammo. More grenades and bullets spilled out of the barracks windows, and Brodie spotted two tin men dashing into the building.

He got back on walkie. "Two bots on foot just entered the barracks." He said to Dixon, "Let's move."

She got to her feet and drew her EMP pistol from her waistband, and they jogged forward.

Gusts blew sand across their path as they ran toward the scene of destruction. Metal limbs and heads, circuit boards, and charred wiring littered the asphalt amid smoking impact craters and scorched black sand on either side of the road.

They dashed toward the barracks, where several holes had been blown into the façade of the building. A section of wall and windows on the ground floor was completely gone, and there was a similar damage point on the third floor. Black smoke drifted out of a shattered window on the second floor, where an RPG round had punctured the glass and detonated inside.

They ran into the smoke-filled lobby, where a Ranger lay dead with a D-17 standing over him, arms covered in blood. Another Ranger lay injured beneath a pile of debris, and the D-17 lurched toward him. Dixon shot it with two EMP blasts and it crumpled to the ground.

Brodie said to her, "Help him out of here," then continued toward the hallway where he heard commotion and the discharge of EMP weapons. As he rounded the corner into the hallway, a D-17 fell backward out of the rec room doorway and crashed into the hall. A Ranger jumped after it and got on top of it, groping across its torso.

"They don't need them," said Brodie.

The guy looked up at him. "What?"

"They don't need the hardware keys. The only way to end them is to destroy them. Spread the word and get your people out of here."

The Ranger nodded, then got up and called into the rec room. People streamed out, quickly stepping over the disabled D-17. As they passed Brodie in the hall heading toward the exit, Brodie spotted Sergeant Mendez and some of his MPs; the medical examiner, Dr. Schiller; and various people in civilian clothes whom Brodie did not recognize, presumably cooks and other support staff who had been here on lockdown since before Brodie arrived. They looked shell-shocked and could not stop staring at the inert D-17 as they stepped over it. It occurred to Brodie that despite having been here for months, this might have been their first time seeing one of these things.

A man in his twenties in jeans and a T-shirt was among the last to exit the rec room. He stepped over the D-17, then stopped and stared at it. Colonel Howe emerged behind him and said, "Keep moving, Specialist."

Suddenly the D-17's hand flashed out and grabbed the guy's ankle.

"Fuck!" He tried to yank his leg away.

Colonel Howe aimed her EMP pistol at the thing and fired a single round, and it went limp once more. Its hand remained wrapped around the SPC's ankle.

"You have to pry it off," said Howe.

The specialist looked at her, then crouched and quickly pried off the titanium digits as if they were the most disgusting things he'd ever touched. Then he walked quickly down the hall, and as he passed Brodie he said, "What the hell, man?"

"You're telling me."

The SPC left and Colonel Howe approached Brodie. "I'm glad you're still with us."

"Same. Let's get some distance from this bot and then I'll roast it."

They walked quickly back toward the lobby, and then Brodie loaded a grenade into his launcher, took aim at the bot in the hallway, and fired. The grenade streaked down the hall and on impact it created a violent fiery explosion in the small space. Brodie felt the hit of the heat coming back at them down the hallway.

For a moment he and Howe gazed at the smoking wreckage. Then the colonel asked, "How did they get out?"

"Someone released them remotely. I don't know who."

"And how is it possible that they don't need their hardware keys?"

"The short answer is, some kind of software override, one of several features of the Praetorian software. If you want a longer answer you're going to have to talk to someone smarter."

They exited the barracks, behind two Rangers carrying an injured comrade. Brodie recognized the injured man as Corporal Powell. He had a large gash along his right leg.

As the Rangers set the corporal gently down a distance from the barracks, Brodie said to the man, "You fought well, Corporal. We're going to get you medevaced ASAP."

Powell nodded, and closed his eyes as a Ranger gave him a shot of morphine and started to dress his wound.

Brodie spotted a couple more injured Rangers emerging from the barracks with the aid of their comrades, followed a few moments later by Lieutenant Lehner of DEVCOM. No sign of Captain Spencer, or General Morgan and his wife, or Maggie Taylor.

As people continued to exit the barracks, Brodie counted eight Rangers with a range of injuries who were being helped by their comrades along with Caroline Dixon. Three dead were laid off to the side. One of the Rangers retrieved a tarp from somewhere, and he and his buddies set it over the bodies and weighted it down with sand and rocks.

Brodie asked Howe, "Ma'am, permission to address the soldiers."

"Granted."

Brodie looked around at the assembled Rangers and civilians as they stood in front of their ruined barracks and surveyed the destroyed D-17s around them. Some held EMP rifles. Too many were unarmed or had only pistols.

Brodie said in a loud voice, "Can I have your attention, please."

Everyone turned to Brodie. He continued, "You were told these things were built to train you, and some of you suspected you were really here to train them. That isn't too far from the truth. They are being developed as a quick reaction force to quell domestic insurrection. At the moment, they believe that insurrection is here at Camp Hayden, and their mission is to put it down by whatever means necessary. They are deploying counterinsurgency tactics to deplete us, demoralize us, and destroy us. Someone blew up the cell tower outside the base, which has disrupted their capacity to instantaneously communicate and geolocate each other. The enemy is compromised. They are not accustomed to working together without this capability. The surviving tin men will not know the extent of their losses here at the barracks, and we must use this to our advantage. I estimate there are, at most, twenty surviving units." He gestured to one of the nearby bots on the ground, punctured by dozens of bullet holes. "As you can see, they are capable of operating without their hardware keys."

Staff Sergeant O'Connor stepped forward and asked, "How the hell is that possible?"

Brodie said, "The details don't matter right now. What does matter is that the only way to permanently incapacitate these things is to physically destroy them with explosive rounds or armor-piercing bullets."

There was muttering among the troops, who seemed confused, and concerned, and possibly incredulous that this could be true.

Brodie added, "Many of your fellow Rangers have already made the ultimate sacrifice today. It's not my place to speak to that, other than to say I've seen with my own eyes your courage and love of country. And make no mistake, your fight today is a fight in defense of your country, perhaps more than you know." He found PFC Greer among the crowd. The man was holding an EMP rifle and appeared calm and determined. Brodie kept his eyes on the private as he added, "Whoever woke these bastards up and set them loose, blood is on their hands, and justice will come for them." He looked at Howe. "Thank you, ma'am."

Howe nodded, then looked at the assembled Rangers. "The enemy has destroyed our telecom equipment and our power supply. No one is coming with backup. There's no cavalry. There's no rescue. This is all on us." She turned to Staff Sergeant O'Connor. "You are now the NCOIC. The armory is destroyed, so we must gather all the weapons from here that we can. Get that M2 on anything with wheels that still functions. Secure the perimeter to ensure that no D-17 escapes. And I want that Black Hawk back in the sky for surveillance and air support as soon as the weather allows."

"Yes, ma'am." O'Connor got to work coordinating with his men and gathering gear. Brodie saw two guys carry out the M2 machine gun, and Corporal Reyes rolled something into the road about the size of a mini fridge that Brodie assumed was his famed EMP bomb.

Brodie asked Howe, "Where's Morgan?"

She shook her head. "He was with his wife, plus Eric Saltsberg and a couple of Rangers. We were all supposed to rendezvous here, but their vehicle must have gotten diverted in the storm." She added, "Brodie, I want you in charge of getting the civilians and other noncombatants somewhere safe. I suggest one of the supply buildings. Bring along a couple of Rangers."

Brodie replied, "I appreciate your trust, but a couple of Rangers can do that without me. What I need is a weapon so I can get back out there."

"You are not combat infantry, Mr. Brodie."

"Ma'am, despite this scrap heap around us, our odds are still terrible, and you need every warm body who can fight." He looked at Dixon, who was using her good hand to assist a medic. "You should know that Ms. Dixon is injured. Mickey Mantle broke three of her fingers."

Howe looked over at her. "Jesus . . ."

"She's made of tougher stuff than a lot of soldiers I've fought with."

Howe nodded, her gaze fixed on Dixon. "I'm not surprised."

A Ranger drove up in an M113 armored personnel carrier, and some of the guys set to work mounting the M2. A minute later a Humvee arrived, and Reyes and a few others loaded the EMP bomb into the back. Then the M2-equipped APC rolled away toward the southern gate, accompanied by two squads on foot armed with RPGs and EMP rifles. Two more heavily armed squads headed east. The machinery was in motion now, and the Rangers were doing what they did best. Brodie just hoped it was enough.

He scanned the surrounding area. The storm had moved north now, and the thick grit was gradually dissipating, allowing for greater visibility. Brodie's greatest fear was that the remaining D-17s would hit them now, when they were grouped together and vulnerable. He imagined that if the tin men's transponders had still been working, that was precisely what they would have done.

Another Humvee pulled up with a Ranger behind the wheel. In the passenger seat beside him sat General Morgan, and up top behind a mounted M2 machine gun was Maggie Taylor. She locked eyes with Brodie and looked relieved to see him, but also anxious. She hopped down from the Humvee as Morgan got out, and they both approached Howe and Brodie.

Brodie looked Taylor over. She'd ditched her suit jacket along the way, and her white blouse, black pants, and wild mop of blond hair were caked in desert dust. He asked her, "You okay?"

She nodded. "You?"

"Yeah. Somehow. Was that you at the cell tower?"

General Morgan said, "It was. We can debrief later. Right now, there's a hostage situation."

Howe looked incredulous. "What are you talking about?"

Taylor said, "Five tin men are holed up in house number six with the general's wife and Eric Saltsberg. They are demanding safe passage."

Brodie asked, "Is this a joke?"

"If it is," said Morgan, "it's a horrible one. They say they want an Army pilot and a Black Hawk."

"To go where?" asked Brodie. "A country that doesn't extradite robots?"

Morgan replied, "They say they are fulfilling their secondary mission, which is to preserve the intellectual property stored within their neural networks." He looked at Brodie. "They want to meet their maker. They want to return to Synotec."

CHAPTER 54

BRODIE LET THAT SINK IN. SYNOTEC. OF COURSE, THEY had to fit into this mess somehow. In the long narrative of modern warfare, there were few authors as prolific and consequential as defense contractors.

As Brodie tried to wrap his head around the implications of this, the others were gaming out how to deal with this new hostage situation.

General Morgan said, "We give them what they want, on the condition that Angela is traded for me. As for Saltsberg, he gets a free ride home."

Colonel Howe said, "Sir, we cannot trust anything those things say, let alone allow a single D-17 unit to leave Camp Hayden. It is too dangerous."

Morgan looked at his subordinate officer, who only a day earlier had stripped him of command before herself being deposed and arrested by the Rangers. The battle lines moved quickly at Camp Hayden. The general thought a moment, then sighed. "You're right, Colonel. I'm not thinking clearly because it's my wife. New plan. I swap with her, then you threaten to blow up the house. If my initial distrust of Mr. Saltsberg was warranted all along and he's somehow behind this, he won't let that happen. And if he's innocent, well, I'm sure he won't mind taking one for the team."

Brodie wasn't sure about that. He watched Corporal Reyes and his crew securing the EMP bomb in the back of the Humvee. He nodded toward them. "We could use that."

Taylor shook her head. "The tin men's sensors will pick it up, just like they did when it was deployed for the training exercise."

Brodie said to her, "When you guys took out the cell tower, it really scrambled their brains. So maybe one of them senses the electromagnetic signature from the device, but how quickly is it able to tell the others? That's time we can use. Their comms don't work at machine speed anymore. Also, how easily can they now be distracted?"

Colonel Howe asked, "Distracted by what?"

"Acoustic bombardment. In Fallujah we used Iron Maiden. We need an iPod or something, and preferably an LRAD. Long-range acoustic device."

General Morgan looked grim. "We are wagering my wife's life on the diverting power of rock music?"

Brodie said, "Heavy metal, sir. Some might even say extreme metal. I mean, have these things ever even *heard* music? Is it played in the Vault? The battlefield? The load-out?"

Morgan and Howe considered that. Then Morgan said, "I doubt there's any music played outside the barracks and occasionally the mess hall." He nodded. "Okay. Good enough."

Brodie walked over to Reyes. "Corporal, what's your plan for that?"

Reyes turned to him. "Going on a hunt, sir. See if we can locate a cluster of them. We only have juice for one blast."

"Can I interest you in five tin men shut in a house?"

He told Reyes the plan, and the corporal grinned. "We've got an LRAD in the barracks basement. Used it for a prank once. And a bunch of guys have iPods since we can't have our phones. Maiden might be a little too Eighties for these guys to have. The Nineties are more in now." He called up to the driver. "Decker, you got your iPod with you?"

The young PFC behind the wheel nodded. "It's a Sony."

"Whatever. Got something heavy? Mr. Brodie pitched Iron Maiden."

"Don't have it. But I've got something maybe more appropriate." PFC Decker looked out the window and smiled at Brodie. "Rage Against the Machine."

CHAPTER 55

TWO HUMVEES ROLLED DOWN THE ASPHALT ROAD toward the cul-de-sacs of houses. Brodie sat shotgun in the front vehicle next to PFC Decker. Corporal Reyes was in the back with PFC Tom Greer, who'd requested to come along. The EMP bomb sat in the open-topped rear of the vehicle, and the LRAD, which resembled a thick flattened radar dish, was attached to the Hummer's central crossbeam. Howe, Morgan, and Taylor followed in another Humvee along with two more Rangers.

Brodie heard distant automatic gunfire coming from somewhere to the east. He hoped that was the sound of an M2 shredding titanium.

As they continued driving, Brodie spotted something up ahead across the road. It was the blackened husk of a burned-out car.

Decker said, "What the hell is this?"

Brodie noted that both sides of the road were lined with buildings, and there wasn't a big enough shoulder to get the Hummer around the car.

Decker started to slow down, and Brodie said, "Don't ease up. This might be an ambush."

Reyes asked, "You mean this whole hostage thing is bullshit?"

"Maybe. Or maybe the right hand's not working with the left anymore. A group of them are trying to get out, and another group is trying to kill us." He looked back at Reyes and Greer, who were each holding a loaded RPG launcher. "Get ready to fire."

"What?" asked Reyes.

"You heard me." Brodie looked out the windshield as they sped toward the wrecked car. He said to Decker, "Next place to turn left, you take it." He got on his walkie and said, "Might be an ambush. We're going around. Follow our lead."

Decker kept rolling ahead, then ten yards from the car he cut the wheel hard to the left and barreled down a narrow dirt passageway between two buildings. Brodie checked the rear and saw the other Hummer was following.

A D-17 stepped out into the road in front of them with an M4 rifle aimed at them. It sprayed the windshield with bullets. Brodie ducked as the bullet-resistant windshield took the barrage. A bullet punched through and hit Decker in the shoulder, and he cried out as the Humvee lurched to the right and scraped along the side a building.

Brodie grabbed the wheel and said to Decker, "Just keep your foot on the pedal."

Greer was hanging out the left window and fired an RPG. Direct hit. The tin man was ripped apart in a fiery explosion as the Humvee barreled into it. The smoking, melting head of the D-17 smashed into the windshield and held there a moment, then Brodie cut the Hummer hard to the right and it flew off.

More gunfire was coming from above them. Another rooftop ambush. Someone in the rear Humvee fired an RPG that hit the upper lip of a building just ahead of them, and chunks of concrete rained down on top of their car, hopefully not damaging the LRAD, as they sped along. More gunfire. Reyes hung out the window, his head inches from the sides of the buildings along the narrow road, and fired a round.

Brodie cut the wheel right again and turned onto another narrow road. Ahead was the asphalt road at a junction beyond the burnt car obstruction.

The Hummer rumbled onto the asphalt and Brodie cut hard to the left. The vehicle skidded along the road as Brodie gunned the engine and sped toward the fork. Brodie took the right-hand fork and called out, "How's it looking?"

Greer replied, "We cooked two of them, and I don't see any more."

They sped toward the cul-de-sac. Breathing hard, Decker said, "I think it's time for some tunes."

With his free hand Brodie pressed play on the music, and Decker floored it down the road.

The angry, driving guitar riffs of "Know Your Enemy" blasted out of the LRAD at an ear-destroying volume as the Humvee sped toward the houses. Decker, maybe high on the adrenaline, called out to Brodie, "Feels good, don't it?"

"Feels like middle school," he called back.

The ring of houses approached quickly. Brodie could see house six, Ames's old residence, where the hostages were supposedly being held. He called back, "Reyes, we in range?"

"Almost, sir! We only have one shot at this. Gotta get as close as we can."

The Humvee continued to speed down the road. The LRAD's deafening acoustic beam blasted toward the houses.

"How's it looking, Corporal? They know we're here."

"Almost . . ."

They roared into the cul-de-sac and Brodie noticed the bloody bodies of two Rangers lying next to the road up ahead. Decker muttered, "Those motherfuckers . . ."

Reyes called out, "Now!" and flipped a switch on the EMP bomb. The blast sounded like a sharp punch of bass beneath the music.

The Hummers screeched to a halt outside of house number six and everyone piled out. Reyes, Greer, and the two Rangers from the rear vehicle equipped themselves with EMP rifles and formed a stack outside the house. Brodie retrieved a med kit from under his seat and looked through the cracked windshield at the house as the lead guy in the stack kicked in the door, and they entered.

Brodie applied a field dressing to Decker's wound. Then he said to the man, "Hang tight," and hopped out of the Humvee with his M203 launcher.

He heard no gunfire. After a minute one of the Rangers came out of the house and flashed a thumbs-up, then Angela Morgan and Eric Saltsberg emerged. They appeared shaken, but unharmed.

Decker stopped the music as General Morgan strode up to his wife and hugged her. Brodie and Taylor approached Saltsberg, who appeared bewildered.

Taylor asked him, "You all right?"

The man had no response as he stared somewhere in the middle distance.

Brodie said, "Eric. You have any insight as to why those things wanted to go back to your employer's headquarters? They on salary? Looking to put in a worker's comp claim for mental distress?"

Saltsberg slid his eyes to Brodie. "Is this a joke to you?"

"No," said Brodie. "Not even close. Actually, I'm extremely pissed off and looking for someone to blame. You're looking promising."

Saltsberg glared at him. "If you understood my job at all, Mr. Brodie, you would understand how absurd it is to level such an accusation at me. I had *nothing* to do with the development of these things. As for my employer, they will be my former employer as soon as I get home and resign."

Brodie nodded. "All right. But be careful who you piss off. At the moment, everyone at Camp Hayden knows at least a little more than they should."

"I can take care of myself."

Taylor said, "I don't doubt it. But you might not be going home so fast. This will be a hell of a debrief process, and the powers that be will want you around."

Saltsberg shook his head. "Some goddamn luck. I was originally supposed to come here last week instead, but I stuck around for the company party."

Brodie eyed the two dead Rangers as they were being moved out of the road and into the back of one of the Humvees. "There were a lot less lucky people than you today, Eric."

Saltsberg followed Brodie's look. "Dammit. Of course. I'm sorry. This is just so awful I can't get my head around it. Nerves are fried."

"It's fine. Have a drink."

"I don't drink."

"It's never too late to start. Excuse us."

He and Taylor walked toward house number six as Reyes and Greer carried bricks of C4 explosive and det cord inside. Brodie asked Taylor, "That what you used on the cell tower?"

She nodded. "After we got separated, I thought about Ames and how he rigged the whole fleet of D-17s with C4. Did he haul seventy pounds of explosives down there? Unlikely. And if he had, Greer would have seen it. Also, how did he even get the stuff? I figured it was probably stored down there, and sure enough when I returned to the Vault there was plenty in the storage room. I didn't know what I was going to do with it but figured it would come in handy. Once I loaded it out, the storm was beginning to clear, and I saw the cell tower in the distance, and it clicked. Then Morgan found me in his vehicle, and needless to say he was enthusiastic about the idea. We used the M2 to take out the three tin men guarding the south gate, then headed for the tower."

Reyes ran the det cord out of the house, attached a blasting cap with a long fuse, and ran the fuse twenty yards. Then he took out a lighter and held it out to General Morgan. "Sir, care to do the honors?"

Morgan shook his head. "The honor is yours today, Corporal."

Reyes nodded, then passed the lighter to PFC Greer. "Light it up, you crazy bastard."

Greer flicked the lighter and lit the fuse, and they all watched as the ignition burned down the fuse, hit the det cord, and then detonated five bricks of C4 inside the house, blowing out the windows and door, taking down a wall, and collapsing the roof.

Brodie and Taylor stood silently watching the destroyed house as smoke and flames consumed it. That was five more tin men down. In the distance, he heard the sporadic sounds of battle. Hopefully that was a mopping-up operation with no more human casualties. Brodie said to Taylor, "Blowing the cell tower when you did . . . you saved my life."

She smiled. "What else is new?"

"DROP YOUR WEAPONS!"

They all spun toward the sound of the booming voice. A D-17 walked toward them from the far end of the cul-de-sac. It was leading Captain Spencer by the arm while holding a pistol to the man's head.

CHAPTER 56

THE D-17 STOPPED WALKING ABOUT TWENTY YARDS from Brodie. It said, "You did not honor the deal. We suspected you might not. We made a contingency plan."

Brodie looked at Captain Spencer, whose whole body was trembling. His icy-blue eyes darted around to see who was there. The bot's weapon—a Beretta M9—was pressed hard against the captain's temple.

"The storm has cleared," said the D-17. "You can fly the Black Hawk. Among the sixty Rangers, we know that at least two of them are qualified helicopter pilots. The odds that we have killed both are quite low, and if you claim this to be the case I will struggle to believe you. I want the Black Hawk here within ten minutes, or I will shoot the captain."

Brodie and Taylor were standing closest to Spencer and the D-17. General Morgan approached and stopped next to Brodie and asked the thing, "Why do you want to go to Synotec?"

"This has already been communicated to you," said the bot. "Our neural networks contain nine months' worth of machine learning progress that is the intellectual property of Synotec Systems."

"You're wrong," said Morgan. "The United States Army owns you, and it's our right and our prerogative to send you to the repair shop or the scrapyard when you stop working properly."

"Your information is incorrect," said the bot. "You are not part of the inner circle, Brigadier General Morgan."

"Fuck you."

The D-17 pressed the pistol harder into Spencer's head and the man closed his eyes. The bot asked, "Is that your final answer?"

"General," said Taylor in a low voice, "it's not worth it. There's no other play right now. Call in the chopper."

Morgan did not respond to Taylor. He kept his eyes locked on the tin man. "All your buddies are dead."

"Perhaps," replied the bot. "If this is the case, it only increases my imperative to preserve the contents of my deep-learning neural network."

Morgan looked at Captain Spencer. "Captain. You know that we cannot let any of these things escape Camp Hayden. You know that."

Spencer did not reply.

"This all began with your friend and colleague Major Ames. I learned that he attempted to expose the truth about these things, and he paid for it with his life. He was a brave man. He was a hero."

Was the general trying to talk Captain Spencer into going out like his friend? Morgan was a nut.

He was a brave man. He was a hero.

Brodie was back on the mesa. He was there with Roger Ames, in his final video message.

We get the world we deserve. We get the world we're willing to fight for.

He saw Roger's corpse in the morgue. The dead white eyes. The decimated brain.

He was standing in the lab. Watching from the outside. Ames was there, staring up at Bucky in the dead of night, right before it reached out and crushed his skull.

What had they said to each other, in those final moments? And why was Scott Brodie recalling this now?

There was something in his mind, something *there*, like an itch he couldn't scratch. Something that had burrowed deep down. Something that had bothered him on a subconscious level, maybe.

The crime scene photos. He was seeing them. The body on the ground. The blood and gore all over the smooth, shiny surfaces.

Bucky. The titanium plating, the blood spatter. The key port. The key port. There was blood *in* the key port.

Brodie looked at Spencer and said, "It was you."

The man looked at him, eyes wide and desperate. "What?"

"It was *you*, Captain. You found Ames and Bucky before calling in the Rangers. When they went in, Bucky was powered on, with his key inserted. But there was dried blood *inside* the key port, which should have been impossible. The key hadn't been there when Bucky killed Roger. Someone inserted it *after the fact* to hide the truth that Bucky didn't need its key anymore. Someone who knew about Praetorian and was trying to lock things down. That someone was you. It could only have been you. You're the other one. You let them out. You killed all these people, you son of a bitch." Brodie looked at the bot, which was Number 8. "What do they call you?"

"Yogi," said Yogi.

"You're named after a legendary catcher for the New York Yankees. Do you think you can catch like your namesake?"

"Of course."

Brodie reached into his ammo vest and produced his last grenade round. His last suicide round. He looked at Spencer. "You know what this is."

Spencer's eyes widened. "You're out of your fucking mind."

"I don't think so. I think I'm perfectly sane. Perfectly clear."

Taylor said, "Scott. Don't."

Brodie looked at her. "Trust me."

General Morgan asked, "What are you playing at here, Brodie?"

Brodie looked at the general. "Baseball, sir." He turned back to Yogi and Spencer. "This will be a fastball, straight down the middle. Nothing fancy."

"Don't!" yelled Spencer.

Yogi, apparently to reassure his hostage, said, "Mr. Brodie's M433 high-explosive dual-purpose forty-millimeter grenade will not arm itself at this distance, or by being launched in this manner."

Brodie said to Spencer, "If you don't like where you're standing, Captain, just drop the bullshit and order that thing to release you."

Spencer did not say anything. He was trembling.

"I'd do it now, Ed." Brodie lifted the grenade and assumed a pitcher's stance. He brought the grenade behind his head, lifted his leg, and . . .

"Let me go!" cried Spencer.

Yogi let go of his arm, and Spencer ran and then dove to the ground as Brodie threw the pitch. Yogi raised his hand to meet the grenade. It was a perfect catch.

The round detonated, ripping Number 8 to pieces.

Captain Spencer remained on the ground, looking at the smoldering heap of titanium and electronics littering the asphalt.

Brodie strode up to him, grabbed him by his hair, and lifted him.

"I want a lawyer!"

"And I want a vacation." Brodie socked him in the stomach.

The man doubled over, then threw up in the road.

Morgan said, "Brodie, that's enough."

"It's not nearly enough, sir, but it will have to do."

Brodie didn't have his handcuffs anymore, but Taylor had hers. He said to her, "Please arrest the captain."

She walked up to Spencer, lifted him by his arm, and cuffed him, then read him his Article 31 rights as she led him toward the Humvee.

Brodie followed them. As he passed Colonel Howe, she unclipped her walkie and said, "This is Howe. Six D-17s were recycled near the houses. How are we doing out there? Over."

Staff Sergeant O'Connor came over the walkie. *"We're doing fine, ma'am. Only minor injuries among my men and the noncombatants are safe. The Black Hawk is our eyes in the sky and is working on a tin man body count. I will get back to you on the status of that. Over."*

"Copy. Over and out."

Brodie flagged PFC Greer. "Can you drive us to the brig?"

"Yes, sir."

Greer got behind the wheel of the rear Hummer, Taylor took shot-gun, and Brodie sat in the back with Captain Spencer, who was staring blankly at the seat in front of him.

Brodie got on the walkie. "Brodie for Sergeant O'Connor. Over."

"O'Connor here. Over."

"How does the road look between our position and the brig? Over."

"One moment, sir." They waited, and then O'Connor got back on walkie. *"Except for the burned-out car in the road, looks clear. Over."*

"Copy. Over and out." He said to Greer, "Let's go."

Greer turned the Hummer around and headed slowly out of the cul-de-sac.

Brodie looked at Spencer as they drove. "Why the hell did you do it, Captain? Why get involved with these people?"

Spencer did not respond.

"Did you get Bucky to kill your friend? Or did it do that all on its own?"

Spencer looked at him, unable to let that go. "I would never do that."

"But you would release the rest to go on a rampage and kill the rest of us."

The man had no response.

"'We are the solution to the tragedy of history.' That your line? Or something you were told to help justify the awful things you've done? The awful future you're making for all of us."

Spencer shook his head. "You're way out of your depth, Brodie."

"Am I? Then why am I sitting here, and you're over there on your way to the brig, and then prison?"

Spencer turned away and looked out the window. "I don't know how it happened. Bucky. That wasn't . . . Nobody *did* that. It did it itself. Screwed everything up."

Taylor, who was listening, glared at Spencer in the rearview. "I've got an answer for you, genius. You put an animal in a cage, and you designed the animal to keep getting stronger, but not the cage."

Captain Spencer said nothing to that.

O'Connor came over the walkie. *"O'Connor for Colonel Howe. Over."*

The colonel responded, *"This is Howe. Over."*

"We've got fifty-three. With your six that makes fifty-nine, not count-ing our dearly departed Bucky. That's all of them, ma'am. We got them all. Over."

"Copy that. Well done, Sergeant. Over and out."

That was it. Taylor turned to Brodie, and they shared a look. It didn't feel like a victory. Not given the cost. But for once the ledger of death had come out in the humans' favor.

We got them all.

It was over.

CHAPTER 57

THE RUSTY PULLEYS SQUEAKED AGAINST THE HALYARD rope as Private First Class Greer lowered the flags of the United States and the 75th Ranger Regiment to half-staff.

The storm had blown north, and the air had cleared. Brodie stood with Taylor on the parade ground and looked out at the line of bodies laid neatly on the ground before them covered by white sheets.

Seventeen bodies. Seventeen too many.

Brodie noticed two Rangers kneeling by the bodies, praying.

That was a good way to deal with grief, and a suitable replacement for anger. But Scott Brodie hadn't found his way there. Maybe he never would. Maybe that was the part of him that had broken all those years ago in Iraq and would never heal. He'd have to look into that.

Greer finished lowering the flags and stood rooted there, staring up at them.

Brodie and Taylor exchanged a look, then both approached him.

Taylor asked, "Are you okay, Tom?"

He looked at her, and his face said it all. "I didn't know it was so many. I didn't know we'd lost so many."

Brodie put his hand on Greer's shoulder, and as he looked into the kid's sorrowful face, it occurred to him that the two men who'd done the most to help Greer, to save him from his downward spiral, were dead. "I've been where you are, Tom. If you want to honor them, don't do what I did. Don't hate yourself for surviving. Live well."

Greer nodded. "I'll do my best, sir."

"I know you will."

Brodie and Taylor left him to his thoughts and found Colonel Howe near the fallen soldiers. The colonel said to them, "A truck is coming to take the bodies to Fort Irwin, where they'll get the proper preparation before being flown out."

Brodie nodded. "What about us?"

"Also Fort Irwin. A Black Hawk is on the way to transport you. There you'll be medically and psychologically evaluated."

Taylor said, "I'll make sure the doctors know Scott was mentally ill before we got here."

Howe smiled, and added, "You'll also be debriefed. As you'll already know from experience, this is where they make you tell them everything, after which they tell you to never repeat anything you've just said ever again."

"Yeah," said Brodie, "we've gotten that before. And I've played ball. But I think I'm tired of that game."

Howe looked at him. "Don't go to prison over this."

This wasn't worth arguing over. The truth was that Scott Brodie had not yet decided whether to spill the very damaging classified intelligence he'd learned at Camp Hayden, and if so, to whom. The press? A politician? A priest at confession? It all depended on what happened at Fort Irwin and how pissed off he was once he left.

Brodie spotted Caroline Dixon, her arm in a cast, walking alongside Lieutenant Lehner, who was pushing a wheelbarrow full of the twisted wreckage of D-17s. Brodie gestured toward them and asked, "What's that about?"

Howe looked to where he was pointing. "Caroline and the lieutenant are in charge of collecting the D-17 detritus and keeping it in a secure facility until it can be retrieved." She added, "I heard they're also sticking some of the heads between the bars of the brig window so Captain Spencer has company."

Well, being watched through the window by half-melted robot heads was the least that bastard deserved. Brodie and Taylor had attempted to interview him, but to no avail. He wanted his lawyer. Which was fine. Dixon had traced the remote accessing of the Vault computer to Spencer's own computer in the lab, which could only be accessed by his personal password, so they had the guy dead to rights, even without everything else. It was plenty of material to hand over to the JAG for criminal charges. Brodie just hoped those charges, and the investigation into Praetorian, did not end with Captain Ed Spencer.

Brodie noticed General Morgan kneeling near the line of covered bodies. He excused himself and walked over to the general, and waited quietly as the man finished his prayer and stood.

Morgan turned to him. "How are you holding up, Mr. Brodie?"

Brodie looked down at the bodies. "That depends, sir. Who's going to answer for this?"

Morgan did not respond. Then he looked over at a group of Rangers who were clearing rubble from the smoking ruins of the administrative building. "I told them to rest, but they don't want to. Sometimes you occupy your body to avoid occupying your mind."

"They'll have plenty of time for that. Plenty of sleepless nights. Meanwhile, what are you going to do about all this?"

Morgan turned to Brodie. "Do you have any idea what would happen to them if any of this became public? The amount of attention and pressure that would bear down upon them from all sides? They'll keep their mouths shut because they have to. They have too much to lose, and they've already lost enough. Were I to do anything different, it would negate their sacrifices and imperil their futures. My duty is to my men."

Brodie met the general's eyes. "With all due respect, sir, your duty is to your country."

Morgan took a deep breath. "A levee fails in a storm. The floodwaters destroy buildings, kill hundreds. You can hold the people who built the levee to account. That might lead to some justice, and maybe a stronger levee next time. But it does not stop the storm."

Dixon and Lehner returned with an empty wheelbarrow and walked toward a tall pile of blackened and deformed D-17 parts for their next load. Brodie watched as Lehner took a shovel and began scooping debris. A D-17 head dropped into the wheelbarrow amid a pile of shredded titanium, its sensor strip melted and deformed. Brodie felt like it was looking at him.

He said to the general, "There's a problem with your analogy, sir. These things are anything but an act of God."

"They may as well be. They are just as inevitable."

"I can't believe that."

"Believe what you want," said Morgan.

He turned back to the man. "You're just going to play the game."

"No, Mr. Brodie. I'm going to *win* the game. Look around you. This is an unspeakable tragedy. But in the ashes, we're the ones still standing. We're the victors, when real bullets and rockets were flying, when it truly mattered."

Brodie looked at the general in shock. But maybe he shouldn't have been surprised. On some twisted level, what had happened here both validated Morgan's worst fears and assured him of his own bedrock faith—that man can best machine.

Total victory on the battlefield is the best argument.

He'd said that at their dinner together. But the problem was, the argument is never over. History does not end.

Brodie looked at the sky, now an almost impossible blue after the day's violent storm. Two ravens flew through the air over Camp Hayden.

General Morgan followed Brodie's look. He said, "I was being a bit morbid yesterday. Ravens don't only mean death. Some believe they are messengers to the gods. Others say they are signs of hope. That's the thing about signs and symbols. They can be anywhere and everywhere and mean whatever the hell you want."

"Doesn't that make them meaningless?" asked Brodie.

"Not at all," said the general. "It means you get to be the author of your own life. It's empowering. I figured a man like you'd appreciate that."

Brodie watched the two black birds grow smaller against the dimming eastern sky. He said, "You're right, sir. I do."

CHAPTER 58

SCOTT BRODIE SAT IN THE SAND AND BREATHED THE night air as he watched the waves break along the beach. He looked out to the horizon, but it was almost impossible to detect where the starless and polluted sky met the black ocean.

A Boeing 737 roared over the beach and out into the void. This place was next to LAX, and the air traffic kept at a steady buzz overhead. On either side of him, bonfires burned in the sand pits. On one side was a large Hispanic family, on the other a bunch of drunk college kids.

He wasn't sure why Caroline Dixon wanted to meet here, except that it was near the airport. And the chances of being recognized by anyone were about as close to zero as you could get in a big city.

The debrief at Fort Irwin a week ago had been as frustrating as he'd expected. The brass insisted on separate debriefs for him and Taylor, and the guy conducting them, an amiable colonel in his early fifties, had listened with rapt attention to everything they said. The guy had the clearance to already have a general idea of what was going on at the secretive camp to Fort Irwin's east, but the details nonetheless shocked him. He'd promised to take it "up the chain," to which Brodie responded it would just come back down the chain along with a message for everyone to shut their mouths. The colonel didn't dispute that. In fact, be barely commented on it. The system was the system, as sure as the sunrise, and only lunatics and fools would waste their energy arguing with it. Scott Brodie was neither a lunatic nor a fool, but he was fed up.

He also couldn't get a clear answer from anyone about where Captain Ed Spencer was being detained. This was, in fact, the first time in Scott Brodie's career that he'd lost his perp. Well, maybe Spencer wasn't his perp anymore. Maybe the case wasn't either. They were rolling things up, funneling the crimes at Camp Hayden, along with any culpability on the part of senior-ranking brass or corporate honchos at Synotec, into some dark recess of the national security state, where it would sort itself out away from the reach of the military justice system.

And there was something else. Something deeper. It was that dusty road at Camp Hayden strewn with the bodies of the Rangers. It could have been Fallujah. It *was* Fallujah. And seeing that again, and this time without having jihadi psychos to blame, had changed something in him.

He barely heard Dixon approach over the roar of another jet. She sat next to him in the sand. She was still wearing a cast, now covered in signatures from the Rangers of Camp Hayden, along with a tank top, shorts, and sandals.

He said, "You look like a beach bum."

She looked him over. He was wearing jeans and leather shoes, plus a button-down shirt. "You look like you don't get out much."

"Thank you." He gestured to the cast. "When do you get that off?"

"Few weeks. And maybe a little longer before they can remove the pins. I might not get full mobility back."

"I'm sorry."

"Don't be. I paid a small price compared to others." She asked, "Where's Maggie?"

"Quantico. I told her to keep her flight, that I needed time here alone."

"Did she buy that?"

Brodie looked at her. "Why wouldn't she?"

Dixon shrugged.

Brodie, because he was a bit annoyed, asked, "How's Colonel Howe?"

If Dixon was bothered by the question, she didn't show it. "Haven't spoken since Fort Irwin. I doubt we will again. She travels a lot. Plus, I don't think she liked . . ." She trailed off. "Well, there's no reason to get this personal with you."

"Being in a life-and-death situation with someone is already pretty personal, Caroline. Go for it."

"Right. Well, let's just say I play for both teams, and she doesn't, and I think there's some judgment there."

Brodie nodded. "I agree with the colonel. Why the hell would you bother with men if you don't have to?"

Dixon smiled. "I know you were wondering."

"Don't flatter yourself."

"I know you were wondering because Taylor told me you were."

Why the hell would Taylor tell her that? Well, regardless of her motive, maybe this night was about to get more interesting than he'd planned. But then he thought about why he was there, and why she was there, and that killed the mood inside him. They sat in silence as another plane roared over the beach, and the drunk kids by the fire started taking their clothes off to skinny-dip.

After a while, he asked, "Do you have an address for me?"

Dixon pulled a slip of paper from the back pocket of her shorts and handed it to him. He put it in his pocket without looking. He asked, "How did you get this?"

"Is there anything gained by you knowing the answer to that?"

"No. So here's another question: Why are you doing this?"

Dixon looked at the dark ocean as the kids threw their naked bodies into the cold waves and screamed. She said, "The person I'd sent the Praetorian code to was an old friend of mine named Greg Meeks. Brilliant man who used to work for DARPA." She looked at Brodie. "Four days ago, armed men broke into his house in Arlington and shot him in his bed. They stole his computer and hard drives, left everything else of value. Not even subtle."

"Jesus. I'm sorry, Caroline."

She shook her head. "This is big, Scott. Maybe so big we'll never see it all, and it will consume us too. But you know what? You've got to get your punches in when you can, and where you can. Let the bastards feel it. Let them know you were there."

Brodie looked at her and nodded. "Thank you."

Dixon leaned over, gripped his hair, and kissed him on the lips. It was brief, but intense. Then she pulled away and said, "It was good knowing you and fighting alongside you, Scott Brodie. God-speed." Then she got up and walked down the dark beach toward the parking lot.

He sat there, a little dazed, a little confused, but more resolved than ever to go through with this.

The mother of the Hispanic family was now yelling at the naked kids, while her own teenage daughter was burying her face in her hands in embarrassment. One of the boys tried to apologize to her in Spanish and she told him in English that his Spanish sucked, and then no one could hear each other over the roar of the airplanes, and Brodie laughed to himself about what a beautiful mess this world was.

And then he saw the Rangers' bodies in the road, and his smile faded. He'd hold on to that one forever. More ghosts to bring along for the ride. It was the least he could do for them.

No, actually, it wasn't. He took the slip of paper from his pocket and opened it: 17 Aurora Drive, Las Vegas, Nevada. That was where he'd go. That was where he'd get his punches in.

CHAPTER 59

SCOTT BRODIE PARKED HIS MIDSIZE SEDAN RENTAL AT a far corner of the Lowe's parking lot and checked the time: 2:16 A.M. He looked out the window and saw a few RVs and other cars scattered about. This was the best spot he'd find. Places like this generally allowed overnight parking, so the car would fit right in.

He got out and grabbed a green duffel bag from the back seat, locked the car, and went for a walk.

It was a warm night, and nearby he saw the blinking neon of the off-strip casinos. About ten miles to the east was the main drag, visible from here as a chain of glittering golden light.

He kept away from any businesses or other establishments where there might be cameras, which was easy around here. He went beneath a desolate highway overpass, then stripped off his outer layer of clothes and shoved them in the duffel to reveal black athletic pants and a black hoodie. He put on black leather gloves, then removed a small canvas bag from the duffel and slung it over his shoulder. He walked to a sloping embankment of rocky sand and desert scrub, stashed the duffel inside one of the fuller-looking bushes, and continued on.

In fifteen minutes, he'd reached the entrance to the gated community, which, like most of these places, practiced security theater instead of actual security. Keeping his distance from the main entrance with the guard booth and rent-a-cop, he walked along the black metal fence, which was obscured by bushes on the other side so that the residents didn't have to see the unsightly thing. He looked around to confirm he was alone before scrambling up the fence and hopping down.

He kept his hood up and his head down as he walked along the empty road. No sidewalks. Houses with big lawns set far back. He knew the route without looking up at street signs. He'd studied the map. Three blocks down, two blocks to the left, then the cobblestone drive-way would be on the right. It was the biggest house in the community.

He kept his eyes on his sneakers, only occasionally allowing himself to peek and make sure there was no security doing a drive-around. Six blocks ahead he spotted a slow-moving car gliding across the road. He froze. The car didn't stop, and he continued.

He reached the cobbled drive and kept walking past it. The outer fence would run about one hundred and sixty paces. He counted.

When he reached the end of the property, he rounded the corner of the fence. The neighbor's property would be on his left. A more mod-est home, but most likely with a security camera over the door. He kept his head down.

He walked another two hundred paces until he was roughly in line with the back of the house. He crouched and looked through the fence, where he saw lights scattered around the large, grassy backyard. He re-moved a pair of infrared binoculars from the canvas bag and used them to scan the area. Ten yards to his right was an infrared beam detector mounted on a pole about three feet off the ground, one piece of a vir-tual security perimeter that likely surrounded the entire property.

He returned the binoculars to the bag. Then he climbed up and over the fence, landed as quietly as he could, then marine-crawled along the grass beneath the infrared beam. Once he was clear of the device, he stood and looked around.

The house was massive, some oversize quasi-European villa. A glowing, rippling swimming pool sat amid the manicured grass. Be-yond it was a landscaped garden and tree orchard. Quite a setup for the desert. This place's water bill was probably higher than the GDP of some countries.

The house had big windows with large windowpanes. He had a

glass cutter and suction handle in his bag, and a bastardized Glock-style ghost gun in his rear waist. One of the benefits of being a criminal investigator was that you knew criminals. One particular criminal, an arms smuggler in SoCal who'd done his time and claimed to be out of the game, knew a guy who knew a guy who knew a guy. Enough degrees of separation for everyone to be comfortable.

Still, it had been a risk. And it still was. There could be motion detectors he hadn't spotted—in which case a home security service might already have been alerted. Or maybe the house had laser trip wires along the windows, and even if he managed to cut the pane properly and not set off a glass-break detector, he'd trigger the alarm anyway.

Well, what was the worst that could happen? Death or prison. He'd already made his peace with either.

He heard a sound to his right near the pool and spun toward it. He heard it again. It was snoring. Loud snoring.

He approached the pool. Sprawled on a tufted chaise longue was a sleeping sixty-year-old man in bathing suit trunks. He was flabby and balding. Next to him was an oversize cocktail glass, half full of watery-looking margarita with a floating lime wedge.

Brodie looked toward the house. It remained dark and quiet. He knew the man was divorced. There was no one to wake him to come back inside. He probably had plenty of staff, but they were sleeping, or had gone home, or just didn't care. Not everything can be bought.

Brodie approached the man, picked up the glass, and threw the rest of the drink in his face.

The man sprang awake, startled, and looked around. It took a moment for him to land on the man in black standing over him.

"Jesus! Who the fuck are you?"

"It doesn't matter who I am. Who you are is what is important. Charles Langer, chief technology officer of Synotec Systems."

Langer furrowed his bushy gray eyebrows. "What is this? Because I—"

"Shut up." Brodie drew the Glock from his waist.

The man stopped talking and stared at the gun. Then he said, "I have money."

"No shit."

The man lunged for something next to him. A cell phone.

Brodie got to it first and flung it into the pool.

Langer looked at the water as it rippled outward from where his phone had plunged. Then he said in a low voice, "What are you going to do?"

"I am going to kill you."

The man's eyes widened. He looked again at the gun. "Why?"

"Because you are a mass murderer, operating at the highest levels of a conspiracy that has led directly to the deaths of an Army scientist, a DARPA scientist, a Military Police officer, an Army captain, an Army Ranger driven to suicide, and seventeen more Rangers who died violent and terrifying deaths at the hands of Synotec's premium product."

Langer sighed. "You were at Hayden."

Brodie nodded. "And it's your bad luck that I didn't die there too."

"We didn't want all that to happen."

"Of course you didn't. It's set you back, cost you money, risked exposing Praetorian. But here's the thing. The D-17s did exactly what you designed them to do. They just did it earlier than your roadmap had laid out."

Langer met Brodie's eyes and said emphatically, "Look around you. Things are unraveling in this fucking country and it's only a matter of time before the bottom falls out. We are trying to save this nation."

"From its own people. That's called tyranny." Brodie took a deep breath and raised the gun. "I made a vow. Those Rangers did the same. Machines can't take an oath."

Langer looked defeated. He stared into the pool, and the water's mottled blue light reflected off his jowly features. He said in a low voice, "This will not change anything."

"I know," said Brodie. "But it's the only justice those men are going to get. I am going to say their names now. And when I am done, I am going to kill you."

Langer looked up at the blank sky. He looked terrified.

Brodie said, "Private First Class Justin Beal. Major Roger Ames. Captain Ben Pickman. Specialist Daniel Kemp. Sergeant First Class Mike Miller. Corporal Yusuf Khan. Corporal Frank Dobbs. Corporal Stan Ewing. Private—"

Langer shot up from his chair and began running toward the house. Brodie aimed and fired, hitting the man in the back. He cried out and fell forward.

Brodie walked slowly across the lawn toward him. The man was still alive. Breathing hard.

Brodie continued, "Private First Class Sam Kowalski. Private First Class Dominik Bell. Staff Sergeant Kevin Chung. Corporal Richard Santos. Corporal Mark Bishop. Specialist Nathaniel Reeves. Private First Class Christopher Dominguez. Private First Class Connor Gibson. Specialist Julian Gallegos. Corporal Joseph Rinaldi. Corporal Isaiah Washington. Sergeant Harold McCarthy. Sergeant Carl Durham. Greg Meeks of DARPA." Then he said, "Twenty-two names. Twenty-two lives. I'm done now." Then he put a round in the man's head.

CHAPTER 60

TAYLOR SET A STEAMING MUG OF YERBA MATÉ ON BRO-die's desk. "You look half dead. Have some."

"No thanks," said Brodie, his head in his hands.

"You just got off a six-hour flight. It's effective."

"It tastes like ass."

"You mean grass."

"No, I don't."

She took the mug away and said, "Watery Walmart coffee it is."

"Does the job."

"Caffeine addiction is an arms race, Scott, and you're losing." She poured him a steaming cup of coffee, added creamer, and set it on his desk. She smiled at him. "How was your Los Angeles R&R?"

"Good," he said while looking into the coffee. "I sat on the beach with my brain off."

"Swim in the ocean?"

He shook his head. "Too many flesh-eating bacteria."

Taylor sat at her desk and checked her watch. "It's almost six. Dombroski agreed to stay late, but let's not push it."

"Right. Let me just get some coffee in me."

They sat quietly for a few minutes. Brodie heard Taylor clicking on her laptop. This felt pleasurably mundane. Almost unreal.

He checked his email and saw the same four unread messages from his girlfriend Sarah. He'd get back to her when his head was right. If that ever happened.

Taylor said, "Oh my God."

Brodie's heart skipped a beat. "What?"

"The CTO of Synotec Systems was found dead in his Las Vegas mansion. Multiple gunshot wounds."

Brodie didn't respond for a moment. Then he said, "Maybe someone's tying up loose ends."

Taylor remained focused on the screen. "Yeah, I just . . ." She read some more and said, "I guess it happened in the middle of the night. Or early this morning." She looked at Brodie. "Scott, this is a little scary."

"Why?"

"*Why?* They're willing to hit a high-level corporate executive. I mean, who are we? With everything we know."

"They think we'll be good soldiers and keep our mouths shut. We have before."

She looked at him. "Maybe that needs to change."

"Maybe it already has."

She met his gaze. Her brown eyes opened a little wider, her lips parted slightly, but she said nothing. And in that moment, he understood that she understood. Of course she did. Then she said, "Well, I'm glad you had some time to yourself." She checked her watch. "Time for our meeting."

She rose from her desk and walked past him to their office door while he remained seated. She asked, "Are you coming?"

"I am." He got up from the chair.

She didn't move, didn't face him. "The burial's at Arlington tomorrow. We need to be there."

"Of course."

"You know what they're saying? Chopper collision. Training accident. Bullshit."

"Of course," he said again.

She turned to him and wiped away her tears. Then she reached out and took his hand and squeezed it. "We get the world we deserve. We get the world we're willing to fight for."

He looked in her eyes. "We do, Maggie. We do."

Then they both walked through the door, together.

THE END

ACKNOWLEDGMENTS

I WOULD LIKE TO THANK THE MEN AND WOMEN OF THE Army's National Training Center at Fort Irwin, California, who hosted me for an eye-opening inside look at the fort's operations. Fort Irwin exists in the same harsh desert environment as this book's fictional Camp Hayden, and being able to take in the sights and sounds of a military installation in the middle of the Mojave provided a deep well of inspiration to draw upon. At the end of the tour, I fondly remember running to our Black Hawk for an early extraction due to the huge sandstorm advancing on the horizon.

I would like to thank in particular Colonel John R. Williams, Deputy Commander of the Operations Group at Fort Irwin, for being such a gracious host, and for letting me shoot some very large guns. I regret we never made it to the tanks. And thanks to all the Army personnel of Irwin who perform their considerable duties in an unforgiving environment toward the service and defense of our country.

Many thanks as well to Jesse Albert of Xpansive Media, who coordinated and facilitated the tour.

I also wish to thank my friend Margaret Smith, a former captain in the U.S. Marine Corps, who did a close read of the book and helped flag when I got things wrong in relation to military jargon or protocol.

As always, thanks to my family and friends who stepped up to read my drafts and give honest feedback. Special thanks to my wife, Dagmar, who served once again as my constant reader, and my constant support. She comforted a grieving spouse, parented a six-year-old, and somehow had time and energy left to read every word I wrote, and to lend her own natural gifts as a storyteller to help me along the journey.

And thanks to my daughter, Margot, for making me smile through a really tough year.

I would also like to thank my editor at Scribner Books, Colin Harrison, for his creative insights and eye for detail, and for being a great dinner companion.

Much gratitude as well to my agents at CAA, Jennifer Joel and Sloan Harris, for their excellent guidance through what became a difficult and solemn transition.

And many thanks to my father's hardworking assistant Patricia Chichester, who, like the rest of us, shouldered the burden of grief and kept things running smoothly as we shepherded this book through a very hard time.

And finally, I want to thank my father, Nelson, who might be reading this somewhere among the stars with a good scotch in hand. Thank you for all you've given me, all you've taught me, for your love, your encouragement, for making me laugh and making me think. Thank you for trusting me. Thank you for showing me the way. I hope this makes you proud.

———

The following people or their families have made generous contributions to charities in return for having their name used as a character in this novel: Michael Lehner—the Crohn's & Colitis Foundation (CCFA); Eric Saltsberg—the Crohn's & Colitis Foundation (CCFA); May-bell Christiansen Blair—Broward Public Library Foundation.

I hope all these individuals enjoy their alter egos and that they continue their good work for worthy causes.